SWEET DREAMS

Dallas though it was incredible: here she was, an innocent runaway schoolgirl in some drunken rake's bed. What could she do to get out of this mess?

"Melanie . . ." Quint whispered, and there was anguish in his voice. "I'm sorry, so sorry. . . ."

In that moment, Dallas would have given anything to be the missing Melanie that Quint so longed for. She tried to move, intent on slipping out of bed, but Quint reached for her, pulling her to him. "No, don't leave, don't leave! We'll have that wedding night you wanted! I owe you that."

Dallas tried to protest, to say that she wasn't Melanie, but suddenly Quint's mouth was on hers, tasting hotly of brandy, sweetly seeking, melting her with his kisses.

His eyes flickered open; they were glazed with undeniable passion. "I must be imagining you," he murmured as he stroked her thighs and moved over her.

"Yes, you're imagining me," Dallas whispered thickly, pulling him ever closer, needing the gift of his love—even though he thought of another woman. . . .

NEVADA NIGHTS

GEORGINA GENTRY

ZEBRA BOOKS
KENSINGTON PUBLISHING CORP.

For Dr. Clifton Warren,

Dean of Liberal Arts, Central State University, Edmond, Oklahoma, and the driving force behind the creation of the Creative Studies writing program. His dreams became students' published realities.

I'm much obliged, Clif'

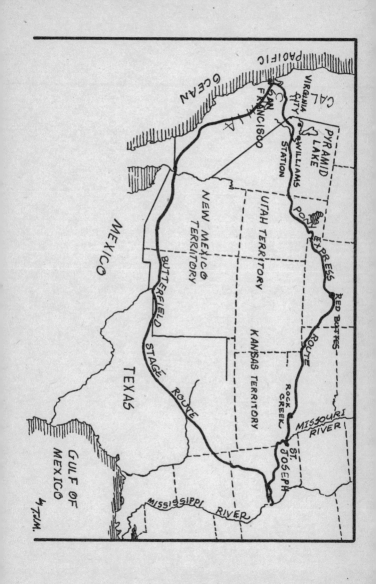

Prologue

The Pony Express ran this advertisement in several American newspapers during early March, 1860: "Wanted—young, skinny, wiry fellows, not over 18. Must be expert riders, willing to risk death daily. Orphans preferred. Wages $25 a week . . ."

Now what do you think would happen if a runaway Texas tomboy cut her hair, masqueraded as a man, and answered that ad? She'd have to be either desperate or loco. But that's how Western legends were made. . . .

Chapter One

Philadelphia, late March, 1860

Dallas already had plenty of trouble of her own when she left work at dark during a sudden snowstorm and found the handsome, well-dressed drunk freezing to death on the doorstep of the *Godey's Lady's Book* building.

For a long moment after she locked the door and almost stumbled over the man sitting on the step, the tall girl only pulled her forest green coat more tightly about her against the chill wind that whipped her long ebony hair around her face. Then she blinked in disbelief.

The hatless man grinned up at her. "Seem to have mislaid both the address and my overcoat," he drawled and then hiccoughed, confusion evident in his hazel eyes. "Tell me, is there a big-stakes card game here tonight?"

Dallas shook her head. "Mister, you're so drunk, you couldn't hit the ground with your hat in three tries if you were wearing one, much less gamble all night!"

"I dispute that." He swayed to his feet, tall, broad-shouldered, and attempted to make a sweeping bow. "No Kentucky gentleman, particularly Quint Randolph, is ever that drunk!"

Off balance, he stumbled and draped a muscular arm around her to keep from falling. "But on the other hand, angel, you might be right." He winked down at her. "I'll tell you what, you help me find that card game, and I'll pay your usual fee for taking your time."

11

"What?" Dallas felt her face flush hotly in the chill night. Evidently, the rake had mistaken her for a lady of the evening out looking for customers. Respectable girls were seldom on the street alone after dark, but she'd lost track of time as she'd worked on the fashion writeup and hadn't realized how late it was.

His arm felt warm on her shoulders, and his face came close enough for her to catch the scent of brandy. Abruptly, his lips came down on hers, hot and tasting of spirits, intoxicating her for a split second. She seemed powerless to stop him from pulling her hard against the fine fabric of his suit. And in that moment, she was not sure whether the rhythmic beating was her heart or his.

"You sidewinder!" Dallas jerked out of his grasp and pushed him. "You may be from Kentucky, but you're no gentleman!"

Quint Randolph collapsed on the doorstep again, looking up at her in astonishment. He rubbed his right hand through his brown hair, a big gold signet ring reflecting the dim street light as he brushed away snowflakes.

In a fury she backed away, unsure whether to be angry with him or herself. If only old Josh, the janitor, hadn't taken sick and left early, leaving her alone at the magazine office. Now there wasn't anyone to help her.

"I reckon I ought to call the police," she blustered, looking up and down the deserted street, and knowing she didn't dare. The authorities all over the East were no doubt on the lookout for the runaway daughter of a big Texas rancher.

The big man smiled sadly, regretfully, looking suddenly much older, although she doubted there was as much as ten years difference in their ages. Something about his handsome face mirrored deep tragedy. "Please don't do that, dark angel. Your virtue is safe, although I forgot myself for a moment. I—I can't . . . that is, I'm no threat to any woman in that way."

Dallas blinked her dark eyes, realization dawning as she took in the humiliation on his face. Was this virile specimen of a man telling her he was impotent?

12

She flushed again. How would she know what he hinted at? After all, she was an eighteen-year-old virgin. What little she knew came from breeding fine horses and cattle on her father's big Triple D ranch down near Austin.

Texas. A wave of homesickness washed over her, and tears came to her eyes. The bluebonnets would be in bloom right now, and scarlet Indian paintbrush blossoms would make the vast prairie look like a wildfire. . . .

"Ma'am," the drunk said softly, "I sure didn't mean to say anything to make you cry."

"Horsefeathers." Dallas gulped and wiped at her eyes. "It wasn't anything you said." She looked up and down the street uncertainly. The chill wind had driven everyone inside. The drunk wasn't her responsibility. She turned to go, paused. "Mister, will you be all right?"

He sighed, looking a bit sad. "If I can find the card game—"

"Well, it isn't here," she snapped, absently pulling at one of her lavender pearl earrings. "You'd better check the address again." She whirled and started down the street.

Behind her, the man called, "Thank you, angel."

She stopped uncertainly, looking behind her. "Are you sure you'll be all right?"

He shivered now on the step, looking sad, weary. "I'll just sit here another minute or so and try to get my bearings. Maybe I'll remember where the game is."

"Don't sit there too long," Dallas scolded. "You might go to sleep and never wake up."

He laughed, but there was no humor in it. "There've been nights this past year when that would have been very tempting."

Well, she'd done her best. There wasn't anyone on the deserted street to help her and after all, he wasn't her responsibility. Dallas walked away, the wind whipping her daffodil yellow hoop skirt around her legs, snow blowing thick enough now to blind her. Cowboys back home called a storm like this a blue norther. It blew in suddenly out of a gray northern sky, sending temperatures plummeting.

13

She listened for footsteps behind her, heard none, turned around again. The tragic man still sat on the doorstep. Even at this distance, she saw his wide shoulders shiver. "Hey, mister," she called, "you can't stay there; you'll freeze to death."

She retraced her path, stood staring down at him.

"Can't freeze to death, he murmured thickly, "got too much alcohol in me for that."

"I reckon we agree on that! You sure cut the wolf loose tonight, didn't you?"

"What?" His hazel eyes looked at her blankly.

Dallas shrugged. "It's just something Texas cowboys say when they go on a drunk." She felt both annoyed and angry that she'd been the one to find the elegant gentleman. Suppose she left him here and he went to sleep on the steps? She pictured coming to work at the magazine in the morning, finding him still slumped in the same spot, all covered with snow and frozen to death.

Horsefeathers. What to do now? She already had more trouble than she needed after having run away from Mrs. Priddy's Female Academy. She'd taken the first train out of the Boston station and had ended up here, hoping to hide out until Papa cooled down and would listen to reason. Dallas didn't want to be turned into a lady; she wanted to go back to the wide open spaces she loved.

Quint Randolph hiccoughed, bringing her back to her dilemma. What she should do was get him on his feet, head him back to his family or even his card game, whichever was closest.

Dallas reached out a hand to him. "Look, I'll help you find a carriage, and you give the driver your home address. Your wife is probably waiting dinner and is worried sick about you."

He stared into space. "She won't worry ever again," he mumbled drunkenly, "Melanie . . ."

"Oh, here, let me help you up."

He reached out and took her hand, his big one completely enveloping hers. "Good Lord, you've got small hands. Can I go home with you, dark angel?"

Dallas laughed in spite of herself. "Not hardly, I live in a strict boardinghouse."

"Then why don't you go home with me?" He hauled himself to his feet, almost pulling her off balance as he did so. She found herself in his arms as she struggled for balance, trying to keep him on his feet. He was as heavy as a side of beef, but the heat of him against her felt good.

She struggled to straighten up and tried to pull her long hair out of her eyes when the wind whipped it. There wasn't any point in arguing with him. She'd help him until she spotted a policeman or a carriage for hire, then she'd be on her way back to her lonely boardinghouse room.

"You need to go home and sleep it off," she scolded, as she would chide any cowboy on her father's ranch who had tied one on. "It must be nearly eight o'clock."

"Morning or evening?"

She started to laugh, then realized from his eyes that he wasn't joking. "Mr. Randolph, how long has it been since you've been completely sober?"

He swayed a little. "I think maybe several days ago when I arrived from Kentucky."

"You're in worse shape than I thought." Dallas sighed and took his arm, draped it over her shoulders. "Maybe I could find you a carriage."

She started walking, helping the tall man along the sidewalk.

"If we don't find the card game, we could go to the Golden Slipper or the Queen of Hearts and have some champagne." He smiled crookedly as they stumbled through the chill darkness.

"Have you been trying to drink this town dry?"

He shivered against her. "I've given it serious thought," he said solemnly. "Should have stayed with my thorough- breds but Sister insisted I come or else!"

Dallas swayed under his weight as they stumbled along. The cold wind took her breath away as it whipped at her skirt and blew icy needles of snow against her face. At least she had a coat. The man shivered again. Dallas

15

looked up at him in concern. "If I don't get you inside, you'll catch your death," she said.

"What I need is a warm brandy." He smiled down at her.

"You've had too much brandy already," she snapped. "If you got near an open flame, your breath would catch fire!"

"For an angel of the streets, you are the most outspoken hussy I ever met! You won't keep any customers if you aren't more charming to them."

Dallas resisted the urge to drop him right on the sidewalk and leave. After all, he was so drunk he didn't know what he was saying. Tomorrow, he'd probably have a splitting headache and a blank memory.

There didn't seem to be any carriages for hire along the street. The darkness and the cold had driven all of them back to the barns.

Quint Randolph said, "I'm not feeling very well."

"That's no surprise," Dallas said, bending under his weight as he leaned on her and they stumbled along. "Just don't get sick right now, you hear?"

He stopped, drew himself up proudly. "I'm a Southern gentleman and, as such, I'll have you know I can hold my liquor."

"That's the problem," Dallas snapped, "you're holding too much, just keep walking." She moved doggedly forward.

"Funny accent, but I like your voice, angel," he said. "Deep and throaty like velvet, what we used to call a 'whiskey' voice. Don't you sing at the Golden Slipper?"

"Where I'm from, Texas, they'd think anyone east of the Mississippi has a funny accent, and no, I don't sing at the Golden Slipper."

"Maybe that was Pearl," he said thoughtfully as they walked, "or maybe that redhead, Tasha, or maybe—"

"Look, Mr. Randolph, I'm not any of your saloon canaries, *comprende?*" She was getting angrier by the minute as they walked. Her shoulders ached from half supporting his weight even though she was taller and

16

stronger than the average girl, and she had worked on big roundups. What was it about this rich drunk that had ever made her think he was sad and sensitive?

She glanced up at him. He shivered uncontrollably, his teeth chattering. In spite of all his conversation, he was very, very drunk. Tomorrow he would wake up with a splitting headache and probably little memory of what had happened tonight. He might even think he'd gone to his card game. No doubt there was some simpering genteel lady sitting on some Kentucky plantation, with a houseful of children, waiting for her erring husband to come back from his business trip in Philadelphia.

She heard the clop of hooves on the cobblestones and sighed with relief as a bay horse appeared out of the mist, pulling a carriage. "Thank God! I was beginning to wonder what I was going to do! Hey, cabbie!"

She waved frantically, propping up the drunken rake. The ragged carriage kept moving. She suddenly realized that they must make a tragic or comical sight, standing under the flickering street lamp in the blowing snow.

The cabbie seemed half-asleep, and Dallas realized as the cab didn't slow down that he hadn't seen her or didn't intend to stop. What would she do if he went on past and left her standing in the street with a half-frozen drunk and no one to help her?

On sudden impulse, she stepped out in front of the carriage, dragging the man with her.

The horse whinnied and half reared in its harness, sending the fat driver almost falling from the seat. "Hey you, girlie! Get outa the street!" He waved her away with one fat fist. "You and your customer find another place to cross! You almost caused an accident!"

If she weren't so desperate, Dallas would have given him a real tongue lashing, but this was no time for taking offense. "I need a cab to get him home."

"Naw." The driver shook his head, pulled his coat collar up. "I'm headin' in. No business to speak of and not a fit night out for man nor beast!"

Quint Randolph seemed to come to momentarily. "The

17

lady and I want to go to the Golden Slipper for some champagne," he demanded. "She's the singing star there."

I don't care if she's the president's lady," the man shot back. "Now get out of me way."

Dallas didn't move. "I'll pay double," she shouted. She wondered suddenly if the rake had that kind of money on him? If she'd had sufficient funds, she wouldn't have taken the job at the lady's fashion magazine, although the editor, Mrs. Hale, was nice enough.

But before the cabbie could answer, Quint Randolph drew himself up proudly. "I resent his tone," he drawled to Dallas. "We'll walk until we find another carriage."

Then he promptly slumped to his knees, almost taking Dallas with him.

The fat driver peered down at them from his seat, but he didn't move as Dallas struggled with Quint's weight. "Girlie, did you say double?"

"Yes! You . . . you bandit, you! Now give me a hand!" How had she gotten herself into this mess? Suppose the Kentuckian wasn't as wealthy as he appeared to be? She certainly didn't have the fare. But this was an emergency. She'd worry about that when they were on the way.

The driver climbed down, stared curiously at them, his hands in his pockets. "Drunk as a lord!"

"Idiot, I can see that!" Dallas retorted. "Just give me some help with him."

The driver looked her over critically, and she felt herself flush at the disapproval on his fat face. "He's a big one, ain't he?"

"Do you charge by the pound? Are you gonna help me?" Dallas lost her temper and screamed at him.

It took the combined efforts of both of them to drag the unconscious man into the carriage. Dallas finally sat next to him, exhausted and breathless, but glad to be out of the wind.

The fat driver peered in at her, stamping his feet. "Well, where to, girlie? You think I got all the damned night to stand out here in the cold?"

"With all that fat," Dallas snapped, "you aren't in any

danger of freezing, although I'm concerned about your poor horse!" She began going through Quint's pockets, wishing she had thought to ask for an address during their discussion. She had the most overpowering urge to have the driver dump him out at the Golden Slipper, wherever that was.

The cabbie looked at her knowingly. "When you get through robbin' him, girlie, leave enough for the fare."

"Robbing him?" Dallas fairly shook with anger; then she realized what it must look like. She found a key in Quint's silk vest. "The Claremore Arms," she said, "and I'll see that he gets there so you won't rob him while he's out."

The cabbie winked. "Girlie, we could split his money. Who'd know but us?" He gestured toward the unconscious man. "He don't look like he'd wake up for Judgment Day."

Dallas had to fight to control her temper. "Get back up on that seat!" she hissed through clenched teeth, "And take us to the Claremore Arms!"

"All right! All right! You don't have to get huffy about it!" The driver shrugged and slammed the carriage door shut.

Dallas waited for the squeak of the springs as he climbed up. When he clucked to the horse, she leaned back against the worn seat with a tired sigh. Young ladies of good family, even in Texas, didn't go out after dark unescorted, and certainly the mess she'd gotten herself into was unthinkable. In the spotty illumination from the street lights they drove past, she looked at Quint Randolph's handsome, aristocratic face, his fine clothes. There was something tragic, almost haunting about him.

Without meaning to, she reached over and brushed his wind-blown hair from his forehead. He moaned softly and she wondered at the torment in his tone. As she would have comforted a sick child, Dallas patted his hand, the one with the gold-crested ring. His hand fumbled for her fingers, found them, gripped them tightly as if he never intended to let her go.

19

Now what? She'd really intended to have the cabbie drop her off at her own boardinghouse, then take the rake on to his hotel. She thought about it a minute, frowning. That cabbie was as crooked as a dog's hind leg, as they say in Texas. If he were to rob the unconscious man, throw him out in an alley to freeze to death before morning, who'd ever know? She felt suddenly protective. The least she could do was see to it that the gentleman from Kentucky made it to the safety of his warm room.

When Quint slumped sideways, she reached out automatically, settled him against her to keep him from falling onto the carriage floor. She felt him shiver and smelled the scent of brandy.

"Yes sir, you really cut the wolf loose tonight," she whispered, "Melanie must be some memory you're trying to drown."

She had never had a man feel that way about her, and she brushed his hair back a little wistfully. Oh, a cowboy or two may have made calf eyes at her, but her papa and her big brother, Trace, would have taken a quirt to any man who tried to get too close to her. Even Mama, who was more understanding, would not be happy with an eighteen-year-old daughter who had gotten herself into such a mess.

Finally the cab stopped. Dallas peered out at a small, select hotel as the driver clambered down and came around to open the creaking door. "Still out cold?"

Dallas decided to ignore the man as she struggled to extract her fingers from Quint Randolph's strong grip.

"He caught you with your hand in his pocket, did he?"

Dallas gave the grinning man a cold, lofty stare. "You polecat! Help me get him out."

The two of them struggled to get Quint Randolph onto the icy sidewalk.

Then the driver held out one dirty hand. "Now pay me, girlie."

She had a sudden vision of the man taking the money, climbing back up on the seat, and driving away. "Uh-uh." She shook her head. "Not until you help me get him up to his room."

He looked sheepish as if she'd guessed what he had intended. "You drive a hard bargain, lady."

"I'm from Texas and I've done a little horse trading in my time," she drawled, "Now give me a hand with him. Let's go around to the back entry so we won't be seen."

The driver shrugged, then shouldered half of Quint's weight and started dragging him around the side of the building.

"Be careful, you'll hurt him!"

"Girlie, you're breaking my heart!"

They got him through the back door and down the hall. Dallas peered at the number on the key, found the door. What would she do if Pearl from the Golden Slipper or, worse yet, a respectable and outraged wife waited on the other side of that door?

She shrugged. Horsefeathers. Her family had fought Comanches to hold their land. She reckoned she had enough spunk to hold her own if it came to a hair pulling with some saloon hussy.

Dallas fumbled with the key, opened the door. In the darkness, she stumbled over to the bureau, found an oil lamp, lit it. With a sigh of relief, she realized there was no one else in the pleasant, small room.

"Whatta I do with him?" The driver grumbled, Quint hanging unconscious off his shoulder.

"Put him on the bed, of course!" She watched the cabbie unceremoniously dump Quint on the bed. Then he turned, held out his hand. "I'm leavin' town tomorrow," he said. "Going back to New York."

"So?" She counted out Quint's money into the dirty hand.

"So if a gentleman goes to the police tomorrow, complaining that a pretty, black-haired girl robbed him tonight, he won't have any witnesses, if you know what I mean."

"Get out of here," Dallas snarled. "Get out of here!"

He flew backward from her fury, stumbling over furniture in making his escape. Dallas slammed the door behind him, locked it and then leaned against it, suddenly realizing she was shivering.

The inebriated man raised his head up when the door slammed, and he looked around, almost seeming to panic when he saw Dallas. "Angel, now whatever I promised you, I didn't mean it. I mean, I can't—"

"I think we both need something to warm us," she broke in wearily.

He raised up on his elbows, brightened. "Good idea! There's brandy in the cabinet by the fireplace."

"You've had enough brandy to float the whole city," Dallas declared. "What I meant was a roaring fire and some coffee."

He watched her, shivering a little as she went over, built a fire, and got it crackling merrily.

She wrapped her arms around herself, waiting for the room to warm, but seeing a tin of coffee, she put on water to boil. "The coffee will take awhile."

"Are we going back out then, to the Golden Slipper?"

She turned and looked at him. "The gambling tables will have to make do without your money tonight, sport. You started in a little too early to make it through the evening."

"It was kind of you to go to all this trouble." He looked a little sheepish and embarrassed.

"Think nothing of it," Dallas shrugged. Still shivering, she searched out the brandy. "Papa says I make a hobby of picking up strays."

"That's what I am, I reckon." He sounded bitter.

Dallas poured herself a slug of liquor, drank it fast, then gasped and coughed.

"Don't I get any of that? It's my brandy."

"You get coffee," she said firmly, and poured herself another drink. The warmth of the liquor began to spread through her. She didn't know when she'd been so tired and cold. Just then wind picked up outside, rattling the window and sending white flakes swirling past the glass.

Damn! Why hadn't she had the cabbie wait and take her on back to her boardinghouse? Because she'd been

22

afraid to be alone with him, that was why. How was she going to get home now? Probably all the cabs had left the streets. Maybe her landlady wouldn't check her room and find her missing, but if her absence caused a scandal, she would be looking for a new place to live on the morrow. Well, she couldn't worry about that now.

Dallas leaned against the window and sipped the brandy, feeling sad and cold. She knew she shouldn't be drinking on an empty stomach, but as the warmth spread through her, she didn't feel too cautious. She poured herself another shot, drank it.

The coffee sent a delicious aroma through the room, and Dallas wobbled a little as she crossed over to it, feeling a little dizzy. "Now, sport, I'll get you warm and sober."

But Quint Randolph had lain back on his pillow. He was out cold.

Horsefeathers. Now what? He was shivering uncontrollably and she went over, looked down at him. Hesitantly, she reached out, felt his coat. Of course, it was damp from the blowing snow. "Mister, tomorrow you'll have a headache so big it wouldn't fit into a horse corral."

She really had to get him out of those damp clothes and under some warm blankets. She hesitated. The Kentuckian shivered again. Who was to know?

Big as he was, it took some doing to get him out of the wet clothing. She tried not to stare at his lithe, virile body as she stripped him, but she was enthralled by the heavy hair on his chest. Without thinking, she reached out and ran a hand over that thick mat. How would it feel against her bare breasts? She decided to leave his drawers on, but she stared at the bulge between his thighs. What on earth was getting into her? Quickly she covered him up, but he shivered noticeably.

What to do? She looked around for more blankets, but there weren't any. Though she poked up the fire, the room was still so chilly with the late spring storm howling outside that she had some more brandy in an attempt to warm herself. Her own clothes weren't too dry.

23

Having finished her brandy, she hugged herself as she stared into the flames, wondering what to do next. She was in a fix all right, she admitted ruefully. One of the other girls at the boardinghouse would put pillows under her blankets to keep the landlady from realizing she hadn't come in, but that didn't solve anything at this end.

Looking at the man on the bed, Dallas realized he was probably out until morning. She took off her damp coat. Then she discovered the hem of her yellow wool dress was wet from dragging in the snow. *Who was to know?* She took it off, too.

So, in petticoats and camisole, she plopped down on the one hard chair, incredibly tired, hungry, and cold. The gentleman from Kentucky must take all his meals out. There wasn't anything but coffee and liquor in the cabinet, and somehow the brandy tasted better.

Dallas had another drink while she tried to decide what to do. First, she would wait for her coat and dress to dry; she'd placed them before the fire. And after that? Would she be able to find a cab on such a night and on this out-of-the-way street? It was too cold and too far to walk back to her boardinghouse.

Quint Randolph moaned aloud, apparently in the midst of some bad dream. "Sorry, Melanie," he muttered. "I didn't mean it . . . if only I could change it . . ." Whatever else he said was lost in sobs.

Dallas sighed, then went over and looked down at him in the dim lamplight. There were tears on his cheeks. Whatever he had done to Melanie lay heavily on his soul, the anguish on his face told her that. She felt both sympathy and a twinge of jealousy. No man cared so much for her.

"It's all right, Quint," she said, patting his face and realizing she was slightly drunk herself. "It's all right now. Don't you know the two saddest words in any language are 'if only' because no one can change what's past?"

The lines in his face smoothed out, and on an impulse, she leaned over and gently kissed his lips, tasting the warm hint of brandy. She looked over at the other side of the big bed. She was tired and cold, and it looked so inviting. Drunk as he was, he'd never know it if she lay down on top of the covers for a few minutes while her clothes dried out.

Giddy with the brandy and her own daring, Dallas tiptoed over, blew out the lamp, and went back to the bed. Except for the flickering firelight, the room was dark as the windswept night outside the window.

Cautiously, she lay down on top of the blankets on the very edge of her side of the bed. Oh, that felt so good! But why was her head whirling so? She must remember not to doze off. Sometime soon, she was going to have to brave the night, try to walk through the blowing snow back to her boardinghouse.

She lay very still, her head spinning slightly, listening to Quint Randolph's heavy breathing. She was cold. She lay there, drunk and shivering, on top of the covers. What difference would it make if she crawled under them? After all, he was past knowing the difference.

She slid under the blankets, very aware that only a few inches away was a handsome man clad in nothing but his drawers. If Papa or Trace were here, there'd be big trouble. She said a little prayer of thanksgiving that they weren't, and was immediately swept up in a wave of homesickness for the ranch life she'd always known and loved. Her mother, the beautiful Cheyenne, Velvet Eyes, had been opposed to sending Dallas off to school, but Papa had been stubborn as only Don Diego de Durango could be. He had wanted her to stay with his rich friends, the Peabodys, in Boston, and learn to be a lady.

A lady. Dallas lay staring at the ceiling and almost laughed aloud. It was incredible, yet here she was, an innocent runaway schoolgirl in a drunken rake's bed. If her Papa or her big brother knew about this, Quint Randolph would be forced to marry her or face the Texans' deadly pistols.

Would Quint marry her to keep from being shot? She played out the scene in her head, imagining Papa bursting into the room, furious at this smirch on his family's honor. She turned her head and studied Quint's aristo-cratic profile in the firelight. He was so very handsome, and so tragic.

Shivering again, he thrashed in his sleep and rolled over so that his arm flopped across her, one big hand on her breast.

Dallas held her breath, keenly aware of the heat of his fingers through the fabric of her sheer camisole. Her heart thumped so loudly, she was afraid the pounding against his palm might cause him to awaken. But his hand only cupped her small breast.

Now what could she do? If she tried to move, he might wake up. She tried to think clearly but the brandy made her dizzy.

"Melanie . . ." he whispered and there was anguish in his voice. "I'm sorry . . . so sorry."

In that moment, Dallas would have given anything to be the missing Melanie he evidently cared so much for. Gingerly, she tried to move, intent on slipping out of the bed, but Quint reached for her blindly, pulling her to him. "No, don't leave . . . don't leave! We'll have that wedding night you wanted . . . I owe you that."

Dallas tried to protest, tried to pull away, but his lips were hot on hers, one strong arm was on her breast, and the other was imprisoning her, pulling her hard against his tall muscular frame.

She must get up and get away, but even as she opened her mouth to protest that she wasn't Melanie, his tongue slipped between her lips, tasting hotly of brandy as he molded her body against his.

She had never made love to a man and this one wouldn't even remember her tomorrow. She felt the heat of wanting him spread slowly through her, much as the brandy had, racing like fire through her veins. His body was warm against her cold one, and the heat of him felt so good, she let him pull her closer. His lips dominated hers, sucking; seeking. His other hand slid beneath her underclothes, pulling the top of her camisole down, strok-ing her nipples, reaching to touch between her thighs.

26

She must get up right this minute, put on her clothes and get out of here. Yet she seemed powerless to move, except to press even harder against him. His hairy chest brushed against her bare breasts and the sensation of it against her swollen nipples made her tremble.

His eyes flickered open. "Who . . . who are you?"

She felt the blush burn her face and turned her head so he couldn't see it. Yet his expression told her that tomorrow he wouldn't remember tonight.

"You're the dark angel of the snow," he murmured. "I must be imagining you."

"Yes, you're imagining me," she whispered drunkenly, the brandy creating a fire in her veins as she kissed him again.

But he pulled back. In the dim light of the flickering fire, she read panic, humiliation on his handsome face. "I . . . I can't," he said. "Not since that day. I'm unable to . . ."

His voice trailed off, anguish in it, and Dallas blinked at him in confusion, too innocent to be sure of what he was talking about. The brandy sang in her veins and the cold wind rattled the window. But here against Quint Randolph's hairy chest was warmth. She slipped her arms around his neck, snuggling closer to him. She might be almost as drunk as he was, she thought in confusion, but it didn't seem to matter. She opened her lips and pulled him to her, hesitant in her inexperience.

"I-I told you I'm unable. . . ." His words ended in a groan as he pulled her to him and kissed her feverishly, his hands running over her body until she thrashed wildly in the throes of the new feelings his touch brought to her.

She felt her body moisten as she pressed up against him, felt his maleness throb strongly against her bare thigh. With more daring than she had ever thought possible, she reached down and touched him, felt him hard and hot in her hand. "Liar!" she whispered.

"Dark angel, if you're only a dream, I hope I don't wake up yet!" Then he parted her thighs and took her, tearing into her virginity as if he had been without a

27

woman a long, long time.

Dallas arched back, spread her thighs, felt him plunge into her as she had seen mustang stallions take a mare; wildly and with utter abandon. There was brief pain as he tore her virgin silk. She winced, then felt her body clasp his, holding him, deep and throbbing, within her. Tomorrow, she might regret this, but tonight she was more than a little drunk and was throwing her inhibitions to the howling wind because she was taken in by a haunting smile on a man's sad face. He gasped and stiffened in her arms and for a moment, she thought he was unconscious again. Then the feeling swept over her, too, and she wept as their passions surged uncontrollably.

He covered her face with kisses. "Don't cry, dark angel! If I'm dreaming, I don't want to ever wake up! Don't leave me. Oh, please don't leave me!"

She clung to him, drunk with both brandy and emotion. At the moment, she didn't care about tomorrow. They clung together, snuggled warmly in the big bed, while the storm raged outside, and within minutes, they were both asleep.

Dallas awakened just at dawn, horror sweeping over her as she realized she lay in Quint Randolph's arms. How could she have done such a thing? It was unthinkable! Her mother had warned her about liquor and now, too late, she realized why.

Her head ached as if she'd been kicked in the head by a mule. Quickly, she slipped out of bed, stumbling around in the darkness to find the wash basin and pitcher so she might clean up as best she could, put on her clothes. Quint Randolph slept heavily. He might not remember what had happened, but it would certainly be humiliating and embarrassing if he awakened and found her in his room. No doubt he would think her one of the girls from the Golden Slipper and try to pay her.

I must have been very drunk last night, she thought as she dressed hastily. Otherwise, I would never have done such an unbelievable thing.

Still, just before she slipped out the door, she tiptoed to the bed and stood looking down at him. Whoever Melanie was, Quint Randolph belonged to her. Dallas had found the man she wanted, but he was married or engaged to another woman. Still, she didn't regret the one night in his arms. He wouldn't remember, but she would never forget.

"Good-bye, dearest," she murmured and leaned over, brushed his lips with her own before fleeing out the door.

Outside the weather was warming, the snow crunching under her shoes as it melted. Dallas paused and looked around, getting her bearings. It wasn't all that far to the magazine building from here. The sun was up, people moving up and down the sidewalks, tradesmen's carts on the streets now. A few of those about looked at her curiously, but it was daylight and her dress wasn't mussed and wrinkled. No doubt they would think she had arisen early.

Dallas stopped at a working man's cafe, had a bite of breakfast. Absently, she reached up to finger her earring. It was gone. Frantically, she reached for her other ear. That earring was there.

Oh, no. The unique pale lavender pearl from the Concho River of Texas, was gone. Where could she have lost it?

She turned and stared before her, thinking. Had she lost it on the street? More likely, it was somewhere in Quint Randolph's room. Dallas cursed silently as she sipped her coffee. Yes, no doubt that's where it was. Horsefeathers. She could forget about it then. There didn't seem to be a nice way to look up a man and say, Beg your pardon, have you found an earring I dropped when I slept with you last night? If so, I'd be much obliged if you'd return it, no questions asked. She tried to picture his puzzled face when he found the earring, drew a blank on how it had come to be in his room.

Could she use that as an excuse to see him again? Dallas pictured herself knocking on his door. *Pardon me, but did I leave an earring in your bed when we both gave way to passion the night of the snowstorm?*

Horsefeathers. Of course she couldn't do that. It had been an unforgettable night, she had to admit that, and so wild. She still couldn't believe she'd given her virginity to some drunk she'd met on the street. Dallas winced as she finished her eggs and stood up. It hadn't been like that — something casual and cheap, at least not to her.

She still had to get to her office in time to comb her hair, look fresh. Now she had yesterday's problems to deal with, plus one more. Though she was reluctant to admit it, even to herself, she couldn't get Quint Randolph out of her mind. But he belonged to someone named Melanie.

With a sigh, Dallas paid her bill and headed toward the *Godey's Lady's Book* offices.

Chapter Two

Quint opened his eyes slowly, staring up at the ceiling.

Good Lord, what a headache! He lay there, listening to the noises passing carriages and people made on the snowy street outside the hotel.

Well, at least the sun was out. He could see its light through the drapes.

What had happened and how had he gotten back to his room? The last he remembered, he'd been fortifying himself against the cold with a little brandy—maybe more than a little, he admitted sheepishly to himself as his head throbbed—then he'd gone looking for that card game. He lay quietly, trying to remember. Perhaps he might have stopped here and there for a drink before continuing on his way. He only remembered being cold, very cold. And something else was tugging at his memory . . . a girl. No, he must have dreamed that.

Quint dismissed the idea with a sigh and sat up, swinging his long legs off the side of the bed.

"Oh, Lord, Quint, you sure cut the wolf loose this time!" He ran both hands through his hair, trying to contain the pounding head which felt as big as a melon.

Cut the wolf loose? Now where did he get that? To his knowledge, he'd never heard the expression before, wasn't even sure what it meant. Well, at least it was the right animal. He stared at the crest on his ring.

He felt too sick to die, and buried his head in his hands, wondering why he had tried to drink himself into oblivion; then he paused, frowning. He knew perfectly well why.

He ought to get dressed, eat something—at least put some coffee in his queasy stomach. Taking a deep breath, he almost imagined he smelled the slight scent of perfume. Puzzled, he sniffed again, looked around. Surely he hadn't gotten drunk enough to humiliate himself by bringing a whore to his room. He bought drinks for the saloon girls. Unfortunately, for the past year that was all he was capable of.

Turning, he peered in growing horror at the hollow on the pillow next to his.

Good Lord, that was what he'd done all right. Well, thank God, he didn't remember any of it; especially not his humiliation when the girl discovered he was impotent. He had enough of them laugh at him this past year. And to think he'd been such a virile stud of a man until . . . He didn't want to recall that day.

Suppose she had cleaned out his wallet? Quint stood up. Swaying slightly, he stumbled over to the bureau, found his wallet, counted the money. He wasn't sure how much he had had to begin with, but there were several hundred dollars here. No, she hadn't taken his money.

An honest whore. He smile slightly, despite his throbbing head. What he needed to do was pull the blankets over his face and wake up tomorrow.

With an uneven walk, he started across the cold floor.

God damnit! Pain stabbed into the sole of one bare foot. With a howl of anguish and annoyance, he lifted it, then hopped and hobbled the few steps to the bed.

He'd have to speak to the maid about dropping pins and tacks so a man couldn't even walk around his own room barefooted. Quint propped the injured foot on his other leg and peered at it, expecting to find a tiny object and pull it out.

Now what the devil was that? He held it in his palm, staring at it, turned it over and over. A tiny gold star with a lavender pearl in the center. A woman's earring, that's what it was. How had it gotten here? Something tugged at his memory and he tried to reach back through a drunken haze and grab it. A girl, yes, the whore who had ended up here must have dropped it.

His gaze dropped to his own lap and that's when he saw the slight smear of dried blood. With alarm, he stared down at himself. That was a very tender spot for a man to injure, yet he didn't remember anything.

Quint examined himself. Yes, it was blood all right, but he couldn't find any wound. Could that mean? No, of course not. Whores weren't virgins. None of this made any sense. He looked from the scarlet stain to the tiny earring. Had he been drunk enough to drag some innocent up to his room, attempt to ravish her? Of course not. He grimaced, ran his free hand through his hair. Attempt would be about all I could do, he thought, remembering the past year's humiliations. He'd been impotent since the day Melanie had died. Maybe God was punishing him. Would He punish him forever? If only . . .

A sharp rap on the door made him start. "Who is it?"

"Ben, suh, Miz Lydia's coachman. I gots a note for you."

Quint groaned aloud. The one person he didn't feel like facing today was his older sister. "Slip it under the door. Ben, tell my sister, I . . . I'm not feeling well. Maybe we can have dinner tomorrow or the next day."

"Ah's powerful sorry, Mister Quint, but Miz Lydia, she say, don't come back without you if ah has to drag you to her house for a late breakfast."

Quint blinked his hazel eyes, scratched at the thick fur of his chest. *Breakfast*. The thought made his stomach churn. He looked at the scrap of paper that the black servant had slipped under the door, stumbled over, picked it up. His older sister's writing always looked as if she took out her fury on the paper, slashing letters, leaving holes in the paper where she dotted *i*'s and crossed *t*'s.

The note demanded he come with Ben. Quint sighed. "Tell Lydia you couldn't find me," he yelled.

"Mister Quint, you gonna get old Ben in trouble," the old man shouted through the door. "You know Miz Lydia ain't gonna believe ah couldn't find you."

Quint pictured Ben getting a tongue lashing from his arrogant, wealthy sister. He couldn't do that to the black coachman. "Just a minute!" He grabbed a robe and, still holding the earring in the palm of his hand, stumbled over to unlock the door. "Come on in. It'll take awhile for me to get dressed."

Ben's white hair was in sharp contrast to his wrinkled black face. "Thank you, Mister Quint, I wasn't wantin' to go back and face the lady without you."

"That's the only reason I'm going," Quint grumbled. "She gets mad enough at me, and no servant should have to take the tongue lashing she gives."

Ben almost nodded in agreement, seemed to catch himself in time.

Quint laid the earring on the bureau, then went over to the wash basin, poured himself some water, began to wash. "She know how long I've been in town?"

"Yassuh," Ben fumbled with his hat. "Someone said they'd seen you so she's been expectin' you all week."

"Then there'll be hell to pay," Quint said, splashing water on his face. "When I got her message, she said it was important, but I didn't really want to leave Kentucky. Besides, the memories here are too painful. And a man deserves a little fun after spending a year away from everyone but servants and horses."

Ben didn't say anything as Quint washed himself. They both knew why Quint had waited to let his sister know he'd arrived. Facing up to a stern sister almost old enough to be his mother was something a man had to work up his courage for. He hadn't been back in Philadelphia since the day of Mother's funeral, two weeks after Melanie's. He hadn't realized how overcome with guilt he'd be at the memories. If only . . .

"Ben, get me some clothes out of the wardrobe and a glass of brandy. Can you shave me?"

"I is a coachman, not a gentleman's personal man," Ben reminded him. "I might cut your throat."

Quint looked down at his shaking hands, took the

sharp, straight razor in the right one, looking at the gold signet ring, remembering.

Very slowly and cautiously, he began to shave himself, while Ben dug in the cabinet for clothes, liquor. "I should have brought a servant with me, but I just got through setting all my slaves free."

"Free?" The old man paused in surprise. "Does Miz Lydia know? All them people on that big horse farm is worth a lot of money."

Quint laughed, then winced as he nicked himself. "I figure she's heard about it and that's why she's demanded a visit."

He took the glass with a grateful sigh, sipped it. "Have one yourself, Ben."

"Thank you, suh, but it's too early for me. Besides, Miz Lydia wouldn't like it if she smelled liquor on a servant."

"Miz Lydia is a hypocrite," Quint said as he shaved. "She won't touch a drink because she knows if she ever did, there'd be no stopping. She'd probably drink the town dry." He finished shaving, his head still throbbing, a few cuts now on his lean face.

He thought for a moment before reaching for his clothes. "Ben, you ever hear the term 'cut the wolf loose'?"

The old black paused in brushing off Quint's boots. "Once I heard a cowboy say that when I belonged to a man over near the Mississippi."

Quint buttoned the elegant silk vest, put on his coat. Cowboy? Quint had never met any cowboys as far as he knew. Now where would he have picked up a term like that? "You have any idea what it means?"

The servant shrugged. "Near's I can recall, it means to have a wild party, get drunk."

"Lord, I reckon that's what I did last night!" Quint groaned again. Facing his sister wasn't something he wanted to do today—or any day. Still if he hadn't come as ordered, Lydia might have journeyed to Kentucky and stayed there for weeks. This way, he could escape back to his thoroughbred farm in the bluegrass country after he got through with this miserable meeting. No doubt she'd heard about his freeing his slaves, then hiring many of them back. He looked at the tiny earring for a long, puzzled moment, then picked it up, put it in his vest. Sooner or later, maybe he'd remember how he'd come by it. "All right, Ben, I'm ready to face my sister now, but I'd just as soon face a lynch mob."

After the carriage deposited him at the door of his sister's elegant Victorian mansion in the best section of Philadelphia, Quint hesitated a moment before ringing the bell. What he really needed was another drink before facing Lydia.

A portly black butler escorted him in. "Miz Lydia had decided you weren't coming, suh, and was about to break-fast without you." He looked Quint up and down. "No hat or topcoat, Mister Quint?"

Where had he left those last night? He remembered starting early at a place called the Lucky Lady, then moving on to either the Golden Slipper or that faro place. After that, events became a little blurry. He did remember trying to find a private, high-stakes card game and being very cold. . . .

"No, it's warming up, so I didn't wear them. I'll an-nounce myself."

Quint brushed past the butler, strode to the dining room.

His sister might have once been a beauty if she had ever smiled. Now the lines seemed too deep to ever be erased. Her expression was as grim as the high-necked black dress she wore. Lydia frowned, looking up at him from the ornate walnut table. Then she went back to her omelet. "It's about time, Quinton. I went ahead without you since it's noon and I didn't think you were coming."

He held his breath while he kissed her forehead so she wouldn't smell the brandy, but she sniffed suspiciously. He went to the opposite end of the long, ornate table, sat down. "Coffee," he said to the butler.

"Bring Mr. Randolph some eggs," Lydia said. "He's been eating hotel food for almost a week and surely is in need of some home cooking."

Quint sighed loudly and folded his hands together, resting his elbows on the exquisite linen. "Lydia, don't start in on me."

"I haven't the vaguest idea what you're talking about, Quinton. I always think of my baby brother's welfare."

She looked like a Randolph, her chestnut hair gray around the temples. Black did not go well with her complexion or her hazel eyes, Quint thought, and her mouth was a grim slash in her aristocratic face.

He watched her reach for a sterling fruit knife, cut a pear with angry, stabbing gestures.

He decided not to rise to the bait. His head still throbbed too badly for him to want to get into a verbal duel with his elegant sister. Just why had he come? To save old Ben from a tongue lashing.

The butler came in, placed a moist, steaming omelet before Quint. Quint took in the smell of eggs and his stomach heaved. "Take it away and bring me some strong, black coffee," he ordered.

"Leave it!" Lydia commanded, her fruit knife poised as if she intended to rise up out of her chair and stab someone.

The butler paused in reaching for the plate, looking from one to the other in embarrassed discomfort.

Quint smiled disarmingly at her. "Sister, with the way I'm feeling, if he doesn't take it away, I may just get sick all over your fine dining table."

Lydia shuddered and grimaced. "Remove the eggs and bring him some coffee. Really, Quint, you are so vulgar! That comes from hanging around with the riffraff, or even servants, who'll go hunting and riding with you."

Quint took the fine china cup from the butler, sipped the strong brew and inhaled the welcome scent. *Here it comes.* "I'm more democratic than you are, but then we never liked the same social circle."

Lydia glared at him, went back to stabbing the pear

with dainty motions. "Someday you'll marry again, have children to carry on the Randolph name. You'll care then about your reputation."

"I doubt both. I've been married and what people think of me has never mattered much."

"Albert and I are certainly aware of that," Lydia snapped. "I'm only glad Mother is gone to her rest now so you can no longer embarrass her. And Charlotte is lucky enough to be far away in California where she never hears about her younger brother's antics, but I—"

"Have to stay in Philadelphia where everyone knows me and hang my head in shame over wild Quinton." Quint finished the sentence for her glibly, and grinned. Certainly he had heard it enough times to know it by heart.

Lydia's cheeks mottled with suppressed rage. In fact, now that Quint thought of it, she'd always seemed to be suppressing rage. He wondered suddenly what went on in his sister's bedroom with that mild little husband who had inherited a chain of dry-goods stores.

Lydia held the knife so tightly, her knuckles turned white. Then, with a sigh, she pushed back her chair and stood up. "Sometimes you make me forget I'm a lady," she said grimly.

"If you ever found a man who could make you do that, believe me, it would change your whole life, Sister." He stood up too, taking his coffee with him.

"And just what is that supposed to mean?" Her tone was scathing.

"Never mind!" He decided he had pushed her far enough. It was something he did out of revenge for having been raised and smothered by three women after his blue-blooded father was killed many years ago in a hunting accident. Quint didn't even remember him.

They went into the morning room and sat down before the fire.

Lydia pulled her needlework frame over before her chair. "You are limping, Quinton. Have you hurt a leg?"

Absently, he reached for the small earring in his pocket. "I . . . stepped on something sharp."

She gave him a searching look before reaching for her needle and stabbing it viciously into the fabric.

He studied the scene she worked on; a wildly abandoned, scantily dressed girl danced in a swirl of handkerchiefs. "What is that?"

"A Biblical scene," Lydia explained loftily, "just like all my others. This is Delilah dancing before Sampson so he will let her cut his hair."

"Looks like she's got more earthy things than that in mind."

The look his sister gave him could have killed. "Only you would profane a Bible story!"

He stared around at all the needlework pillows on the furniture: Salome, Bathsheba, Eve, Jezebel. All whirled and danced half-naked, frozen in his sister's needlework for all time. He wondered again about her choice of subjects. "Why have you sent for me, Lydia?"

She looked insulted, went on stabbing the needle through the fabric. "Do I need a reason to want to see my only brother? I worry about you, Quinton, living on that horse farm with nothing but a bunch of Nigras. What you need is a wife to look after you."

He closed his eyes briefly, guilt sweeping over him as he remembered good, obedient Melanie. "I had a wife; remember?"

"Do you think anyone in Philadelphia society has forgotten?" Her tone was biting. She stabbed the needle through the fabric again.

Quint held the cup between his hands, staring into the fire. "You can't make me feel any guiltier than I already do about that day, Lydia. You waste your breath trying."

"I-I shouldn't have said that." Her face flushed, and she turned the needle over and over in nervous fingers.

A great sadness came over him, and he stared into the fire. Melanie had been small and blond, and she had loved him. But he had not loved her. "Is there any whiskey?" He stood up suddenly, favoring the injured foot.

"You know there's sherry, nothing stronger. You keep that up, you'll be just like Father."

He went over to the cabinet, got the decanter, poured himself a drink. He thought about lighting his pipe, decided that was pushing his sister too far.

"I'd think you would have learned your lesson after what happened on your wedding day. If you hadn't gotten so drunk at the reception, if only—"

"Will you please stop!" Quint screamed. His hands were shaking so badly the sherry sloshed over his fingers. He couldn't control the urge to throw it, but he did manage to keep from throwing it at her. Instead, the glass slammed into the fireplace.

"That was a piece of my best lead crystal," Lydia said with prim satisfaction, glad that she had pushed him over the edge. She returned to stabbing the needle into the fabric.

Quint leaned against the mantel with both hands and closed his eyes. "I know you won't believe this, but I've relived that day a thousand times in my mind, wishing I could go back, change things. There's no way to change what's in the past. But, believe me, I've paid for my sins in ways you couldn't imagine."

He thought of his impotence, brought on by guilt. Oh, Melanie, I'm so sorry, he thought, I'd give my own worthless life to bring you back.

She had loved him so, and he had loved her not at all. That was why he'd been so drunk at the reception. If only he had let old Ben drive the phaeton. If only . . .

Lydia's voice interrupted his troubled thoughts. "You really should marry again, Quinton. You can't live in the past forever, and, after all, the year of mourning for Melanie was up yesterday."

That was why he had been drinking, he remembered that now. Quint sighed and turned to look at her. "What is it you want, Lydia? I'm expecting a lecture on the freeing of my slaves, so get it over with and let's get on to something else."

"I did mean to speak to you about that, too. Do you realize what a good slave's worth?"

He grinned wryly. "That's the sort of comment I would

40

expect from you. Besides the fact that it seemed the humanitarian thing to do, there's a civil war looming and they'll be freed sooner or later."

Her stern face paled as she no doubt considered the financial loss. "That's one of the things we need to discuss."

Quint shrugged. "My thoroughbred farm is probably in a good spot to catch hell from both sides if it comes to shooting. Both North and South will be requisitioning my horses, and I might lose some in the shelling."

"You could make a good deal of money selling your stock as officers' mounts." She looked up from her sewing, her eyes gleaming. "And then you could move back East—"

"Why in the hell would I want to do that? There's nothing for me to do here."

"Oh, but there is!" Lydia allowed herself the luxury of a smile. "Albert says if war comes, the Union will need uniforms for its soldiers. We plan to build huge factories, hire hundreds of seamstresses, and buy some of those new sewing machines."

A suspicion began to build in his mind. "That sounds like it would require an enormous amount of capital, much more than Albert has and certainly more than my horses are worth, not to mention where you'd get the cotton or the mills to make the fabrics."

"I've worked it all out," Lydia said triumphantly, "and you would be in charge of the manufacture."

"Bossing sweatshops full of starving immigrant girls?" Quint snorted. "I think not. I'm considering gathering up my horses and reopening that Spanish land grant the family's owned all these years."

"The Wolf's Den ranch? Quinton, you can't be serious! You're the fifth generation of Randolphs and the only son. What a waste that would be! The West is full of cactus and wild Indians."

"And maybe solitude and peace for me." He closed his eyes, trying to remember the dream that kept pushing its way into his brain . . . a girl with very dark eyes and long

41

ebony hair blowing about her face. She must have been an angel because he remembered tiny stars and her mouth warm on his as she came into his arms . . . warm, giving, making a man of him again.

". . . and that's it, Quinton, what do you think?"

He started, then looked at his sister. "What? I'm not sure I heard you."

Lydia was visibly annoyed. "Must I go through it all again? You remember the friends I made in Boston while you were at Harvard?"

He nodded, although he didn't. At least she hadn't reminded him that he'd been kicked out of that university because of his wild and unconventional behavior. Quint went over and sat down, conscious of the dull ache in his head. "I haven't been in Boston since I attended the Shaw's New Year's ball two years ago."

"That's who I mean."

He thought a moment. "I think Austin Shaw announced his engagement that night, but I don't remember ever receiving an invitation to the wedding."

"Because there wasn't one!" Lydia was maliciously enjoying the gossip. "His intended was Summer Van Schuyler from Miss Priddy's Academy. Ran away to the Indians, she did," Lydia wrinkled her nose in distaste. "Imagine! Indians!"

He felt impatience. "So what's the point, dear sister?"

"The Shaws have the mills, and a connection in Georgia, the St. Clairs, raise cotton. Shaw is stockpiling it, figuring there'll be a shortage when the war starts."

"Such astute businessmen," Quint said dryly, wondering how soon he could make an excuse and leave.

"So you see," Lydia said triumphantly, "all we need is the capital and we're on our way to a fortune. We thought Banker Peabody might provide that."

Quint searched his memory. "Oh, yes, I remember him now. I think I danced with his clumsy daughter, Maude, at the ball. You can forget about borrowing from old Peabody. He's as tight as a cork in a bottle."

Lydia didn't look at him, concentrating on her needlework instead. "He wouldn't be tight about financing a son-in-law's business venture."

"He hasn't got a son-in-law," Quint snorted, "and if you'd ever met his fat daughter, you'd know why. I . . ." A sudden suspicion pushed into his mind. "I hope this isn't what I think it is, Lydia."

"I don't know what you're talking about," she protested, her eyes a bit too wide for her denial to be believable. "Why, here you are a widower and Maude is a lovely girl—and an only child."

"Maude's as big as a beached whale, and has brains to match. Besides, she never shuts up."

"She's from a fine family."

"A *rich* family," Quint said.

Lydia shrugged. "Same thing. I was in Boston just a couple of weeks ago and I invited the dear girl to come to Philadelphia for shopping."

"They don't have stores in Boston?"

"She'll arrive tomorrow for a visit," Lydia said. "I thought you might join us for dinner."

Quint now knew why she had sent for him. He was so angry, he had to struggle not to grab her and shake her. Instead he stood up. "No."

She gave him her most pleading look. "Do think about it, Quinton. I can hardly cancel my invitation at this moment; Maude is surely already on her way. After all, I'm only thinking of your own good—"

"You never stop meddling, do you? A little more than a year ago, I recall a similar conversation about how my marrying a local society girl would make my dying mother happy!"

"Melanie was wildly in love with you," his sister protested, "and I was only thinking of what was good for everyone concerned—"

"Lord protect me from people doing things for my own good," Quint snapped, running his hand through his hair distractedly. "I let my sisters and my mother pressure me into marrying a girl I didn't love. But I won't again. I've had all the tragedy and guilt I can deal with! Was there

43

anything else, Lydia, before I go?"

She looked as if she might argue, then reconsidered. "I have a buyer for some of your horses. He's in town now staying at the Tradition Hotel."

"Good, I could use the money. Is he interested in racing?"

"Something about a fast mail delivery." She got up, went over to the desk, got a pen and paper, scribbled something, handed it to him. "Quint, won't you reconsider? It's been a year; you ought to marry. Melanie was such an angel."

Angel. He looked at the paper in his hand; the slashing marks of his sister's handwriting. She almost seemed to use her pen as a weapon. There was some clue to her personality here, but he wasn't quite sure what it meant.

Angel. With the word, a face came to his mind, the dark angel of his dreams. Could she possibly be real? "You know, Lydia, maybe you're right."

She actually smiled at him. "I don't know why everyone resents it so when I try to give advice. I'm only doing what's best for all."

"Yes, I'm seriously considering remarrying," He folded the paper, put it in his silk vest. "But I intend to choose my bride and this time I will marry for love, not because of family or inheritance."

She clenched her fists. "What does love matter in the long run? In a marriage, it's good family and wealth that count!"

"Do they?" He looked around at the needlepoint pillows with Biblical heroines dancing wildly, and suddenly felt very sorry for Lydia. "Is that what's wrong with your own marriage?"

Then, while his sister sputtered with rage, he turned and strode from the room. While Ben brought the carriage around, Quint turned and looked through the window. The elegant lady was gripping one of the needlepoint pillows. Her face was buried in it, and her shoulders shook with sobs.

Quint felt a twinge of pity and guilt. He half turned to

44

reenter the house, then paused. Lydia had always bullied him, bossed him. He was not going to take it anymore, nor would he let her choose a wife for him, not again. What he was going to do was try to figure out if the dark angel in his dream could possibly be real, and if so, he'd move heaven and earth to find her.

Ben brought the carriage around. Quint wanted to go back to bed because his head still ached, but curiosity got the better of him. He gave the coachman the address of the Tradition Hotel.

Thaddeus Barnes greeted Quint warmly and introduced himself. "Come in, come in! Your sister tells me you have the best horses in all Kentucky!"

Quint shook hands with the lean, tanned man, liking him instantly. "Well, I do take pride in my horses, always looking for better blood to add to my pedigrees."

Barnes took up a decanter. "Drink or coffee?"

Now that he was away from Lydia, Quint didn't feel the driving urge for a drink. He accepted coffee, lit his pipe. "Are you interested in racing, Mr. Barnes?"

"In a way; but not as you think of it." The Westerner poured himself a drink, then sat down. "Would you believe me if I told you someone's going to attempt to get mail from St. Joe, Missouri, to California in ten days?"

Quint was thunderstruck. "Lord, what an exciting idea! But, of course, it's impossible! It takes six weeks now by ship around the Horn, and three weeks by Butterfield Stage, over the Southern 'Ox-bow' route."

Barnes sat down, leaned forward as he sipped his drink. "You heard of Russell, Majors, and Waddell, the freighting company? They're going after the government mail contract Butterfield holds."

Quint laughed and blew out fragrant smoke. "That'll be hard to take away. Butterfield's a friend of President Buchanan."

"But not impossible!" Barnes said, leaning back in his chair. "Remember the election is this fall and there'll be a new President in 1861. If the Pony Express proves it can carry the mail and do it faster over the central route, maybe they can take that contract away from Butterfield."

For the first time Quint felt his heart beat with excitement over a business venture. "And you're buying fast horses? How many?"

"Possibly as many as four hundred. Some of them we've already bought. On the California end, we'll use mustangs. If we make a deal, Mr. Randolph, could you deliver them yourself?"

Quint thought about it with growing excitement. "Sure I could! What do you call this new venture anyway?"

Barnes grinned. "The Pony Express. It begins running first week in April. You'll deliver your horses to the jumping off place, St. Joe, Missouri."

Quint's headache suddenly faded. "I can see we've got a lot to talk about, Barnes. Can I be your host and show you a little of the city tonight?"

Barnes smiled, a little embarrassed. "What I'd really like to see is a minstrel show."

"A what?" That was definitely not what Quint had had in mind.

"And I'd like to meet a real actress," Barnes added. "Now that's what I'd call cuttin' the wolf loose!"

Cutting the wolf loose. Quint saw her in his mind then with sudden clarity, the smoldering dark girl with the deep, velvet voice. Of course she existed. He could remember her now, he just couldn't remember where he'd met her. But, by God, he was going to turn this town upside down before he left to deliver those horses. He intended to find her.

"Barnes, I just happen to know a real actress; Lillie's an old friend, matter of fact. And I'll find us a minstrel show to attend. I'll pick you up tonight at eight. Now, let's talk horses! This Pony Express sounds like the stuff legends are made of!"

Chapter Three

Dallas got to her office at *Godey's Lady's Book,* freshened up, and was at her desk before the editor, Mrs. Sarah Hale, arrived.

The plump, gray-haired lady stopped by her desk. "Is anything wrong, my dear? You look so preoccupied."

Dallas started. "Oh, no. Nothing. I was just sitting here wondering where I'd lost an earring."

The older woman clucked sympathetically. "That lovely pair with the unusual lavender pearls? What a shame! I've often wondered about those."

"I don't know much about them myself," Dallas said. Actually her papa had had them custom made for her birthday. The gold stars represented Texas, the Lone Star State, of course, and the pastel pearls were Concho River pearls, of a color almost never found anywhere else.

"You know, dear," Mrs. Hale peered at her absently, "it occurs to me that I haven't found out much about you, either, in the two weeks you've worked here, except that you're doing some very good writing about the latest fashions from Paris."

Dallas shrugged. "Not much to tell. I just had a burning ambition to work on one of the few magazines that actually had a woman editor." It wouldn't do for the motherly woman to ask too many questions. If she knew Dallas was a runaway, no doubt she would consider it her duty to contact the school, the Peabody family, or Papa.

"I've tried hard, in my own way, to help women. I've

shown that a woman can hold a man's job—be an editor."

"And don't forget your drive 'to turn' Thanksgiving into a national holiday," Dallas reminded her.

"Haven't yet succeeded at that," Sarah Hale said with a sigh, "but this is an election year. Once the new president is in office, I'll try again on the Thanksgiving thing."

Dallas smiled encouragingly. "I'm sure you'll be successful."

Sarah Hale began to turn away. "The next thing I want to do is help Mr. Vassar organize a women's college. But sometimes I have a sinking feeling that future generations will never know how hard I worked to improve women's position in this country. If I'm remembered at all, I'm afraid it will be because of that silly children's poem I wrote some years back."

"Poem?" Dallas looked at her blankly, her mind actually on Quint Randolph.

"You know, 'Mary had a little lamb, its fleece was white as snow. . . .' "

"Yes, of course," Dallas said, and she looked down at the papers on her desk, hoping the editor would move on.

"Well, I've got work to do, too." Mrs. Hale walked away, leaving Dallas to try to concentrate.

It was nearly impossible. Try as she might, Dallas couldn't keep her mind on the fashion article before her. "Hoops will be getting larger, skirts fuller over the next few years," she read. So what? That will just make it harder for women to do things like ride horses.

Dallas yawned. It was a bit ridiculous that a Texas tomboy who preferred to wear men's pants and a denim shirt should be working on a fashion magazine, but she'd been so good in grammar at Miss Priddy's Academy. She made a face as she thought of that awful, snobbish place. Maude Peabody had been nice, but everyone else had been cruel to the girl from the Texas hill country. And several weeks ago, that alumna, the snooty Mrs. Albert Huntington III, had provided the final straw when she'd visited both the school and the Peabodys.

Dallas stared out at the melting snow, her emotions in

turmoil. She must have been loco or drunk or both last night. Now that she remembered it, she could hardly believe she had given her virginity to some wealthy rake she'd met on the street. Maybe she had only dreamed it.

But no, when she closed her eyes, she remembered every detail. The taste of his hot brandy-flavored mouth, the feel of the thick fur of his broad, hairy chest rubbing against her sensitive nipples. Even now, as she thought about it, a wet warmth spread between her thighs and she remembered virile stallions rearing and plunging into eager fillies at the Triple D.

Horsefeathers, she said to herself, it has to be the most loco thing I've ever done. And he was a man about town, intent on conquest. No doubt he won't remember who I am if he sees me. If only . . .

No. She shook back her hair. She must not have regrets, wish she could change the past. The two saddest words in the whole language are these: "if only." The past can't be changed and people who continually look behind them, wishing it were otherwise are doomed to sadness. Think about what happened to Lot's wife in the Bible.

But as Dallas stared out the window at the passing people and carriages, and tried to work, her mind went continually to an aristocratic but strong face and a tall figure with hazel eyes. He belongs to someone named Melanie, she reminded herself. You were only an evening's entertainment for him. Besides, you have all the trouble you need without getting mixed up with that handsome, drunken rake.

But that didn't keep her from staring out the window for the rest of the day or sighing and imagining that he was galloping up to the office building on a great, white charger, striding in, running one hand distractedly through his chestnut hair.

"Lord, I've been out of my mind with worry, my angel," he would say. "You don't know how I've turned this city upside down trying to find you!"

Dallas leaned back in her chair and closed her eyes, imagining the feel of his fine silk vest against her face as he swept her to him. "I thought you belonged to someone else," she murmured. "I didn't think you cared about me at all."

"Care about you! I adore you! Now, my little Cinderella, I have the equivalent of the glass slipper you dropped as you fled the other night." With a sweeping bow, he returned her missing earring. "I believe this belongs to you."

"But I thought you were married?"

"Me? No, there's some mistake!"

"Oh, Quint, what happens now?"

"Now? Why, what happens in every Western legend!" he'd say forcefully, sweeping her up into his arms. "I put you on my horse before me and we ride off into that eternal sunset to live happily ever after on my ranch!"

"Yes, dearest, yes!" Dallas said aloud, feeling his imaginary lips on her cheek. "Of course that's how it ends in all the fairy tales. I'd go anywhere with you!"

"Dallas? Who on earth are you talking to?"

She came out of her fantasy with a start, feeling her face turn crimson as she looked into the curious eyes of one of the other girls, plain little Nell Cromwell.

"What, Nell? Oh, I was just thinking aloud." Did other women have such fantasies? Dallas didn't know and was afraid to ask.

Nell adjusted her wire-rimmed spectacles. "You work too hard, never have any fun. My cousin is the ticket taker at the minstrel show, and he gave me free passes for tonight. Would you like to go?"

"What?" Dallas looked at her blankly, her mind still on the elegant gentleman from Kentucky.

"The program's nothing special, although the Christy Minstrels will be here next week. But I think it's daring to even consider going out unescorted!"

Daring. Dallas almost laughed. She'd lived in the untamed country of stampedes, rattlesnakes, and Comanches. But, even in Texas, women were sheltered. "It don't make me no never mind," Dallas said ruefully. "Might as well."

"You sure talk funny!" Nell peered at her nearsightedly. "Does that mean yes?"

Dallas nodded. "What time shall we plan on meeting before the show?"

As she and Nell took their seats at the theater, Dallas regretted coming. She found herself craning her neck, looking around.

Nell brushed a wisp of drab hair back into her bun. "Who are you looking for?"

"Nobody." She felt a little foolish and slumped back in her seat. Of course she would never see him again. Why did she look at every man and hope? Because a woman never forgets her very first man, Dallas thought. Oh, she'd made such a mess of things, given away her virginity so recklessly! If only . . .

The house lights dimmed and the curtains opened. A group of white actors, their faces covered with black makeup, their lips painted white in exaggerated grins, danced out onto the stage.

"Oh, I wish I was in de land ob cotton, Old times dar am not forgotten, Look away! Look away! Look away! Dixie Land. . . ."

Dallas nudged Nell. "If civil war does come," she whispered, "that'd make a great song for the South!"

Nell rolled her eyes. "They say the author is a strong Union man. He'd be furious if that happened!"

Dallas only half listened to the jokes and songs as the program progressed; her mind was occupied with her own problems.

Now the minstrels marched across the stage behind a fetching actress smeared with light brown makeup so she would look like a mulatto. The leader carried a Texas flag.

Dallas almost stood up automatically. Then realizing how noticeable she'd be in the theater full of Northerners, she sank back in her seat.

"There's a yellow rose in Texas that I am going to see; no other darky knows her; no darky, only me. She cried

51

so when I left her, it like to broke my heart, And if I ever find her we never more will part. . . ."

Even Dallas caught herself tapping her foot to the good rhythm. In the South, a light-colored black girl was called a "high yellow." Even though the song had a good tune and rhythm, Dallas wasn't sure how a song celebrating the charms of a mulatto girl would go over in slave-holding Texas.

". . . Her eyes are bright as diamonds, they sparkle like the dew, You may talk about your dearest May and sing of Rosa Lee, But the yellow rose of Texas beats the belles of Tennessee."

Now it was intermission. Dallas stayed in her seat, while Nell went out in the lobby.

Just before the house lights dimmed again, Nell came back in a rush of excitement. "Guess who I saw? Lillie La Femme, the actress!"

"A real actress?" Dallas perked up. To go on the stage was the most daring thing any girl could imagine. "Did she have on rouge and lip color?"

Nell nodded, obviously hardly able to contain her excitement. "Isn't that daring?"

"You know some of the most fashionable and adventurous women are trying cosmetics now. But I hear some of that face powder has arsenic and lead in it."

"Who'd care? If my mother would let me, I'd wear it," Nell said, "but she's mad enough because I've gotten a job instead of getting married. She says I'm disgracing the family."

Disgracing the family. Dallas winced. That was probably what Papa would say about her getting kicked out of Miss Priddy's school. "What does Miss La Femme look like?"

"She's beautiful and elegant," Nell gushed. "She's with two men, and one of them is the most handsome man you can imagine!"

"I doubt that," Dallas said. "I've met the world's most handsome man already and—"

"Here they come now!" Nell pointed excitedly at the trio

seating themselves in the ornate box above them.

Dallas stared upward, blinked. No, it couldn't be. Her mouth went dry as she looked again.

Just then, the house lights dimmed and the show began. Dallas barely heard the banjo music. Her heart pounded in sudden excitement and embarrassment. In the box sat a beautiful, highly painted woman and two men. One of the men looked like a cowboy, the other was a tall, aristocratic gentleman with chestnut hair and hazel eyes.

Without thinking, Dallas let out a sound of anguish.

Nell looked over at her. "What's the matter? You look sick."

Dallas couldn't take her eyes off the man in the box. Last night he had taken her virginity and tonight Quint Randolph was out on the town with a beautiful actress. "I . . . I think I do feel ill." She half rose from her seat just as the man seemed to turn and look directly into her eyes.

Nell caught her arm. "Are you really sick?"

"Shhh!" hissed several people, the reprimands audible over the brassy music.

He seemed to be staring straight at her. Or was it only her imagination? "Nell, I . . . think I'd better leave. I feel faint."

Nell peered at Dallas over her spectacles. "If you think we should go—"

"No. You stay and enjoy the show," Dallas said quickly. "I can get home all right."

Before Nell could protest, Dallas got out of her seat and fled up the aisle, her heart pounding with anger and humiliation.

Quint peered through the darkened theater. That sultry brunette down below looked almost like the girl in his dream. He must have drunk too much again. Puzzled, he leaned over the box rail, trying to get a better look.

His old friend Lillie, glanced at him. "What's the matter, Quint? You look like you've seen a ghost."

"Is that the same as seeing a dream?" He squinted. The

girl below looked stricken, and appeared to be about to leave her seat.

The actress's beautiful face furrowed with puzzlement. "What are you talking about?"

If he tried to explain about the girl in his dream, would Lillie laugh? Quint decided not to find out as he stared down at the lovely dark girl. The actress was usually a good sport, and he often asked to accompany him to the theater. There wasn't anything between them, though. Most men of wealth were afraid to be seen with an actress, but that didn't bother Quint. His reputation had been ruined years ago by his hell-raising at Harvard . . . and then by what had happened on his wedding day.

The girl below him was out of her seat, running up the aisle.

Quint half rose, looking at the fleeing figure. Suppose he chased her down, grabbed her, and she turned out to be a complete stranger and screamed for the police? Suppose . . . ?

Lord, suppose the girl in his dream was real and he passed up this chance to face her, beg her to marry him?

"Quint?" Lillie's voice was full of surprise, but he had no time to explain. He ran from the box, took the steps down to the lobby two at a time. It was full of people who were moving back toward their seats. He frantically elbowed his way through them.

"Excuse me. Please! Make way!" Peering over the crowd, he looked for the dark-eyed angel. He didn't see her anywhere, but then, she'd had a head start.

Finally he made it to the front doors of the theater, ran out on the sidewalk, looked both ways. The night air tasted cool and fresh as he took a deep breath, wondering which way to go. People walked along through the melting slush, the remains of last night's storm, and they jostled him as they brushed past.

He had lost her. With a sinking heart, Quint ran to the corner, peered around it. Plenty of people, but no tall, slender girl with long ebony hair. Was he losing his mind or was the brandy making him see things that existed only in his imagination?

That must be it. He had wanted the girl from his dreams so badly, he'd thought the girl in the theater resembled her. With a sigh, he trudged back and took his seat next to Lillie.

"What was that about?"

"Nothing." Quint turned toward the blackface comedians on the stage, and pretended to smile at their joke. "I-I thought I saw an old friend, that's all."

As he stared at the performers without really seeing them, a plan began to form in his mind. He'd already arranged to go back to Kentucky, deliver the horses himself to St. Joe for the new Pony Express venture. But he was going to spare no expense in attempting to track down the mysterious dark beauty—that is, if she really existed outside of his fantasies. If she was in Philadelphia, Quint was determined to find her.

Yes, Lydia, he thought with satisfaction, automatically applauding the entertainers as they took a bow, I do need to marry again and I've got her all picked out—if she'll have me. And as for plump Maude Peabody, you invited her, Sister, you deal with her. I've already chosen the girl I want!

The next day at the magazine office, Dallas had to face Nell.

"I was worried about you," her companion said. "Are you all right?"

"Of course." Dallas's response was a little too bright. "I just got a little sick at my stomach, that's all." She thought about Quint Randolph sitting in the box with the notorious actress. "Well, maybe more than a little sick."

Nell clucked sympathetically. "Glad you're feeling better."

"Uh, yes. Much obliged for your concern."

The girl peered at Dallas over her glasses. "What did you say?"

Dallas laughed. "I sometimes forget Easterners don't

55

understand cowboy talk. Much obliged is what Westerners say instead of thank you. That's how you tell an authentic cowboy from a dude."

Nell shrugged and returned to her desk, and Dallas tried to work. But she found herself staring out the window, wondering about Quint Randolph. She hadn't realized how much he meant to her until she'd seen him at the theater with a beautiful woman. Philadelphia was a big place by her standards, still it might not be big enough for the two of them. How humiliating it would be to run into him again.

Absently Dallas tapped her pen against her teeth, and stared out at the carriages running through the dirty slush. What if the next time she bumped into him he was with his wife—or worse yet, a whole passel of children?

Maybe she needed to consider leaving town. She cursed the foolish impulse that had gotten her mixed up with a rich rake. Didn't she already have enough trouble? It was hard for a girl to find a job, except as a maid or governess. She toyed with the idea of contacting her papa, wondered if he had cooled down yet. Even with her mother's moderating influence, she was afraid Papa would insist on sending her back to Miss Priddy's Academy.

A carriage slowly passed by, and Dallas stared at it absently, stiffened, took another look. It couldn't be. She was far away in Boston. Dallas's heart beat faster as she stared out at the slowly moving carriage, at the girl in it.

It couldn't be, but it was. There was no mistaking the plump, sallow face, the large, deep-set eyes, that garishly bright mauve dress. Why did she invariably wear colors that were wrong for her?

Maude Peabody. It couldn't be, but it was. Dallas dropped the pen with a clatter, stared after the carriage disappearing down the street. Why would Maude be in Philadelphia? Could it be that she and her banker papa were looking for their ward who had run away from school? If the Peabodys were in town, no doubt someone had wired them that the runaway schoolgirl had been seen. The net must be closing in on Dallas. Now who in

Philadelphia might have told someone in Boston?

She closed her eyes, put her face in her hands. She couldn't imagine any reason for Maude to be there unless the Peabodys had been contacted about their missing charge. Could Quint have told them where she was? Papa might be offering a big reward. Quint Randolph didn't need money—or did he? Could there be another reason?

Could he be afraid she might run into his wife in a chance encounter, like the one at the theater? That didn't make any sense if he was brazenly going about with that actress. Could the man who'd been in the box with him be a police officer? No, he looked like a cowboy. Maybe a sheriff?

Possibly Quint was afraid Dallas would try to blackmail him, or that she might tell his wife about their brief affair. She knew he'd tried to catch her last night; she'd hidden in the shadows while he'd stood on the corner and looked up and down.

What was she going to do? Desperately, she tried to think of alternatives. There seemed to be only one. She was going to have to get out of town as soon as she could. Where would she go? Heaven only knew, and she had only the two weeks' wages due her from the magazine.

Horsefeathers.

Chapter Four

Quint was up at dawn, making plans. It seemed there wasn't anything money couldn't buy with no questions asked. Before breakfast, he'd secured the services of a seedy investigator who promised that if the girl was in Philadelphia, he'd find her. But he pointed out that it was unfortunate Quint could give him so little information. Quint mumbled and turned red.

It wasn't the way it looked. He'd met the girl on the street in a snowstorm. No, he didn't know her name or where she lived or anything else about her, except that she was dark and mysterious and beautiful — and he had to find her because he wanted to marry her. But in her hurried flight, she had dropped an earring. Quint held it out.

The seedy man smiled. *Like Cinderella, huh?* All he had to do was find the girl who had the matching lavender pearl.

Quint resisted the urge to hit him in the mouth, and paid a substantial sum to start the man on his search. Then he put the precious earring back in his silk vest and went out. He couldn't just sit in the hotel and wait. He'd look for her himself.

If only he could remember where he'd met her . . . In frustration, he ran a hand through his hair, stared at the animal on the gold signet ring. *Cut the wolf loose,* her deep, velvet voice drawled in his ear.

If only he had been sober, he might remember more

than the hazy encounter that he might only have dreamed.

For several hours, Quint walked the streets aimlessly, peering into each passing face. Once he chased down a tall, ebony-haired girl who, from the back, looked very much like his dark angel. But when he caught up with her and grabbed her arm, she wasn't the girl from the snowstorm, and an indignant young lady whacked him with her parasol and threatened to call the police.

He stopped for lunch at one of his favorite restaurants and sat smoking his pipe and staring out at the passing cabs. *A cab.*

Of course. He remembered now. Excited, he went to a cab company, asked about the routes, the drivers. No clues. The bored old man behind the desk said they'd only had one driver out after the storm started last night but he'd left for New York today.

"Did he leave a logbook or anything that would provide information about his riders?" Quint demanded.

The man sucked his teeth and looked at him as if he'd lost his mind.

Discouraged, Quint took a carriage back to his hotel. What was he going to do if she wasn't found? He had to leave now and get to Kentucky to fulfill his contract.

The short desk clerk called out to him as he passed, "Message in your box, sir."

Could the investigator have found the girl already? With shaking hands, he grabbed the note, but the slashing handwriting and the holes in the paper where *i*'s had been dotted, or *t*'s crossed, told him it was from Lydia.

"Quinton Dear: Miss Maude Peabody has arrived and is out shopping this afternoon," he read. "She hopes to copy some of the latest *Godey's* styles at our dry-goods store for her trousseau." He smiled as he noticed Lydia's choice of words. "We are expecting you to join us for dinner at seven. Love . . ."

Sister dear, you are in for a long, dull evening, entertaining Miss Maude for nothing, he thought as he crumpled the paper, threw it away. I've spent my whole life letting you and Mother and Charlotte boss me, even to

59

choosing my wife, but that's all over. Quint suddenly felt very free.

The little clerk peered at him. "Shall I send a reply, sir?"

Godey's. Godey's Lady's Book. Now why did that seem so familiar to him?

"Yes." He turned to the desk. "Send my sister my regrets and say that I am unwilling—no, unable—to join her for dinner."

Why be rude to Miss Maude who had really done nothing except hope some man would marry her? Sorry, it wouldn't be Quinton Randolph. Lydia would have to find another way to finance her business deal.

He turned to go to his room. But something tugged at his memory. *Godey's.* It was an elegant fashion magazine here in Philadelphia. Quint had no interest in Parisian styles. Why did the name keep pulling at him so?

Slowly he walked about, lit his pipe, thinking. He wasn't sure he even knew where the office was located, yet, for some reason, when he thought of the name he almost shivered.

Cold, very cold, he thought absently. He stopped, blinked his eyes. In his mind, he suddenly saw a round of parties, many drinks at several of the best gambling houses in town. Then he heard of a high-stakes card game and decided he would go, even though it was getting dark outside.

Quint paused in the lobby. He had a vague recollection of several gentlemen attempting to talk him out of going, but he'd been drunk and stubborn. In his mind's eye, he pictured himself standing on the street, trying to hail a carriage, but they were all headed back to the barns because of the mounting storm. Failing to get one, he had lost his temper and had decided to walk.

His excitement mounted as he smoked and fitted pieces of the puzzle back together. Cold—very cold. No carriages. He remembered that he had walked some blocks before realizing he'd forgotten his overcoat and the address. Or maybe the wind had blown it out of his hand. The hell with the overcoat! he'd thought. He'd been determined to find that card game.

Godey's. Now why did that seem to be a missing piece of the puzzle? Had he met someone who had that name? He sauntered back outside, still lost in thought. It had been cold that night and very dark. Quint had realized how drunk he was when he'd stood, lost and bewildered, on a sidewalk in front of a building, looking at the sign on the front of it. Would anyone hold a high-stakes card game there? He'd been too tired and cold to look any farther. He'd decided to rest a moment on the step and then move on.

The step. The building. The girl. *Godey's Lady's Book* building!

Quint shouted triumphantly, causing passing pedestrians to start and then look at him strangely.

Ignoring them, he ran to a nearby carriage. "Can you get me to the *Godey's* building?"

"Sure." The wizened driver nodded as Quint jumped up on the seat beside him and then took off at a fast clip.

When the carriage stopped, Quint looked up and down the street. Yes, this was where he'd been that night, he was sure of it. He paid the driver and then stood across the street from the *Godey's* building, his heart beating with excitement. He started to go over to it, but changed his mind. Suppose he was wrong? Suppose she'd just been passing by instead of coming out of the building? If he went inside, asking questions, would they think him crazy or eccentric?

He took out his pocket watch, checked the time. Offices would be closing in less than an hour. He was so impatient, he wasn't sure he could wait here that long. What he wanted to do was go inside, run from office to office until he found her, then sweep her up in his arms and carry her off. But he didn't want to scare her—if she was there. Besides, maybe it would be smarter to follow her, see where she went. Suppose she was married? He would wait until quitting time, then watch the employees as they left.

If his dark-haired angel was among them, he'd see her.

Yes, that was what he would do. Quint leaned against the lamp post and smoked his pipe. He'd waited his whole life for this great love; he could wait another hour.

Dallas stared out the window, torn between horror and hope as the tall man got out of the carriage. No, it couldn't be.

He started to cross the street, hesitated, then lit a pipe and leaned against the lamp post. There was no mistaking that aristocratic profile. It was Quint Randolph, all right. How and why had he tracked her here?

Did his presence have anything to do with Maude Peabody? With a sinking heart, Dallas realized all the pieces came together. The Peabodys were responsible for her safety. No doubt they had posted a reward, had hired an investigator to find her. That had to be it. Quint Randolph was an investigator, tracking her down for the reward.

Maybe he had even pretended to be drunk that night, so he could strike up a conversation with her as she came out of the building. No, she was certain he had been as drunk as a *caballero* at a cock fight.

What could she do now? If she didn't do something, and quick, tomorrow she'd be on a train, heading back to the snobbery and humiliation of Miss Priddy's. Dallas winced, remembering the final incident that had triggered her running away. That snooty Mrs. Huntington . . .

She tapped the pen against her teeth, torn between wanting to throw herself into Quint Randolph's arms or to attack him with her fists. No doubt he'd notified Maude Peabody and her father. That was why Maude was in town. Quint probably planned to catch Dallas when she was coming out at quitting time. He'd offer to take her for a bite of supper, but instead, he'd take her to the police station and turn her over to the Peabodys.

He'd tricked her, the damned charming skunk! Now what was she going to do? She licked dry lips and stared

62

up at the loudly ticking clock. In less than an hour, the office would close. She could pretend to have work to do, stay late. Maybe when she didn't come out with the others, he'd get tired of waiting and go away.

Horsefeathers. She peered out at him. He looked as if he were prepared to stand there forever if need be. She had to think fast. If she went out the back door, grabbed a few things at her boardinghouse . . .

Mrs. Hale entered the office just then, interrupting Dallas's thoughts. "Is something wrong, child? You look upset."

Dallas was an honest person, straight as a string as they say in Texas, but she decided she was going to have to fib a little to save herself.

"Mrs. Hale, do you see that man out there?"

The older lady leaned forward and peered out to where Dallas pointed. "My, he's handsome, isn't he?"

Dallas took a deep breath. "Ma'am, I've been working here under false pretenses. I-I'm a runaway!"

"A what?"

"It's true," Dallas admitted. "My father's trying to force me to do something I don't want to do; he's trying to force me to marry a man I don't love."

Mrs. Hale's mouth dropped open. "Is that the man? Why, I can't imagine why any young lady wouldn't—"

"No, it's a mean old man," Dallas blurted out. "That handsome varmint out there's just the investigator who's been hired to bring me in."

"You poor girl!" The portly lady fairly bristled with indignation as she glared out the window at Quint Randolph who was lounging against the light pole. "Why, some men would do anything for money!"

"That's why I've got to escape!" Dallas grabbed her arm. "I hate to leave on such short notice, but if I could get my pay and go out the back door before he comes in, starts asking questions—"

"Certainly!" Mrs. Hale said. "I'll help you."

Dallas looked out at Quint and couldn't help smiling a little as she turned to follow the editor to her office. "And one more thing, ma'am, there's no telling what he'll tell you or anyone else."

"Don't worry your head about it," the older lady commanded. She reached for the small cash box on her cluttered desk. "Before closing time, I'll have passed the word about that villain waiting out front—and what he's up to. No one will tell him a thing!"

Dallas accepted her pay, said a few quick good-byes, and fairly flew out the back door. She paid her bill at her boardinghouse, threw a few clothes into a valise and counted what she had left in her purse. Not much, but maybe enough to get her by for a week or so until she found another job.

It probably wasn't smart to carry it all in her purse. Suppose that got stolen? Very carefully, she took half the money, wrapped it in her extra petticoat, and slipped it in the valise. There, if something should happen, she had emergency funds put away in her luggage. It didn't pay to put all one's eggs in one basket.

Now what? Soon the office would be closing and that handsome rascal would discover she'd slipped through his trap. He might have gone inside already, discovered her missing. Were the police even now combing the streets, looking for her?

In her own good time, she intended to contact her parents and let them know she was all right. But first she wanted to give Papa's fiery temper time to cool down. And if she could prove to him that she was independent, that she could hold a job and look after herself, maybe he'd change his outlook on forcing her to attend that miserable school. What Dallas really wanted to do was stay on the ranch and live the life she loved.

She hurried to the train station, knowing she must get out of town before Quint Randolph tracked her down. As she stood in line to buy a ticket, her heart was beating very fast.

Where should she go? She really didn't have any idea, but her destination would certainly be governed by the price of the ticket and by which train was leaving right away. She reached up automatically to touch the gold Lone Star earring, and, as she thought, remembering she had lost one, tucked the other in her camisole for safekeeping.

The line moved slowly toward the ticket window. Dallas glanced around uneasily, expecting to see a tall, broad-shouldered frame appear in the station, to hear that gentlemanly drawl: *Stop that girl! She's wanted as a runaway!*

She didn't have any idea where to go. She thought about it frantically as the line moved up.

Behind her, two men talked.

"So why you going to St. Joe?"

"Lots of excitement there with the Pony Express starting up soon. Hope this line moves a little faster or I'll miss the train."

Now it was Dallas's turn. *What to do? Where to go.*

The clerk looked at her from under a green eyeshade. He had a crooked nose. "Well?"

She looked at the money in her palm.

"Well, lady?"

Behind her, there was grumbling about the slowness of the line.

At least she'd be closer to Texas than she was now. That cheered Dallas some. "Do I . . . do I have enough to buy a ticket to St. Joe?"

The clerk peered down his crooked nose at the money in her hand. "Just barely. You'd better hurry, lady, if that's your destination; train's leaving in less than five minutes."

That settled it. She paid her fare. "I'm much obliged," she said politely, accepting her change.

"What?" he stared back at her blankly.

"It's what folks say in the West, instead of thank you."

He scratched his head. "Why?"

"I don't know why, we just always have, that's all."

Someone behind her grumbled about the delay, so, grabbing up her small valise, Dallas fairly flew to catch her train.

Once aboard, she collapsed on a seat and gasped for

breath, then pressed her nose against the dirty window, peering out. Even as the train began to move out of the station in a cloud of smoke and soot, she expected to see the man from Kentucky run onto the platform and try to stop it.

He didn't. She was safe—at least for the moment. Dallas took a deep breath, drawing in the scents of immigrants and drummers with sales samples. There were few families on the train. She didn't have much money in her purse, but the rest was safely tucked away in her luggage. What she would do when she reached St. Joe, she didn't know, but she had some time to decide on that before she arrived.

Quint glared at the seedy investigator whose greasy hair reflected the light. "You say you still haven't found her?"

The man shrugged. "Spent all day yesterday looking and talking to people. If you ask me, them ladies at the magazine ain't telling the truth."

Quint didn't think so either, but he didn't know what to do about it. There was no telling what that mysterious girl had told the grandmotherly editor.

"Lord, I've got to find her!" He ran a hand through his hair distractedly, took the tiny pearl earring out of his vest, and stared at it. "Keep looking, and wire me at my place in Kentucky or at the Patee House in St. Joe. That's the finest hotel they've got."

"St. Joe?"

Quint nodded, then returned the precious earring to his vest pocket. "I've got a contract to deliver some horses, so I've got to leave right away. But you have the name of my hotel, and remember, there's a big reward."

He closed his eyes and saw the dark-haired angel, her long hair whipping about her face. But her features were a blur. He cursed himself for having drunk so much that night. Could he actually recognize her if he did see her? He wasn't sure.

He wanted that girl back in his arms more than he had

ever wanted anything. With his eyes closed, he could taste the sweetness of her lips, feel her small breasts crushed against him, even smell the slight scent of her perfume.

"Keep looking," he ordered. "And remember, if you find her, I'll be in St. Joe in a few days!"

When Dallas finally got off the train several days later in St. Joe, she wasn't at all sure she'd made the right choice. She held onto her small valise in the chill of late afternoon, being pushed and jostled by the rowdy crowd while she tried to decide what to do next.

Slowly and uncertainly, she left the station and headed down the sidewalk. St. Joe was a bustling place, filled with people and excitement, she decided. She felt a little more hopeful. Maybe with everything that was happening here, she might be able to find a job.

The streets were filled with covered wagons, soldiers, and settlers. Dallas saw a scout or two, and an occasional Indian. As she stood on the wooden sidewalk, being buffeted by the crowds, she recalled that she'd been told on the train that St. Joe was the jumping-off place for wagon trains that would follow the Sante Fe and Oregon trails. It was on the Western edge of settled country, so it got railroad and river traffic, being on the Missouri. This was also the Westernmost telegraph depot, which was why St. Joe had been chosen as the starting point for the Pony Express.

Dallas was a little scared, even though she'd always been spunky. She tried to reassure herself as she walked along the street, especially when rowdy cowboys turned and looked at her.

Then a beautiful, but highly painted blonde drove past in a red-wheeled buggy.

"Come to the Naughty Lady tonight, gents!" she called out as she waved at the men. "We'll show you a real good time!"

Some of the men laughed, made ribald comments, and waved back. "We'll be there, Margo! Don't start without us!"

Dallas looked after the blonde's buggy and flushed as she realized what the girl must do for a living. There were only two kinds of women in the West—wives and whores. She thought about how she'd thrown herself into Quint Randolph's arms. Which kind was she?

Well, she had to find a respectable boardinghouse, eat, clean up, and start looking for a job in the morning. What could she do? If she sewed as well as her mother, she might get a job as a seamstress. She rode and handled a gun as well as most men; her brother had seen to that. But she wasn't sure she could find a job doing those things. Her stomach rumbled as she thought of supper.

Gunfire interrupted her thoughts as two men shot it out on the street. The crowd hardly noticed. By the rules of gunfighting, it was the loser who was wrong. It occurred to Dallas that she could disappear here and her parents would never know what had happened to her. What she would really like to do was go home to the Triple D.

By now, her parents must be frantic with worry. She thought of them tenderly. Would Papa be ready to give a little? She made a decision and headed toward the post office.

But, once there, she stared at the blank paper she'd purchased, tapped the stub of a pencil against her teeth. Should she let them know where she was, beg for a chance to do things her way?

Hesitantly, she began to write: *Dear Momma and Papa: I know you must be worried to death about me, but I am fine, really I am! I've found a respectable job here in St. Joe.* (That is a lie, she thought, but I will find a job tomorrow.) *I just want a chance to prove I can be independent and that I don't need that awful school. I hope you will reconsider sending me back when you realize how well I've done on my own. Please don't be angry with me. You can write me here in care of General Delivery.* She wet the stub of pencil in her mouth. *Your darling daughter, Dallas.*

She tried to picture Papa's face when he got the letter.

Surely he would write back immediately and say all was forgiven. The very worst he could do would be to send her big brother Trace or Uncle Luis to fetch her home while he decided whether to send her back to Miss Priddy's. Alone and homesick, she stood there addressing the envelope, almost hoping someone would come and get her.

The clerk said, "Ma'am, if that letter's going out on the stage loading up, you'd better hurry. They say when the Pony gets running, you'll get a letter to California in ten days."

The old man standing across the room snorted. "Ten days! That's *loco!* Delivering mail clear across the country in ten days is an impossible dream."

The clerk took Dallas's letter and shrugged, waiting for her to dig in her purse to pay the postage. "All I know is what everyone says. In less than two years, they plan to have the telegraph laid clear across the country to California, so important messages can get there in a matter of hours."

"Progress!" the old man said in awe. "Why, what will they think of next?"

Dallas gave the clerk all but five cents of the money she had for postage. When she got into a boardinghouse, she'd get out what she had hidden in her luggage so she could eat. But she didn't want to open the valise in front of people, reveal her underwear and maybe let thieves see her take the money out.

She wanted to make sure the letter got on the stage, so she watched the red-faced man stuff it into the mail bag, which he carried out and threw onto the dusty coach.

The driver cracked his whip, and the stage creaked as it lumbered away. Dallas watched it roll down the street, carrying her letter to her parents. Maybe in a few days, she'd get a letter with a few dollars in it and a note saying Papa was coming after her.

Horsefeathers, she told herself, shaking her long ebony hair back. You mean to show them how independent you can be, remember?

But she didn't feel very independent. She suddenly felt

alone and hungry in this rowdy, lawless place. It occurred to her that she'd be safer if she could pass herself off as a boy; the settlement was full of them. Dallas was tall and slender for a girl, and she had small breasts. She could put on boy's clothing and put her hair up under a hat.

And do what? She laughed to herself as she watched the stage pull out of sight in a cloud of dust. No, she'd find a respectable boardinghouse run by a nice, motherly type, and tomorrow she'd see if anyone in town would hire an unattached female.

She was so hungry, she felt like a posthole that hadn't been filled. And her arm ached from carrying the valise. As she stood there, looking around, singing from a saloon drifted on the air.

"Buffalo gals, won't you come out tonight, Come out tonight, come out tonight . . . Buffalos gals won't you come out tonight, And dance by the light of the moon. . . ."

Somewhere a woman laughed. Men pushed and jostled her and each other. She smelled sweat, horse manure and leather. The late afternoon air carried the scents of a wood fire and of stew from a room over one of the stores.

Dallas's head ached almost as badly as her arm. With a weary sigh, she set the valise down on the sidewalk and rubbed her arm. Her suitcase was too heavy; she'd brought enough to be able to live out of it for a while.

Shouts and curses rang out, and Dallas turned. Two men were fighting it out in the street, one knocking the other up against a buggy.

"Fight! Fight!" Men shouted encouragement to the combatants, then surged forward, taking Dallas with them. As she struggled to turn and grab her precious valise, she saw a seedy-looking tramp snatch it up.

"Stop, thief! Hey, stop that man!"

But the crowd around her was elbowing its way closer to the street fight, and with the shouts and curses, no one seemed to hear Dallas.

She swore, though doing that was unladylike, and tried to fight her way back through the crowd. "Stop, you varmint! That's my valise you've got there!"

The seedy little man looked back over his shoulder once, but kept on running. Dallas tried to pursue him, shouting for him to stop. Everything she owned was in that valise. If she caught that low-down skunk, she was mad enough to whip him herself!

But even as she tried to push her way through the crowd, she realized he was slipping away.

Her heart beating faster from both fear and fury, Dallas finally broke free of the crowd and, lifting her skirts, ran after the thief. But the seedy little man seemed to have melted into the crowd.

Frantically, Dallas looked up and down the street, ran up an alley, then back the other way. But he had disappeared as surely as if the earth had swallowed him.

Oh God, what would she do now? She had no money, no clothing, and she didn't know a soul in this rowdy town. Dallas, she thought, stubbornly blinking back tears, you've really got yourself in a mess this time!

71

Chapter Five

Now what was she going to do? Dallas looked around in frustration, her stomach rumbling with hunger. Here she was in a wide open frontier town with no job, no clothes, and almost no money.

She opened her purse, recounted her pennies as if hoping the sum had mysteriously grown in the last few minutes. There wasn't even enough for a meal, much less a hotel room.

First she'd better notify the law about the theft of her valise, although she couldn't even give much of a description of the thief. She asked a passerby for directions to the sheriff's office.

That place stunk of dirt and stale coffee. A deputy sat reared back in a chair, his feet on a littered desk, spitting and mostly missing a tin spittoon.

Dallas glared at the whiskered man. "Don't bother to get up," she snapped pointedly, but the irony of the remark seemed to escape him. "You need to clean a little. It smells like hell on housecleaning day!"

He yawned and spat a stream of brown juice at the spittoon. "Ain't paid to clean. What can I do you fer?"

"I've just had my valise stolen."

"If that's the worst thing I have to deal with while the sheriff's out of town, lady, I could sleep mighty peaceful tonight."

Dallas sighed. He looked so stupid, she wasn't sure he could track a fat squaw through a snowdrift. She wasn't going to get much help here.

She didn't. After she described the luggage and the thief, the deputy only yawned again. "Not much of a description and not much chance of catchin' him. Lots of people and excitement in town 'cause of the Pony; lots of trash comin' in. Be glad when the horses finally arrive and the big day's over. Then things'll settle back down."

"Are you telling me you aren't going to do anything?" Dallas bristled, reached over to push his feet off the desk. "And stand up when you address a lady!"

He stumbled to his feet, properly chastised. "You must see there's not much I can do, ma'am. Law's stretched mighty thin with all these folks crowding into town to see the Pony start runnin' in a few days. But if you'll leave me word as to where you're bunkin', I'll let you know if'n I find anything."

She didn't have the price of a room, but was too proud to tell him. "I-I'll get back in touch with you."

Turning in a dusty swirl of full skirts, she marched out of the building. There isn't much use in checking back, she thought despondently. He isn't going to do anything.

Maybe she'd better look for a job that afternoon, and if she found one, ask for an advance on her pay. What could she do? She'd been writing articles for the magazine. St. Joe wouldn't have a magazine, but there'd be a newspaper.

It was not far from sundown when she located its offices. By now, her stomach thought she'd died and forgot to lie down. The stooped editor, smudged with ink, was just locking the front door when she walked up. "Mister, I'd like to interview for a job on your paper."

"Sorry, ma'am, I do the cleanin' myself."

"I meant as a reporter."

His eyes widened as if he couldn't quite believe what he'd heard. "A what, miss?"

Horsefeathers! Is he deaf? Dallas smiled and tried to hide her hunger and irritation. "A job," she said loudly. "I want to write for your newspaper. I've had experience on a magazine in Philadelphia, and—"

"You don't have to shout, I ain't deef!" He locked the

73

door, stared at her curiously. "A woman wants to write for my newspaper? Are you one of those suffragettes?"

"As a matter of fact, I think it would do wonders for this country to let women vote." Dallas let her temper get the best of her. "I hope I live to see the day that Congress finally approves such a bill."

"Ain't likely," he said scornfully, and turned to go.

"But about the job?" Dallas insisted.

"I'd just as soon turn my office over to my wife's cat."

At that, Dallas lost her temper completely. "I think your paper already has all the animals it needs," she snapped, "with a jackass for an editor!" And she spun on her heel and marched away, leaving him standing there, staring after her.

What next? Dusk had fallen over the bustling town while she'd confronted the editor. Soon it would be dark, and the weather was chilly even though it was almost April. No place to go and nothing to eat.

Probably she could track down the minister of some church, ask for lodging and food. But she was proud as only a Texan can be. Besides, if she stooped to asking for a handout, the preacher might start wondering why such a young girl was out in the world alone. She didn't want to end up being held in that smelly jail while the law tried to track down the parents of the runaway.

Dallas walked slowly back up the sidewalk, thinking about her problems. The scent of fresh bread came to her and she took a deep breath, savoring it. Maybe she could work for a meal in a restaurant.

She followed the aroma to a tiny, crowded cafe run by a Chinaman. When she tried to make him understand that she wanted a job, he shrugged and pointed to a large number of Chinese already clearing tables and serving. His expression, as he looked over her expensive, though dusty, dress, let her know he didn't think she knew how to work hard anyway.

She thought about the few pennies in her purse, but her heart sank as she looked at the prices painted on the wall. Obviously in a boomtown like this, prices were higher than a cat's back.

The pearl earring. That ought to be worth something. Ignoring curious stares, she reached into her bodice, pulled it out, held it out to the Chinese. "Trade for a meal." She smiled hopefully.

He took it, peered at it a long moment before shaking his pigtailed queue and handing it back. "No. One earring no good. Can't sell. Need two. Go away."

He dismissed her with a wave, went back to waiting on customers.

It was the hardest thing she had ever done, but Dallas had to walk past an empty table on which a plate full of leftover steak and potatoes sat. She almost had to clench her fists to keep from reaching out and grabbing the food. But she had the pride of a turkey gobbler. Reminding herself that her father was one of the richest, most powerful men in the Lone Star State, she walked with that little strut known as "Texas Proud."

But that didn't fill her empty stomach. Forlornly, she went back outside into the coming night, wondering what to do next. She certainly couldn't be any worse off than she was now.

Her most immediate need was food. Could she bring herself to steal a few crackers or maybe a pickle from the big barrels found in general stores? She drifted on down the street. I should have thought of that a little earlier, she told herself as she passed two such stores, realized they had closed for the night.

St. Joe was too rough a town for a woman alone. Why on earth had she acted on impulse and ended up here? Maybe she should admit defeat, holler calf rope, as the cowboys did. If she turned herself in to the sheriff or contacted some local church, she'd be looked after until Papa was contacted—and then it would be back to Miss Priddy's awful school, probably.

She wondered just how angry Papa was. She'd know in a few days because when he got her first letter, he'd write, send her brother, Trace, or ignore it and wash his hands of her. What would she do if Papa did that?

75

Abruptly, she lost her bravado and felt keenly aware that she was just an innocent girl from a Texas ranch, with little knowledge of the world.

At that point, Dallas felt like flopping down on a step and weeping in misery and frustration, but she was far too stubborn and proud to do that. Many of the streets were dark as night fell, and she was drawn by the lights to the string of rowdy saloons she'd seen earlier.

Music, light, and laughter drifted from the Naughty Lady.

Listen to the mockingbird, listen to the mockingbird,
The mockingbird still singing o'er her grave. . . .

Dallas hesitated out front. She was tall for a girl, almost as tall as most half-grown boys, so she could see over the batwing doors. There was a big, bustling crowd inside, lots of music and laughter.

Listen to the mockingbird, listen to the mockingbird,
still singing where the weeping willows wave. . . .

Two laughing soldiers came through the doors, almost bumping into her.

"Great free lunch," one said, sucking his teeth as he brushed past.

"Wasn't it though? I et more than I needed!" The other picked his teeth as the pair sauntered on down the sidewalk.

Free lunch. She'd forgotten she'd heard that in some of the better saloons, they put boiled eggs, pickles, and crackers out for the men to eat while they leaned on the bar and had a few drinks.

Now just how did one get some of that free lunch? You were supposed to buy a drink, of course. And respectable women didn't go into saloons.

Dallas hesitated, hunger gnawing at her. Then, in the light streaming through the windows, she opened her purse and counted her pennies as if they might somehow have multiplied since the last time she'd looked. Five pennies was all she had. But that was the price of a beer, wasn't it? At least, she thought she remembered hearing that was what one cost in the tiny *cantina* in the village near the Triple D.

Maybe she should take her nickel and go back to that cafe, lower herself to asking for a loaf of bread for the money.

But suppose when she got there, it was closed? She didn't know whether she had the strength to walk much farther. Besides being hungry, she was bone tired from being on the train so long.

Would they serve her a beer in the Naughty Lady? Right then she wished she were a man so she could move about without being stared at.

From inside, a woman's laughter echoed, and Dallas thought of the highly painted girl in the buggy. Even if the bartender wouldn't serve her a beer, she might manage to snatch a handful of boiled eggs and pickles before they threw her out. And perhaps she could get a job here, even washing mugs.

Dallas's hunger made her bold. *Horsefeathers!* All they could do was refuse to serve her. And while she argued with the bartender, she could eat some of the free lunch.

Inside, an off-key piano pounded out a song. Men's voices accompanied it. " '. . . talk about your dearest May and sing of Rosa Lee, but the yellow rose of Texas beats the belles of Tennessee. . . .' "

Dallas took a deep breath and pushed through the batwing doors into the noise and light. The place seemed full of boisterous, singing men, and laughing, painted women. Her nose wrinkled as she looked around. Stale smoke hung blue on the air, and even the gaudy red walls seemed steeped in the scent of stale beer.

Only a few people noticed her as she primly made her way through the crowd to the ornate mahogany bar along the wall. But those who did stopped singing and stared at her, wide-eyed.

" 'She's the sweetest rose of color this darky ever knew, her eyes are bright as diamonds. . . .' "

Dallas elbowed her way to the bar, and men made way for her, their mouths falling open in surprise. There was the free lunch. She grabbed a boiled egg.

The bartender, a tough-looking hombre with hair parted down the middle, came down the bar, wiping his hands on his apron. "Are you lookin' for your daddy? You should have sent some man in here after him. Nice girls don't come in here."

Dallas gave him a cold lofty look, which was hard to do since she was choking on a mouthful of dry boiled egg.

"I'll have a beer." If she were a paying customer, they couldn't throw her out until she ate her fill . . . could they?

The bartender blinked as if he couldn't quite believe his ears. "A what?"

"You do serve beer, don't you?" Dallas said this as disdainfully as she could with her mouth full of eggs.

"We serve beer." The big man scowled. "What we don't serve is ladies."

Dallas grabbed a pickle and gestured toward the dancing girls on the saloon stage. "There're women here."

"I said *ladies*." He emphasized the word. Around them, men turned to look at Dallas, stopping their conversations in midword to stare at what was obviously a respectable girl in a place that was not.

The bartender looked up and down the bar as if not sure of what to do next. Possibly he had never been in this situation before.

The talk gradually died out as men poked each other, and they all turned to stare at Dallas. She felt about as popular as a wet dog at a parlor social. But while everyone hesitated, she took advantage of the moment to grab a small bite of ham from the platter.

The bartender paused, shrugged, and extended his hands, palms up, as if asking for advice from the crowd. "Okay, ma'am, one beer and then you skedaddle out of here before you run off the customers."

Dallas only nodded; her mouth was too full for her to talk. As she kept stuffing food in it, the silence kept spreading. By the time the bartender had brought her a foaming mug, one could have heard a field mouse tiptoe across the scarred floor.

78

She grabbed it, washed the eggs down.

The bartender held out his hand. "Now I'd be much obliged if you'd pay and get out of here."

Dallas finished the last of the mug of beer, politely held back a dainty belch and fumbled in her purse for the pennies, counted them out on the scarred bar. She was almost full anyhow. By now, even the old piano player had stopped playing and was craning his neck to look.

The bartender stared down at the pennies as Dallas turned to go. "Just a minute, miss, that's not enough."

She had a sudden, uneasy feeling in the pit of her stomach, but she gracefully wiped her mouth. "That'd buy a beer in Texas."

The scantily dressed girls on the stage had stopped dancing when the music had ended, and now they, too, craned their necks, staring. Dallas recognized the one called Margo by her yellow hair, carmined lips, and red dress.

"Texas! I might have known from the accent," the bartender groaned. "You can always tell a Texan, but you can't tell 'em much! Now, gal—"

"Clark, what the hell's going on out here?" A tall man stuck his head out of the back office. He looked a little like Quint Randolph, except he had a cruel mouth. He wore a flowered vest and a string tie, and his Southern drawl was thick as syrup in winter time.

"Nothing, Mr. Yancy, sir," the bartender said respectfully. "This little lady came moseyin' up to the bar, drank a beer, and now can't pay for it!"

A wave of laughter swept through the place, and Yancy's face reddened angrily. Obviously he felt his establishment was the butt of some kind of joke.

Dallas bit her lip. "I-I just didn't have quite enough money, I reckon."

He came out of the office, striding toward the bar. "Let's get the music going again," he drawled soothingly, and gestured to the piano player. "Now you men have another drink and go back to your cards. This one's on the house!"

The men cheered and pushed forward as Yancy took Dallas's elbow. "Maybe we'd better talk in my office, miss."

She knew from his accent that he was a Southerner, but he looked like a tinhorn gambler. Dallas let him lead her back to a richly decorated, but gaudy, office. It was dimly lit by one elegant oil lamp. He gestured her into a chair, stuck a gold toothpick in the corner of his mouth, and sat down.

"Now then" — he smiled reassuringly, but she realized he'd had more than a little to drink that evening; she could smell the bourbon on him — "what seems to be the trouble? You were sent by my competitor to stir up trouble, right?"

"Oh, no, Mr. Yancy. I just got here from Philadelphia a few hours ago!" Dallas hastened to explain that she was hungry, and had decided on her own to come into the saloon.

Yancy clucked sympathetically, but he didn't really look as if he believed her. "Ah can certainly understand, Miss . . . Miss?"

"Da — Delilah." She'd almost told him her real name, which might not be wise. There was a box of cigars with that brand name on his fine desk.

"Delilah?" He paused, leaning back in his chair, then sat up very straight and stared at her. "I wasn't expecting you to make contact this way, I thought I was to wait for your letter . . ."

She didn't have the least idea what he was talking about and said so.

He seemed very flustered, and his hands shook as he put the toothpick in his flowered vest, reached for a cigar. "Forget what I said. Now, you tell me the truth."

Dallas watched him light up, knew then he wasn't really a gentleman. No gentleman ever lit up without asking a lady's permission. But then, she conceded, not many ladies went around stealing the free lunch off bars.

She didn't tell him everything, just that she was alone with no money, had arrived in St. Joe that afternoon, and was hoping to find a job, but her luggage had been stolen and she didn't have the price of a meal. "So you see, Mr. Yancy, I'm sort of in a bad spot. I never meant to walk out without paying for the beer."

He threw back his head, laughed as though amused by her pluck and her outrageous behavior. "Damn me! You're as sassy as a pair of red shoes! Where you from, Delilah?"

"Texas." She watched him smoke the cigar. He was looking her over in a way that made her uneasy.

"I should have known from your accent that you're as Southern as I am," he drawled. "I'm from Biloxi. Drink?"

She shook her head, watched him pour a tall tumbler of bourbon for himself, although he was drunker than a peach-orchard sow already. She didn't think it would help her situation to tell him her Papa was a strong supporter of Governor Sam Houston who'd brought Texas into the Union and was determined to keep her in it, even if the other Southern states finally seceded.

Yancy drank his bourbon, smoked his cigar, and looked at her. "I've only been here a few weeks myself. St. Joe is an uncivilized town, a Yankee town. But there's work that may need doing for our great cause. . . ." His voice trailed off as if he realized that he shouldn't discuss some things.

"I'd be willing to pay for the beer and all the food I ate when I finally get a job." She leaned forward.

"A job? Beggin' your pardon, ma'am, but you are obviously a lady of breeding. You can't convince me that you ever held a real job."

She wanted to smack the smug, shocked grin off his handsome face. "I worked on a lady's fashion magazine."

He snubbed out his cigar and laughed. "Let me assure you, Miss Delilah, there's not too many fashion magazines hereabouts. St. Joe's an uncivilized place, not at all like Atlanta or Savannah."

"If you dislike it so, why are you here?"

His expression was suddenly guarded, as if he had something to hide. "I might ask you the same thing, my dear."

She looked away, but figured her guilt must show on her face. "I . . . thought I had an uncle here, but he's died."

"What was your uncle's name?" His gaze bored into her in the dim, smoky glow of the lamp.

"Uh . . . Smith, John Smith." Idiot, she thought, is that the best you could do? She wasn't used to lying.

"Unusual name," he said dryly, sipping his drink.

She had to change the subject. "I-I'm desperate," Dallas admitted, shame-faced. "I'd even clean off tables, wash glasses at your bar."

He studied her over the top of his glass. "Would you now? Although it goes against my principles as a Southern gentleman, perhaps I could find some way to give you gainful employment."

Dallas almost clapped her hands with relief. "Oh, Mr. Yancy, how kind you are! Why, I'll clean your office, iron your shirts—"

He held up a hand and shook his head as though embarrassed by her thanks. "It's the least I can do for a real lady. Now, let me find you something to wear."

"Wear?" She looked down at her dress, realized how dusty it was. "Oh, of course."

Though a little unsteady on his feet, he led her to another room, dug through a closet. "I think maybe some of these things previous girls have had might fit you until you can do better. Just try this on, and then come show me how you look."

The scarlet dress looked a little bright, but Dallas realized she would seem ungrateful if she pointed that out. Yancy left, carefully closing the door behind him.

Dallas uneasily inspected the dress, the jewelry, and shoes. This didn't look like what kitchen help would wear. She'd at least try them on. But standing in front of the mirror once she'd buttoned everything, she felt embarrassed.

Perhaps the gown had once belonged to a much smaller girl. Besides that, its former owner had apparently lost the jacket because the top revealed the swell of Dallas's small breasts and too much of her bare shoulders.

She slipped on the shoes and jewelry, turned again to the mirror. She looked like a dance-hall girl in the spangled, bright red dress that clung to her slim body so tightly it revealed way too much. Yancy probably didn't realize what he'd given her, drunk as he was. Well she'd go show him and he'd apologize and find her something else to wear.

Music and laughter drifted from the saloon area as she tiptoed down the hall, knocked on his office door.

"Come in."

She barely heard him over the sounds of the bar's customers and the whirling of roulette wheels.

She entered the room. "Mr. Yancy, there must be a mistake. I'm sure this is the wrong dress—"

"Close the door, my dear, and let me see you in it." He stood up slowly, drained his glass, set it on his desk as he started over to her.

Something about the way he looked at Dallas made her uneasy. "As you can see, it's way too tight and shows too much—"

"I wouldn't say that," he drawled. "I shorely hadn't realized how pretty you are. Delilah is a good name for you, after all."

He ran his tongue over his lips in a slow way that upset her, and then he moved so that he stood between her and the door.

"Mr. Yancy, I feel almost naked in this. Wasn't there a jacket or something?"

He came over, reached out, and put one hand on her bare shoulder. "Never hide the merchandise, honey. I don't know who you really are or why you're here, but let's drop the innocent act, shall we?"

She recoiled from his hot, sweaty hand as it touched her bare skin. He knew she was on the run. What could she do to keep him from telling the sheriff? She needed time to think. "I-I don't have the least idea what you're talking about."

"I don't believe that for a minute." He winked at her,

83

weaving a little unsteadily on his feet. "Now, honey, if the law's lookin' for you, you're safe here at the Naughty Lady." He ran his hand along her shoulder to trace her throat with the tips of his fingers, then the swell of breasts above cheap satin.

What in the name of goodness was she to do? In all her sheltered life, she had never met a man so blatantly disrespectful. Her heart was pounding so hard, she was sure his trailing fingers could feel it. Then he slipped his arms around her.

"Yancy, I . . . I think we ought to stick to business."

"This is business." He tilted her head back, kissing her neck, while she wondered whether to scream and bring a crowd running. Maybe she could talk her way out of here.

"I could bite you and tear out your jugular vein, you know that, Delilah?"

She was dealing with a madman. His teeth nipped along the column of her throat. She was too terrified to move.

"I can feel your pulse pounding against my teeth, honey," he said thickly, as she felt his hot breath on her neck.

If she struggled, would he really sink his teeth into her flesh?

His lips worked down the column of her neck to the hollow of her throat as his hands pulled at her dress.

Dallas's fright began to give way to fury. How dare him paw her this way? "Why don't we find a more comfortable place?"

She smiled up at him, her heart still pounding. If she could get his hands off her for a moment, maneuver him around so that he was no longer between her and the door, she might escape.

"You can think of that at a time like this?" he gasped, pulling down her bodice, stroking her breasts. "I'm gonna take you the first time right across my desk. Lying on your soft belly has to be the most comfortable position in the world!"

Dallas murmured something undecipherable, forcing herself not to shudder as his hands found her nipples while he backed her up against his desk. She reached behind her, her shaking fingers closing on the heavy goblet he'd just drained. She glanced at the door, then went into his arms again, gradually moving him around so he wasn't between her and the only escape from this room.

He pulled her hard against him, his mouth hot and wet on her breast. "Delilah, my Delilah . . ."

Dallas took a deep breath, fear seizing her as she felt his manhood, hot and throbbing, through his clothes. The heavy goblet rested in her grip.

You may only get one chance. Make sure you do it right the first time!

Thinking that, she pulled slightly away from him, smiling with fear-frozen lips. "Give me a chance to get this dress off."

He stepped back, smiling at her with that cruel mouth.

Now! Dallas thought, and she brought her knee up with one hard movement, catching him squarely between the thighs even as she cracked him across the skull with the goblet.

"Bitch!" he screamed and bent double, clutching himself as he collapsed onto the floor.

That was all Dallas needed. As he fell, she stumbled backward, fairly flew out the door.

Did she dare stop for her clothes? Already she heard Yancy cursing and shouting for someone to stop her.

In terror, she ran down the hall to the back of the building, searching for a way out. Behind her, she heard a creak as the door swung open and Yancy limped out into the hall. "Where'd the bitch go? Someone stop that girl!"

Desperate to get away, Dallas ran down the dark hall, trying doors. A storage room. A closet. Would she never find a way out without running back into the saloon?

Behind her, Yancy yelled. She had never been so frightened. At the end of the hall was another door. Where it led, she didn't care as long as it got her out of this hallway.

Horsefeathers! It was stuck! For a long heart-stopping moment, she tugged at it while Yancy was shouting and searching behind her. Then the door came open and she ran out into the cool darkness.

Dallas took off like chain lightning. She ran blindly through the night, stumbling over the uneven ground, running into things. Perspiration beaded on her satin skin, ran down between her small, bare breasts. It seemed she could still feel Yancy's wet mouth on her nipples, his teeth on her throat. There was no telling what he would do to her if he caught her.

Finally, breathless and stumbling, she leaned against a barn and gasped cold air into her straining lungs.

Early in the evening, she'd thought she had as much trouble as she could possibly handle. How wrong she'd been! Then she'd only been without luggage and money. Now she'd lost her clothes, her purse; and she was wearing a skimpy, gaudy dress.

Worse yet, Yancy was looking for her. Dallas leaned against the side of the barn and shook all over. With a man like Yancy, killing was probably the most merciful fate she might expect.

Her thoughts suddenly went to Quint Randolph, and she longed for the warmth of his arms. But of course, he was far away in Philadelphia, and she would have to deal with this trouble by herself.

What in God's name was she going to do?

Chapter Six

Dallas leaned against the barn and shook for some moments. She wondered if Yancy had his henchmen out combing the streets for her.

Where should she go? She was cold and exhausted, even though she managed to get enough to eat from the free lunch on the bar. Certainly she couldn't stay out in the street all night, not in this outfit and with Yancy's men searching for her.

Dallas crept to the livery stable, slipped inside. The scents of hay and horses smelled good to the ranch-raised girl. A horse in a nearby stall whinnied at her and she crept over, patted his velvet nose. "Easy boy, don't give me away. I don't need anyone coming to investigate a noise."

She climbed the ladder into the loft, settled into the soft hay with a sigh, and drifted off to sleep.

But tomorrow came all too soon. Dallas was awakened by men in the stable below, feeding and saddling horses. She watched them from a crack in the loft floor. After the morning rush, things got quiet again and she crept out of the barn. Peeking around the corner, she realized she was on a deserted back street.

She looked down at the dance-hall dress she wore. She'd certainly be noticed if she went very far in this outfit. What was she going to do without proper clothes or money?

Briefly, she thought of the letter that was even now headed for Texas. At this point, she'd be relieved if Papa did send her brother after her. Right now, even that awful school didn't seem so bad. What was it the cowboys always said? *Any time you need a helping hand, look at the end of your arm.* She'd gotten herself into this mess, she'd have to get herself out.

What could she possibly do to get a little money so she could buy a respectable dress and some breakfast? It was tough to be a woman alone in a frontier town. Dallas almost wished she were a boy. Boys didn't have to worry about men trying to take advantage of them, and they could easily find jobs in a town as bustling as this one.

She washed her face and hands as best as she could in the horse trough, and tried to comb the hay out of her long, tousled hair with her fingers.

From a cafe somewhere down the street, the scent of bacon and hot biscuits floated on the early morning breeze. Dallas took a whiff and sighed. At home, there was always steak for breakfast and prickly pear jelly for the biscuits, washed down with coffee the way Texans liked it, strong enough to float a horseshoe—and for her, full of rich cream from the ranch cows.

Maybe she could offer to wash dishes or wait tables at that cafe to pay for breakfast. *In this dress?* She looked down at the gaudy satin. *Not likely.*

Her mind busy with possibilities, Dallas started down the sidewalk, passed a small shop. La Boutique, the sign read, The Latest in Paris Fashions For My Lady. Dallas studied the dresses and wigs in the window. The styles were several years behind the ones in Philadelphia, but out on the frontier, they always were. A smaller sign caught her eyes: We Buy Quality Hair.

Hair? Of course. For all the fashionable switches and hairpieces women used when their own hair was thin or wouldn't grow long.

Dallas picked up one of her long luxuriant locks, looked at her reflection in the store window, then shook her head. No, she couldn't even consider it.

The scent of bacon drifted on the breeze again. She was so hungry, her belly felt like it had grown to her backbone. She half turned to walk away, then stopped, reconsidered. A plan began to form in her mind.

Could she pull it off? Did she have any alternative? After all, hair eventually grew back. Before she could change her mind, she entered the shop, which smelled like old fabric and dust.

The elderly lady proprietor looked as if she'd been weaned on a sour pickle. She frowned in obvious disapproval of Dallas's appearance.

"You buy hair?"

"Sometimes." The woman's attention went to Dallas's tresses, and she took up a lock of them, inspecting it critically. "Most of the hair available comes from young innocents about to enter convents in Europe, or so they tell us. But you know what the rumor is?"

Dallas shook her head, leaned closer.

The stern lady inspected Dallas's hair and smiled, obviously liking what she saw. "The rumor is"—she lowered her voice conspiratorially—"that it's really cut from the heads of fever victims around New Orleans just before they bury 'em!"

Dallas's horror showed on her face. But now that the older woman had ruined the girl's day, she was almost cheery. "Don't think you can get a fortune from me just because you have nice hair," she warned.

But Dallas had grown up watching cowboys do horse trading. Nobody, but nobody, could best a Texas cowboy on a deal. When she got through, Dallas had a nice piece of change in her pocket, and she'd sent the old lady over to the dry-goods store to buy a pair of boy's pants, a shirt, and boots.

Within moments, she stood dressed like a boy, her small breasts flattened by the band; her hair short and curly as a boy. The old lady frowned in obvious disapproval. "Don't know what you're up to, young lady, but can't say as how I approve."

"I'm hiding out from a man who's trying to force me to

work in his saloon," Dallas said. "I reckon I might be safer if I can pass myself off as a boy." It occurred to her that the old lady might gossip about this. "If I were you, ma'am, I'd keep mighty quiet about this. I reckon he isn't going to be too happy with whoever helped me."

She looked startled. "Maybe I'd better turn this into a wig quick then. Don't want him to come in here and find the evidence." She looked admiringly at the luxuriant hair she'd just cut from Dallas's head. "I figured you had to be desperate to cut and sell hair like this."

Dallas tried not to have regrets. "It'll grow back in a year or so, and in the meantime, maybe I'll be safe from men."

She looked herself over in the store's mirror. Yes, with her tall, slender frame and her breasts tightly wrapped to disguise them, she really might pass herself off as a boy.

"Be seein' you," she said, running her hand through her short, black curls and sauntering out the door. She had a sense of freedom she'd never felt before as she headed for the main streets of town.

Remembering to walk like a man, Dallas went directly to the cafe down the street. She must remember to hang onto what little money she had until she decided what to do next. She sought out the cook. Could she really pass for a boy? This would be her first test. Thank goodness her natural voice was low and whiskey-soft.

"Mister, you got something I can do to earn a meal?"

The harried cook hardly glanced up. "Sure do! Boy who usually sweeps up is sick this morning. Start cleaning off those tables, carry out the garbage, and then grab a broom!"

Dallas obliged, trying not to stare too hard at the cowboys and soldiers wolfing down their breakfasts. She was strong from years of riding horseback and helping in roundups, but she struggled with the heavy garbage. Still she was happy when she finally finished her chores and gobbled down some food in the midmorning lull. If she could fool the cook, maybe she could fool everyone. She asked him, "Could I get on steady?"

He shook his head, wiped sweat from his florid jowls. "I'd like to keep you; you're a good hand. But my wife's nephew usually has this job. Maybe if he gets sick again . . . by the way, what is your name, son?"

Dallas gasped, thinking fast. "Uh, Dal; Dal Dawson."

"Maybe later, Dal."

Full and with her problems temporarily solved, Dallas ambled down the street, absently looking in windows. She didn't realize what a good job she was doing passing as a boy until she started to enter a general store ahead of a girl and the young redhead huffed with displeasure and whacked Dallas with her parasol. "Where I'm from, gentlemen open doors for ladies and let them enter first!" the redhead said sharply.

I must remember my manners. Little things like that will give me away faster than anything. "Excuse my rudeness, miss," Dallas said gallantly, as she stepped back to open the door for the snippy girl. "I was so taken by your beauty, I plumb forgot my manners."

The redhead paused. Then she smiled and batted her eyes at Dallas. "You're forgiven," she said softly. "My family's with the wagon train leaving for Oregon tomorrow. I don't suppose you're coming on that trip?"

Dallas stared back at the girl in confusion. Then she smiled. She was beginning to enjoy her masquerade. "For you, miss, I'd consider it."

The girl smiled again, reached out to touch Dallas's hand, and then went on into the store, leaving Dallas staring after her with delight.

She had passed the toughest test of all—fooling another girl. Did she want to join a wagon train? She thought about it, decided Oregon held no appeal for her. She'd lived in the warm and arid Southwest too long to be happy on the Northwest coast. But passing as a man opened up possibilities she'd never dreamed of.

For the next several days, Dallas did odd jobs to pay for her meals while she thought about what she might try as a permanent job. She could rope, ride, and shoot as well as almost any man on the Triple D. Maybe someone needed a cowhand. After she'd proved to Papa that she could make it on her own, she'd go home in triumph.

Horsefeathers. She ran her hand through her short curls. Mama would faint when she saw her tomboy daughter's hair, and Papa might be angry. But when she explained that she'd done it because masquerading as a man was the best way to protect her virtue, even he would understand.

Virtue. She'd lost that in a bed in Philadelphia. She thought of Quint Randolph sadly. Why was she so attracted to the tall dude when he seemed so different from every man she'd ever known? She wondered how he'd fit in on a ranch, then scolded herself for even thinking about him. But when she closed her eyes, she remembered his mouth dominating hers, his tongue teasing hers. Even the thick hair of his broad chest had tantalized the sensitive tips of her nipples. With her eyes closed, she could remember every sensation of that brief night; the heat and the touch and the taste of the man. No use thinking about him now.

But, absently, she reached for the earring tucked safely in her shirt pocket.

Dallas sat down on a bench in the shade, picked up a newspaper someone had abandoned. Maybe there'd be a job in the advertisements. Someone needed an apprentice at the harness makers. She shook her head; that didn't appeal to her. The newspaper needed a printer's devil to set type. That was tempting.

With a grin, she thought about applying for that one. She even daydreamed a little about being such a success at it that the cranky owner offered to take her in as a partner. She imagined over and over the grand scene when she revealed herself as the girl he had turned away earlier. But she knew that was taking too big a chance, she dare not risk the man recognizing her.

She scanned the paper slowly and then saw a big advertisement: "Wanted — young, skinny, wiry fellows, not over

18. Must be expert riders, willing to risk death daily. Orphans preferred. Wages $25 a week. . . ."

Puzzled, Dallas looked at the address, recognized it. The Pony Express, that's what it was, advertising for riders to carry the mail. She looked at the salary again. Why they were offering almost as much a week as cowhands made in a month!

A daring plan began to form in her mind; it was so daring it even shocked Dallas. She was young, wiry, and a better rider than most boys her age. She could also handle a gun. Could she possibly walk into the Pony Express, fool them into thinking she was a boy, and get one of these jobs?

She stood up uncertainly. It was obviously dangerous work. The company must be having a hard time filling the jobs if they still needed riders when the regular runs were scheduled to begin in only a few days. She smiled in spite of herself. It was worth the gamble, with the money being offered and her needing a job so badly. All they could do was throw her out of the office.

She shook her head. No, it was too dangerous and daring even for her. She'd find something right here in St. Joe to do until she got enough money for a stage ticket home. By then, Papa might have cooled off enough to listen to reason about that stupid school. Riding west for the Pony Express, into territory where all sorts of dangers threatened and hostile Indians awaited, could be dangerous indeed.

Where should she begin to look for a job? Perhaps the livery stable needed a boy to curry horses. Or maybe she could get taken on at the general store, helping stock shelves.

Dallas spent the next several days working at odd jobs and sleeping up in the stable loft at night. But her wages were low. Every time she had to buy a meal, she looked at her pitiful handful of coins and thought about the princely salary the Pony Express boys would be making now that the first run was scheduled for April third.

She'd finished sweeping out a store and was heading down the street, remembering to walk at a slow saunter without swinging her hips. As she passed the train station, a big engine huffed and hissed as it pulled in with a swirl of smelly smoke.

Curiously, Dallas wandered over to watch the train pull in, as did many of the people standing around on the streets. Passengers disembarked, conductors called out instructions. The crowd bustled around the busy station as the train spewed black smoke over the crowd.

The most interesting thing about the train was that it pulled two open flatcars carrying some of the finest horses Dallas had ever seen, and she'd seen many good ones. Thoroughbreds. She pressed closer, admiring the fine mounts, wondering where they were destined for? Her first thought was the army at Ft. Leavenworth, Kansas Territory. But then she shook her head. No, the army couldn't afford horses as fine as these.

She pushed closer, reached out and patted a velvet nose. Bays, chestnuts and sorrels. Without a doubt, these were some of the biggest, finest horses she had seen. The rancher who had bred these certainly knew his bloodlines. The long, clean legs showed a capacity for speed and stamina. Where were these being shipped?

Then a hired hand, motioned everyone away. "Stand back!" he shouted, "Stand back, folks, so we can unload them!"

Dallas blinked in surprise and yelled to the man as he directed some men to put a ramp in place. "These horses are getting off here?"

The man nodded, "Came all the way from Kentucky for the Pony Express!"

Murmurs of excitement and admiration came from the crowd as the hired hand turned away to talk to a tall, broad-shouldered man who had just descended from the train.

"For the Express," an old lady said at Dallas's elbow. "You know, I didn't think it was possible to deliver mail across the country that fast, but now that I've seen these horses, I almost believe it."

But another woman shook her head. "I don't know. Ten days to get a letter to California is lightning quick. I'll withhold judgment till I see if they really can do it. Two thousand miles is a long way! What do you think, sonny?"

Dallas suddenly realized that the woman had spoken to her. She doffed her hat politely as a cowboy would. "Reckon I don't know what to think, ma'am. It does seem like a might big undertaking."

The old lady smiled at Dallas. "Hear they need about eighty or a hundred boys. Good wages. You thinking of applying, young man?"

Dallas's attention went again to the tall, broad-shouldered man standing with his back to her. There was something vaguely familiar about that figure. "Reckon not," she said. "They say it's mighty dangerous, and the Injuns far west is restless. My scalp's worth more than the Pony'd pay."

The hired hands had the gate down now, and were leading the fine horses down the walkway and into a waiting corral. Dallas watched the thoroughbreds come down the ramp, powerful hooves flashing, manes blowing in the wind as they shook their heads and neighed, obviously glad to be on solid ground after the long trip on the swaying train.

Dust swirled and Dallas put her hat back on, wiped her face, and took a deep breath of the pleasant scent of sweating horses.

No, she reckoned she wouldn't ride for the Express even though she yearned to throw a leg over one of these quality horses. The job was too dangerous, and she had no reason to leave St. Joe. Then the broad-shouldered man turned and looked straight at her.

For a moment, Dallas stood frozen in surprise, staring back at him. She'd been wrong. She did have a reason to leave this town now—a very good reason. Part of her past had just caught up with her.

She stood there, trying to decide whether to run to him or from him. She'd have to decide quickly even though her feet seemed unable to move. Torn between horror and remembrance of his kisses, Dallas couldn't move as Quint Randolph strode down the ramp toward her.

What was she going to do? Would he make some ribald reference to her ending up in his bed? Would he—?

Quint flipped her a silver dollar. "Here, son, go tell the livery stable I've arrived and would like a buggy brought around."

Sonny. He didn't recognize her, thought she was a boy. She didn't know whether to be relieved or disappointed. The more she thought about it, standing there and looking from him to the tip on her palm, the angrier she got. He'd been in bed with her and that experience hadn't been memorable enough for him to remember her?

Quint frowned. "Sonny, did you hear me?"

"I-I heard you, mister. I'll go get the buggy."

Quint ran a hand through his hair. "Did we ever meet before, kid? Somehow, when I look at you—"

"You want a buggy?" Dallas gulped, backed away. "I-I'll go get a buggy."

She turned and fled. Behind her, she heard Quint say to one of the hired hands, "That poor boy must be either a little retarded or a little deaf."

The nerve of that hairy-chested idiot! Dallas fought an impulse to run back and throw the coin in his aristocratic face. But, if she did that he might remember where they had met before.

Matter of fact, once he thought it over, he still might. How humiliating that would be for both of them! Here she'd thought she'd hang around St. Joe until she decided what to do next and Quint Randolph showed up. Had he trailed her here, hoping to find her and turn her in for the large reward that was surely being offered? She couldn't imagine any other reason for him to be in St. Joe.

She shook her head, thinking he didn't look like a man badly in need of money. But she knew from their first meeting that he gambled. Maybe he had big gambling debts to pay. Perhaps he was here to play cards.

She had the livery stable deliver the buggy to the station, watched it pass by with Quint driving at a fast clip. It was heading directly to the Patee House, St. Joe's finest hotel.

Just what was he doing in town if not looking for her so he might collect the reward? And suppose he decided to stay on for some weeks? Surely if she kept running into him, he'd finally realize she was the runaway who'd ended up in his bed. Dallas suddenly wondered if that confession of impotency was a trick with which he lured unsuspecting innocents into his embrace. After all, what woman could resist a challenge like that, to see if she could be the one with enough allure to obviate his problem.

Dallas decided she had to get out of town as quickly as possible, but she didn't have enough money for a train or stage ticket. She walked past the Pony Express office, saw the sign posted in the window. She stopped, read it again, laughed at her sudden idea. The gossip she'd heard indicated that this end of the line was civilized and not dangerous. It was the far end of the line, in the part of Utah that was rapidly becoming known as Nevada, where there were deserts, mountains, and wild Indians on the warpath.

Standing in front of the window, Dallas read the ad again, her mouth starting to curl into a grin. Wouldn't it be a joke on Quint if, while he was searching for her, she got away again—as a Pony Express rider?

Before she could give it further thought, Dallas marched into the office. "I want to ride for you," she said in her huskiest voice.

The weathered man at the desk looked up, and Dallas's blood almost froze in her veins. He was the genial, cowboy type who had been at the minstrel show that night with Quint and the actress. But he showed no sign of recognition. He stood up, reached out to shake Dallas's limp hand. "I'm Thaddeus Barnes. You look wiry and lean enough. Do you ride well?"

"You think I'd apply if I didn't?"

He motioned her to the chair in front of the desk. "Sit down, boy, and we'll talk. What's your name?"

What was it she had decided to call herself? "Uh, Dal. Dal Dawson. When do the runs start anyway?"

Barnes shrugged. "April third. Lots of pomp and speechifyin' involved in something historic like this. Hear the president himself may send a message of greeting to the state of Californy. Besides, we're short of horses; expecting some on contract right away."

"Oh, maybe that's them being unloaded now down at the station. I just came from there."

Barnes stood up. "Well, that's good to know. Reckon I'd better go look into it, soon's I get you signed up. Then we can all relax and celebrate . . . unless Mr. Majors shows up. He's real religious; plans to give all the riders a Bible and make them swear not to drink or use foul language."

She wondered if Mr. Majors had a rule about girls who ran away and then masqueraded as men? She finished giving him the information he needed.

"Can you write your name, boy? If not, just make your mark."

"I can write and read, too." Dallas knew many on the frontier couldn't. She signed.

"Well, I'll keep in touch," she said lamely, turning to walk away. She was already regretting her impulsive act. Even though the money was good, could she pass for a man well enough to fool all those boys she'd be riding with? She shrugged as she went out onto the street. So far, so good.

Despite herself, she found that her feet were carrying her over to the Patee House. She just wanted to spy on him, make sure he was checked in and not already out on the street looking for her, she told herself. But her more sensible side told her she was asking for *mucho* trouble by going anywhere near him.

She stood in the lobby, her Western hat pulled low over her eyes and watched people come and go. Leaning against a potted fern in the ornate Victorian lobby, she began to indulge in a fantasy.

Quint would come down into the lobby, dressed in an elegant outfit, perhaps even wearing a cape like the man about town he was.

Dallas would step forward, take off her hat, and confront him. "I've decided to admit that I'm the dark angel from a few days ago."

Right there, he would fall to his knees, clasp her hand in his with a glad cry. "Thank God, I've found you, my dearest angel! I was going mad with worry. Swear we can be married and never be parted again!"

Then, before she could answer, he would stand up and sweep her into his arms. "Don't even think of saying no! I intend to take you back to a fine mansion in Philadelphia — as my bride!"

Even as she protested that she wouldn't consider saying no, he would carry her off. But Philadelphia? God's country was anywhere in the West; Dallas didn't like towns and cities. If he really wanted to live in the city, perhaps . . .

But suppose he looked puzzled when she admitted to being the missing dark angel, ran that hand with the big gold ring on it through his light hair and shrugged. "Dark angel? I haven't the least idea what you're talking about! Are you sure you haven't confused me with someone else?"

No, never, she thought, running the tip of her tongue across her lips, remembering his kisses. When she thought of him, she thought of his hairy, muscular chest pressed against her breasts, the brandy taste of his mouth. She didn't know whether she felt relieved or disappointed that he hadn't recognized her. Maybe a little of each.

She half turned to go, still imagining the scene. Would his lips curl with scorn and loathing? "Of course I remember you, you shameless tart! How can a man forget a hussy who'd fall into bed with some drunk she picked up on the street? Tell me, do you do that often?"

Tears came to her eyes. Only once, she thought, and only you.

Then she recalled the words meant for a girl named

Melanie. With a sigh, Dallas finally admitted to herself that she'd only come to the hotel in the hope of getting the merest glimpse of him. If he came down that sweeping curved staircase right this minute, could she stop herself from running to him? Before, she'd been too shocked at seeing him in St. Joe to do anything but stand and blink.

Reluctantly, she turned to go as Thaddeus Barnes and a couple of younger men came into the lobby, laughing and talking.

"Hey, Dal," Barnes yelled and motioned to her. "I'm takin' some of the Pony Express boys out for a drink; join us!"

"I-I think not," she said, backing toward the exit. If she spent any time with them, they might figure out real quick she wasn't a boy. But the tanned manager caught her arm. "Aw, kid, you too good for us? We're celebrating the horses getting here. That's the main thing that's been holding us up."

How could she get out of this without looking snooty or arousing suspicion? "I was just going back to my room to get me a chaw of tobacco," she said, gesturing at the door. "You know how we all are about a good chaw!"

"I'm Tom Ranahan, Happy Tom, they call me. One of the riders." The young man with the broad, Irish face grinned. Then he reached into his pocket, pulled out a plug. "Here. Have some of mine; save yourself a trip."

"It ain't my brand. I'm mighty partial to the brand I been using." *Please, God, don't let him ask what brand; I can't rightly remember the names of any I've seen the cowboys chew.*

But the boy pressed the tobacco into her hand, "Try this," he insisted. "It's new and I really like it."

The others nodded encouragingly, and there was nothing Dallas could do but bite off a hunk, put it in her jaw.

"See ain't that good?"

The young men looked at her as she rolled it around in her jaw. "The best!" She gulped, eying the spittoon over by the potted fern. If she dribbled juice down her chin while spitting, she'd give herself away. "What're you doing

100

here, anyways?"

Ranahan shrugged. "Same as you most likely, I reckon—watching the swells come and go—but we got to meet a man so we can buy him a drink. After all, he's brought the horses in so we can begin our runs. This here's Bill."

She shook hands with the other rider, choked on the tobacco juice. *How in the name of bluebonnets could men put this nasty stuff in their mouths?*

"Yep," Barnes said, gesturing toward the stairs. "Here he comes now, so we can all go over to the Naughty Lady and celebrate.

The Naughty Lady. That was the last place in the world Dallas wanted to go. She started to protest even as she turned to look at the gentleman who had provided the Pony Express horses. He was Quint Randolph.

Chapter Seven

Dallas stood choking on the tobacco and gaping at Quint as he joined the group.

"Good to see you again, Barnes." Quint slapped him on the back. "My horses will get your mail through in record time."

Barnes grinned, introduced the other riders, then turned to Dallas. "Say howdy to one who just hired on this afternoon. Quint, this is Dal Dawson."

Quint took Dallas's limp fingers in his own, shook them. "Haven't we met before, young man?"

She stared up at him, keenly aware of the warmth of the strong hand grasping hers. She resisted the urge to shout *Of course! I spent the night in your bed!*

What she finally said was, "We . . . we met at the station, remember? You sent me to bring a buggy for you."

"Oh, of course. I knew you looked familiar. . . ."

Barnes grabbed them both, holding each by an arm. "Quint, we're all headed over to the Naughty Lady for a drink. I just hope old Majors doesn't find out."

The crowd guffawed good-naturedly.

Dallas felt a little sick from the chaw of tobacco, and she was gradually choking on the juice. "Couldn't we go someplace else?"

Immediately, the others protested. "Naw! The Lady has the best action at the card tables — and the prettiest women."

Barnes winked at Dallas. "My boy, if'n I was your age, I'd be like a stud bull among all those heifers at the Lady."

Quint laughed agreeably. "If that's where the prettiest girls are, I'm sure that's where Dal and I want to go!"

"I-I was thinking of turning in early," she said.

"By yourself?" Tom Ranahan laughed suggestively. "Maybe if you get lucky tonight, you can have Margo herself."

Quint slapped Dallas on the shoulder. "Maybe Dal and I will both be interested in this gal!"

Dallas smiled weakly, resisting the urge to give him a swift kick in the seat as he turned away from her and started toward the door.

Still, there was nothing she could do but follow as the men trooped outside, and sauntered toward the ornate saloon.

At least, she could spit out the wad of tobacco. A few more minutes of that and she would have been as sick as a poisoned hound.

She still felt a little queasy, but there was nothing to do but accompany the men as they walked toward the bright lights of the saloon. Dallas had a sudden vision of being sick enough to throw up in front of Quint Randolph. If she did, she hoped she'd just lie down and die after so she could skip the humiliation.

She hadn't realized how charming and witty Quint was when sober. As they walked, he entertained them with a ribald story and the others seemed to be hanging on his every word. All she could think about was whether he would finally remember why she looked familiar to him . . . and what would happen in the Naughty Lady if she should come face to face with Yancy? The saloon owner had been a little drunk when he'd met her, but maybe not that drunk.

The five of them entered the rowdy saloon, pushed their way through the laughing, talking crowd.

The piano in the corner banged away: *Buffalo gals, won't you come out tonight, Come out tonight, come out tonight, Buffalo gals, won't you come out tonight, And dance by the light of the moon. . . .*

Quint used his wide-shouldered frame to clear a path to the ornate mahogany bar. "Belly up, boys! I'm buying in honor of the Pony Express and the best damned horses in the world! Mine!"

Somehow in the confusion, Dallas had ended up next to him, and he put an arm around her shoulders. "Dal, you'll carry that mail in record time on my thoroughbreds."

She nodded and stared into the big mirror behind the bar, keenly aware of the heat of the muscular arm resting on her shoulders.

Quint looked down at her. "You're trembling, boy. You cold?"

"I-I thought I was coming down with the grippe earlier," she mumbled. Why didn't he take his arm off her shoulders?

The bartender brought the drinks, and she pretended to sip hers. *Thank God, it's a different one tonight.* Any minute now, Quint would recognize her or Yancy would come out of his office and spot her.

The piano player began a new song and a bunch of drunks sang along: " 'Listen to the mocking bird, listen to the mocking bird, The mocking bird still singing o'er her grave . . .' "

Grave. Dallas almost wished she were in hers. She put one small boot on the brass rail, relieved yet furious that she'd made such a small impression on this elegant Southern gentleman he didn't remember her. Well, she'd never forget him or that night.

Quint took his arm off her shoulders, lit an expensive pipe, and then felt in his pocket for cigars, offered her one.

Dallas shook her head. "Prefer a chew myself," she almost whispered, afraid someone would offer her another.

Quint refilled the glasses of those around him. "Another toast!" he sang out. "Here's to the brave boys, like Dal here, who are going to risk their lives to get the mail across the country!"

Barnes held up his glass, nodded. "The Pony has a slogan, men, and we intend to carry it out; the mail must go through!"

"Hear! Hear!" Quint said, and he tipped his glass up. Then he looked at her. "Dal, boy, you aren't drinking my toast? That's an insult."

She hesitated, glass in hand. Liquor had gotten her into trouble before, she was afraid of what it would do to her inhibitions. But the men were all looking at her. There was no help for it; she drank the raw, strong whiskey.

Barnes motioned for the bartender. "Now it's my turn to buy a round in honor of President Buchanan and Mr. Randolph's fine horses!"

"I'll drink to that!" Quint said, and all of them turned their glasses up again.

There was no way out. Dallas drank the whiskey, feeling it burn all the way down.

She looked over, saw Yancy come out of his office, stand looking over the crowd. Had he seen her? Would he recognize her? She leaned on the bar and turned her face so he wouldn't get a good look at her profile if he glanced her way. She wished there were some way she could excuse herself and get out of there without attracting attention.

Margo, the highly painted blonde Dallas had seen riding in the carriage, finished singing her number; then came over to the bar. All the men called out to her, offering to buy her drinks. She stood looking them over, as if making her choice. Then she sidled up to Quint. "Hello, good-lookin'. You wanna buy a lady a drink?"

Quint put a hand on her bare shoulder. "Sure! We're celebrating the Pony Express tonight. History will remember it and St. Joe forever."

Margo leaned her curves against Quint while Dallas, in a fury, watched. "Good-lookin', I think maybe we could make a little history of our own."

Dallas saw Margo smile up at Quint who winked broadly. "Maybe we might at that."

Dallas controlled herself. But she was mighty tempted

to reach over Margo's shoulder, pour a drink down the front of the blonde's gaudy, low-cut dress. The only reason she didn't was that would create a ruckus and bring people running. She dared not attract attention.

A petite brunette sauntered up to Dallas. "Hey, cowboy, my name's Rose. What say we go upstairs?"

Dallas blinked at the girl deliberately pressing big breasts against her arm. "Upstairs? I-I can't afford it; haven't drawn any pay yet."

Quint laughed. "Aw, Dal, let me treat you in honor of the Pony Express."

"I wouldn't want you to spend your money, Mr. Randolph."

The brunette pressed even closer. Dallas could smell the perfume she wore, feel the warmth of her body. She wanted to jump back, give the girl a good smack, but knew she couldn't.

"A Pony Express boy, huh?" Rose said. "I want to see if this rider can really ride!"

The others laughed.

Quint slipped an arm around Margo. "Depends on how spirited the filly is, I'd say. Isn't that right, Dal?"

Dallas swore silently as she tried to smile. All she could think of was Quint's arm around that blonde. Damn him! How was she going to get out of this without arousing suspicion? Yancy seemed to be staring at the group with open curiosity.

Dallas said, "I don't think—"

"Aw"—little Rose was hanging onto her arm—"I'll give you a good time, cowboy. You don't know what a wild filly I can be!"

The men all laughed again, and Quint nudged Dallas in the ribs. "Go on, Dal, I'll pay for it. In fact, I may be right next door." He gave Margo a flirtatious look and handed Rose a fistful of silver dollars.

Dallas hesitated again, but the brunette had her arm, was pulling on it. "Come on, cowboy," she whispered, "Yancy's lookin' at us. If he thinks the customers don't like me, I might lose my job and I need it."

Yancy was indeed staring at the group. If Dallas turned the brunette down, would it arouse the saloon owner's suspicions? Would it arouse Quint's?

Quint's arm was draped familiarly around Margo's bare shoulders. The blonde looked up at him with frank admiration. "Why don't we go upstairs, too, so your little friend won't feel so uncomfortable going up alone?"

Quint hesitated, shrugged. "Sure. Why not?"

Damn him! He was going to bed with that tart! Dallas was almost speechless with anger. But she didn't have time to think about that because little Rose had her by the arm and the four of them were climbing the stairs while Yancy stood, thumbs tucked in his vest, nodding in obvious approval.

Dallas stood uncertainly in the upstairs hall, the girl clinging to her arm. How was she going to get out of this mess? Quint started through a door with Margo, came back to pat Dallas's shoulder. "Is this your first time?"

She felt her face flame. In that split second, she remembered being in Quint Randolph's arms. It had been wild, wonderful and warm.

"No." She shook her head, sad that he didn't remember. Maybe it hadn't meant much to him. "It isn't."

The girl on her arm smiled. "I'll bet I've got a few things I can teach you anyway, cowboy."

Quint and Margo went into a room, closed the door. Dallas was in such a fury at thinking of him in there with the blonde that she could hardly keep her mind on the mess she was in and figure out how to get out of it.

Uncertainly, she walked over to peer over the railing at the boisterous crowd below. Yancy was standing in front of the door, looking up. There was no way to get out that way without getting past him.

The brunette had her by the hand now. Dragging Dallas into a room, she kicked the door shut. "Now cowboy, I've had my eye on you ever since you came in." She began to unbutton her dress.

"Uh, I think I've changed my mind," Dallas said. But the girl backed up, leaned against the door.

107

"I want to be able to say I've made love to a Pony Express rider, especially a dark, handsome one like you. Ain't you part Injun?"

How am I going to get out of this? "I'm part Indian and part Spanish," Dallas said. Perspiration was breaking out in the hollow between her bound breasts.

"Ain't that romantic?" Rose said, stepping out of her dress. She wore a lace camisole and petticoat, big breasts swelling above the lace.

She came over, put her arms around Dallas's neck, looked into her eyes. "I really like you, Dal."

Dallas tried to disengage Rose's arms. Maybe she could distract her. "I really like you, too. You've got the prettiest hair; black as a crow's wing."

The girl smiled, noticeably pleased. "You really like it?" She reached up to stroke her locks. "I'll tell you a little secret; it's a wig. Bought it this morning at La Boutique—"

Dallas threw back her head and laughed. It was her own hair! She was admiring a wig made from her own hair!

"You laughing at me?" The girl pulled away, frowning.

"No, of course not," Dallas said quickly. "Something just struck me funny; that's all. I think you're pretty, really."

The girl threw her arms around Dallas's neck again. "Then let's stop wasting time."

Dallas felt Rose's warm curves as the girl pressed against her. Now Rose's hand was fumbling with the buttons on Dallas's pants. If Rose got Dallas's pants off and discovered she was about to bed a girl in man's clothing, she'd probably scream loud enough to bring Quint and Yancy and everyone else in the place running.

Dallas reached out, caught the girl's hand and brought it to her lips. "I've got to level with you. We . . . we can't go through with this."

"Why not? You don't like me?"

"Like you?" Dallas managed to free herself; stepped away. "Why, if I was looking for a gal, you'd be the very one I'd choose. I don't reckon I've ever seen one I thought was as pretty as you are, but you see, I've got to be faithful to my love."

The whore blinked. "What?"

Dallas sighed wistfully. "I couldn't talk about it in front of that bunch because I know they'd hooraw me and laugh about anyone being faithful to an old love."

The brunette dabbed at the tears gathering in her eyes. "That's the sweetest thing I ever heard! There ain't many men faithful like that."

"There sure ain't!" Dallas snapped, thinking of Quint in the next room with Margo. She had meant less than nothing to him, but she would never forget him. "It isn't that I don't think you're pretty, Rose, but I've pledged my love to another and I just can't get that one off my mind." *Wasn't that the truth?* Quint Randolph hadn't been off her mind since she'd fled Philadelphia.

"I respect that," Rose said solemnly. "You're one in a million, Dal."

If you only knew, Dallas thought with relief. If you only knew . . . "So now we'll go back downstairs, and nobody need know I was too faithful to my sweetheart to end up in bed with you."

Rose nodded happily, reaching for her dress. "I didn't think men like you existed anymore, Dal. You've restored my faith in men; you're so sentimental and honest."

"I wouldn't carry it that far," Dallas said guiltily.

"If you ever leave that other girl, I'd be mighty interested in seeing you again." Rose wiped her smudged eyes and then led the way to the door.

"I'll remember that, Miss Rose." Dallas released a sigh of relief.

They went out into the hall, down the stairs. Dallas leaned up against the bar, waved at Rose who gave her a melting smile, before joining a group of men playing poker.

Barnes looked at Dallas in surprise. "You weren't gone long."

"How long does it take to get the job done?"

"For a hot young stud, not much time, I reckon. Boy,

that lady looked really happy. You must have done something special."

Dallas shrugged and tried to look casual. "That's between me and the lady." She turned to the bartender. "Bring me a beer."

She leaned against the bar, sipping the beer and looking up the stairway toward Margo's closed door. All she could think of was Quint in that blonde's arms, rubbing his hairy chest against her bare breasts. Dallas had to force herself not to run up the stairs, throw the door open. She was miserable and furious. What was keeping Quint?

Ranahan looked up the stairs and laughed. "He's sure taking a long time; must really be enjoying himself, that old stud hoss!"

Barnes nodded. "He looked like he had a lot to give—if you know what I mean."

Dallas tried not to blush crimson at the men's jokes as she drank her beer in silence. But she kept imagining Quint in Margo's arms. She hadn't been willing to face how much he meant to her until she'd envisioned him in the grip of the blonde's long, slender legs. Just what the hell was going on up there behind that closed door?

Quint lay back on Margo's bed, sipping his drink and slowly watching the blonde undress. Just how had he ended up here with a woman who didn't interest him?

Because he'd felt an unnatural attraction to the boy, Dal, and he'd panicked at the idea that his problem with women hadn't been caused by guilt after all. Suppose he was one of those men who preferred boys and was just now discovering it?

"You're awfully quiet," Margo said, stepping out of her lace pantaloons and going over to sit naked on the edge of the bed.

He put his drink on the bedside table, sighed and reached out to squeeze her breast. He knew what it was that women wanted to hear. "Just thinking how beautiful you are, that's all."

110

She smiled, leaning to kiss him. "I like you, too."

I'll force myself to make love to her, he thought, pulling her close, but he remembered the feel of the boy's shoulder beneath his arm, the soft darkness of Dal's eyes. When he'd stood close to the boy, he'd had an impulse to touch him. He'd thrown his arm familiarly across the boy's shoulders, had wanted to pull him close. Only at one other time in the past year had he felt such desire, such arousal.

Quint stroked Margo's hair absently, and thought about his dark angel. Maybe she didn't even exist except in his imagination. He felt for the pearl earring in his vest and it reassured him. There *had* been a woman, but that was all he could be sure of. Maybe her beauty was only the product of his drunken longing. If he really met her, the girl from the storm would probably turn out to be an ugly old whore.

He kissed Margo . . . and felt no eagerness, no wanting—no heart-pounding drive to lie between her legs, pump his seed deep within her. He put one hand on her soft thigh, then stroked the light silk at the vee of her legs. She was satiny wet in her readiness, and she caught his hand, urged him to explore even deeper while she spread her thighs and tilted her body up to meet his fingers.

Yet all he could think of was the slight boy he'd met that night. Quint cursed himself for being a filthy, unnatural man and pulled Margo close, kissed her.

She ran her hands up and down the fur of his chest. "I like a man with a hairy chest," she whispered. "It's sort of like being made love to by a bear."

"I'll make you think 'bear.' " He kissed her again, determined to drive away the memory of a dark girl with long curls wind-whipped around her face.

She laughed and murmured in his ear as he held her, but his mind was a thousand miles away, in another place and time. He had never taken Melanie's virginity. She had loved him so, and he had killed her. Then, because of his guilt, he had been unable to perform with any woman—until the dark angel had come out of a snowstorm and

111

given him the sweetest, most unselfish love he had ever had.

Since that cold night, he had had no woman, had wanted no other but the mysterious girl from the streets of Philadelphia. What was wrong with him? Here he was with a beautiful whore in his arms, yet his thoughts were on one of the young boys who rode for the Pony Express.

Margo arched herself against him, nibbling at his nipples with sharp teeth. "I got all night, honey. You can start anytime."

The throbbing that had built in him, when he'd thought of the girl who'd come out of a winter's storm and into his bed, began to fade. If he couldn't have her, he didn't want a common whore. He was suddenly aware of the scent of stale perfume on Margo's skin; of the slight scent of other men's sweat, other men's seed.

He suddenly sat up on the edge of the bed.

"What's the matter, honey?" She laid her head in his lap, her tongue warm and wet, smearing his maleness with her bright lip rouge.

"Nothing." He remembered with sudden clarity the bright red of Melanie's blood all over her white lace wedding dress; the virgin blood of the dark angel on his manhood. For a moment he closed his eyes and swallowed heavily, willing himself not to be sick. "I-I've just change my mind—feel a little queasy."

Margo sat up, pouted. "That always happens when men drink too much. It would happen tonight, when I want you so bad."

He didn't want her. That was the trouble; he wasn't all that drunk. Here he was in bed with a blonde with satin nipples as pink and moist as fresh cherries. And his mind was on that boy, wondering if he was enjoying the tiny brunette Quint had bought him.

Lord, I must be going crazy! Quint looked down at the gold signet ring, ran his hand through his hair distractedly. "I've just changed my mind; that's all! Maybe some other time."

She looked at him, sitting on the bed all satin and

naked, her breasts full of pleasure for some man's eager mouth, her body ripe for a man's plunging dagger. "There ain't many men who wouldn't kill for a chance to share my bed," she said softly. "You're a strange man, Quint, and maybe a tortured one. What I'd like to know is, who was she?"

"I don't know what you're talking about!" He grabbed up his clothes, savagely pulled them on. "I just changed my mind, that's all."

"If you say so," Margo shrugged. "But I think I'd like to trade places with her, have a man be that crazy in love with me."

Lord, did it show so much? Every day he'd hoped there'd be a message from Philadelphia saying that they'd found her. Yet he had been so drunk, he wasn't sure he'd recognize the girl if the man he'd hired did find her.

He smiled gently at Margo, reached for his wallet. "I'm really sorry."

"Don't be." She waved his money away. "But if you ever get over her and I'm still here, look me up."

"Thanks." He turned and strode out of the room, went down the stairs to the noisy saloon below.

He elbowed his way through the crowd to the bar. Dal was leaning against it, sipping a beer. Quint couldn't stop himself from reaching out, rumpling the boy's hair. "So how was the brunette?"

Dal shrugged, flushed. "Good, I reckon, as good as any. How was the blonde?"

Quint signaled the bartender to bring him a drink. "Does she know how it's done! I tell you, kid, next time pick Margo; she really can drive a man wild!"

The boy looked almost angry. "Reckon you've had enough women to know."

"Enough," Quint admitted.

"You ever find a real special woman?"

Quint hesitated, thinking of the ethereal girl who had come to him out of a snowstorm, given him her virginity, and disappeared. But she was too special, too precious to laugh and joke about with other men. "They're all special," he said, turning to place both elbows on the bar behind him.

He began to tell wild sexual tales about all the women he'd made love to, while the others listened. He had a terrible urge to reach out and put his arm around Dal. Two people had drawn Quint sexually, and one of them was a boy. Men had been gelded and lynched in the West for what he was thinking about now.

He needed to get far away from St. Joe and this appealing boy—and soon. Barnes had invited Quint to go on West with him, to look over the Pony Express stations that were placed every ten to fifteen miles along the two-thousand-mile trail the Pony would take when it finally began its historic runs tomorrow night.

Quint thought a moment sighed. Yes, he'd take the man up on that offer, go over the whole route and look around the area called Nevada. At least it would get him away from this appealing boy before he did something he'd be sorry for.

Dal finished his beer. "Reckon I'd better go," he said, shaking his curly head. "Exciting day tomorrow."

Quint fumbled with his pipe and grunted. "Suppose I should go, too." He wanted more than anything to leave with this boy, but he wasn't sure what he might do when he got the kid out in the dark. Damned if Dal didn't have a mouth as soft looking as any girl's.

Dal frowned at him. "You still got the rest of the night, Mr. Randolph. That should give you enough time to make love to every other woman in the Naughty Lady."

With that, the boy turned and marched out, his back ramrod stiff. Quint scratched his head. Now what was the kid mad about? Had he wanted Margo himself? He shrugged, lit his pipe, and blew smoke into the air.

Damn Quint Randolph! Dallas marched out of the saloon and went back to the livery stable to bed down. He was as randy as some big, hairy bull, mating with every available female who crossed his trail.

114

Why had she wasted her virginity on that faithless, womanizing rake? Obviously she'd been taken in by a man skilled in getting women to let him make love to them. No doubt he often went around telling them he was impotent, knowing that was like waving honey before a bee. What woman could resist a challenge like that? There wasn't a woman alive who didn't think she could cure a man of impotency. And she'd been stupid enough to fall for a lie like that!

How long was Quint going to be in town? Surely, now that he'd delivered his horses, he'd leave. She didn't know when she'd be sent on her first ride, and if he hung around St. Joe, she might keep running into him. She finally admitted to herself that she cared for Quint, cared too much. She felt betrayed because he'd gone to bed with that Margo at the Naughty Lady.

She lay sleepless all night, staring out the window, but seeing nothing. Finally the first gray light heralded dawn. In another half-hour, the sun would be a bright red ball peeking over the hills to the east.

She sat up with a sigh, still staring at the coming dawn. Had her letter to her parents ever reached Texas?

Surely it had arrived at the Durango ranch by now. Would Papa forgive her? He was known to be a harsh man—except where her mother, the beautiful Ojos de Pana, Velvet Eyes, was concerned. He had rescued the Cheyenne beauty from the Comanche when he'd been a Texas Ranger riding with the famous Jack Hayes. She could only wish Quint Randolph adored her as Don Diego adored her mother.

Resolutely, Dallas reached for her boots. If Papa did decide to track her down, the Pony Express office would forward his messages—if there were any. In the meantime, she had to get away from Yancy—away from Quint Randolph—before she was recognized. Besides, it hurt too much to be around Quint, knowing he cared nothing for her.

Dawn would break soon, even down in the desolate plains of Texas. Dallas stood up. She had made her decision. The Pony Express wanted a volunteer to take the first mail sack west late that afternoon. Dal Dawson might go down in history or be forgotten all together. Whether Papa forgave her when he got her letter or not, she was leaving St. Joe. She would be the one to carry the first mail out.

Chapter Eight

The young half-breed Comanche boy sat his paint pony along with the rest of the war party. From the isolated butte, he could see the first lavender gray of dawn to the east of the country the white eyes called Texas.

Eagle's Flight did not want to be here. His mother, a captive called Annie Laurie, had wept when his uncle had forced him to accompany the war party on this raid to kill some of her people.

Now as the dawn broke pink and purple, Eagle's Flight saw the thing that looked like a box pulled by six galloping mules come over the hill.

The boy turned eyes as gray as a gun barrel toward his uncle, the savage warrior, Pine da poi. "What in this thing?"

The hatchet-faced warrior snorted with contempt and displeasure. "It is called a stage coach, and it carries more *tavibo,* whites, into our country all the time."

"My mother says the whites have need of this land, too. We only roam it; they will use it to grow food for the hungry ones in their cities."

For a moment, he thought the ugly Comanche would strike him. "It is good my brother, Blood Arrow, did not live to see the sniveling pup his white captive produced as a son for him. Eagle's Flight, hah! The one called Annie Laurie would be wise to stop trying to turn you into a white man."

He *was* white. In his heart he was as white as his Scots-

117

Irish mother, the boy thought proudly as he watched the stage roll even closer. The alkali dust swirled up in clouds and coated the lathered, galloping mules. If his father had lived, he might have thought of himself as a Comanche, but his uncle, Pine da poi, Whip Owner, was not the man he would want to be.

No, deep in his heart, the gray-eyed boy was as white as Annie's ancestors. He was certain that someday the whites would rescue both him and his mother, and the two of them lived only for that day.

Pine da poi's eyes gleamed in the coming light as he looked around at the other members of the war party. "We will wait for the stage to get closer and then we will take it by surprise." Scarlet war paint was smeared, like congealed blood, across his dark countenance.

A murmur of excitement ran through the small war party. "There will be guns and ammunition on the rolling box," said one brave, holding in his stamping dun pony.

"Maybe there will be the bright, shiny metal things to decorate our hair and use for ornaments," said another.

"Money," Eagle's Flight said. "My mother says the whites call it money."

The half-breed knew by the sudden silence he was still considered an outsider. He was only ten years old, in reality too young to be taken on a war party. He suspected his uncle hoped he would be killed. When Blood Arrow had died, Pine da poi had taken the white woman his dead brother had stolen from a Texas ranch. As was the Comanche custom, he shared her with his other brothers. When he was drunk, he shared her with any buck in camp who offered him a little whiskey. And he beat her son when the boy tried to prevent that.

Eagle's Flight felt sick as he watched the stage move even closer. He could see white faces now, inside the box on wheels. Because of his mother, he thought of them as his people, and he had a terrible urge to fire a shot in warning so that the driver might speed up, perhaps outrun the ambush.

From his vantage, he saw the driver and the guard

beside him, heard the sharp crack of the whip over the running team. Of those inside, he got just the barest glimpse. His heart turned over. There was at least one white woman.

Pine da poi laughed deep in his throat. "Women! I think there's women! I will keep one and trade this cowardly pup's mother off!" He sneered as he looked over at the half-breed boy.

One of the warriors grunted. "They are almost close enough, crawling like a bug into our web! Only a little while now and we will have them before they know we are here."

Eagle's Flight closed his eyes and took a deep breath. He knew what his mother, Annie Laurie, would want him to do. But his uncle would beat him for it. In his mind's eye, he saw his mother's plain little face, her big, gray eyes. Funny, no one ever thought her pretty until she smiled. But to the boy she was the most beautiful, wonderful person in the world. And someday, when he was a grown man, he intended to free her. They would both escape from the Comanche forever.

Taking another deep breath, Eagle's Flight knew what he would do now, even if it cost him his life. In his heart, he was white—white as his mother's people.

He fumbled with his rifle, pretended he nearly dropped it, and fired it.

"White spawn of the most cowardly bitch!" He saw the blow coming and tried to duck, but the warrior caught him across the face with his fist, momentarily stunning him.

The shot echoed and reechoed. Even as Eagle's Flight had hoped, it reverberated off the distant rocks, alerting the stage coach.

The driver looked up toward the bluff, whipping the mules in sudden alarm. White faces appeared at the stage windows, peering up at the war party on the bluff, pointing, shouting.

Pine da poi swore. "They've seen us now. There'll be no surprise, thanks to this stupid cub! We must attack!"

119

Eagle's Flight hung back as the war party started down the rocky incline, whipping their mustang ponies as they galloped after the moving stage.

Silently he urged the stage on, hoping it would outrun the Indians. There would be punishment for him when he got back to camp, but if his warning shot had saved the whites, he did not care. They might ridicule him, hurt him, or even kill him, but they would never make a Comanche out of him. Someday, as his mother had told him, they would return to the white world, so she had taught him that most magic of all things: she had taught him to read the magic marks white men used to talk to each other.

For a long moment, as he loped along after the others, Eagle's Flight thought the stage would escape. And then the lathered mules began to tire and the stage slowed. The boy urged it to move faster. He prayed to his spirit animal to give the stage wings and take it from this place.

The whites were shooting back. Shots and shouts and the crack of the whip echoed through the still Texas dawn. He shot his rifle without aiming, not wanting to hit the whites in the stage. The guard clutched his chest, half stood, fell under the hooves of the pursuing horses. There was the acrid scent of powder; the scream of a warrior suddenly hit broke the early morning quiet. They were going to overtake the stage after all.

A great dread began to take hold of Eagle's Flight. If this thing must be, he hoped none of the whites were taken alive. Comanche could keep a wounded man alive a long time, killing him slowly by torture. And if there were women . . . He winced, thinking of what his dear mother had endured from the warriors.

The driver looked back over his shoulder at the war party gaining on the stage, cracked his whip over the backs of the galloping mules. Eagle's Flight saw fear on the white face, and knew the man realized it was only a matter of moments until it was all over. White men fired from inside the coach and a warrior screamed, clutching at his bare chest as hot, crimson blood sprayed from it, then tumbling from his running horse.

Pine da poi cursed loudly as he saw the man fall. He will make the survivors pay for that loss, Eagle's Flight thought.

Then the coach hit a small rock in the road. For what might have been an instant or a lifetime, it wavered, balanced on three wheels, and then turned over in a cloud of dust.

Eagle's Flight would always remember the screams and the wheels spinning in the empty air; the way the mules broke free and kept running, still held together by the harness.

With shouts of triumph, the Indians reined in around the wreckage.

The driver lay crumpled at an odd angle, his neck broken. From inside the coach came the sounds of a woman weeping, and a man said in English, "Remember I love you, darling." Then a shot rang out.

Pine da poi screamed in rage at realizing what had happened and the war party charged the coach, dragged the injured man out. He was handsome, with a sandy mustache.

"I saved her," he whispered in English, blood running from the corner of his mouth. "I loved her enough to save her."

Eagle's Flight slid from his pony, walked over and stood looking down at the man. "I'm sorry," he said in English. "Forgive us."

The man looked up at him a long moment, coughed up more blood. "I loved her enough to keep her from falling into their hands," he gasped. "Used my last bullet . . . it was worth whatever torture they put me through."

Pine da poi laughed. "Now, my weakling nephew, you will help us torture this *tavibo* for doing us out of the woman."

Eagle's Flight looked down at the man, then over to the lovely woman lying inside the coach. The white man had shot her behind the ear.

"You'll never torture him," the boy said, looking at the

man. "He just died."

Pine da poi went into a rage because he had been cheated of his pleasure. While the half-breed boy watched, his uncle began scalping the corpses, looting the stage. Warriors tore into the strong box, keeping the coins for ornaments, throwing bank drafts and documents to the winds.

The boy did not tell them some of the paper was valuable. It pleased him to think they were throwing away something of value, too ignorant to know any better.

His uncle dragged a canvas bag from the stage boot. "What is this?"

He shouted with rage and disappointment as he tore it open with his knife and more paper fluttered out.

"Mail," Eagle's Flight said, looking away from the dead bodies the warriors were mutilating. "The whites send messages through the magic marks on the paper."

"Then we have stopped their messages from going through!" The hatchet-faced brave shouted in triumph. "We will burn the stage and all their magic messages!"

The others shouted in agreement. "Burn them! They may be messages from the white soldiers about moving against us, about forcing us onto reservations!"

While the boy watched, heartsick at the slaughter, the renegades finished their looting and threw the letters up in the air, tearing them into pieces so that they blew about like snow in the winter blizzard.

Then they took matches from the coat pockets of the dead white men and set everything on fire while they danced about and whooped a victory song.

The young boy narrowed his iron gray eyes, watching smoke spiral upward like a black snake against the pink pale dawn of the desolate Texas landscape. He would force himself to forget what he had seen that day, block it from his mind forever. But he could not forget how the brave man had used his last strength to save his woman from torture. He wondered if he could be that strong, care that much.

The fire roared like the mythical thunderbird's wings

flapping as they brought the rainstorms. The stage was a mass of flames, as were the crumpled bodies. Now the mail sack caught fire and the letters blazed.

Somewhere, people were waiting for these letters. They would not get them, probably would never know they hadn't. Yet lives might be changed because those missives never arrived. Curiously, Eagle's Flight leaned over, picked up a torn scrap of paper. Only part of the letter was still legible:

Dear Mamma and Papa: I know you must be worried to death about me, but I am fine, really I am. I've found a respectable job here in St. Joe. . . ."

The dainty handwriting was that of a woman. The parents she begged for forgiveness would never see her plea. Would the woman ever know that the letter wasn't received, or would the lack of an answer make her think she was unforgiven? Who knew how many lives were being affected because the Comanche had waylaid a Texas stage? There was no way to know.

The boy felt both shame and sadness as he tossed the scrap of letter back into the flames, watched it crumple and turn black as the greedy fire consumed it.

The flames rose higher and higher as the sun lighted the scene. He turned away, blocking the sight from his mind. Somehow he would wipe this horrible day from his memory. If he did not, he thought he could not live with it.

Pine da poi threw back his head, shouted a victory cry that echoed and reechoed through the desolate country. "I know where there are ranches with fat cattle and horses to steal!" He grinned without mirth, the war paint ochre and crimson on his cruel face. "You! Half-breed coward, mount up! We will hit a ranch this day!"

The war party gathered up booty—guns, jewelry, a man's hat, and silver coins. Then they shouted and urged their prancing mustangs away up the trail.

Behind them, the stage burned. As the smell of burning flesh came to the boy's nostrils, he blinked back tears and urged his pony into a lope. Smoke rose in lazy curls over the vast, empty landscape as the war party turned and galloped away. The boy with eyes as gray as a gun barrel forced himself not to look back.

Don Diego de Durango looked up at the dawn as he hurried out of the magnificent *hacienda* to meet his foreman. "Sanchez, is there still no news? We'd hoped for a letter."

The Mexican rubbed his face with his deformed hand, the missing finger denoting a roper. It was a common enough injury among cowboys. "*Dios,* boss, I ask at the village, but they say no letter from Señorita Dallas."

"It's my fault." Graying hair fell into the tall man's dark eyes as he lowered his head. "Her mother begged me not to send her to Boston, but I was too stubborn to listen to my Velvet Eyes."

Sanchez shook his head. "Perhaps there will be a letter yet. Perhaps instead, Señorita Dallas will come riding in one day and surprise us all."

"Pray God it be so." Don Diego crossed himself reverently. "Maybe she is dead, or has decided not to forgive me for my foolishness. If she weren't angry with her papa, she would write us."

Sanchez pulled at his mustache. "The Peabodys have heard nothing then?"

Don Diego thought for a long moment, then shook his head, blinked back tears. "Nothing at all. And they warn us war talk grows stronger every day. If war should break out between North and South, we will no longer be able to search for her."

The foreman patted his shoulder. "Trace says someday Dallas will return to this place that she loves."

"Do you think so?" Don Diego couldn't stop himself from grabbing at every straw. "Perhaps she is too angry with me for sending her off to school. My brother says maybe she has run away with a man and will never come back."

The Mexican foreman frowned. None of the help liked Luis very much, and even Don Diego had to admit he had always spoiled his handsome, younger brother.

Don Diego sighed. "Well, I guess I must now tell her mother that there is still no news."

Sanchez comforted him. "There will be. Señorita Dallas will write and tell us where to come after her; you'll see. Maybe the letter will come tomorrow."

"*Sí,* tomorrow." With a heavy heart, Don Diego looked up at the new day that had just dawned. Sighing, he straightened his shoulders and went inside to tell his beautiful Cheyenne wife and his son, Trace, that again, there was no word from their beloved Dallas.

Yancy frowned at the rising sun as he stood in the St. Joe train station. *Damn me! I don't remember the last time I had to get up this early.*

He grinned in sudden remembrance as he stuck the gold toothpick in the corner of his mouth. Yes, he could. He had been big for his age, a poor-white-trash boy in a shack on the outskirts of Biloxi. He'd started out weeding the rich widow's garden early in the morning. Before it was over, he'd been in her bed on those mornings and she had paid him a helluva lot better than she'd paid a yard man.

The train whistle blew in the distance as the locomotive chugged toward the station. Yancy took out the letter, read it again. Almost as interesting as the command to come for further orders was the slashing style of the handwriting. It showed poorly concealed frustration and rage. The paper actually had holes where a pen had crossed the *t*'s and dotted the *i*'s.

The train screeched into the station with a burst of steam. Yancy picked up his valise and boarded, thinking about the identity of the writer whom he had never met.

A woman, he thought, probably middle-aged with crepy skin and sagging tits like the widow in Biloxi. The widow had bought him his very first gambling establishment because he'd done stud service in her bed so long. Leaning back in his seat as the train pulled away, Yancy stuck his thumbs in his brightly flowered vest and wondered if the widow had ever found out he was also servicing her married daughter and her black slave girl?

He reached up and gingerly touched the place on his head where that fiesty girl had struck him with the tumbler. He needed to be more careful about his drinking and his women before he got into serious trouble. He'd almost given some of his secret away that night.

Yancy took out the letter again, stared at the handwriting, the signature. "Well, Delilah, all I've got is your address and a mental picture of you. I reckon you were afraid to put too much in a letter so now you want me to come to Philadelphia."

He was still wondering about it several days later as he rang the bell of the imposing Victorian mansion.

The door opened suddenly as if he'd been awaited by the tall, elegant woman in black with graying chestnut hair pulled into a severe bun.

"I'm looking for Delilah."

She glanced up and down the street as if to make sure no one had seen him. "Are you Yancy? Come in."

He followed her into the parlor. "Usually, ladies don't answer their own doors."

"I doubt a tinhorn gambler like you knows very many *ladies*." She emphasized the word as she spread her skirts before sitting down on a burgundy horsehair sofa. "It's the servants' day off and my husband is out of town on business."

"Of course." He decided to ignore the insult as he leaned against the mantel. "Couldn't you have just written your instructions?"

"And take a chance on them being intercepted?" She pulled her needlework frame over, went back to working on a scene of a half-naked woman dancing in wild abandon. "Besides, I like to meet someone I'm paying. All I

126

had before was the word of acquaintances in the South that you would do anything for money."

He sucked the gold toothpick and grinned at her, refusing to be insulted. "Well, maybe almost anything."

"My associates and I know there's a lot of profit to be made during the coming war, and we intend to get our share."

"By helping to encourage the conflict?" he said suggestively. She sneaked a look at the crotch of his tight pants, then glanced up suddenly, realized he had seen her, flushed.

"It's going to happen anyway," she said, stabbing at the cloth with her needle. "Someone always makes money off a war; it might as well be us."

She's like all the other lonely women, he thought. Even if she didn't realize the significance of those slashing marks she made on paper, he'd been around enough to know.

He studied the needlework pillows on the furniture. Half-naked women cavorted in every scene.

Her gaze followed his. "Scenes from Bible stories," she said haughtily.

"If you say so. Aren't you even going to offer me a drink?"

She went on sewing. "There's sherry in the sideboard." She indicated it with a nod.

"Sherry!" He snorted. "Don't you keep drinks for *real* men. Or have you never had a *real* man in this house?"

Two bright spots of color came to her pallid face. "Let's talk business."

"You talk, I'll listen." He grinned easily at her, put away the toothpick, sauntered over to the sideboard. While she talked about her plans, he filled two glasses to the brim, brought them back over, and sat down next to her.

She broke off and moved ever so slightly away from him. "I don't drink."

Her gaze dropped to his tight pants again, to the noticeable bulge.

He handed her the glass anyway and leaned back on the

cushions. The one under his hand depicted a half-naked girl cavorting wildly. He ran his hand over the pillow, stroking the figure's bare belly. "What is it you want me to do?"

For a long moment, she didn't answer and her hazel eyes watched him stroke the cushion. "I — my brother — sells horses to the Pony Express."

He looked up in surprise, watched her sip the sherry. "Randolph? I've seen him, heard the name. He was in the Naughty Lady the other night. Didn't know he was your brother."

"That's just as well." She looked down her nose at him. "My associates and I want you to disrupt communications with the West coast. Do whatever is necessary; rile the Indians or something."

Yancy shrugged, watched her sip her drink. "When your own brother is supplying the horses? Drink up." He almost commanded it.

She hesitated, looking at him, then grimly drained the glass. He got up, took her glass to the sideboard, refilled it, came back, handed it to her.

"Quint's made his profit and should be on his way back to Kentucky by now."

"I take it Brother doesn't know and wouldn't approve of all this?"

She took a big gulp. "Quint is very naïve in some ways. If this is going to be much of a war, someone needs to help the South a little; disrupting the Pony Express is just one of many plans."

He put both hands behind his head, flexed his shoulders, and spread his legs so she would get a better look at the bulge of his pants. And he let her see him staring boldly at her breasts. "Delilah, you're talking treason!"

"Or patriotism!" she snapped, then sipped the sherry.

He ran his hand over the pillow again, gently stroking the figure's breasts. "Somehow, my dear lady, I think you don't know the meaning of the word. You don't give a damn who wins or who dies; you're only interested in profit."

128

"That's the way wars are fought," she said thickly, and finished the drink. "There's a lot of profit in this for every one."

He looked at her, running the tip of his tongue over his lips ever so slowly. "And what else?"

"I-I don't know what you mean." She flushed.

Somehow, highborn ladies had always held a fascination for him, even when they were old and their flesh sagged. He liked to bring them down to his level.

"Sure you do, Delilah." He reached over, put his hand on her shoulder, fiddled with the lace at the high neck of her somber dress.

She drew back. "Get your hands off me, you piece of trash, or I'll scream!"

"Will you now?" He grinned easily, and his fingers moved ever so slightly so that they stroked her throat. "You just do that. If anyone should hear you, which I doubt, you'd have to explain how a tinhorn gambler got into your parlor in the first place."

She stood up a little unsteadily. "I'm going to have to ask you to leave!"

"Not yet." He rose, in control now. There had been many women just like this one in his past. "You don't want me to leave yet . . . not when I want to make love to you."

She half turned as if to run from the room, half opened her mouth as if to protest when he grabbed her, pulled her to him in a brutal embrace. His hands held her against the bulge of his manhood while his tongue forced its way into her mouth. She struggled slightly and pushed at him with her hands, but he held her. Gradually she began arching against him with her breasts and belly, her hands going up around his neck while she made little sobbing noises deep in her throat.

He reached up to take the pins from her hair, sending a gray-streaked, chestnut cascade down her shoulders for him to tangle his hands in. Yancy knew what women liked to hear. "I've wanted you since the first minute I walked in here; just a few kisses, that's all."

"I-I'm old enough to be your mother."

Isn't that the truth? "Naw, you're beautiful; desirable."
He pulled at the tiny buttons at the neck of her dress,
knowing that if he could just get his hands on her
breasts . . .

"No! No. . . ." She shook her head slightly, stood there
with her eyes closed, trembling violently while he opened
the collar of her gown, put his hand inside, cupping her
breast, stroking her nipple.

He kissed her again, pulling her down so she sat on the
sofa. "Just a few innocent kisses," he whispered, unbuttoning her dress still more. He had both hands on her
breasts now, stroking her while she threw her head back
and gasped, breathing through her mouth.

This was an awkward, uncomfortable place to do it, but
he knew she'd balk if he tried to get her clear into the
bedroom. Still, if he could get enough liquor in her, she'd
be dancing naked, just like the women on those damned
pillows.

Yancy pressed her back against the sofa with his body,
began stroking her thighs. She tried to protest, but he
slipped his tongue between her lips, grabbed her hand and
put it on the hard bulge of his manhood.

She attempted to take her hand away, but he held it
there a moment. "Stroke me, Delilah, make me want you
the way you dream of making men lust after you; make
me take you in wild abandon."

When he shifted his hand to her thigh, she didn't take
her hand off his hardness. Very gradually, as he kissed her,
he pushed her skirt up. He knew at this point, she
wouldn't let him undress her completely. Probably her
own husband had never seen her completely naked.

"No, I . . . I shouldn't." But now she ran her tongue
between his lips, stroking him while he gradually worked
his hands up under her clothes.

"Delilah," he whispered. "Beautiful, ravishing Delilah
who's never had a man treat her like a Jezebel. That's
what you want, isn't it? To have a man take you with heat
and passion."

She was shaking in his embrace, pulling him gradually on top of her as she slowly slipped into a reclining position on the sofa. "I shouldn't. Oh, please. . . ."

He still had a hunger on him for a woman, a hunger the stormy brunette had built in him and left unsatisfied when she'd hit him across the head and fled. If he kept his eyes closed, he wouldn't see the crepy skin and sagging breasts the elegant lady was offering to his lips while she dug her nails in his back.

Yancy always took a perverse pleasure in seducing high-class ladies, making them beg for it. "Delilah, tell me what you want," he said.

"Oh, please, please. . . ."

He slipped his fingers into her, stroked her. This stud service was going to cost her double what she had intended to pay him for sabotage.

He reached down, unbuttoned his pants, put his throbbing maleness on her bare thigh so she could feel the heat of him. They were half on, half off the sofa; not a good position for riding her hard, like she wanted, like the slashing motions of her pen on paper.

He pulled her off the sofa onto the thick Persian carpet, amused by the thought of the sight they must make tumbled on the floor amid a swirl of skirts. What a comedown for a lady. He kept his eyes closed and pretended he had that ebony-haired bitch from St. Joe beneath him. The thought made him throb with desire, and he took the elegant lady, ramming into her with hard strokes while she arched against him and dug her nails into his back.

In a few hours, he'd be headed west to do her bidding, but until then, he was going to amuse himself at the expense of the gentry. This was revenge for all the uppity bitches who had mistreated the poor-white-trash kid from Biloxi.

Chapter Nine

Tuesday, April third, dawned cool and clear. The whole town of St. Joe was jubilant. The Pony Express would begin its historic run late that afternoon, and St. Joe was full of Eastern newspapermen and dignitaries.

Dallas went into the Express office, almost had to elbow her way through the crowds.

"Here he comes, folks," Barnes shouted. "Here's that boy you've been wanting to interview!"

Newspaper people crowded around Dallas, shouting questions. "What made you decide to be the first rider, son?" "Are you scared of riding through hostile country?" "Tell us about yourself!"

Dallas hesitated, her heart hammering. She'd volunteered simply to get out of St. Joe fast, be away from Quint Randolph; but now everyone was interested in her.

"Well," Dallas drawled, keeping her voice low and her head ducked, "don't think there's much to tell. I took the job because I needed the money. I ride well, and the company tells me there aren't any hostile Indians except maybe in Nevada. I don't expect to be going there."

The reporters looked disappointed. Obviously the boy wasn't flamboyant enough. He wasn't going to say anything quotable. The newspapermen edged away, intending to interview the district manager of the company, or Mayor Thompson, who was at the office to declare this a glorious, historic day.

A man stuck his head in the door. "Hey, here comes the

fellow who's providing the horses for the Express!"

Dallas froze in place as Quint, looking elegant and self-assured, pushed his way through the crowd and into the office.

Oh, horsefeathers! She had hoped to avoid running into him today. Why hadn't it occurred to her that he'd be right in the midst of the action?

Newsmen shouted questions, but Quint motioned for silence. "I'm sure you've already heard the details, but I'll tell you as much as they've told me. The route will stretch almost two thousand miles—from here to California—with a relay station for changing horses every ten to fifteen miles along the way."

Someone in the crowd whistled low. "Sounds like a tremendous outlay of money."

"It is." Quint nodded. "Russell, Majors, and Waddell are gambling everything they own that they can get the mail from here to California in only ten days."

"Ten days! Unbelievable!" A murmur went through the crowd.

"Mr. Randolph, you don't sound like you're from these parts, what do you think of the West so far?"

Quint grinned and tipped his hat back. "From what I've seen, I think I've found where I really belong. I'm considering moving my thoroughbreds to a ranch I own in Arizona and staying out here."

He looks so calm and in control, Dallas thought as she watched him light up. She had forgotten how tall and handsome he was. Her heart skipped a beat.

"Mr. Randolph"—the reporter pushed closer—"some of us are having trouble believing mail could ever be delivered across the whole country in ten days when it takes weeks now by Butterfield stage."

The crowd murmured, but Quint held up his hands for silence. "Remember the stage takes the southern route while the Express will take the central route, which is shorter."

"But the central route goes through the mountains," a man reminded him. "And no one thinks mail can go

133

through mountains in the winter time. Remember what happened to the Donner party?"

Dallas remembered. It was one of the most horrible events of American history. In the winter of 1846-47, a wagon train had gotten itself stranded in the Sierra Nevada mountains and had resorted to cannibalism to survive.

Quint ran a hand through his hair. "We'll see what happens next winter. On this end of the line, they're using some of my best thoroughbreds, and on the Western end, tough little mustangs; so they've thought of that. Less than a hundred riders and four hundred of the fastest horses in the country are going to keep the Pony Express promise: 'The mail must go through!' "

His enthusiasm brought a cheer from the excited crowd.

"And when does the run start, Mr. Randolph?"

"Five o'clock tonight."

"Seems late," a newsman said. "Why so late?"

Quint shrugged. "Mr. Barnes tells me we're waiting for a train to bring historic mail. A message from the president to the governor of California will be in that first *mochila.*"

"And how does the system work?"

Thaddeus Barnes answered. "Two riders will start at the same time," he said, "one of them leaving California and bringing mail from the West coast, one from here, late this afternoon on one of Randolph's fine bay mares, Sylph."

He seemed to spot Dallas for the first time. "In fact, there's the boy who's going to carry the first *mochila.*"

Quint waved at Dallas, then went over and rumpled her hair, looking troubled. "How you doing today, kid?"

"All right, I reckon." Dallas tried to appear casual, but the touch of his hand made her remember that night in Philadelphia. She stood there stiffly, hoping, yet dreading, that he might reach out and touch her again.

The reporters didn't appear to have much interest in interviewing the close-mouthed boy a second time. They turned back to Barnes while Dallas watched Quint out of the corner of her eye. She could smell the slight scents of tobacco and bay rum hair tonic on him. For a long moment, she wondered if he had spent the night with Margo? She didn't even want to think about it. The sooner she got away from this randy rake, the better off she'd be.

She tried to act casual, listened to Barnes explain what a *mochila* was.

"It's Spanish for knapsack," the manager said. "It fits down over the saddle so the rider can just yank it off, throw it over a freshly saddled horse, and take off at a gallop."

The reporters crowded around Quint again, eager to hear what the wealthy, handsome gentleman had to say. In the confusion, Dallas slipped away.

She hid out in the livery stable loft, knowing people were probably looking for her, but past caring. She didn't want to risk bumping into Quint Randolph again, and she didn't want to face any more reporters with nosy questions.

Finally she curled up in the hay and dozed off, pretending that she slept in Quint's arms. In her sleep, she reached for him, tasted his kisses, felt his hard-muscled body respond to hers. The thick mat of hair on his massive chest brushed her nipples as he pulled her close.

Dark angel, he whispered, *I've looked everywhere for you. I want to marry you.*

You don't care that my hair is cropped like a boy's?

Hazel eyes sparkled with amusement as Quint ran his fingers through her short curls. *What does it matter? It'll grow out eventually.*

But you're such an aristocrat, your family probably wouldn't approve of me. And you have a wife already—Melanie.

No. He shook his head as he kissed her. *There's been some mistake. Dark angel, we're going to be married. I want you . . . I want you. . . .*

"Yes, oh, yes," Dallas whispered, and then her eyes blinked open and she realized it had only been a dream.

Nothing had really changed. With a sigh, she sat up, peered at the sun through a hole in a weather-beaten board. What time was it?

She got out the bright red Pony Express shirt and blue pants she'd been given to wear for the ceremony. But she also gathered up a worn buckskin outfit to change into once she got away from St. Joe. The fancy scarlet shirt might look flamboyant, but it would also make a good target if anyone decided to shoot at her. She pulled her Western hat down over one eye at a jaunty angle, so it shadowed her face.

With both excitement and dread, Dallas made her way to the barns. Would Quint be there? Probably. Would the reporters be there? Certainly. Why hadn't those possibilities occurred to her when she'd volunteered to be the first rider? She had only been intent on getting out of town, and hadn't realized so much fuss would be stirred up. But the galloping pony had fired the country's imagination like nothing had in a long time.

Wouldn't it create real excitement if they all knew she was a girl? If they did, she wouldn't be allowed to ride. Women weren't even allowed to vote, much less do something wild and dangerous like this.

That gave her cause to think. As she pushed her way through the rowdy crowds, she had second thoughts about the job she had accepted. A woman, she would be riding alone across vast expanses of desolate country. Even though she would have a pistol and a rifle, and knew how to use them, she suddenly wished she had not volunteered.

For a split second, she imagined herself standing before the crowd of reporters and saying, I have a real story for you! The first rider out of St. Joe is a woman! Dal Dawson is actually a runaway, Dallas Durango from the Triple D ranch in the Texas hill country near Austin.

Would the papers have a field day with that! She imagined the headlines in Texas, imagined her proud old Spanish papa reading them and being embarrassed and humiliated because his unmanageable daughter had done such a scandalous thing.

And what would Quint say? She winced at picturing him finally learning the 'boy' Dal was the girl who had so recklessly fallen into bed with him. How could she have done such a shameful, unthinkable thing?

But when she closed her eyes, she saw Quint's face, tasted his lips, and knew that given the chance, she would do it all over again. She loved him, right or wrong.

The bay mare stood all saddled and bridled, held by a stable boy. People pushed forward, pulling hairs from Sylph's tail for souvenirs until Dallas said to the boy, "Why don't you put the mare back in her stall until the messenger arrives? She's gettin' nervous."

Dallas looked around. Neither Quint nor Barnes was anywhere in sight. She turned to the boy. "What's happened?"

The pimply-faced boy shrugged. "The fella bringing the mail from the East missed his connecting train. The telegraph says the railroad has arranged for a special engine, the Missouri, to make top speed from Hannibal just to get him here! He's already late."

As the boy led the mare back in her stall, the crowd milled about restlessly, complaining about the delay. But no one left. They all wanted to witness what promised to be one of the most festive and historic happenings the bustling town of St. Joe had ever seen.

The speeches of various dignitaries filled the time while they waited for the delayed messenger from the East. It was almost dark.

Dallas felt people staring at her. "Is that the rider? Why, he's just a boy!"

"They're all just kids," a man said. "Young and lightweight. They've got to be good riders, and able to handle a gun. How would you like to face a war party by yourself like some of these young fellows will be doing?"

That question didn't make Dallas feel any better.

A cheer went up from the crowd. "Here they come! Here they come with the letters from back East!"

Her heart pounding with excitement and apprehension, Dallas turned to see the tall Kentuckian and Thaddeus

137

Barnes shouldering their way through the crowd and bringing a bearded man with them. The newcomer waved a packet triumphantly. "Letters from President Buchanan for California!"

The crowd cheered again. The stable boy led the fine thoroughbred out. Quint patted her velvet nose. "Where's that boy who's making this ride?" he asked.

Dal kept her hat low as she came forward. "Here I am, all ready to go."

She saw the puzzlement in his hazel eyes. Sooner or later, he might make the connection and she wanted to be safely away before he did. If he realized who she was, he might offer to make her his mistress, and she wasn't sure she would be able to say no even though she knew it was wrong.

Barnes took the packet from the messenger's hand. With a great flourish, he locked it in one of the four little pockets of the *mochila*. Three of the pockets contained mail for the West Coast. All were safely locked up. They would be unlocked by the Express man in California. The one unlocked pocket contained mail to be distributed at stops along the way.

A lady standing near Dallas said, "What does it cost to send a letter anyway?"

"I hear five dollars a half-ounce!" a fat woman whispered back. "It'd have to be mighty important mail to spend that much sending it."

"I reckon so! That's a week's pay for a cowboy."

Quint held the stamping, impatient horse, yelled at Dallas. "Come on, Dal, boy. You're already behind schedule because of the messenger missing his train! You'll have to make the time up!"

Almost numbly she pushed through the milling crowd to Quint and the horse.

Barnes pushed his hat back. "Now, Dal, the ferry's waiting for you at the dock. After that, you're on your own to the next station. You'll be riding in the dark, but you're armed." He motioned to the weapons on the horse. "Good luck to you!"

She started to mount, and Quint assisted her. For a moment, when he touched her, it was all she could do to keep from crying out, "Were you so drunk that you don't remember? Don't recognize me?"

For a split second, as he boosted her up, they stared into each other's eyes.

Then he looked troubled and glanced away. Suppose he had recognized her, and was only pretending he hadn't? That wild night in the snowstorm would be embarrassing for him, too, if anyone found out about it—especially his wife.

He reached up awkwardly, shook her hand. "Good luck to you, boy! You've got one of my best horses under you so make up that lost time and Godspeed!"

His big hand was so warmly reassuring on hers that she had to force herself to turn loose and rein the mare in as it danced about. "Clear a path!" she shouted. "Clear a path through the crowd!"

Ahead of her, people pushed to get out of the way while Dallas held in the nervous thoroughbred. Seven o'clock. Lights blinked on as people lit lamps in their houses. At the western edge of town, on the Missouri River a ferry waited to take the first rider across into Kansas.

Quint looked up at her. "Are you ready, Dal? This is a historic moment the country will never forget!"

She blinked back tears while staring at the path that had been cleared for her run. The smells of new spring grass and sweating horses came to her, the noise of the crowd was almost deafening. And then the cannon boomed to announce the historic departure.

Dallas reared the mare up on her hind legs, then she took off her hat and waved it at the crowd. In that split second, she glanced at the eager reporters and shouted the Pony Express slogan, " 'The mail must go through!' "

The crowd cheered as she spurred her horse and took off along the cleared path. Along her route, people had gathered to see the first rider out. Men shouted, women waved handkerchiefs. Old men held up their grandchildren so someday they could say that they had witnessed this historic moment.

Dallas galloped along the street, waving her hat. " 'The mail must go through!' " she shouted and the crowd roared its approval, everyone knowing that things would never be the same after this historic moment.

Almost dizzy from the excitement, Dallas galloped along, aware of the hot power of the horse between her legs, the excitement of the crowd. She thundered through the streets of St. Joe, the wind blowing against her face, her heart pounding; spurring the horse toward the river where the ferry, *Denver,* waited to take her across to Kansas.

She shouted as her mount loped down to the dock and thundered onto the deck of the waiting vessel.

Immediately, the ferry tooted its whistle, began to move away from the dock. Dallas slid from the mare's back, patted her soft nose. "Good girl, Sylph, you did us both proud!"

The captain came out of his small quarters. "We been waiting for hours, was beginning to wonder what had happened."

Briefly, Dallas explained about the missed connection and the special train.

"Ain't modern technology a wonder, though?" The captain grinned, displaying gapped teeth. "They say they'll actually have the telegraph all the way across the country in a couple of years and maybe later, the railroad."

Dallas thought about it. "Imagine being able to ride a train completely across the country."

He nodded. "It do give us something to think about. Maybe the Pony is just the beginning of it all."

The Pony. She was part of making history. She looked down at her fancy red shirt. "Where can I change out of this outfit?"

The captain laughed and pointed back to his quarters. "Wouldn't do to have you change right here on deck. Some old lady with a spyglass might see you from shore and complain to the mayor."

Dallas laughed, then grabbed her buckskin garb out of

the saddlebags and went to change. So far, so good, she thought, checking the band around her breasts. Would there come a time when she would have to change or relieve herself in front of men? She should have given more thought to things like that, but it was too late now.

The captain shouted at her. "Almost there, young fella. Get ready!"

Swiftly, she gathered up the fancy clothes and ran out to mount the horse. The mare stamped her feet and snorted, looking at the riverbank in Kansas Territory, obviously eager to run again. Quint raises good horses, Dallas thought as she held the mare back while the ferry docked.

When it was tied up, the captain said, "Good luck to you, young fella."

Dallas waved and then guided the mare off onto solid ground. She urged Sylph forward, and they galloped away toward the next station — Elwood, Kansas Territory.

Past that lay other stations where she would change horses and leave the one she rode to rest and munch hay. She galloped through the night, aware of the need to make up time. There was just enough moonlight for her to see her way. Somewhere a coyote howled, but that didn't bother her although it was a lonesome sound. Coyotes were wily but timid animals. They posed no threat unless rabid.

The big prairie wolves were something else again. She patted the Navy Colt she carried on her saddle, wondering if she would ever use it. She'd even carved her initials in the butt although she'd been ordered to try to outrun any trouble, not stop to deal with it. Time was precious to a company gambling hundreds of thousands of dollars on being able to cut the mail delivery time and to convince the president to give the Pony the mail contract.

She hunched down over the mare's neck, galloping through the darkness, and wondered if her parents had received her letter? Shouldn't she be getting an answer by now if all was forgiven?

Feeling sad and disheartened, she concentrated on following the road. Because the roads and stations for this part of the Express route were already used by stagecoaches, the trail should be in good shape.

How long could she keep up this masquerade as a boy before she got caught? She set her mouth stubbornly, kept her attention on the road ahead. She wouldn't think about that. She was making more than a cowboy would make, and she needed the money if she was going to be on her own. What she would do in the long run, she wasn't sure.

Only one thing saddened her as she rode northwest across the lonely Kansas landscape. With every minute, she was putting more distance between herself and the man she loved. It could never work, she told herself, urging the horse on. She had to put as much distance between her and Quint Randolph as possible.

She was giddy from the speed and excitement of the ride, the scent and the creak of the saddle, the heat of the horse between her thighs.

For a moment, she was again in Quint's bed, her legs locked around his powerful, hard-driving hips as he plunged into her. No wonder men didn't want their women riding astride. They didn't want them to discover the thrill of controlling that hot power, rubbing against the saddle. No wonder they insisted on the prim sidesaddle.

Stop thinking of him. That's over, she commanded herself. But she couldn't stop her heart from yearning for him, couldn't stop her body from wanting him.

She grasped the saddle horn and immediately remembered his hard manhood in her hand as she'd guided him into her, the sensation of his hot mouth on her breasts.

The April night was cool, and Dallas shivered in spite of herself. But the mare was lathered and blowing as they galloped on. Faintly in the distance, she saw the glimmer of lanterns.

"Keep on, Sylph." She patted the mare's neck encouragingly. "See? There's the relay station up ahead where I pick up a fresh horse and you get some feed and a rest!"

The mare's hooves drummed like thunder. In the vast

emptiness of the prairie, hoofbeats seemed to echo and reecho.

Dallas had been given a small bugle to blow as she approached the station, but she realized she wouldn't need it. A dog barked to announce the incoming rider, and people came out of the small building, hurried about in the moonlight.

Another minute and she thundered into the station yard, reined in. A man stood in front of the stable, holding an already saddled horse. "What kept you? We expected you a couple of hours ago!"

Dallas swung down, grabbed her *mochila,* threw it up over the saddle, swung up on the fresh mount. "Delayed and trying to make up time now. You give that mare a good rubdown, you hear?"

He nodded while reaching up to hand Dallas a warm piece of corn bread full of fried meat and a canteen full of hot coffee.

Dallas nodded her thanks, then galloped away toward the next station, leaving the stationkeeper holding the mare and staring after her.

She rode at a lope and ate the food. The corn bread was hot and crusty, the meat crisp and juicy. She hadn't realized how hungry she was until she'd smelled the warm food and then bitten into it.

Again she headed at a gallop for the next station. It's peaceful riding along under the diamond dust of stars, she thought with a sigh as she finished the food.

Somewhere on the other side of the country, another rider was galloping her way, carrying news from California to St. Joe. There would be many riders, many horses, but somewhere in the vast middle of the country, two riders would finally pass each other with whoops and waves of hats; one galloping west, the other east.

The horse's hooves seemed to beat out a rhythm. *Quint. Quint. Quint.* Would she never get him off her mind? She would force herself to think about something else. Horses. She would think about horses. Quint certainly did raise good horses. She didn't know when she'd ridden better.

But she was tiring now, glad that at the next station, a fresh horse and a fresh rider would take over and she could finally get some rest. Her body ached from hours of riding and she felt dirty. Would there be a place to take a bath and, if so, would there be men around so she dare not? She wouldn't think about that right now. Primitive as most of the relay stations were, the few men at them probably slept on the floor, fully dressed and wrapped in blankets.

The night deepened as Dallas galloped across the still landscape. An owl hooted from a scraggly tree, and a fox glided across the trail, startling the horse so that he broke gait for a split second, then smoothed out and galloped on, his long legs eating up the miles.

Dallas's muscles ached, but she loved the ride, the wild, free feeling of racing across the prairie through the darkness, carrying the precious mail. At this cost, no one would send a letter that wasn't of the utmost importance. Ordinary people couldn't afford to use the Pony Express. Yet even at those prices, Russell, Majors, and Waddell would lose money unless they finally got the government-subsidized mail contract.

Up ahead, she saw a tiny faint light—the next relay station—and breathed a sigh of relief. The horse was lathered and blowing, and Dallas ached all over.

"Not much farther, boy," she leaned over and whispered. "We're almost there. Someone else will take over for both of us now, and we can rest."

The horse tipped his ears back as if he understood, while racing toward the light where a fresh horse and a new rider were waiting to accept the *mochila*. But there was no movement at the station as Dallas galloped down the rise toward the lights. A sixth sense told her something was wrong, but she didn't rein in her horse.

Indians? There hadn't been any trouble lately that she knew of. Besides, on her tired and stumbling horse, she wouldn't be able to outrun them.

Robbers? A rider didn't carry anything but mail, nothing worth stealing. Maybe it was only her imagination. Gripping her pistol with a clammy hand, she galloped into the station yard. An old man limped out of the barn leading a fresh, saddled horse.

"Thank God!" Dallas exclaimed, reining in and sliding off. "I was beginning to think something was wrong!"

She turned to pull the *mochila* from her own lathered mount, whirled around. Then it hit her. "Where's my relief rider?"

The old man hesitated, pointed toward the station. "He's here, but useless as a knot in a stake rope," he whined. "I been tryin' to sober him up."

"Are you telling me he's drunk?" A feeling of dread swept over Dallas. She was so weary, she wasn't sure she could even walk inside to investigate.

"Drunker than a fiddler's bitch!"

Out of sheer frustration and weariness, she began to curse. "Help me sober him up!" She stumbled inside.

"Sober him up?" the old man scoffed as Dallas knelt next to the man on the hearth. "Son, Willie won't wake up 'til tomorrow, and then he'll feel like he was dead and didn't get buried!"

Dallas leaned over the young man. Willie held an empty bottle close to his chest as if he were afraid someone would take it away from him. He had a whiskey breath so strong it'd crack a mirror. "You're right, old man. There's no chance of sobering him up tonight."

She put her head in her hands. *Horsefeathers.* What in God's name was she to do now? She was so tired, she wasn't sure she could throw a leg up over a horse, much less ride on. "Is there anybody here but you two?"

The old man shook his head. "I'm powerful sorry, young fella. You kin see I'm in no shape to ride."

Dallas nodded. *The mail must go through.* The whole country was waiting to see if the Pony Express really could get mail across to California in the lightning-fast time of ten days. Everything the three partners had was riding on the Pony, as were the other riders' jobs. A sense of pride swept over Dallas.

Slowly, she stood up, keenly aware that time had been wasted. "You got some food for him?"

"Yep, but he ain't in no shape to eat it." He pointed to a small knapsack on the table.

"Well, I am." Dallas grabbed the food, headed for the door. "When I tell them what happened, Willie'll be out of a job, so you might as well tell him to pull his picket pin and move on. I'll take the mail to the next rider."

"You? But, son, you've already ridden a long way tonight."

"And I've got to ride a lot farther, thanks to that no-account, drunken varmint." She swung up on the fresh horse. "Be sure and cool that horse out." She nodded toward the weary mount she'd come in on, then turned her new mount slightly toward the north. "Where does Willie's run end?"

The old man sputtered. "Rock Creek station, but that's a long ways from here, son, just across the line in Nebraska Territory. And you're tired already!"

That was true. Every bone in her body ached. But she'd sworn to take that mail to the next rider, and if that meant riding to Rock Creek, that's where she was headed. It would take hours to get there. At least dawn would be breaking soon, so she wouldn't be riding the whole run in the dark.

Dallas spurred the horse forward, waved her hat at the old man. " 'The mail must go through!' " She yelled and her words echoed and reechoed across the Kansas plains as she spurred the horse and took off for Rock Creek station.

Chapter Ten

Quint had never felt such confusion as when he'd helped Dal into his saddle. For an instant, he'd fought an urge to take the boy in his arms. Then, horrified, he'd stifled the urge and had lifted the boy into the saddle, watched him ride away on the first historic run.

What kind of unnatural man was he to be attracted to a young boy? Maybe it wasn't guilt over Melanie's death that made him unable to perform with any woman but the dark angel from the streets of Philadelphia. Maybe it was something more horrible than that.

One of those. Oh, Lord, no! But he was almost certain the boy had felt the magnetism between them. There had been some deep emotion showing in Dal's dark eyes.

It was a good thing he was gone. That solved the problem for both of them. Quint heaved a sigh of relief as the bay mare disappeared over a little rise, galloping toward the river ferry in the growing dark.

Barnes clapped him on the back. "Well, it's finally begun! What a night to remember! Let's go have a drink at the Naughty Lady."

"Aren't you afraid Majors will hear about it?"

The manager chuckled. "I won't tell him if you won't!"

Quint grinned to hide his inner torment. "I'll buy."

The saloon was full. Any excuse to celebrate was good enough for the regulars.

Quint ran a hand through his hair, surveyed the crowd. "Everyone's excited about the Pony. I hope my horses give a

147

good account of themselves."

Barnes nodded. "I wouldn't worry about that." He sipped his drink and turned to watch the women dancing on the small stage. "By the way, are you still interested in mustangs? Remember I'm headed out West to check on some of our stations, make sure things are running smoothly. You're welcome to come along."

He had piqued Quint's interest, and had almost taken his mind off his strange fascination with that boy. "Mustangs? I understand those are the mounts on the Western end, but I confess I know nothing about wild horses. Still, I'm interested in any horse that might improve my own bloodlines." He lit his pipe, shook the match out.

Barnes rubbed his chin. "Mustangs roam the West by the thousands. They're descendants of conquistadors' mounts that escaped several hundred years ago. There's one stallion up in the Sierra Nevada Mountains that's become a legend."

Quint leaned closer, straining to hear over the whirling of roulette wheels and the off-key piano. "How many Pony Express stations are there?"

"One hundred and eighty."

"It'll be a real undertaking to keep them all supplied and operating."

"Don't I know it?" Barnes sipped his drink. "You might enjoy seeing one or two. And if you're lucky, you might get far enough west to see this legend of a horse."

Quint took a deep puff, savored the taste. "Your offer begins to interest me. I might go along. This stallion sounds like one I'd like to own."

Thaddeus Barnes threw back his head and laughed. "So would a lot of people! I think every man in the West has tried to capture the Medicine Hat stallion but no one has yet. I'm not sure he even exists. Maybe he's just one of those Indian tales that grow better with each telling."

Quint watched the little brunette with the very black hair sidle through the crowd toward him. "Why do you call him the Medicine Hat stallion?"

"It's peculiar markings on a pinto horse that many Indi-

148

ans think is big medicine; you know, magic. Those who claim to have seen him say he has a blotch of black shaped like a war shield on his chest and a blotch on his head that covers his ears. That's powerful medicine, the Injuns say."

Quint snorted derisively. "This sounds like a 'windy,' you know, a tall tale."

"Doesn't it, though?" His companion shrugged jovially. "I ain't sayin' I've seen him because I haven't. A lot of men have chased him and been killed trying to catch him, even Indians, but no one has added that big, powerful brute to his string."

Quint thought about it. "Is he real or only an Indian legend?"

"Who knows?" Barnes said. "He gets bigger and smarter with each telling. I'm beginning to think he's a myth like that flying horse from the Greek tales."

"Pegasus," Quint muttered. Like all men, he was enticed by the difficult and unattainable. He imagined Medicine Hat's bloodlines mixed with his thoroughbreds'. "Thaddeus, when you leave in the morning, I think I'll go with you."

"Good! Now, if you'll excuse me, I see a game starting over there. You interested?"

Quint shook his head. He saw the little brunette, Rose, looking at him. He smiled at her. "No, you join the game, I see something that interests me."

Barnes noticed the girl. He winked at Quint, then moved away from the bar to take a chair at the card table.

Rose came up to Quint, rested one elbow on the bar. "I remember you from the other night."

"I remember you, too." He almost frowned, for he was thinking that this was the girl young Dal had taken upstairs. He burned with humiliation, remembering. While he'd failed to perform with Margo, no doubt Dal had played the virile stud with this girl.

He signaled the bartender to bring Rose a drink. "I never forget a really pretty girl," he said smoothly. Knocking the ashes from his pipe, he put it in his pocket.

Rose's face softened into a smile. "Well, ain't you the

149

gallant gentleman, though!"

"I'm from Kentucky," he drawled. "It's bred in us."

The bartender brought the drink and she sipped it, smiling up at Quint. As he looked down at her, he saw that the full swell of her breasts was visible above her bright purple dress and he felt a sudden need for a woman, which surprised him. Except for the girl from the streets of Philadelphia, he hadn't had a woman, hadn't wanted one, since before Melanie had been killed.

Or was it only that Dal had had this girl? Did he want to prove to her, to himself, that he was every bit as virile, as potent as that young stud had been?

She leaned on her elbow, brushing the softness of her breast against his sleeve, and his manhood swelled. He was remembering another dark-haired girl. He looked at her. "Let's go upstairs."

She put her glass down, ran the tip of her tongue over her lips in a slow, suggestive manner. "Thought you'd never ask, Kentucky gentleman."

He followed her, watching her hips sway as she walked, seeing light reflecting off the purple satin that sheathed her curves.

Quint swallowed hard, imagining her spread under him so he could drive hard and deep into her, his hands grasping her small bottom and tilting her up to take his full length right up into the center of her womb, deep in her silky belly.

By the time they got to her room and she closed the door and began to undress, his groin throbbed and was aching for relief. She was standing with her back to him. He saw only ebony hair and satiny bare skin showing beneath lace underwear.

He went up behind her, pulled her hard against the swollen maleness in his pants. "Dark angel," he whispered, burying his face in her ebony hair, "Oh, I've looked and looked for you. . . ."

He felt her unbutton her camisole, reach to take his hands, cup them over her breasts. But they were large breasts with big nipples, not the small, firm ones he re-

150

membered.

He felt his maleness start to soften. Desperately, he whirled the girl around, kissed her deeply. He would take her as Dal had, with heat and savagery, even though as he held her, he could no longer fool himself into thinking she was the girl he had sworn to find.

Her tongue flicked along the edges of his mouth, gradually invaded it. He tried to convince his body that he wanted her, but his erection was softening.

She led him to the bed, lay down beside him, fumbled with his buttons.

He reached out and caught her hand, kissed the tip of each finger. Surely she would do something to excite his body so that he could complete the act. Or was he doomed to be forever faithful to a girl who might only exist in his imagination?

Rose unbuttoned his shirt, ran her hands through the thick hair of his chest, bent her mouth to his nipples. He moaned aloud, closed his eyes, but in his mind, he remembered a girl in Philadelphia and how her tongue had traced those same tips.

She moved so that her full breasts hung over his face, and he reached up, pulled them down to bury his face between them; wanting to want her.

"Oh, Kentucky," she gasped, "I don't know when I've wanted a man so bad; I'll bet you're good with women."

"Better than that boy, Dal?"

She went on unbuttoning his pants. "Don't mention that kid to me."

"Why? Wasn't he any good?" Why did he want to know? He was horrified to realize it was because he envied Rose for having taken Dal to bed. Quint closed his eyes as he felt the warm heat of lips kissing his flesh. Still, his manhood was losing its rigidity.

He closed his eyes, remembering the dark angel, wanting her; wanting no other. He couldn't fool his own body. With a curse, he sat up, swung his legs over the side of the bed.

"What the hell?" The girl sprawled naked on the bed, eager for him. He could smell the hot, aroused scent of her.

151

"I've just changed my mind," Quint said, standing up, reaching for his clothes.

She looked up at him bewildered. "I must be losing my touch! Last night, it was that Dal Dawson; tonight, you're backing away from me like I'm poison."

Quint paused as he finished buttoning his pants. "What?"

She was seething with anger now, bright splotches of red coloring her full breasts. "I said you're just like your young friend! Get me up here all panting and eager, then stop sudden and leave."

Quint looked at her, bewildered, as he reached into his vest, tossed five silver dollars on the bed. "Dal didn't make love to you, either?"

She shook her hair back in angry, jerky gestures. "At least he had a story about being faithful to a sweetheart. What's happened to men lately? Don't know whether they can't or won't!"

He turned toward the door. "I wish I knew the answer to that myself, Rose. I think for me, it was just because you look a little like the girl I love; that's all."

He left the saloon and went back to his room at the hotel. There was a telegram in the box, from Philadelphia.

STILL NO TRACE OF THE GIRL YOU SEEK.
STOP. NOT SURE SHE EVER EXISTED. STOP.
AT LEAST, NOT SURE SHE'S IN THIS CITY.
STOP. SHALL WE KEEP LOOKING?

Quint scribbled a note to the seedy little man to continue his search, offer a bigger reward if necessary; and he gave it to a boy to take to the telegraph office.

Then he reached in his vest, staring at the tiny earring in his palm. Where in the world did lavender pink pearls come from? If he knew that, it would give him the clue he needed? He didn't even know where to ask about such things.

He'd go crazy waiting here or in Kentucky for the investigator to turn up something. Should he go back and help him look?

He was already doubting his own sanity. In fact, if it weren't for the solid evidence of the pearl, he would have thought he'd dreamed the girl up.

Still the investigator seemed to be doing everything he could to find her, so there was nothing to take him back to Philadelphia. And his hired help would keep the bluegrass farm running.

He looked down at the big, gold signet ring, on it the family crest of his English ancestors. Until the girl was found, he would go west with Barnes, maybe go to Arizona to reopen the Wolf's Den ranch. Quint thought about the legend of the horse. The Medicine Hat stallion presented an interesting challenge. Though everyone else who'd tried had failed to capture it, Quint wanted to be the one to put his brand on its mottled body. Or was that, too, only a dream like the missing girl of the snowstorm?

Barnes came into the lobby. "If we're going to get an early start, we'd better turn in."

Quint nodded, and they went up the stairs. "What time we leaving?"

"See you at dawn. We'll make our first stop at the Rock Creek station."

They separated and went to their rooms, but Quint couldn't sleep. The wind picked up and rattled the window panes. It sounded like a dying woman's moans. *Melanie*.

He rolled over and dozed off while the wind whimpered throughout a night that was cold and raw for the first week of April.

His mother and two older sisters had raised him since he was a toddler, from the time his father had been killed in a hunting accident. Quint had never told them that the servants had said his father had killed himself; there had been no accident. Maybe that and his drinking were the only things about his early life that were not humdrum. . . .

Quint hadn't wanted to marry Melanie Griswold, the heiress from Philadelphia. But his mother was dying of cancer, and she said it would make her happy to see him wed. And he had caused her so much heartache by being

153

rebellious and getting kicked out of Harvard when she had set her sights on his being a lawyer, he'd agreed to do so.

It was one of the biggest society weddings Philadelphians ever saw. At the reception, Quint got very drunk because he felt he'd been cheated and he was cheating the shy, pliant girl he'd married.

But she loved him. It showed in her eyes every time she looked across the crowded room. All he could feel was anger at the smug satisfaction on his older sisters' faces. Why had Lydia been so set on this particular girl? And why had his mother suddenly agreed with her? He had always figured he would marry someday, but his mother's plea to make her happy before she died had made him feel so guilty, he'd let them push him into proposing to Melanie.

He drank a lot of champagne at the reception, delayed leaving because he suddenly realized that on this cold March evening, he would soon be in bed with a girl he hardly knew. And Melanie seemed so shy, he thought his wedding night would be little more than rape on his part while she did her "wifely duty."

Then old 'Ben was at his elbow. "I done brought the phaeton around in front of the house, Mister Quint, so's you all kin leave the party." His dark face furrowed anxiously. "You sure you don't want me to drive you and Miss Melanie?"

"I am perfectly sober!" Quint slammed his glass down with a crash. "And it's not dark yet. You think I want to take a driver along on my honeymoon?"

In truth, he didn't even want to take his bride. She came over to him then, her long ivory lace dress not as pale as her face. "Quint, dear, speak a little more softly, everyone is looking."

"Let 'em look!" All his life, women had bossed him, bullied him, except for the times when he'd escaped their company and sought out the stable boys and hired help. Even though his mother had disapproved, he'd been stubborn enough to enjoy that little bit of companionship with the men who'd taught him to ride, shoot and hunt.

His mother and sisters glared at him from across the

154

room, making Quint feel guilty because his mother was dying. Hadn't she whipped him into line by reminding him of that often enough lately?

And, suddenly, he was sick of the whole scene, the society people who were friends of the females in his family. Had he suggested inviting his friends, their names would have brought a frown to Melanie's face and to the faces of his sisters and his mother.

"Let's go," he said gruffly. Melanie took his arm and they went out the door unsteadily, in a shower of rice and amid shouts of congratulations.

Old Ben helped him into the phaeton, saying, "Mister Quint, you sure you don't want me to drive you?"

But Quint shook his head, reached for the reins and the whip. "Not far. The inn is only a few miles away. We'll be there just after dark."

The wind, which had turned cold, was moaning and whipping the veil around Melanie's face. Quint cracked the whip smartly, and the fine bay started off at a brisk trot.

He heard Melanie sigh audibly and relax next to him as they drove away from the big house, and he looked back at the crowd standing in the twilight waving good-bye.

Then he felt even more angry and guilty at letting himself be pressured into marrying a girl he did not love.

"Well, it's done," he said. "I-I'm sorry it's so obvious that I regret it already."

"I know that," she said, one hand on her light hair to keep her veil from blowing. "But I love you enough for both of us."

He glanced over at her sad eyes and felt sorry that he didn't love her, sorry that he would be spending the rest of his life with this girl who seemed almost a stranger to him. Somehow he had hoped marriage would be more than just a legal contract. Lord, what had he gotten himself into?

Maybe it would work out all right. He reached over and put his arm round her, tried to pull her close, but she was stiff and wooden in his embrace.

"Quinton, I-I want you to know I'm prepared to do my duty as your wife."

"Duty?" He looked over at her, put both hands back on the reins. Her tone had told him she dreaded what was coming this evening after they reached the inn. "Melanie, my dear innocent, do you even have any idea of what it is men and women do together on their wedding night?"

Even though it was almost dark he could see the sudden flush of her face. "I . . . I have some idea." Her chin came up bravely. "I'm prepared to let you do that to me . . . each time we want another child."

"And only then?" He had hoped for a wife he would love as she loved him, a woman who would come into his arms without hesitation and match his heated passion with her own. He had a sudden vision of Melanie lying wooden and submissive beneath him while he took her virginity in a joyless union.

"Surely you don't expect a respectable girl to carry on like a saloon tart?" She sounded appalled.

He whipped up the horse, both angered and saddened by the turn things were taking. They were on a long stretch of deserted road now.

"Quint, slow down. You're driving too fast. There's no hurry. You did remember to make reservations at the inn, didn't you?"

In truth, he had forgotten to notify the management that they were coming. But what difference did it make if they weren't expected? The small country inn wouldn't be crowded on a cold March night.

"You sound exactly like the women in my family!" he snapped, urging the horse to go even faster. "I intend to be the man in my own house. Lord, no wonder my sisters and mother liked you. Behind that sweet face, you're as bossy a bitch as any of them."

When he glanced over at her, she held onto the seat with tense hands. "Quint, don't talk to me like that. I'll tell my daddy and the deal will be off!"

"What deal?"

"Nothing." She was hiding something. Her tone told him that.

He had a sudden suspicion. "No, tell me. I've wondered

why my mother and sister chose to push you at me."

He heard her open and close her mouth several times as the phaeton raced through the darkness. He ought to slow down, he knew; for there was a sharp curve in the road up ahead. But he was too drunk and too angry that he'd let his mother bully him into marrying by using her illness as an excuse.

"Tell me, Melanie!" He cursed and cracked the whip, urging the horse to go still faster.

"For God's sake, slow down, Quint! I . . . I'll tell you! Your sister Lydia's husband is having financial troubles. I set my cap for you and begged Papa to help me."

"And?" Wild-eyed, Quint shouted at her as the buggy clattered along the road at breakneck speed. "Tell me, Melanie or I swear I'll smash us up!"

"I—he went to your mother, promised to help your brother-in-law if she'd see that you married me." Melanie began to sob. "You were never to know!"

"You conniving bitch! Behind that sweet face, you're as ruthless as Lydia ever dared to be!"

"Slow down, Quint! The curve—"

He saw it too late. Although he tried to rein the horse back, slow the buggy, the wheels skidded in the loose gravel.

Always he would remember her high, shrill scream, the way the veil whipped around both of them as the buggy skidded toward the steep bank. The horse neighed wildly, fighting to stay on the road.

Too late he tried to slow the buggy, too late he fought to keep it upright as it skidded, in a clatter of rocks, toward the edge. And then it was forever too late.

It seemed an eternity that he twisted through the air as the buggy went over the edge in a tangle of harness and white veil. He was not sure whether the shriek he heard came from the horse as it hit and broke its neck, or from Melanie who was still in the buggy, which was rolling over and over.

Then he hit the ground. Vaguely he was aware of bones breaking as he landed and rolled. He remembered thinking it was a good thing he was drunk so he didn't fully feel the pain of what was happening. The next thing he remembered was the scent and taste of cold earth against his lips as he finally came to.

"Melanie?" How long had he been lying here? What had happened? He searched his memory. Oh, yes, they had left the reception and there'd been an argument. . . .

"Melanie?" He tried to get up, but some of his limbs didn't work. He had never been so cold as he was lying on the ground in the dark with the March wind whipping through the stillness.

He heard a moan. Thank God, she was still alive. He crawled on his belly toward the wreckage. It seemed to take a long time to reach it. He didn't know whether that was because he was so drunk or because he was hurt.

The moon came out, and he stared at the buggy wheels. Funny he had never noticed they were bright yellow before. It was eerie the way the wind made them turn as if the buggy were moving.

"Melanie?"

She moaned again and he crawled over, found her lying in a tangle of harness and white satin.

"Melanie? Oh, Lord, you're all right! I'll make it up to you, you'll see, I—"

He had turned her over as he babbled and he saw in the moonlight that she was not all right. A deep crimson stained the white satin gown, and when he held her, it was warm and sticky and smelled coppery sweet.

Her eyes flickered open. "I never meant for you to find out," she whispered. "I thought I loved you enough for both of us, that I could make you love me. . . ."

"I'll spend the rest of my life making it up to you," he gasped. "I'll get you some help. If only I hadn't drunk so much! If only I hadn't hit the curve so fast! If only . . ."

"Hurt so much, get help. . . ."

"Yes! Hang on, Melanie. I'll get help and we'll pretend this never happened, make a fresh start."

She had lapsed into unconsciousness, and he gently laid her down and looked up toward the road. The gully beneath the curve was deep enough to hide the wrecked buggy. It looked a million miles to the top, where the road ran.

It was torture to move, but he had to get help for Melanie. He began to crawl on his belly, the rocks cutting into his hands.

He cursed himself as he crawled inch by slow inch. Back at the wedding reception, they would have no way of knowing what had happened. And the inn wasn't expecting them, so no one would be alarmed when they didn't arrive.

His head ached and he tasted blood from his cut lip. The wind cried like a hurt woman as he struggled toward the road. "Help!" he yelled, but it came out as only a weak cry. "Oh, Lord, please help! She's hurt. . . ."

He called out every few minutes as he crawled, but finally his voice became only a raspy sigh in the blackness of the cold night.

Above him on the road, he heard a wagon approaching, the creaking of wheels, the slow plodding of a team of big draft horses. And singing; many people singing.

" 'Row, row, row your boat, gently down the stream, merrily, merrily, merrily, merrily, life is but a dream. . . .' "

A hayride. That's what it was; a church group out on a hayride. As it moved closer, the singing and the shouts grew louder. " 'Row, row, row your boat, gently down the stream. . . .' "

"Help!" Quint gasped. "Help me . . . please!" He tried to cry out loudly but even if he could have, the singers probably wouldn't have heard him over their own noise.

He guessed the wagon must be even with the wrecked buggy now. The singing and laughter was louder, the wheels creaked slowly past. " 'Row, row, row your boat. . . .' "

He had to crawl up there in time to stop the wagon, he knew that. This was a fairly deserted road after dark. It might be morning before anyone else came along.

Sweat stood out in big drops on his forehead as he forced his broken bones to move inch by agonizing inch up the incline. If he hadn't been so drunk, he might have fainted

159

from the pain. But all he could think of was that Melanie was injured and it was his fault. He had to get help for her, no matter how much he hurt.

He was halfway up, but the slow-moving wagon was past him now. The song drifted on the cold black night.

Suddenly the singing stopped. Someone on the wagon shouted, "Will there be hot chocolate when we reach the inn?"

"Of course, and a roaring fire!"

A fire. Quint shivered and kept crawling. He had never been so cold. Now while they were quiet he must call again.

"Now everyone, let's do another chorus!"

"Help!" Quint gasped, "Please help. . . ."

" 'Row, row, row your boat gently down the stream,' " someone sang. Then others joined in. " 'Merrily, merrily, merrily life is but a dream. . . .' "

They had passed him and moved on down the road. Quint forced himself to crawl up the incline even though his hands were raw and bleeding; every inch was pain. "Help, oh, help me!"

" 'Row, row, row your boat. . . .' " The sound was fainter now. He had to get up there in time to stop them. He kept crawling, his face torn by the gravel. He must get help for Melanie. The hay wagon moved slowly on, those aboard laughing and shouting out the words of the song.

Exhausted, Quint crawled up the slope, but the music drifted back faintly now. Still, if he reached the road, someone might look back and see him lying there. He kept crawling.

" '. . . Life is but a dream. Row, row, row. . . .' "

It wasn't a dream; it was a nightmare of crawling upward with broken bones screaming out their pain. Sweat ran down his face as he struggled. Finally he reached the top.

He lay there in the road looking after the hay wagon, the cold wind bringing the echo of voices, the scent of hay. The lanterns on the back of the wagon swayed in the darkness like tiny fairy lights.

Quint raised his torn, bloody face up out of the road, reaching vainly after them, willing them to return. If only someone would look back and see him in the road . . .

"Help," he gasped. "Help!"

" '. . . Life is but a dream. . . .' "

The night swallowed the creaking wagon up as it moved on toward the inn. That was it, he would crawl to the inn. How far was it? Three miles? Five? He had to do it. He crawled down the middle of the road, determined to find help for the girl who had loved him enough to do anything to get him.

Oh, God, just let her live. I'll make it up to her. If only I hadn't been drunk. If only I hadn't driven so fast. If only . . .

He kept crawling although every move was agony. He would change the past, relive the mistake he'd made, make it up to Melanie.

His last conscious thought was that there wouldn't be any wedding night for both of them to dread.

In the frosty dawn, a wagon delivering milk to town found him lying unconscious in the middle of the road. He had crawled two miles on his belly with two broken ribs and a broken leg.

If only . . .

Quint came awake suddenly, sat up in bed, sweat running down his face. He was in St. Joe and the sky to the east had turned a silvery lavender. It was ironic. He had never been a husband to Melanie, yet his guilt made him unable to perform with any other woman . . . except one.

When he had confronted his mother and sisters, they had denied everything. What difference did it make? Melanie was dead, and the worst of it was that he'd never loved her.

He stood up, went over to the bowl and pitcher to wash. Today he was headed for Rock Creek station. Then he'd go on to Nevada to look for the legendary Medicine Hat stallion.

He took out the little earring, stared at it, tucked it back in his vest. If only he hadn't been so drunk, he might remember more clearly what she looked like, so he could describe her. *If only . . .*

No, he shook his head. What was it she had said about the futility of trying to change the past? *The two saddest words in any language . . .*

Okay, he'd look to the future and close the door to the past—except where that mysterious girl was concerned. If the investigators found her, he'd pay any price—go anywhere—to find the dark angel of the storm!

Chapter Eleven

It was late in the morning when Dallas finally rode into Rock Creek station, but she'd made up much of the lost time. She saw the big rock building up ahead, the small rider waiting with his horse as she galloped in, slid off her lathered mount.

A big, young man with light hair ran out of the barn, caught her as she almost collapsed. "Where's Willie? Wasn't this his route?"

"Drunk," she said wearily. "Dead drunk. I had to ride a double stretch." She reached up to pull the *mochila* from her saddle, tossed it to the eager boy waiting with the fresh horse. "Here you go!"

He threw it over his saddle, mounted, and loped away.

Dallas stared after him as he disappeared in a cloud of dust.

The big, handsome boy whistled low. "You mean you been in the saddle that long? Can you walk?"

"I can walk," Dallas said stubbornly, handing the reins of her horse to a stable boy who led the weary animal away to be watered and fed. "I'm Dal Dawson."

"Howdy," the tall boy shook hands, gestured toward the station. "I'm Jim Hickok. Come on in and get some grub. We've got a bunk for you."

Dallas look at him curiously as they headed toward the main building not far from a small lake. "You a Pony Express rider?"

He laughed. "Not hardly! I'm too big, so I work around the place. The riders all have to be little guys like you. Under a hundred and thirty pounds, I think the requirement is.

163

Heavy riders slow the horses down and speed's all important in this business."

Hickok opened the door. "But I got big plans for later on. I'm good with a gun. They say a man who can handle himself well can always make a name."

Dallas looked the broad-shouldered, handsome Hickok over. "Well, Jim, you got the looks to become a legend, if one of those back-East writers ever decides to take an interest in your exploits."

Hickok reddened modestly as he led her inside. He gestured her to a table in the large main room, handed her some coffee. "The cook saw you coming. There'll be steak and potatoes in a minute. We're a big stage stop, you know, so we feed pretty good. Tell me the news from St. Joe."

Gratefully, Dallas slumped down on the bench and warmed her stiff hands by placing them around the steaming cup. She filled Hickok in on what had happened so far, including the drunken Willie.

He frowned. "Well, there's one S.O.B. who'll be out of a job. We're expected to get that mail through, no matter what! The Pony's reputation and the future of that government contract depend on it!"

Dallas turned so she could look out at the small lake shimmering in the early evening sunshine. What she wouldn't give for a bath. Maybe after dark, she could sneak out and swim when no one was around.

Hickok's light eyes followed her gaze. "Mud Springs, they call it," he offered by way of explanation. The fact that there's a natural spring and lake here, where the buffalo watered for hundreds of years, makes it a perfect site for a stage stop. There'll be a big heifer dance here tomorrow night."

Dallas yawned, reached eagerly for a fork as the black cook came in, set before her a platter of fried steak and potatoes, and some hot biscuits with rich butter and home-made jam. "Oh? A heifer dance?"

"You know out here, we don't always have enough gals to go around, so we make do with what we've got. Sometimes boys wear a handkerchief tied to their arms and they take the place of girls."

"I don't know whether I could dance backward." She went on eating.

"Some of it's square dancin'. Lots of locals will come off the nearby ranches and farms for it," Hickok said. "A dance is such a treat out in the wilderness that folks will drive for miles to attend."

He winked and nudged Dallas. "The station manager, Wellman, has a pretty daughter, Thelma. You're about her age, Dal. You'll get a chance to dance with her."

Horsefeathers. Just what I need, Dallas thought. She shoveled in more steak and reached for another biscuit. "I-I don't dance very well."

"I bet Miss Thelma would be willing to teach you. After all, you'll be here a few days before you have to carry another mail sack back the other way."

Dallas finished her meal, sipped the strong, hot coffee. "Right now, all I want to do is sleep the clock around."

She stood up and stretched the way she'd seen men do.

Hickok stood up, too. "I got chores to do, Dal, but I'll show you to your bunk."

He led her to a comfortable back room full of bunks. There was no one there at midmorning. She wrapped herself in a blanket, fell across her bunk, and slept until late afternoon.

Dallas was so sore and stiff she could hardly move when she finally awakened and went to the outhouse, carefully closing the door before pulling her pants down. Thank goodness the mail only came through once a week. That would give her several days to rest up before heading out again, back to St. Joe with the mail coming from the West. It was a mild afternoon. No one paid much attention to her, not with a stage coming through and stopping to change horses, and with the other chores to be done around the station.

She sat out in the sunlight, leaning up against the building. Miss Thelma, a pert girl with a pug nose, came out and introduced herself, but Dallas wasn't overly friendly. It was hard enough to keep passing herself off as a boy, and it was anyone's guess as to how long she could do this before she got caught.

She stared out at the small lake and wondered about her letter. Was there any chance Papa hadn't gotten it? She shook her head. Probably he was just too angry with her to answer. Maybe later he would cool down or Mama would prevail on him to change his mind and send Trace after her. In the meantime, she had to support herself, and riding for the Pony paid well.

That night, when it was finally quiet and everyone at Rock Creek station was asleep, Dallas got clean clothes and a bar of homemade soap from her saddle bags, and sneaked down to the water.

She hadn't realized the cool spring water would feel so good on her perspiring, dusty feet. She was more than ready for a bath and a change of clothes.

Making sure there was no one around, she stripped and swam across the small pond, the water pulling at her breasts. Then she turned over and floated lazily, looking up at the stars. Idly, she wondered where Quint Randolph was tonight? Probably headed back to Philadelphia or Kentucky now that he had delivered the thoroughbreds. Dallas had to admit the ones she had ridden ranked with the best mounts she'd ever had.

Why couldn't she get that faithless rake off her mind? He belonged to another woman, and what she had done with him was wrong. Still she would never forget him.

She stood up in the shallow water, reached for the soap, scrubbed her slender body down, shampooed her short, curly hair. Then she dived and swam like a water nymph for a few more minutes before drying herself off and reaching for the clean clothes. First she bound her breasts down with the band so they didn't show under the oversized shirt.

Miss Thelma would wash her dirty things for a fee just as she did for the other travelers.

Dallas went back and crawled into her bunk with her clothes on. It wasn't going to be as hard to pass herself off as a boy as she had thought. All the men slept with their clothes on. In fact, they were glad to have a bunk; in the more primitive stage stops, all they got was a blanket and a spot in front of the fireplace.

She lay there listening to the snoring around her, smiling to herself. Only a few short weeks ago, the idea of sleeping in a roomful of men would have horrified her, but now, all she thought about was the loud snoring. Since everyone thought she was a boy, she was perfectly safe. Still, as she drifted off to sleep, Dallas found herself wishing she was sleeping against a big, hairy chest and Quint's arm held her protectively.

The next day, she felt a little better and went hunting with some of the stable boys. She was a good shot and brought down a number of fat, juicy quail for supper. It was late afternoon when they went back to the station.

Hickok waved from the barn. "Oh, there you are, Dal! I was afraid you boys wouldn't get back in time for the dance. A couple of important men rode in early this afternoon, one of them from the company."

She nodded and went out back to wash up by the well. She certainly didn't intend to go to the dance. She'd hide out in the barn loft until it was over, and plead sickness. She didn't care who the important men were. The more people she could avoid, the better her chances of not being discovered.

The important men missed supper because they were off looking over the pony route, and Dallas was relieved that she didn't have to share a table with them.

Immediately after the meal, the help started clearing out the tables and moving chairs against the wall to make room for dancing on the rough floor. Buggies began arriving before sundown, a little later some frontiersmen rode up and tied their ponies out front.

Dallas fled outside and watched the people gather. But when the fiddler first started to play, she was sorely tempted. Being from Texas, she knew many of the old Western dances and was good at them.

The music drifted through the spring night: *Jimmy, crack corn, and I don't care, Jimmy, crack corn and I don't care Jimmy, crack corn and I don't care, old massa's gone away. . . .*

Maybe she could get cleaned up and just slip inside, lean against the wall, and enjoy watching. She entered through the back door, went to the bunkroom. Thank goodness it was empty so she could change clothes.

Dallas sighed as she slipped into a clean shirt and pants, continuing her masquerade. How she yearned for a lace petticoat and a full hoop skirt! When she looked in the cracked mirror, remembering her long locks tied up with a ribbon, she almost wept. Well, hair eventually grew.

She went into the big front room, lounged against the wall. The place echoed with music and hand clapping. The worn, board floor creaked with the stamp of dancing feet.

The old fiddler and a man with a mouth organ struck up one of the cowboy's favorites.

Put your little foot, put your little foot, put your little foot right there. Put your little foot, put your little foot, put your little foot right there. . . .

She watched the crowd, itching to dance.

"Yoo-hoo!" Thelma waved. Dallas tried to pretend she didn't see the pert girl, but Thelma stopped talking to a burly farmer and pushed through the crowd.

Dallas looked around for an escape, but Thelma had her trapped against the wall. "Ah declare, Dal, I've been waiting for you to ask me to dance."

"I don't dance very well, Miss Thelma, and as pretty as you are, every man in the place is hopin' to dance with you." Dallas scuffed her boot against the floor.

But the pug-nosed girl was not to be discouraged. "I'll teach you," she said. She caught Dallas's arm, dragged her out onto the floor.

Dallas had never felt so ridiculous as she did when Thelma came into her arms and the music started again. *Why did I ever come to this dance?*

"Dal, this is called a waltz." It happened that Dallas was a skillful waltzer, but Thelma frowned up at her.

"What's the matter?"

"Dal, you are supposed to lead and I'm the one who dances backward."

Blood rushed to Dallas's face. If she didn't watch out, someone would suspect she was a girl from the way she danced. "I told you I don't dance very well."

"That's quite all right, I'd just as soon go outside and talk anyway."

Before Dallas realized what she was up to, the girl had danced her out the door.

"Miss Thelma, your reputation might be questioned if anyone saw you come out here with me."

The pert girl had a tight grip on Dallas's arm, preventing her from pulling away. "I'm sure if anyone smeared a lady's reputation, you'd call them out, wouldn't you, Dal?"

"Uh, of course. Wouldn't any gentleman?" Dallas turned and looked wistfully toward the station. *Horsefeathers. Now what?*

Thelma hung onto her arm. "You're as nervous as an unbroke colt, Dal. Honest, I'm not worried about my reputation. I'm sure if it was questioned, you'd do the right thing by me."

"What?"

"You may kiss me, Dal." Thelma closed her eyes, her face turned up toward Dallas.

"Miss Thelma, I respect you too much to take such liberties. Let's go back in for some punch!" Dallas turned and fled back inside to the safety of the dance.

She almost collided with the big man called Hickok. "Oh, there you are, Dal. We been wondering where you were. There's not enough gals and so we thought you'd fill in. One of those important men is on the other side of the room, wanting to dance."

Dallas shook her head and began to back away. "No, I don't think—"

"Nonsense!" He winked. "Be a good sport!" And while Dallas tried to protest, Hickok tied a handkerchief around her arm.

"Come on and meet this man," Hickok said, taking her by

169

the arm and pulling her along while she protested over the loud music, saying she didn't dance very well and didn't think she could dance a girl's part.

But by then they were across the room. The fiddle stopped just as they came up behind a tall, broad-shouldered man with chestnut hair. Why, he looked like . . .

Quint Randolph turned around. For a long moment, Dallas didn't know whether to scream or throw herself into his arms. He reached out, shook her limp hand with his big, warm one.

"Why, Dal! Nice to see you again, son." He looked at the handkerchief and laughed. "They got you tagged for a heifer! All right, we can both go along with the joke."

"No." Dallas shook her head and began to edge back. Her emotions were going wild, for she was horrified yet glad that Quint had ended up here at Rock Creek station. "I-I don't think I feel like dancing."

But about that time, the fiddler shouted. "Let's polka, folks!"

Quint grabbed her, whirled her out onto the floor to the lively rhythm while she tried to protest. All she could think of was the feel of his arm around her waist, his hand clutching hers warmly. She wasn't sure whether the giddy feeling sweeping over her was due to their whirling or his nearness.

Quint grinned down at her. "Why, Dal, I don't know why you didn't want to dance the lady's part. You dance backward like you've been doing it all your life!"

"Uh, I learn fast," she gulped, concentrating on the steps. As they danced past Thelma and her partner, the girl smiled and waved.

Quint laughed. "Looks like you've made a conquest! After a while, you ought to take off the bandana and dance with the young lady."

Dallas looked up at him, thinking what a firm chin he had, how golden his hazel eyes were. "I don't think she was waving at me; I think she was waving at you!"

"I'm almost old enough to be her father. No, make no mistake"—Quint grinned—"she's interested in getting you out under the cottonwoods for a stolen kiss, young man."

Dallas sighed heavily. This masquerade was getting more and more complicated.

Quint looked down at her as the music ended. "Are you okay, Dal? You look sort of peaked."

"As a matter of fact, all the cigar smoke is making it hot in here."

Quint took a handkerchief out of his silk vest, wiped his own face. "For the first week of April, it is hotter than hell with the lid off. Let's go outside and cool off."

"I don't know. . . ." Miss Thelma winked again and looked as if she might be thinking about pushing through the crowd to join them. "Maybe you're right," Dallas said hurriedly. "We'll go outside for a cigar."

Quint looked at her. "I thought you chewed tobacco?"

Dallas remembered that night in St. Joe. "I . . . decided little cigars are something more acceptable to women," she sputtered.

They went outside, leaned against the hitching rail.

"In that case, have one of mine. I always carry extras." Before she could say no, Quint handed her one, lit his pipe. There was nothing to do but accept his match.

She tried striking it on the seat of her pants the way she'd seen her brother do, failed miserably. "Must have gotten wet," she said.

Quint struck a match with his thumbnail. For a moment, he hesitated, looking down at her in the glow of the flame. Then he lit her cigar, shook the match out.

Dallas tried not to cough as she stood there with it in her mouth. To her it tasted like burning rope. "Ah, nothing like a good cigar! What are you doing so far out, Randolph? I thought you were heading back to Kentucky after you got your horses delivered."

He shrugged and smoked, his eyes sad, pensive in the moonlight. "I was awaiting a personal message from Philadelphia, but nothing came of it, so when Thaddeus Barnes invited me along to see how the Pony operates, I came."

Personal. She thought of his wife. Had the woman found out about his escapade with Dallas or that blonde, Margo?

Were they estranged?

She studied his profile in the moonlight, smelled the fragrance of his tobacco. The fiddle music and the stomping and clapping drifted on the night air. Of all the places in the world she would want to be, standing here with Quint Randolph was her first choice . . . if he weren't married and if she could let him know she was a girl.

"You aren't smoking your cigar," Quint said. "Not your brand?"

"What?" She was jolted out of her thoughts. "Uh, no, I like mine a little stronger."

His face furrowed in the moonlight. "I'd swear we've met some place before. Do you have a brother or a sister anywhere who looks like you?"

"A brother, Trace. He's in Texas." She thought about her family with tenderness.

He shook his head. "Don't reckon I've met him then. I met a girl from Texas once in Philadelphia. . . ."

She waited breathlessly for him to continue. "Yes?"

"A gentleman never discusses ladies."

"Oh." She turned, took a couple of aimless steps toward the lake. Had he meant her? What had he thought of her? She'd give a year of her life to know.

"Pretty little lake," he said and came down to stand beside Dallas, holding his pipe and studying the water.

She leaned against the trunk of a giant cottonwood, listened to its leaves tremble softly in the breeze. The moon reflected off the water.

She had a sudden vision of swimming naked, diving and surfacing like mythical creatures. She would swim underwater and he would capture her in the depths, kiss her as they clung to each other in the quiet green of the water. Then he would lift her, kiss her wet breasts and belly. Later he would lay her down on her back in the shallows and take her, the water washing gently at them while he drank shimmering droplets of it off her nipples. His thumbs and forefingers would hold her turgid nipples captive as his mouth explored the velvet secrets of her own. . . .

"Did you hear me?"

172

"Oh, yes," she lied, looking at him. "It is a nice lake."

He knocked the ashes from his pipe against the tree trunk, dropped it in his pocket. "I was asking about how Sylph and the other horses ran? You must have your mind on a sweetheart."

"I suppose I do," she answered truthfully. "Your horses were outstanding; you can be proud of them."

"I'm going on to Utah Territory, that section they call Nevada when I leave here tomorrow," he said. "There's some legendary wild mustang that I'm hoping to add to my herd. They call him a Medicine Hat."

Dallas turned, looked at him. "That color is sacred to the Indians, big magic."

"You don't believe that nonsense, do you?"

Dallas hesitated. She was half-Cheyenne and that was one of the tribes who considered the unusual markings to be strong medicine. "I just don't think the Indians will like the idea of a white man capturing their legend, dragging it away to Kentucky."

"I've got an old Spanish land grant in Arizona," he said. "Thinking about reopening the ranch. This Western landscape gets into your blood. I sure never expected to run into you out here. I wouldn't admit this to anyone else under torture, but I . . . I can't deal with the attraction you have for me."

His face reddened and suddenly he looked both sick and angry. "Forget I said that, boy. I wouldn't want you thinking I was one of these men who—"

He broke off and swore under his breath, turned to stride back to the station.

Dallas didn't even stop to think of the consequences. He was walking away from her, walking out of her life. She didn't care about right or wrong or what exposing her masquerade might lead to. She thought only of how much she loved him. "Quint!"

And when he paused, half turned, she threw herself into his arms, kissed him on the mouth.

Chapter Twelve

Quint stared down at Dal and the boy stared back up at him in horror.

"Randolph, I — I mean, it was just a joke, that's all! I've had too much to drink, and with them tagging me as a 'heifer,' I just got carried away with the joke!"

Quint was more horrified than the boy was. A distant memory pulled at the edges of his mind, but all he could think about was how his senses and emotions had reacted to that kiss. He had to fight himself to keep from grabbing the boy, kissing him again.

He backed away, swearing under his breath. He had to face it. Despite all his denials, he was that kind of man, and Dal must be, too. That was the reason the boy had not performed with that whore, Rose, in St. Joe.

He stood frozen, staring down at Dal, wondering why, if he were that kind of man, he had been able to perform like a stallion with the dark angel of the storm in Philadelphia?

Dal finally said. "Quint, for God's sake, say something! I-I told you it was a joke. I've had too much to drink." The boy laughed, but it sounded forced — hollow and unsure.

What was the memory that kept pulling at Quint's mind? The kiss. What was it that was so familiar about that kiss?

The boy shrugged. "I reckon I shocked you and you're mad, the way you keep staring at me. Maybe we'd better go back inside."

As Dal turned, the moonlight lit up his small face and Quint frowned, trying to remember what it was that had distracted him when he'd danced with the boy. Now, in the moonlight, he looked again and realized what it was that had puzzled him. The boy had tiny holes in his ears, as if . . . as if. . . . No, that was a crazy idea. Quint decided he must be dead drunk to even imagine such a thing!

And yet . . . He stepped closer, caught the boy's arm, stared down at him. "Just a minute, Dal."

Tiny holes in his ears. Like . . . like girls have who wear earrings. Unbelieving, he reached out, put his fingers under the boy's chin, turned his face up.

"Randolph, why do you keep staring at me like that? I told you it was just a joke, okay?" Dal tried to pull out of his grasp. "I've been drinking and they got me tagged as a 'heifer' for the dance and I got carried away."

Well, I'll be damned! Quint stared down at Dal, wondering whether he had been blind or drunk that night he hadn't recognized the girl with her hair cut short? He was torn between grabbing her and kissing her or turning her over his knee for what she'd put him through.

The longer he stared down at her, the madder he got. All this time, she had recognized him and had been playing cat-and-mouse games with him.

"Randolph, are you all right? You're shaking. Are you mad or something?"

Dal tried to pull out of his grasp.

Quint couldn't remember when he'd been more furious— or more relieved. Damn, she deserved a scare for what she'd very deliberately put him through. The little hellcat! He was going to give her what she so richly deserved!

He moved closer. "Now, Dal boy, I think we might as well stop fighting this thing. It's bigger than both of us!"

She backed away. "I beg your pardon? Mr. Randolph, I don't think I understand." She looked both upset and confused.

"What I said, Dal, was that we should realize we're special, different in that we're attracted to each other."

She withdrew another step toward the edge of the lake. If she backed up any farther, she was going to be standing in water. "No, there seems to be some confusion here. I . . . I don't know what you're hinting at."

175

But the desperation on her face told him she did. He advanced one more step, and she was trapped. "Oh, but I think you do, boy. This was common enough in ancient Greece."

"No!" She tried to run past him, but he reached out and caught her.

It was hard to keep up the pretense when he wanted to pull her into his arms, shake her, and say, "Let's stop this nonsense! What have you been up to with this ridiculous masquerade?"

But he was furious over what she had put him through over the past several weeks. To him, it was cruel and irresponsible of her to make love to him, then disappear, and finally turn up dressed as a boy. What on earth was she up to? Was she a spy of some kind and for whom?

But he didn't care anymore, all he cared about was having her in his arms at any cost.

"Let me go!" Her voice rose. "Do you hear me, you terrible man, let me go or I'll scream and everyone will come running!"

He was too annoyed with her not to bait her further. "Scream? Why, Dal, that doesn't seem like something a man would do! A man would defend himself with his fists, now wouldn't he?"

She took a swing at him, but he caught her hand and dragged her to him. "Dal boy, this is bigger than both of us! Let's forget about what other people think and just love each other, man to man!"

"No, Quint. You must be out of your mind! No!"

While she struggled to break away, he kissed her.

For a long moment, she fought him though his tongue invaded her mouth and he held her hard against him. Then, with a soft moan, she clung to him, returning his ardor with her own.

He held her very close, rubbing his throbbing hardness against her while his hands roamed down her back. Good Lord, what was that she had on beneath her shirt? Some kind of band? What a clever little minx! He almost laughed aloud at the sheer relief of finally holding her close again.

She looked up at him, her eyes as round and horrified as a doe's. "You . . . you like boys?"

"Not just any boy, Dal, just you. There's no point in either of us pretending any longer. And, oh, by the way, Cinderella"—he reached into his vest, pulled out the little earring—"I believe you dropped this when you fled that night."

She pulled back, blinked up at him, then slowly held out her hand and stared as he placed the earring in it.

There was a long moment of silence as realization sank in. "Why you rotten polecat!" she sputtered. "You scared me to death just now for nothing!"

He grinned, pleased with himself. "Turnabout's fair play, I think, angel. By the way, what is your real name?"

Her fist clenched over the earring. "Dallas. It means 'spirited.' "

" 'Spirited', huh? Can't imagine why anyone would give a sweet, shy filly a name like that."

"Why, you unspeakable varmint! You stood here and scared me to death, let me act the fool? Of all the rotten contemptible—"

Before he realized what she was up to, Dallas brought her knee up, caught him between the thighs, then turned and fled.

Quint moaned and doubled up. Angel? Why the hellcat had just tried to emasculate him with one swift blow.

As he dropped to his knees, Dallas turned and ran back. "Oh, Quint, I didn't mean to hurt you."

"Get away!" He groaned, motioning her to leave. "I must be crazy to be attracted to you! You've been nothing but trouble to me since the first time we met!"

"But if you're hurt—"

"Just don't touch me, okay? Just don't touch me!" He flopped into a sitting position in the dirt.

She gestured helplessly. "Why do you have to act like the injured party, when—"

"Because I am the injured party! Lord, why did I bring this upon myself by getting mixed up with a hellcat like you!"

"As I remember," she said frostily, "if I hadn't got mixed

up with you, you'd have frozen to death like some common drunk back on that door step."

He stood up slowly. "So you came along, rescued me, and then deserted me. In my bed, then out again — like a paid trollop."

"Trollop?" Her voice rose. "You, a married man sleeping around, you have the nerve to talk to me about morals?"

"Damned if I know what you're talking about now." He reached out, caught her shoulder, looked down at her.

"Damned if you don't! I'm talking about your wife, you philanderer!"

He had been about to pull her to him, kiss her. Now he paused. "What?"

She turned her face away as if she had read his mind. "Oh, don't act so innocent. I know about Melanie."

What had he revealed that night when he was drunk? He shrugged. What difference did it make if he had bared his soul to this girl? She owned it anyway.

"Dark angel," he whispered, "we've got a lot to talk about, but first I want you to know I'm a widower. Maybe that's the reason I was more than a little drunk that night. Melanie was killed on our wedding night before I ever even made love to her for the first time."

The face looking up at him softened. "Oh. You must have loved her very much."

He turned away, slammed his fist against a tree. "No. And that's the damned shame of it! I didn't love her at all."

"Then why — ?"

"You'd be amazed why people marry," he answered bitterly, "and maybe love is at the end of most lists."

She dropped the earring into her pocket, came over, put one hand on his arm. "It shouldn't be."

"You're such an innocent." He smiled at her, but without mirth. "Maybe that's what attracted me to you. You see things so simply. You'd do anything for love, wouldn't you?"

"Anything." She emphasized the word and didn't take her hand from his arm. He could feel the heat of it through his coat.

He wanted to ask a thousand questions such as why a girl from Texas was in Philadelphia, why she had run from him. But for now, it was enough that she was here, standing close enough so he could reach out for her.

Very gently, he slipped an arm around her shoulders, ran the other one through her short dark curls. "What the devil did you do to your hair?"

She laughed self-consciously. "I needed money. Rose is wearing it."

"What?"

"I sold my hair to a shop that makes ladies wigs."

He threw back his head and laughed. "No wonder that tart looked so attractive to me! If you needed help, why didn't you get in touch with me?"

"Because you were part of the reason I was on the run."

He waited for her to tell him more, but she hesitated, stopped. There was something she wasn't telling. . . .

She reached up to brush her hair out of her eyes. "I suppose I look a fright."

"Not to me," he whispered, and he bent his head and kissed her very gently.

"Oh, Quint!" She clung to him, sobs shaking her. "It's been so scary, all alone as I was! My valise was stolen, and I was so desperate!"

He held her close against the shelter of his big chest. "Hush, angel. Everything's fine now, I'm here."

She must have had some close calls in the last several weeks, he thought. It upset him just to wonder what she had had to endure alone.

"I-I thought I was so independent, that I could take care of myself." She wept.

Her tears fell, hot and damp, onto his jacket. "You didn't do too bad a job," he said. "Although it's going to be hard for historians to believe the first Pony Express rider out of St. Joe was a girl."

Dallas wiped her eyes and looked up at him, an impish smile curving her lips. "Maybe they'll never find out."

"Maybe."

He kissed her then, long and lingeringly. Her arms went

up around his neck, and she pressed herself against him. He had never felt such a burning desire for a woman.

They clung together, each feeling the other's heart beat, tasting the sweetness of the other's mouth. Somewhere on the other side of the small lake, a frog croaked rhythmically, and music and laughter from the dance floated in the air.

She pulled back. "We ought to go in. They'll wonder what happened to us."

"Let them." And he pulled her to him again, swung her up into his arms, carried her over into the shadows under a tall cottonwood tree near the water.

He reached out, slowly unbuttoned her shirt. "What is this underneath?" Then he realized and chuckled. "You could have gotten into serious trouble out here in the West, running around without a man to protect you."

"Why do you think I dressed as a boy?"

He lay down next to her, slowly undressed her. Fireflies hovered in the blackness like Indian ghost lights. "I'm going to make love to you just as I've dreamed of doing a million times since I let you slip away from me, angel."

"And as I've dreamed of." She unbuttoned his shirt, ran her hands over the mat of hair on his massive chest.

At last I'm in his arms as I dreamed of being so many times. Dallas kissed his nipples, not able to get enough of him, of the taste and the scent and the feel of him.

"You keep that up, this won't last long."

"I don't care." She stroked the hair on his wide chest, feeling him hard and throbbing against her.

His lips covered hers, kissed at the corners, then he probed deep with his tongue. Releasing her mouth, he sucked at her earlobe, ran the tip of his tongue, hot and wet, into her ear.

She shuddered at the sensation he was provoking as his mouth moved down the column of her neck, found her small, firm breasts.

"Ahhh!" She couldn't stop herself from arching up against his hot mouth, putting her hands on the back of his head to draw his face closer still against her nipples.

As she writhed under him, his mouth became more demanding, sucking her breasts into firm, pink tips. Then his mouth moved down to touch her navel.

She felt the dew of wanting between her thighs, and his hand came down, stroking there while she shivered at his touch.

She reached out, grasped his maleness. It was hammer-hard and throbbing in her grasp.

He pulled away from her, moved to spread her thighs. "I'm going to do something to you I've never done to a woman before," he whispered. "Never wanted to." His lips kissed and caressed her thighs while she trembled. Then he put one hand on each and began to spread them.

"Quint, you aren't going to—"

Before she could say more, he bent his head and kissed her there.

She started to protest, but the feel of his hot mouth—probing, teasing with the blade of his tongue—was an overpowering sensation. It felt too good. With a sigh of surrender, she let her thighs part so that he could do whatever he wanted to her body.

Such a caress would never have even occurred to Dallas, but as the tip of his tongue ran up and down the velvet ridge, chills and shudders of pleasure ran through her.

Then his tongue plunged deep within her as he turned and lay so she could kiss his maleness.

Until that moment, the idea would have shocked and horrified her, but this was Quint and she loved him so. . . .

She felt him surging between her lips even as his tongue caressed and stroked her velvet place. She relaxed her lips and threw her head back in complete surrender, letting him—no, encouraging him—to plunge deeper and deeper. His mouth was doing wonderful things to her, his tongue teasing and tantalizing. And then that crashing feeling began to build within her even as his manhood throbbed.

She locked her thighs around him, not wanting him to ever stop what he was doing to her even as she ran her tongue around the sheaf of his sword. He gasped and moaned as he gave up his seed with a shudder, and she reached a crescendo of feeling and then blacked out for a moment.

When Dallas finally became aware of objects and sounds again, he lay next to her, cradling her against his chest. "You little hussy, I never had a woman do that with such fire before!"

Her face burned. "I'm sorry, I didn't mean—"

"And I want you to do it again and again." He gently kissed his seed from her lips. "As innocent as an angel, but the ability to drive a man as wild as any high-priced whore can."

She wasn't sure what to say to that. They lay naked in each other's arms, and he stroked her back, ran his hands down to cup her small bottom. Time seemed suspended as they embraced.

"We'll be married," he said finally, "just as soon as I get back from capturing that horse."

"What horse?"

"There's a stallion that has become almost a legend in the Nevada area, I'm going looking for him."

She sat up, "And what am I supposed to do in the meantime?"

He grinned down at her. "Well, you sure can't go with me!"

"What about the Pony Express?"

"I think Barnes has bad news for you. He told me on the ride over that some bigwig's nephew wants the job and he's going to tell you that you're being placed on standby."

After all she'd been through? "You mean I'm fired?"

"Well, not exactly. You do have a choice. You can work at the Western end of the run where there's more danger. So, of course, you'll quit." He reached for his shirt, began to dress without looking at her.

"Will I?" Had he arranged this? But he hadn't known who she was until now.

He looked at her. "You're not upset, are you, Dallas? I assumed you'd quit and go back East until I get back from

Nevada."

"How about letting me make my own decisions?" She couldn't keep the slight edge from her voice. The thought of returning to the East depressed her, but obviously that was where he expected her to live.

"You could be the standby rider or go on out West, but that's out of the question."

"Is it?" Dallas wanted to be with him, but not back East. She had hated it there.

"Well"—Quint grinned as he dressed—"you could just hang around here and try to keep little Thelma out of your bunk. I think she's decided she wants to be Mrs. Dal Dawson."

"What a choice!" Dallas began to dress, still uncertain about her decision.

The dance must be breaking up, she thought. The music had stopped and people were drifting out of the building. Soon someone might come looking for them.

He draped an arm over her shoulders. "Maybe you ought to keep up that masquerade for the time being, it's safer for you."

She saw Hickok's tall form silhouetted in the light of the doorway. "Dal? Quint? Where are you two?"

Quint pulled away from Dallas, hurriedly lit a cigar. "Down here, Jim."

Hickok ambled toward them. "What are you two doing out there?"

Quint reached over, stuck the lit cigar in Dallas's hand, "Uh, just enjoying a smoke and skipping stones across the lake." He lit another cigar for himself.

Would Jim wonder what two men were doing down by the lake? Dallas stuck the cigar in her mouth, took a deep puff, and had to fight to keep from choking on the smoke.

Quint drew on his cigar, grinning as the big stock tender joined them. "There's nothing like a good cigar," he declared.

"You're right there, Quint." Hickok took the smoke

Quint offered, bit the end off, spit it out. When Quint lit it for him, Hickok took a deep puff. "Ahhh! By the way, Dal, Miss Thelma is looking for you. Said something about going for a stroll in the moonlight. I reckon she's set her cap for you."

Dallas choked, then took the cigar out of her mouth and pretended to study it. Should she reveal her true identity? Maybe Quint was right. It would save a lot of explaining if she kept up her masquerade.

"To be honest, Hickok, I understand I'm being transferred West. I won't be around to go traipsin' through the moonlight with Miss Thelma."

The startled look on Quint's face was a reward to Dallas.

"Yep," she said, feeling a little green, but too stubborn to throw the cigar away, "now that I've thought it over, I definitely am taking that assignment on the Western end of the run."

Quint said quickly, "Oh now, Dal boy, I think you should reconsider. After all, it is rough, dangerous country, what with that uneasy truce with the Paiutes."

He'd thought she'd submit weakly, go back East. *Horsefeathers!* She was going with him, whatever the danger.

"I've thought it over and I've made up my mind," she said as the three of them started walking toward the station. "Dangerous or not, Nevada, here I come!"

Chapter Thirteen

The two of them rode out at dawn the next morning, headed west, following the Pony Express trail which was the same route the telegraph lines were following now that they were under construction.

The lines were going up faster than expected, Quint had said. The Pony would be put out of business by the magic wire, probably in less than two years. But those next two years were of utmost importance because of the trouble between North and South.

Thaddeus Barnes had taken a different route, to check out a station that was having management problems. He'd been apologetic to Dal, but she, still in her boy's disguise, had assured him that riding at the Western end of the line was agreeable to her.

When they crossed the plains, she and Quint passed a herd of buffalo that looked like a brown, undulating sea as it moved slowly across the prairie.

Dallas threw her leg up across her saddle and sighed. "Beautiful, aren't they? As long as there're plenty of buffalo, the plains tribes like the Cheyenne will run wild and free."

He leaned on his saddle horn with both hands, shook his head. "Then I expect they'll soon be targeted to be wiped out. Farmers are already talking about how much wheat and corn could be raised out here if they could get water and fencing, and if they can do something about the millions of buffalo and the Indians."

She clucked to her horse, and they moved on. "I think,

Quint, that what I know and love will not last very long, maybe not even through my lifetime."

He smiled sadly. "If only we could make it last. If only—"

"Remember what I told you," she scolded gently, "about the two saddest words in any language?"

He nodded. "I'm trying to learn that, angel."

They rode on, enjoying the early spring weather. Quint had thought it wise for Dallas to continue her masquerade as a boy, although he'd told her he wasn't about to let her ride with the Express anymore. It was too dangerous. When they reached the station in Nevada to which she'd been assigned as standby, he wanted her to turn in her resignation.

It was in a tiny settlement in the Rockies that they found a preacher and decided to go ahead and get married.

"Dearest," she said, "later would you take the faith so our union could have the blessing of a priest?"

"Of course, angel." He kissed her forehead. "But this will have to do for now. I'm sorry you have to do without the fancy dress and the elaborate wedding."

She smiled up at him, loving him so very much. "All that matters is I'll finally be your wife in the eyes of God."

The elderly minister's wife rummaged around and found a dress, although it was a bit big for Dallas's slender frame, and she provided a lace scarf to cover the bride's close-cropped hair.

Quint picked a bouquet of wild flowers for Dallas, and then they stood in the tiny chapel before the plump preacher whose wife was playing a wheezy organ. The church handyman and the minister's dumpy sister were witnesses.

"Dearly beloved, we are gathered here today before God and these witnesses. . . ."

Dallas smiled up at Quint, her heart too full, her eyes overflowing.

"Do you, Quinton Randolph, take this woman, Dallas,

for richer or for poorer, in sickness and in health, 'til death do you part?

"And do you, Dallas Durango . . ."

She heard the words and yet she did not, for she was concentrating on the face of the man she loved more than life itself.

"By the power vested in me by God and the authorities, I now pronounce you man and wife. What God hath joined together, let no man put asunder!"

Quint kissed her then, crushing the bouquet between them while the old minister smiled gently and clasped his Bible against his broad belly. In the background, the two ladies sniffed noisily and even the handyman took out his bandana and blew his nose with a honk.

The minister's stout sister ran a picturesque little hotel and that was where they spent their wedding night, in a cozy Victorian room done up in red velvet and lace curtains.

It started to rain as the raw-boned hired girl set a supper table before the crackling fire in their room, gave them a knowing smile, and left.

Dallas picked up a crisp white napkin and sat down at the table. "Our own little world."

Quint stared at her gravely across the damask tablecloth. "*You* are my world, angel. I'm sorry you had to settle for this instead of a fancy wedding and a honeymoon in a grand hotel."

She shook her head, reveling in the sound of rain on the roof, the growing twilight, the crackle of the fire, and most of all the nearness of the man across from her. "Horsefeathers. It couldn't get any better than this."

"Oh, it can." He winked at her, his eyes promising more.

Her pulse quickened and she blushed in spite of herself. "Doesn't the food look good?"

"If you say so." But his adoring gaze never left her face.

Dallas turned her attention to the crisp, fried quail, the hot rolls dripping with butter. They ate with gusto, then finished off the meal with steaming coffee in delicate cups

187

and crusty wild-plum cobbler.

Their dinner eaten, Quint moved to a big wing chair before the fireplace, and Dallas poured each of them a glass of homemade blackberry wine before curling up in his lap.

She held up her glass, watching the reflections of their faces and of the firelight in the crystal. "To the future."

"To the future." He agreed and they sipped the wine. Then he bent and kissed the top of her head. "Oh, angel, I love you so!"

"And I love you, dearest, so very, very much!" She savored her wine, put her head against his wide chest so she could hear his heart beat, and stared into the flames. Whatever the future might hold, they had tonight. No one could ever take that away from her.

They set their glasses to one side, and Quint lit his pipe. With a sigh, Dallas closed her eyes and breathed in the scents of tobacco and of wood burning. "I could sit here all night."

His big hands held her close. "All night?" he teased, "What about that big feather bed with piles of pillows on it?"

She turned in his lap to look at the old-fashioned four-poster. "Well maybe not all night," she admitted, snuggling deeper into his embrace. "But I do wish I had a lace nightgown. Every bride should have a lace nightgown."

"Why?" Quint rumpled her hair playfully. "How long do you think you'd get to wear it?"

She kissed the underside of his jaw. "I'd be disappointed if it were very long."

And yet they sat for quite awhile, cuddling before the fire in the quaint, Victorian room until the flames died down to glowing coals. It almost seemed they had to hold on to every moment, make it last; pack a lifetime into this one night.

Finally Quint sighed and put down his pipe. "That feather bed looks better and better to me." He stood, swinging her up into his arms.

She looked at him in alarm. "You aren't going to sleep, are you?"

"Did I say that?" He grinned wickedly in the flickering

glow of the dying fire and the light from the oil lamp on the bedside table. Quint carried her over, pulled back the plush velvet spread with one hand, and laid her down. Then he sat on the edge of the bed and undressed while she watched him.

Something had been bothering her. "Did you really make love to Margo at the Naughty Lady that night?"

He lay down next to her, propped his head on one hand. "Of course not. All I could think of was that I must be losing my mind. I was in a bedroom with a desirable woman, but I couldn't get the boy in the next room out of my mind."

She watched his hands as he slowly undressed her. "More desirable than me?" she asked in a small voice.

He had her clothes off now, and his gaze seemed to caress her bare body. "Good Lord, no, Dallas. No one is more desirable than you are."

She shivered in the cool night air. "I'm cold."

"I'm about to make you very warm, angel." Quint pulled her to him, almost covering her with his massive body.

She pressed her naked breasts against his hard chest, enjoying the sensation of brushing her nipples against the hairy fur on it. Then she settled her head into the hollow of his shoulder, sank into the soft feather bed.

They lay snuggled in the big four-poster, listening to the rhythmic patter of rain on the roof. His fingers caressed her bare skin, sending little shivers of delight through her. She felt her nipples swell and harden into small rosy peaks. Her back arched so that they were offered up to his warm mouth while his fingers tantalized and teased between her thighs.

Why had she ever thought he might be impotent? Even now she could feel him hard as steel, throbbing against her thigh. She thought of him plunging deep inside her and trembled all over.

He pulled her even closer, kissing the corners of her mouth. "Are you still cold, angel?"

"No."

He raised up on one elbow and looked down at her in the dim light. "You aren't afraid of me?"

"I'm only afraid I might wake up and find out that I'm not really your wife, dearest." She reached out and pulled him down on her, slowly flicked her tongue along his lips.

"This is forever, Dallas," he promised. "Like the words said, ' 'til death do us part.' "

"Please, Quint, take me — take me now. . . ."

He spread her thighs and came into her, holding onto her slim waist so he could plunge deeper, and her body began to convulse, wanting to hold him within it. A heat began to rise in her, almost like a fever. Faintly, she remembered the sound of the rain, the crackle of the fire, and the feel of the hair on his chest brushing her swollen nipples. Then he moaned and stiffened. Her body responded to his spurting seed, grasping him, holding onto him. Even as she faded into the blackness of rising desire, she thought what a glorious night was before them. She was, finally and eternally, Mrs. Quinton Randolph.

The next morning they were on their way again. Usually they stayed at Pony Express relay stations as they headed west, so Quint could inspect the mustangs in use as mounts in that part of the country. At the stations Dallas maintained her disguise as a boy. It wasn't really all that hard. Most of the men slept in their clothes anyway, and bath water was so hard to come by, there wasn't any mass bathing. When they did find enough water, the two of them swam. And at night, out under the stars, they camped and made love. Dallas began to wish the trip would last forever, but Quint was relentless about moving on. He'd set his heart on capturing that stallion in the Sierra Nevada mountains.

They had stopped at a relay station called Red Buttes, on the western side of the Rockies, and had just sat down for a meal of "Sonuvagun" stew when a stable boy cried out, "Here's comes the Pony!"

Chairs overturned as those who'd come in by stage rushed out to see the never-to-be-forgotten sight. Dallas and Quint rushed outside, too.

The relief rider stood with a saddled mustang, waiting for the incoming rider to hand off the *mochila*.

A dude stood on tiptoe, craned his neck toward the distant horizon. "I don't see anything."

"Listen!" Dallas admonished. "You'll hear him, before you see him."

All held their breath. In the vast silence of the prairie, there was no sound save a cricket and the soft fluttering of the breeze. Then the rhythmic sound of a running horse drifted to them faintly, grew louder.

The grizzled station manager pulled out his big watch, nodded with satisfaction. "Sounds like Will is right on time! They did away with the bugle they used to carry, after it dawned on everyone that in the silence we could hear the pony's hooves pounding long before we could see it coming."

Dallas watched the empty horizon. Away in the distance, a black speck came into view. "Here he comes!"

Even though she had ridden the line herself, it was thrilling to see the rider galloping toward them. To think that such a gallant undertaking as keeping the two halves of the continent in touch depended on less than a hundred boys, some of them barely old enough to shave, galloping through some of the most desolate and hostile countryside in the world. It was enough to bring tears to her eyes.

The rider galloped even closer, a slight boy hunched low over his bay's neck.

The station manager grunted in satisfaction. "Get ready, rider. He'll be here in just a couple more minutes. You checked your saddle girth?"

The boy nodded and all eyes turned back toward the lathered, blowing horse galloping toward them across the desolate landscape.

Dallas said aloud, "It's such a moving sight! I think if you've ever seen a Pony rider, you'll never forget it!"

"You're right, boy," the manager said. "I get a little thrill of patriotism every time a rider gallops in."

The rider raced closer, hunched low over the saddle. He

rode into the station yard, reined in sharply in a cloud of dust.

Why, he really is very young, Dallas thought. He couldn't be more than fifteen years old.

The handsome boy slid from the exhausted horse, yanked the leather *mochila* from his saddle, threw it to the new rider waiting in the station yard with the fresh horse.

As they watched, the second rider tossed the mail pouch up onto his saddle, and his wiry little gray mustang took off at a gallop even as he stepped into the stirrup.

"The mail must go through!" he called out, and the Pony's slogan echoed back at them.

The little group stood staring after him until he was lost to sight, but the rhythmic sound of hooves still sounded in the air.

The dude turned back toward the building. "He wasn't carrying a rifle. I thought they was all supposed to be heavily armed."

The handsome newcomer handed the reins of his lathered horse to a stable boy, and the crowd turned back toward the station building. "New order out the last couple of days. A rifle's heavy and we wouldn't have much chance to use it anyways. We're better off tryin' to outrun Injuns if they come after us."

He looked at Dallas as they all trooped back in. "What route do you ride?"

"I've been transferred," Dallas said as they all sat down to eat in the dim lamplight. "I'll be a relief rider in Nevada. I'm Dal Dawson. This is Quint Randolph."

The boy offered his hand, shook with Dallas and Quint. "Glad to make your acquaintance. I'm Will Cody."

Quint looked him over critically as they shoveled in the rich stew made from odds and ends of leftover meat. "Son, you don't look old enough to hold a job like this."

The boy's eyes twinkled. "I'm old enough, mister. Every one of the riders is young."

Not as young as you are, Dallas thought, but she went on eating. "How'd you start, Will? You answer an ad like I did?"

"No, I was already working for Majors in his freighting business." The boy dug into his stew with his spoon. "My pa died in a knife fight three years ago, and I'm the sole support of my mama and sisters."

Quint looked at him a long moment. "Big responsibility for one so young."

The boy shoveled food into his mouth. "I aim to be rich and famous before I'm done, and the West seems to be the only place a man can still start with nothin' and make a name for himself. Already, everybody's talking about 'Pony Bob' Haslam. He's becoming famous on the west end of the run."

"I'll bet you'll become famous, too, Will," Dallas declared as she reached for another crusty piece of corn bread.

Quint pushed back his tin plate, ran his hand through his chestnut hair. "So, Cody, you know the country west of here. You ever heard of the Medicine Hat stallion?"

The station manager belched. "Who hasn't? I think he's just a fairy tale, an old Indian legend."

Will Cody looked around the table at everyone. "I not only heard of him, mister, I've seen him!"

Immediately, talk ceased and all eyes turned toward the boy. Even Dallas felt her heart skip a beat. It was almost like hearing that Pegasus, the flying horse, or the unicorn were realities.

Quint leaned closer. "Tell us what you know."

"Well . . ." The boy tipped his chair back on two legs, obviously enjoying being the center of attention.

Whatever he ends up doing, Dallas thought, watching young Will, he wants to be the star.

"It was late afternoon, almost sunset," the young rider said, and everyone leaned closer. "He's big, maybe sixteen, seventeen hands high."

A murmur of appreciation went through the little group. Horsemen measure a horse by the width of a hand from the ground up to the withers where its powerful neck starts. Sixteen hands or more is a big horse.

Quint nodded. "Sounds like just the stud I need for my own herd."

The boy frowned. "You ain't planning on trying to catch him, are you?"

"I sure am!" Quint blew smoke toward the cabin ceiling. "That's why I've come all the way out here."

"The Injuns in that region been chasin' him for years without puttin' a bridle on him, and so has every rancher in the mountains. You may never see the Medicine Hat and his herd of mares, but if you do, you darn sure won't get close enough to get a rope on him!"

"I'll take that bet!" Quint said, his hazel eyes bright with excitement.

Dallas felt uneasy. From a Cheyenne mother, she had heard of medicine horses. Maybe this animal was meant to be left running wild and free. "Tell us more," she urged Cody.

The boy raised his voice dramatically. "The Injuns call him Sky Climber because he has this habit of watching you from a high ridge with the moon all big and gold behind him. When you see that black and white pinto silhouetted that way, with his long mane and tail blowing out behind him, you really do wonder if he's a real horse or a ghost legend like the Injuns say he is."

Quint snorted. "He's just a stallion like any other. Nobody's been smart enough to get a rope on him, that's all."

"Maybe," Will brought his chair down on all fours with a bang. "But, mister, if you ever see him rearing up and neighing a challenge at you, those front feet pawing the sky like he's about to climb the horizon, run through the clouds, and disappear behind a rainbow, you'll feel a chill go down your back and you'll wonder in your own self if he ain't magic."

There was silence as the boy's words painted a picture of the great horse rearing and pawing the sky before he took off at a gallop.

Dallas gasped. Will Cody had a talent for drama that easily could make him the center of attention wherever he went. There were bound to be bigger things ahead for this young Pony Express rider.

Quint looked thoughtfully at the boy. "Indians in that area friendly?"

"The Washoe are the saddest, most defeated bunch you'll ever meet," Cody said. "They're almost what we call 'digger' Injuns, just barely surviving at the edge of white areas on whatever they can beg or scrap for. I hear this past winter was bad for both them and the Paiutes, lots of them just flat starved to death."

"Serves 'em right," the station manager grunted. "I been warned that if the Express has any trouble, it's gonna come from that young war chief, Timbi, and his clan."

Dallas knew little about the Indians of the Great Basin although she was half-Cheyenne herself. "Timbi's a Washoe?"

"Not hardly!" Cody said, "He's Paiute. They're a proud, fierce bunch, relatives of the Bannock and Shoshoni. They defeated the Washoe in battle some years back and won't even allow that pitiful bunch to own or ride a horse. The Washoe got to walk."

Quint frowned. "This Timbi sounds like he'd be a real problem if he ever takes to the war path."

He glanced over at Dallas, and she had a sudden feeling he was thinking of sending her back to safety. *Horsefeathers.* She was going with him. If he was going to Nevada, so was she. After all, she was safe enough in her disguise.

"He ain't a problem yet," Cody shook his head. "But that's only because Winnemucca, the main chief, and old Chief Truckee, have tried to keep the peace. Those miners up in the Virginia City area are trespassin' onto Indian lands, doing all sorts of things to make the Injuns mad."

Quint looked over at her, and she gave him just the slightest shake of her head. If he thought he was sending her back, he was in for a surprise. Besides, it sounded as if the Paiutes were still peaceful.

Later, in private, Dallas and Quint had quite an argument that left things between them strained. But she was determined not to sit around and wait for a stage to come through headed east. If Quint tried to leave without her, she would follow him.

Seeing as how he couldn't change her mind, they started out again the next morning headed west.

Quint glared at her as they rode. "I believe you are the most damned stubborn girl I ever met in my life!" He ran one hand through his hair distractedly, the gold ring reflecting the light. When he looked at her, it seemed there was some question he wanted to ask but dared not.

Dallas puzzled over it, decided not to mention it. If he wanted to ask why she'd been in Philadelphia or why she'd run away and joined the Pony riders, he finally would. She wasn't about to tell him about her abrupt departure from the elegant boarding school because she wasn't yet sure just what he would think about it.

It had been a humiliating experience, that final, miserable day at Miss Priddy's Academy. She would never forget sitting in class on that last day of February.

"Girls," portly Miss Priddy said as she swept into the room in her severe gray dress, "today we are all fortunate to have a former graduate of this school, and a prominent member of society, Mrs. Albert Huntington III, visiting us."

While politely applauding all the girls had sneaked looks at plump Maude Peabody who'd tried not to look too pleased. Gossip had flown through the school, a rumor that the social leader was actually in town to arrange a match for her brother and Maude.

Mrs. Huntington stood before the class, looking elegantly grim in her black dress as she glanced around the room. Her gaze stopped on Dallas. "Well, standards have certainly been lowered since I went to school here! This used to be a place where young ladies were taught manners! The next thing I know, the Academy will be accepting darkies!"

Maude looked over at Dallas sympathetically as if not quite sure what to do. Some of the other girls who were jealous of Dallas's looks tittered with delight.

But no one could humble Dallas. She glared right back at the elegant Mrs. Huntington. "Down in Texas, we judge ladies on their good manners. Obviously, you don't qualify!"

The snooty woman's cheeks mottled with suppressed rage while the class hid smirks and Miss Priddy wrung her hands. "C-class dismissed!" the upset woman finally said.

Dallas made her decision right then. The snobbish socialite would be staying with the Peabodys a few days while a possible engagement was discussed. Dallas decided she couldn't bear one more hour of associating with the woman. This was the final climax of her whole terrible time in the north. That night, she took what little money she had in her purse, packed one small bag, and caught the first train leaving Boston, which just happened to be going to Philadelphia.

She and Quint rode on west. Late that afternoon, the temperature rose, making the sun feel hot on her skin. She was relieved when they came to a spring that was a watering place for deer. A few of those gentle creatures started and sprang away as the riders approached.

"At last! I feel just filthy!" She dismounted and watered her horse, then began to undress. There was rich mud on her side of the spring. It oozed up, warm and comfortable, between her toes as she pulled off her boots, waded in.

Quint chuckled as he unsaddled the horses and hobbled them so they could graze on the grass under the pines. "You look like some water sprite out there swimming around."

She rested her knees on the bottom of the tiny pool and turned, arching her body so that her small breasts jutted out proudly.

He gave her a long, smoldering look, and began to unbutton his shirt, never taking his eyes off her breasts.

"Come on in." She smiled very slowly at him, cupping her breasts with her hands offering them to him.

"I will." His eyes never left her as he unbuckled his pants, stepped out of them. His maleness stood out, hard and throbbing, as he stepped into the water.

She laughed coquettishly, then dived beneath the surface like a mermaid and came up almost under him as he stood where the pool was waist-deep.

Away from the spring, the water was warm from the sun; warm as a lover's mouth on her body. She came to him and he reached for her, but she laughed again and swam away. "You'll have to catch me."

"You teasing little hussy!" He grinned at the challenge. "Why did I ever think of you as an angel?"

She was caught off guard by his talk and while she paused, looking back at him, he dived suddenly and caught one of her slim ankles, upsetting her in the water.

She came up, dripping and coughing, in the circle of his arms. "That was an underhanded, ornery thing to do!"

"Was it?" He knelt in the shallows, pulling her to her knees.

The water felt very warm there, pulling at her body, washing between her thighs. The sun reflected off it, and she thought it was fascinating how the hair on his chest seemed to float on the surface between them. She could feel his maleness against her belly as the current moved.

Dallas looked up at him, drops of water dripping from her hair, her breasts wet and slippery as he pulled her against him.

"Oh, angel . . ." He kissed the drops from her face, then stood up suddenly, holding her against his hot, throbbing maleness as they clung together.

Without a word, he carried her over to the warm mud of the shore, set her down.

"Not yet." She shook her head. "I don't want it to end too soon. Make it last."

The mud didn't seem dirty, it was warm and soothing and soft on her wet skin. After all, she could always wash it off.

He reached out, picked up a handful of the warm wet earth, and spread it on her bare belly. "You ever make mud pies, Mrs. Randolph?"

She giggled at the memory. "In my best dress, just before a party. Mama was upset. I reckon the reason kids like to play in the mud so much is because it's always forbidden to them."

The mud was soothing, or maybe it was only his touch as he spread it in ever-widening circles on her flat belly. She closed her eyes, relaxing with a sigh, enjoying the feel of his big hand putting more mud on her breasts, stroking there. She felt her nipples go turgid with desire as he ran his hands over her skin. "I hadn't realized playing in the mud could be so much fun."

He didn't answer, but his hands moved up her breasts to her neck, then started down to her thighs.

She took a sharp breath, suddenly wanting him very much. "Now," she said. "Now!"

But he smiled smugly and lay down in the mud beside her, clasping his hands under his head. "You said make it last, remember?"

She sat up, the mud still slick on her body as she rolled over on top of him. "It's lasted long enough."

She straddled him, looking down at him, awaiting his next move, but he only smiled up at her.

Damn him, he was teasing her! She reached over, got a handful of mud, rubbed it into the hair of his chest. His maleness come up hard against her hips, and he pulled her down so that her breasts rubbed against him. The warm mud felt silky and erotic between their two bodies.

"Let's wash it off," he whispered, and she moved off him. Together, they swam out into the water, then his hands reached out to wash the mud from her. She hadn't realized how callused and hard a man's palms were, the excitement their touch created as he deliberately brought his big hands down across the tips of her sensitive nipples.

She clung to him and he held her tightly against him in the water, his mouth forcing hers open so his tongue could probe the inner recesses of hers.

"Now, you," he ordered, and hesitantly she slipped her tongue between his lips, let him suck it deeper still.

He held her so hard against him, she could feel the hard planes of his hips while his hands cupped her bottom. "Ready?"

"Do you have to ask?" She shuddered from the feeling that swept over her as he held her tightly against the wet hair of his powerful chest.

With a low moan, he swept her up into his arms, carried her through the water to the shore.

She saw urgent, intense passion on his face; knew she couldn't stop him from taking her now if she wanted to. Dallas spread her thighs wide as he fell on her, took her hard and deep.

Three hard strokes seemed to plunge deep into her very being, and she opened her thighs still wider as if offering up the flower of her womanhood on some primitive altar in a ceremony of mating.

Three hard strokes followed, with all the power a virile male could put behind them, and then she heard him gasp and hold his breath as he exploded inside her, sending his hot seed spewing deep into her belly. She seemed to feel it leave him as she meshed with him, their bodies straining hotly against each other. And then her body responded, wanting what his body had to give.

She felt her insides convulse as if to grasp him, squeeze every vital drop from him. Then the black waves began sweeping over her, and if the world had ended in that moment, she wouldn't have known or cared.

When Dallas finally became conscious of things around her again, Quint held her tenderly. He was kissing her eyes. "Oh, we'll have such a good life! I'll build you an elegant mansion, near my sister's house. She lives in the most fashionable district of Philadelphia, you'll like it."

Philadelphia? She felt depressed. Somehow, she hadn't thought he'd want to live in a big city, but then, that was where he'd been when she'd met him. Why should she be surprised?

"Of course," she said, and tried to smile and look enthused. She got up and washed off in the spring while she thought about it. "I didn't know you had a sister in Philadelphia."

"Yes." His expression betrayed nothing as he got up, washed off, started dressing. "She's very social. If you're going to be anyone in that city, you have to have Lydia as a friend. Anyone will tell you Mrs. Albert Huntington III is a force to be reckoned with."

Dallas stopped, looked at him. But he didn't notice her staring. He went on putting on his boots.

Oh, God, it couldn't be! But how many women could there be with a name like that? Still she didn't want to believe it.

"Is . . . is your sister an alumni of Miss Priddy's Female Academy in Boston?"

He laughed, reached for his boots. "Miss Priddy's must be well known if a girl from Texas has heard of it. Funny you should mention that. She was back up there just a few weeks ago to visit her old school, came back all enthused about marrying me off to Maude Peabody. You'd have to have met Maude to know what I'm talking about."

Dallas almost said she had, but managed to stop herself. She stood there, while her whole world lurched and then crumbled. She had married Quint, and now he'd expect her to live near his cold, arrogant sister who had treated her so cruelly.

"What's the matter, Angel? Go ahead and get dressed. I'll shoot a couple of fat rabbits while you get a little fire going so we can eat."

Numbly, she did as she was told. She considered telling Quint the whole story, then decided against it. Even if he sympathized with her, that wouldn't change the fact that she had married into a family that would despise her and would try to break up her marriage. The Philadelphia socialite would be an impossible sister-in-law.

Why had she ever thought two people from such diverse backgrounds could make a go of a marriage?

Long after they had curled up in their blankets that night, Dallas stared into the red coals of the dying fire. She heard his gentle breathing, felt the heat of the arm thrown across her. In their case, love might not be enough. His family

201

would try to destroy the marriage. If they could live far away from them, it might work, but Quint wanted to build a mansion near his sister's. Dallas didn't think she could ever live in town, she hungered to get back to ranch life.

She lay a long time, thinking. She finally decided to continue on to Nevada with him, acting as if nothing were wrong. From there, it was only a short distance across the mountains to California. In her disguise, maybe she could sign on as cabin boy and sail around the Horn or even catch the Butterfield stage back to Texas.

No, she had no money for stage fare. And her parents didn't want her back. Well at least she could write them again from California, see if Papa's anger had softened. If not, she might just lose herself there and find a job. She hadn't been married by a priest, so maybe the marriage could be annulled . . . except in her own heart. Deep in her soul, she would always be Mrs. Quint Randolph, no matter what happened. *Hadn't the preacher said ' 'til death do you part'?* What should she do?

Quint commented on how quiet she was as they rode into Nevada. Absorbed by the struggle in her own heart, Dallas said little.

It was late afternoon several days later when they finally rode into the isolated trading post known as Williams' station.

They dismounted and Quint led the horses over to the barn while Dallas stopped to wash the dust off her face at the well.

A tall, light-haired man came out of the station. Dallas barely glanced at him until he spoke in a thick Mississippi drawl. "Hello, boy. What's the news from farther up the line?"

She thought for a moment she had imagined she recognized the voice. But as she slowly raised her head and looked into the handsome face, saw the cruel mouth, she knew there was no mistake. It was Yancy.

Chapter Fourteen

Atsa peered over the rocky ledge and watched the white people at the adobe building below. She often sneaked off from the Paiute camp to spy on the whites and satisfy her curiosity, although it was a long way to walk over rocky trails. Her brother, Timbi, would not approve of her being here, so no one knew she did this but her best friend.

At the age of sixteen, Atsa knew she should be making plans to attract a young man to marry, but in the deepest part of her, she hungered to be a white man's bride. Someday she would get up the nerve to go to the station and offer herself, but for now, she was content to spy on those who came and went and to wonder about their ways.

She shifted her position, shaking back her coarse black hair, and watched a tall man and a boy with short black hair dismount in front of the station. The man's lighter hair gleamed in the midmorning sun as he led the two horses away to the barn and the boy went over to wash his face. As she watched, a man came out of the building. He was about the same size and height as the other one. He seemed to carry on a conversation with the boy. Then the first man joined them and they all went inside.

Frowning, Atsa scrambled around on the rocks, but she couldn't see inside the building. She considered creeping down to look in the windows, but was much too shy to do that. What would she do if they saw her? The Paiutes were not at war with the whites; still, her brother said it was only a matter of time. But then Timbi hated the whites, and with good reason.

She lay there a while longer, hoping the black-haired boy would come out again. He looked young and handsome. Would he be interested in marrying a Paiute girl, taking her away to the white man's town?

The early spring sun beat down on Atsa, but she did not leave. She hoped something interesting would happen, rewarding her for her patience. In the past, she had seen the boys with the mysterious leather packets gallop by. Sometimes they stopped a minute before dashing away. What could they be carrying that was causing all the speed and excitement?

At another time, she had seen a box on wheels, with white women in beautiful dresses inside it, stop at the adobe building. She'd looked down at her own antelope-skin shift with a frown. By Paiute standards, she was well dressed, thanks to her brother's hunting skill. Most Paiute women wore only a skirt woven of reeds or sagebrush bark, topped off with a rabbit-fur cloak in cold weather.

She watched and waited in vain. Finally, she decided she'd better return to camp. At least she had seen something interesting to tell her friend, Moponi, about. Moponi was as small as her namesake, the mosquito. Being newly married, she was busy with women's tasks, but her eyes always brightened at hearing Atsa's stories. Someday Atsa would convince her friend to come along and see these interesting sights for herself.

Forlornly, Atsa brushed a fly from her face and started back toward the camp. What she dreamed of was a white husband who would buy her a carriage and a closet full of real dresses in her favorite color, red. In fact, her name meant "red" in her language. She kicked at a lizard with her beaded scarlet moccasins, and it scurried away. Red moccasins were supposed to protect one from rattlesnakes.

The sun was directly overhead before she got back to camp. Her older brother, Timbi, sat before their *karnee,* repairing a bow. "Where have you been?"

"Out picking berries," she lied, pointing vaguely off toward the hills. She thought her brother was fierce looking when he scowled, though all the girls thought him handsome.

"Your friend's husband tells me you sneak down to spy on the whites."

"Moponi should not share my secrets with her husband," Atsa snapped. "She promised not to tell."

Timbi glared at her. "Moponi is a good friend and she worries about you. You should be doing what she has done. Learn the womanly tasks and look again at those young men who try to catch your eye."

"Just because you are old, do not tell me what to do!" Atsa flung the taunt at him recklessly. But he was old, maybe ten winter counts older than she.

He laid down his bow, stood up. He was big for a Paiute, and wide-shouldered. His name meant "the rock," and it suited him. "Remember your place, little sister. Not many would speak thus to a chieftain."

She was at once contrite, for she knew he felt great love for her. She had always been spoiled and pampered. "Forgive me, Timbi. I know you are only cross because you care about me."

It was not seemly for him to show much affection to a young sister, so he sat down before the fire, cross-legged, and began work on the bow. "Atsa, we have only each other after what happened last fall. . . ." He hesitated, didn't continue.

"I know. I do wrong to worry you." She sat across from him and poked the fire so that she could start a meal. For a while after the great tragedy, her brother had been so morose over the loss, she had wondered if he would throw himself over a cliff. "You should take another wife. There are many girls who look at you and wait, hoping you will notice them."

"I can only love one way, with my whole heart, and I will not marry again, although I might take a captive to warm my blankets."

"A Washoe?"

"Would a Paiute stoop to that?" Timbi sneered. "Washoe are white man's Indians. They hang around his mining

205

towns, dig through his garbage for food. I wouldn't want one of the Pit River tribe."

She reached for a waterproofed basket full of their major food, ground piñon nuts, added water from a canteen. "Now that the cold is gone, our relatives, the Bannock and the Shoshoni are gathering to talk about the whites who invade our land; maybe they will bring along a captive."

"Maybe." He shrugged as if the subject were of little interest to him. "If she can cook and give me sons, that's all I need."

Atsa lifted hot rocks from the fire, dropped them into the basket that had been waterproofed with pine pitch. The heat would gradually cook the pine-nut soup. Some in the tribe had traded for iron pots at the Williams brothers' post, back before all the tension had started over the poison water. But her brother was proud and vowed to live by the old ways. He would not even carry a white man's rifle, relying instead on bow, lance, and knife.

Timbi accepted the small bit of food and the dried *cui-ui* fish without comment. Finally, his curiosity seemed to get the better of him. "What do you see when you spy on the whites? Are there soldiers?"

He must have caught her expression, for he added quickly, "It is a chieftain's business to know such things so we can be prepared for attack."

"Once in a while, a soldier passes by, but seldom. A few of the wagons with fabric over the top come through, headed on across the mountains. Most who stop are miners. You can tell because they have tools and donkeys to carry them."

He directed a Paiute curse at the miners, his eyes moody and angry. Atsa regretted that she had mentioned them.

"Something else," she said, hoping to distract him from his dark mood. "Sometimes I see a young boy gallop in, and then gallop away again."

He looked at her, his straight, black hair hanging loose almost to his wide shoulders. "Other warriors speak of these boys." He nodded gravely, went on eating. "All wonder what magic thing is in the pouch that they always take with them when they get a fresh horse?"

"White man's magic." She shrugged, and ate her food with pleasure. Last winter had been one of the coldest in memory. Not only Indians had starved. Word had come that many of the white miners, those who dug in the hills for the gray metal they called silver, had also gone hungry and frozen to death.

Timbi set aside his bowl. "Little sister, I forbid you to go spy on the whites again. They have no respect for Indian women. They will use you for their pleasure if they get a chance, and then no warrior would want to take you for a wife."

She wiggled the toe of one red moccasin in the dust, and avoided his stern gaze. If he knew that she aspired to marry a white man, live in a house instead of a *karnee* made of willow branches covered with dried cattails, he would be angry with her.

She thought of the young boy with the short, black curls she had seen for the first time that afternoon when he'd ridden into the station. He was handsome and slender, but the older one with the chestnut hair was more likely to have the yellow and gray rocks that could be traded for red cloth and ribbons.

Timbi sighed and stood up. "I'm getting a late start, but perhaps I will get a chance at the great stallion when he comes to the pool just before sundown."

"You are going looking for the Medicine Hat *again?*" She emphasized the word, annoyed that her brother was so obsessed with capturing and taming the legendary wild mustang.

"He is a fitting mount for a chieftain who may yet be leading his warriors against the whites."

"Old Winnemucca is still chief and he is for peace. He even sends his daughters off to the white man's school."

Timbi gathered up his things before answering. "Winnemucca is very old and very trusting. Now that our relatives, the Bannock and the Shoshoni, are gathering to council, I think the vote will be to fight!"

"How long will you be gone? You should take Moponi's husband with you."

Timbi shrugged. "I'll be fine. Have I not been raised in

these deserts and mountains? Besides, the new husband is still too lovesick to leave her for even a day or two. You stay with them."

Atsa nodded. She would tell Moponi of all she had seen from the rock ledge. Sooner or later, she wanted to go inside that adobe building and look at the trade goods. She was a little hesitant to go alone, and she hoped her friend would go with her. "Many things can happen to a man alone in the hills."

"Everyone is busy, and I can't risk one of the other braves capturing Sky Climber when I want him so badly. Besides, if something happened to me, my roan would return to camp and you could backtrack him. I'll be home when I capture the Medicine Hat."

"*If* you capture him," Atsa pointedly reminded him.

He sighed as if in great annoyance, put his hand up to shade his smoldering dark eyes. "Five is the magic number of our people; I had a vision that the number would bring me good medicine soon. Maybe it means that in five days' time, I will be back with the horse. The other vision I didn't understand at all. . . ."

His voice trailed off, and he looked troubled. "Little sister, do not worry about me. I intend to bring Sky Climber back this time, to break and ride to the council when the tribes gather."

Reluctantly, she followed him out to where he mounted the roan gelding from the small pony herd. He was all the kin she had left and she loved him. She handed him his rabbit-fur robe, a canteen, food, and a lariat to tie on his saddle. "Timbi, some of the old ones say the horse is magic, that he is not really a horse at all, but the spirit of the Paiute people."

He looked down at her from the roan and scoffed. "Sky Climber is a horse like any other. I will break him and keep him as I would any horse. The ones who frown on capturing him are the ones who have tried and failed. They don't want any warrior to tame him."

She watched him turn the roan. "Maybe," she said. "But some think he should be left to run wild and free forever, like the ghost of a great warrior."

He laughed and waved, nudged the gelding with his heels, and took off into the purple hills at a slow lope.

Timbi knew these mountains well. Many times as a boy he had roamed through them. That was before the white men had come and cut down the piñons to provide fuel for their fires or timbers to shore up the tunnels they dug in the ground like gophers while searching for the yellow and gray metal.

He swallowed hard at the memory that came unbidden to his lonely heart. How were innocent Indians to know the runoff from the streams the whites used to wash the metal contained poisons that polluted . . . and killed.

He would not think of that sad time now, he would block it from his mind and think only of how proud he would be to ride the great horse into the camp, how warriors would look at him with even more respect when they gathered to say the five prayers and pass the pipe five times around the circle. Even the old ones would listen gravely to his words if he had captured the magic horse.

His heart ached with pain as he thought of what he would say. War, he would shout, the whites have wiped out all my family save one young sister. I want to avenge the lives they took!

And even that would not be enough to ease the dull hate that never left him for very long. He had buried mother, father, and, most hurtful of all, his woman, her belly swollen with his unborn child who never drew a single breath. His wife had drunk the runoff from the creek and had died in agony with the others. Timbi had been the one to find them, all contorted and in anguish as they screamed and died.

The whites owed him life for life. His hatred was fed by the memory. Sooner or later, he would go to war and kill every white man he ran across. But it would not bring his family back to life.

The day was warm for so early in the season. The sun felt good on his bare brown shoulders as he remembered how many of the tribe and their horses had been lost in the cold weather. Even now, the gelding he rode was bone thin and without stamina.

Too soon, winter would be here again, and there would be even less piñon nuts and grass because of the whites who came like a light-colored wave, sweeping everything before them. Some of them took their big covered wagons and went on, crossing the mountains to get to that place they called California. But many—too many—stayed, and the fragile desert country could only support a few people, a few animals.

Timbi rode slowly, his gaze on the ground, seeking any clue that might set him on the great horse's trail. While he would never have admitted it to his little sister, there were times he, too, wondered if the big black and white stud was only a horse after all. After being outsmarted and outmaneuvered by it so many times, he could almost believe it was a spirit animal, returned to run the endless mountain trails forever with a band of real mustangs.

His eyes missed nothing as he rode; a bent blade of grass, a slight hoof impression in the dust. He realized with mounting excitement that he was on the trail of a small wild band, maybe Medicine Hat and his harem.

That made him think of the vision again and it troubled him. What did it mean? He considered carefully, shook his head. Maybe it was no great medicine vision at all, only a nightmare disturbing his dreams as he thrashed in his blankets and reached for a woman's soft body that was not there, that would never again be beside him. He winced, realizing he was lonely for the sound of a girl's soft, rhythmic breathing, for skin warm on his as he took her. He must stop thinking about what was in the past that could never be changed. He would salve his grief with white man's blood when he finally got the chance.

The ones called Mormons had come and taught a few Paiutes, including Timbi, to speak their language. But they had gone back to their farms in Utah. And the miners were not like the Mormons, who'd sought only to live in peace and spread their faith. The miners were greedy. They raped the Paiute women, despoiled the land. Their intrusion was building to a climax that could only end with bloodshed.

Timbi followed the trail for several hours. He had been about to decide this was just another wild band when he heard a warning whinny and looked up, gasped in awe.

The great black and white Medicine Hat stallion stood posed on a cliff above Timbi. The sun reflected off the mustang's gleaming hide, and the breeze caught his long mane and tail, blew them out behind the horse like banners. Sky Climber arched his powerful neck, sniffing the breeze as he stared down at horse and man.

There was no mistaking that mustang, there was not another like him in all the Sierra Nevada. Even as Timbi stared upward, the big horse reared, pawing the sky as if he would start at the edge of the horizon and walk right up into the heavens.

His heart beating with excitement, Timbi watched, unable to do more than stare. The Medicine Hat tipped his dark ears forward, and then reared again, shaking his great head, neighing a challenge that echoed and reechoed through the sagebrush-covered hills. Then he reared once more, pawing at the sky with powerful front legs as if any moment, he would use the white and pink clouds as footholds to gallop across a sky pale as a mountain wild flower.

Timbi's vision came to him again, but he had no time to think of anything but capturing the great horse. Still, even as he reached for his rope, he had a feeling deep inside that this stallion was indeed magic and should be left to run wild and free with the other mustangs forever.

But as he wavered, he saw himself riding the horse into the Paiute camp, saw the admiring looks of his people, heard their compliments.

Timbi dug his moccasined heels into the thin roan's sides and took off after the big stud as it wheeled and ran. Sky Climber had the advantage of being above him on the trail, but Timbi knew every rock and each twist through them and he used that knowledge to his advantage.

He rode as if he were part of his mount, so expert was he, and he urged the gelding on. On a straight stretch, Timbi had no chance because he knew no horse could outrun the big stud. Still, because Timbi knew the hills so well, he could anticipate each turn, each ravine. Besides, the Medicine Hat would never desert his mares and wobbly-legged foals.

The thin roan gained the top of the bluff and took off after the stallion. There were only a dozen or so mares and several half-grown yearlings. But four or five new foals were stumbling about on young legs. Their coloring showed the unusual chest shield and hat markings of their sire.

Timbi felt a rush of excitement. He was actually gaining on the big horse as Sky Climber hung back, nipping the fillies and new colts to keep them running when tiny legs began to fail.

That is a smart horse, Timbi thought with admiration, realizing the stud stayed between him and the foals, determined to protect his family at any cost. As any worthy male would, Timbi felt a twinge of conscience.

His own horse was lathered, sweating hard between his thighs as Timbi readied his rope, but gaining steadily on the great stud that would not desert his little family to save himself from capture. Sky Climber seemed to know he was in danger of the rope, for he neighed frantically and snapped at the foals, keeping them running on their long, unsteady legs.

Timbi's roan stumbled, almost went down. He expertly shifted his weight so the gelding could regain his balance and keep running. If he didn't rope the big horse soon, his own mount would tire and stop, unable to go farther. But Timbi was still gaining on the little herd because of the new colts.

He was close enough now to see the lathered foam on the great horse's sleek spotted coat; he could almost smell the scent of sweating horses. The sun beat down on his back as Timbi widened his loop. His mouth tasted dry and salty, but there was no time now to reach for the small canteen on his crude saddle. Later he would stop and drink his fill.

Timbi's muscles ached, and dust raised by churning hooves blew back in his face as he galloped after the thundering herd.

He was slowly gaining on the virile stallion only because the big pinto would not desert the bandy-legged foals that were tiring and slowing down. His muscles tense and straining, Timbi leaned forward over the roan's withers, his hand-braided rawhide loop ready.

Only a heart-stopping second more . . . He knew he might get only one chance to throw his loop, so the first attempt had to be good. They were all galloping up an incline now, loose rock clattering around them as they ran.

Now! Timbi threw the lasso as he rode almost even with the paint stud's beautiful head. He had him! Timbi almost shouted with triumph as he watched the loop snake through the air, settle around the powerful neck. The stallion dodged away as the rope went taut.

In alarm, Timbi felt his roan being yanked off balance by the sudden movement, and the gelding had already been struggling for footing on the steep slope.

No! He thought with alarm, as the stallion lunged against the taut rope jerking the smaller roan off balance. That split second seemed like a lifetime as Timbi shifted his weight, trying to keep the gelding on its feet. But nothing could save it as the great stallion reared and plunged. The roan stumbled on the slope and fell with a scream.

Timbi saw the fall coming, vainly struggled to jump clear. He didn't make it. Even as the roan crashed to its side with a broken neck, the stallion reared one more time, broke the rope, and galloped away with the loop still dangling from its mighty neck.

Timbi fell with the horse, even as he struggled to jump clear. Then gravel bit into his bare flesh and he knew great pain as the roan fell across his leg.

For a long time, Timbi lay unconscious. And when his eyes finally did flicker open, he was aware only of the pain in his leg and heat and thirst. At least he wasn't dead. That fact registered with him as he lay there. What had happened?

Oh yes, he remembered. . . . In his mind he saw the great stallion running, the loop flying through the air, and the roan's wildly flaying legs as it went off balance when the Medicine Hat jerked against the rope. Well, when his roan limped into camp, Atsa would spread the alarm and a search party would come looking for him.

213

He raised up on one elbow, looked around. No, they wouldn't. Not for at least a week. The dead roan was the weight across his right leg. He cursed himself for having been an arrogant fool. He couldn't survive trapped this way for a week.

The desert and the hostile mountains were beautiful but savage, and they deserved to be treated with awe. The man who did not fear them and respect their dangers deserved to die.

Was the leg broken? It didn't feel like it, although it was so numb it was hard to tell. He was only lucky that the roan had landed on a big rock which had kept the full weight of its body off his leg.

Could he free himself and try to limp the many miles back to camp? He pulled with all his might, but the dead horse held him tighter than a trap. Someone would have to move the roan before Timbi could escape.

The sun beat down on him, and he had never been so dry and thirsty in his whole life. He had brought along a canteen, and that small amount of precious water would keep him alive a day or so if he rationed it. By then, Atsa might have sent someone to look for him, or perhaps a hunting party would pass this way and find him.

Timbi licked his dry lips, tried to sit up, search for the canteen. He hoped the Pit River tribe weren't the ones to find him. The Paiutes were not on the best of terms with those renegades because Paiutes were often blamed for the attacks on isolated ranches that were carried out by the Pit River Indians.

With alarm, he noted the dark stain in the dry sand under his trapped leg. Was that blood? No, he was not that lucky. With a sinking heart, Timbi realized the source of the moisture—his leaking canteen. The same sharp rock that had taken most of the roan's weight when it fell, thus saving Timbi's leg from being crushed, had also pierced his canteen. The precious water, more valuable to him than his blood, had gradually soaked into the arid sand.

Perhaps he could suck the moisture from it. He clawed frantically at the damp sand, put a handful of it in his mouth, immediately regretted it. The water had already dried up, and the sand left him with more thirst than before. He spat the sand out, wiped his cracked lips.

The late afternoon sun beat down on him as he lay there, blinking at some object that reflected light like a mirror from over in the rocks. Maybe he could take his knife, cut himself free somehow. He searched around him for the weapon. Not there.

With despair, he suddenly realized what the shiny object reflecting the light was. It was his knife. Only a few feet away, it might as well be on the other side of the mountains. Timbi laughed bitterly.

If only the relentless sun would set, so his sweating body would cool and his thirst would let up. A shadow fell across his face and he looked up to see a buzzard slowly circling overhead. With a shout, Timbi threw a stone at it, waved his arms. The scavenger squawked and flapped away. But tomorrow it would return and bring the others. Timbi knew he could only shout and throw stones for so long. He hoped he was at least unconscious before the filthy birds of prey began to tear his living flesh with their sharp beaks and claws.

The sun finally sank, in a burst of flame and purple; over the hills to the west. Timbi breathed a sigh of relief that he would have a few hours of respite before its blazing rays tortured him on the morrow.

But as the chill desert night descended on the Great Basin country, Timbi began to shiver. He had brought along the rabbit-fur cloak that most warriors owned, but it, too, like the canteen, lay under the dead horse and he couldn't get to it. Only the furry edge of the cloak showed a bit. If he had his knife, he would strip the hide off the dead roan, wrap his shaking body in it.

Could he do it with a sharp rock? He saw one lying, like the knife, just out of his reach. He scraped his skin raw stretching and straining to bridge those hopeless few inches, trying to claw his way toward the rock.

The moon came out, big and golden, but it brought no warmth, only light to the cold, black darkness. Timbi hunched himself into a ball as much as he could, trying to draw heat from the stiff, dead body of the horse. He had not been so cold, no, not even during last winter's long storms when so many of his people had starved and frozen.

In sheer frustration and anguish, he bit his lip, tasted his own blood, warm and salty. His trapped leg ached and his tongue had swollen so that he swallowed with difficulty. Timbi tried to hunch against the dead horse for warmth and drifted in and out of consciousness.

The vision came to him again of the great horse running wild and free along the crests of the hills. And gradually, in his vision, Timbi rode the great horse, merged his heart and soul with it, so that he was the pinto stallion, his mane blowing behind him as his powerful legs drummed out a rhythm on the rocks he galloped over.

He felt himself rear and neigh a challenge before galloping away again, forever free, through the hills. It would be better to be the ghost spirit of the great horse than to go to the eternal hunting ground the Paiute medicine man spoke of.

The wolf. The giant lobo was part of his vision. Timbi tried to remember how it fitted into the dream legend as it howled and the lonely sound echoed and reechoed through the still, snow-clad peaks. What did the vision mean?

The howling echoed and reechoed, jarring him awake. Over on a ledge, a big lobo watched him, wailing at the starlit sky. Timbi was helpless and he knew it. He thought of the vision again and shivered.

If the wolf realized he was helpless, would it attack him? Coyotes were cowardly, but the big lobos were afraid of nothing. He could not reach a rock or anything that might be used as a weapon, not from his trapped position.

Even as terror came into his heart, he heard the challenging neigh of the giant stallion, saw it gallop onto the ridge, and the wolf retreated and slipped away into the darkness.

Timbi heaved a sigh of relief. In his vision, he wasn't sure that was the way it ended, with the horse as victor. He watched the stallion and it watched him, the moonlight reflecting off the white hairs of its coat making it look like glacier ice from the Sierra Nevadas. Was the horse protecting him . . . or gloating over his plight?

All too soon, the blackness of the night had passed and the relentless burning sun rose again to the east. If he had been choking with thirst yesterday, it was as nothing compared with this day's agony. Timbi drifted in and out of consciousness as the sun moved upward. Sometimes when he became conscious, he felt as if the sun were a molten gold coin that was laid with a sizzle against his dark skin.

If he'd had his knife, he might cut a piece of the dead horse and eat it raw, sucking the juices from it. But he had no knife; it lay gleaming in the sun out of his reach. And his stomach rebelled at the thought, because by now the dead horse reeked and had drawn a swarm of flies that lit on it and Timbi in a black cloud. Weakly, he brushed them away again and again.

If he had a knife, he might cut off his trapped leg. But he would bleed to death before he could get help and even if he lived, of what use was a one-legged man? He would be a burden to his sister. He almost prayed that he could find a way to take his own life, end his ordeal.

Timbi shook his head. That was a coward's way out and he was a Paiute warrior. He would struggle and fight to escape up unto the moment of his death. He clasped his arms over his face to ward off the blazing sun.

Within moments, he felt rather than saw the shadow that crossed over him. He heard a hoarse call, looking up with a start. A flock of buzzards circled on lazy wings overhead, gliding on the hot air currents. Yesterday's bird of prey had returned and brought others, as Timbi had know it would.

The wolf howled again and he saw it on a ledge, watching him. The lobo must be hungry to show himself so openly in daylight.

Which predators would finally get up the nerve to move in? Timbi could only pray to the spirits that he would be unconscious, not feel the sharp beaks or teeth that would finally tear into his bloody flesh before he was even dead.

When he closed his eyes and drifted off to sleep, one of the smelly buzzards landed on the dead horse with a squawk and a flutter of wings.

In a panic, Timbi jerked awake, waved his arms wildly and shouted. His voice came out as a weak croak, but it was enough to send the bird of prey flapping away.

It would be back, he knew. How long could he find the strength to frighten the rank bird away before it and the others realized that he was only meat like the horse to ease their vicious appetites?

The sun marched across the sky and Timbi dreamed of *ki-ebe,* the mountains. He was at the summit of *Kurangwa,* the Paiute holy mount the whites called Mt. Grant. The damp, cool fog, *pogonip,* descended and hugged the mountain tops like an icy veil.

Now he imagined he swam in *Coo-yu-ee Pah,* that the whites knew as Pyramid Lake, the giant remainder from the inland sea that had once covered much of the Great Basin. He dreamed that he and his woman swam in the cold water, laughing and diving deep after the big *cui-ui* fish that were also left from that time millions of years ago and were found no place else but this lake venerated by the Paiute.

Timbi dreamed of splashing the water, diving deep into it, drinking gallons and gallons of it until he could swallow no more of its cold sweetness. The woman in his dream was not his wife, but she had deep, dark eyes, soft skin, and she came to him, took him in her arms. Her skin was burning hot against his nakedness. . . .

With a start, he came awake, the sun searing into his flesh; and looking down at him was a giant buzzard that had perched on the dead horse and was watching him, its ugly head cocked.

Cursing in his own tongue, Timbi swung his arm, chased the bird off into the sky again. The sun moved past noon. He had lain here already a whole day. He wondered just how long a man could live under this scorching sun without food or water? A weak man might already have died, but Timbi was a chieftain and he'd not die without a struggle.

In his thirsty agony, he began to long for sundown again although he knew it would bring the bone-chilling Nevada night with it.

The dead horse smelled so rotten that several times, he gagged and would have vomited, but there was nothing in his stomach and he no longer had the strength to retch. Well, he thought, I will die of thirst and exposure before I die of starvation anyway.

Had this come about because he had dared to try to capture the sacred Medicine Hat? Were the Gods punishing him? Did not the Paiutes, over many generations, tell the legend of this stallion, that he was a spirit meant to run the hills, proud and free forever?

The buzzards were roosting on some nearby cliffs, from which they could watch him. They seemed to smile as they preened their black feathers and waited.

Timbi did not think he would live to see the sun set, he only hoped he would not feel it when the big birds or the coyotes attacked him.

But he was a Paiute warrior, and was determined to die as bravely as he had lived, giving no quarter and asking none. He began a rhythmic death chant, low in his throat. When that Dark Rider came for him, Timbi intended to meet him with a challenge on his lips.

The buzzards watched, their ugly heads cocked as if they listened to the singsong challenge and wondered. Somewhere, a pack of coyotes yipped their sad refrain. This might be his day to die, but Timbi would not be taken without a fight!

Chapter Fifteen

Quint wondered if Dallas might be ill because her face had turned pale. He had come back from putting away the horses to find her talking to Yancy, the fellow who ran the Naughty Lady in St. Joe.

"Never expected to see you two clear out here, although the boy rides for the Express." Yancy indicated Dallas with a nod, held out his hand to Quint.

Quint shook it, wondering why the man was this far away from St. Joe, deciding it wasn't his business to inquire. "Dal came out as a standby rider, and I'm searching for some mythical stallion that's supposed to be roaming these hills."

As a matter of fact, he had no intention of letting Dallas ride for the Express ever again. When he captured that horse, he intended to take her back east or wherever his angel wanted to live.

While an old Mexican woman served dinner, Quint sat at the end of the table, drank his coffee, and watched Dallas. Obviously it hadn't occurred to either of the Williams brothers or Yancy that she was any different from the dozens of skinny boys who rode for the Express.

In that case, he wouldn't have to worry about any man bothering her. He puffed his pipe and sipped the coffee, watching Dallas fill a tortilla with chili peppers and beans. He almost shuddered at the way she ate those hot things with such relish. "You Texans must have cast-iron bellies." He winked good-naturedly at her.

She smiled back. "Texas young'uns are weaned on panther milk spiced with chili peppers."

Quint laughed. "I believe it!"

Later, after the others had retired to their bunks, the two of them slipped out into the cool desert blackness.

She sighed, stretched as they walked. "A Nevada night; full of stars, ripe for passion."

They went out to the small shed of a barn, climbed into the hayloft. Lying in the sweet, soft hay, Dallas breathed in its scent, looked up at the bright stars showing through the cracks in the roof.

Quint glanced over at her. What would his sisters say when they finally met his half-breed bride with short, black curls and the habit of riding astride like a man?

He laughed aloud. Charlotte might or might not be understanding, but he could count on sheer venomous rage from Lydia, especially since he had refused to have dinner with that Maude Peabody she'd wanted him to marry.

"What's so funny?"

"Nothing, angel. I was just imagining my sister's reaction to you." Quint reached out to pull Dallas to him. He didn't give a damn about what his sister thought; he had made his choice, and was happy in a way he had never thought possible. It was almost as if a piece had been missing from his personality all these years and now it had been found.

"You're saying she won't like me, aren't you?" Dallas snuggled against him, that I'm too much of a tomboy to ever fit into Philadelphia society, that my accent and everything about me is wrong for a place like that."

He brushed back her hair, kissed her forehead. "Maybe they're wrong, not you."

She didn't say anything for a while. "What do you suppose Yancy is doing out here in Nevada?"

"Would you believe I don't care?" Quint shrugged, cradled her in his arms.

"I don't really feel married," she whispered. "Let me wear

your ring and let's see how it looks."

He slipped off the big gold signet ring, placed it on her finger, then turned it so that only the wide gold band showed. "I swear that looks natural on your finger, angel. When we get to a city and you drop this foolish masquerade, I'll buy you a real wedding ring with jewels in it. What do you fancy? Rubies? Diamonds?"

Dallas looked at the ring a long moment, before she pointed up through the cracks of the roof. "I'd like real stars out of a Nevada night."

"Sorry, can't get those for you; Nevada gets to keep them. I don't even know what 'Nevada' means." He nuzzled along her jawline.

"It's Spanish; means 'snowy' or 'snow-clad,' I reckon because of the mountains," she murmured.

"Does it now?" He didn't want to talk anymore. He wanted to take her in his arms and make love to her.

She unbuttoned his shirt and rested her face against his hairy chest. "You really think there will be war?"

"Yes, I do." He started to tell her about his sister and the others who wanted war, not caring who won or who died, thinking only of the profits to be made. Would Dallas want to live in desolate Arizona? He was afraid to ask her, afraid he would find she might be like Melanie after all, wanting a fine mansion in the best part of Philadelphia, stylish clothes, and an elegant carriage. If she were like the other women he had known, he did not want to hear it yet.

Something was bothering Dallas, something deep inside. He could feel she was holding something back. Had she already regretted marrying a man so much older and from such a different background? Was a young cowboy waiting for her in Texas? If only he knew . . . If only . . .

The two saddest words in any language. He must not think, only hope she loved him. It was too late for regrets.

"Make love to me, Quint," Dallas whispered, and turned her face to his.

"No, you make love to me," he countered, rolled over onto his back and pulling her on top of him.

She smiled impishly, slowly unbuttoned her shirt, pulled

222

off the cloth that bound her breasts down. "You know how hard this is gonna be with both of us wearing pants?"

"Who's wearing pants?" With a laugh, he upset her, grabbed the legs of her britches, pulled. They ended up rolling naked in the hay until she lay on her belly and he lightly lay down on top of her. Leaning over, he slipped his hands under her arms, cupped her breasts while he kissed the back of her neck.

She leaned on her elbows, reached down to cover his hands with her own.

His lips ran along her naked shoulders, sending evident chills of pleasure down her body. "Umm," she shivered all over, "you give me goose bumps."

"I love you, angel." His hands kneaded her breasts into hard peaks of desire.

"I thought you wanted *me* to make love to *you?*" Dallas protested.

In answer, he rolled her over on top of him. "I'm waiting," he whispered.

She became embarrassed, flustered. "I-I feel funny about this."

"As a certain Pony Express rider would say," he scoffed, "horsefeathers!"

"I may not do everything right."

He reached up to cup her face between his two hands. "You'll do it right, angel. You do everything so right!"

He had to resist the urge to turn her over, ride her in a frenzy. They were going to take this one slow and easy. She sat straddling him with her naked body. He could feel his pulsating manhood beneath her small hips.

"Ride me, Dallas. Ride your stallion!" And he truly felt like one—potent, big, and virile. He felt he could mate her a dozen times and leave her smeared with his seed, sleepy and satisfied, yet still be wanting her again.

He began to stroke the small ridge of her womanhood with the tip of his finger. He knew it excited her from her sudden gasp, the way her warm thighs squeezed his body. "Now raise up, angel, and come down on me; come down on me hard!"

With tantalizing slowness, Dallas raised up on her knees.

He reached to stroke between her thighs, found her wet and warm with desire. His own maleness seemed swollen to bursting, standing up rigid as a sword that she now slowly impaled herself on.

He fought himself to keep from grasping her slim waist, bucking to completion under her. Instead, he reached out and stroked her small, hot ridge of flesh. He felt her insides grasp him, hold him tightly within her as she began a rhythmic rising and falling.

He clasped her waist, pulling her down hard on his staff, and fought to keep his body under control, wanting to drive her wild with desire before he finally satisified himself.

"Oh, Quint, I love you so."

Why did she sound so despairing? "I love you, too, Dallas."

He began to raise up under her in spite of himself, wanting to push deep into her womb and leave his seed in her belly.

And as she rode him, she leaned over, tangled her face in the thick hair of his chest, then rubbed her nipples against him before she leaned over and nibbled his.

No woman had ever driven him quite so mad with the wanting of her as this one did with her stroking hands and sharp little teeth, nipping and sucking at the tips of his nipples until they were swollen and sensitive.

He couldn't stand any more. Quint caught her small waist in his two big hands and moved her up and down on him in a frenzy. As his seed exploded deep inside her, she fell forward, gasping and convulsing in his arms. Slowly he came back to consciousness and kissed her lips, her face.

She broke down and wept in his arms as he held her and whispered endearments under the bright stars of the Nevada night.

The next morning, when Quint announced his intention to search for the stallion, he was met with whoops of derision.

At breakfast in the trading post, the bearded Williams brother, Oscar, chortled with laughter. "A dude like you is going after the stallion that all the seasoned cowboys in the

224

ACCEPT YOUR **FREE** *GIFT AND EXPERIENCE MORE OF THE PASSION AND ADVENTURE YOU LIKE IN A HISTORICAL ROMANCE*

Zebra Romances are the finest novels of their kind and are written with the adult woman in mind. All of our books are written by authors who really know how to weave tales of romantic adventure in the historical settings you love.

Because our readers tell us these books sell out very fast in the stores, Zebra has made arrangements for you to receive at home the four newest titles published each month. You'll never miss a title and home delivery is so convenient. With your first shipment we'll even send you a **FREE** Zebra Historical Romance as our gift just for trying our home subscription service. No obligation.

BIG SAVINGS AND **FREE** *HOME DELIVERY*

Each month, the Zebra Home Subscription Service will send you the four newest titles as soon as they are published. (We ship these books to our subscribers even before we send them to the stores.) You may preview them *Free* for 10 days. If you like them as much as we think you will, you'll pay just $3.50 each and *save $1.80 each month* off the cover price. *AND you'll also get FREE HOME DELIVERY.* There is never a charge for shipping, handling or postage and there is no minimum you must buy. If you decide not to keep any shipment, simply return it within 10 days, no questions asked, and owe nothing.

Get a Free
Zebra
Historical
Romance

*a $3.95
value*

ZEBRA HOME SUBSCRIPTION SERVICES, INC.
P.O. BOX 5214
120 BRIGHTON ROAD
CLIFTON, NEW JERSEY 07015-5214

Sierra Nevada have been unable to catch? Are you funnin' us?"

Quint glanced over at Dallas. In her mannish disguise, she was sipping coffee and eating biscuits and ham. "If that means am I making a joke, I assure you I'm not. As far as my chances of catching him, I know a lot about horses and their habits, so I figure mine are as good as any. Now if I could hire one of you as a guide . . ."

"Nope." The older brother, Dave, the one with the broken front tooth, shook his head. "The Injuns around here won't take kindly to a white man lookin' for that stud. He's some kind of a legend. Only a brave should own him, if anybody."

His brother broke in. "Dutch Phil, one of the local guides will be back from Virginia City in a few days, he'd take you out if you'll wait."

Quint shrugged. "I'm restless. I might just ride out a ways, look around for a day or two. I've got a compass to keep from getting lost, and anyway, if I should, I'll bet I could just ride to the top of a ridge and look for the smoke from the chimney here. I'll wager you can see it for miles." He looked over at Yancy as the old Mexican woman poured more coffee. "You interested in going?"

The handsome gambler shook his head. "I'm here to do a little business with the trading post, maybe go on to California to find some pretty dancing girls for the Naughty Lady. Besides, I like my comforts, and sleeping out in the desert ain't my idea of soft. What about taking Dal here along?"

"I don't think the kid wants to go either," Quint said, casting a pointed look at his wife. Actually, Dallas had begged to go, but Quint had been adamant in his refusal. He wasn't sure what kind of dangers he would run into in that hostile desert, and the Indian unrest was another concern. In her boy's disguise, Dallas would be safer staying at the trading post until he got back, he'd decided.

He thought about the Indians a moment. "Any real Indian trouble?" he asked.

Dave of the broken tooth shook his head. "It simmers. Oh, we sell 'em a little whiskey now and then, which we ain't supposed to do, and trade with the Washoe and a Paiute once

225

in a while. The Pit River bunch are the real troublemakers. We just hope it stays peaceful; the Pony Express comin' through will eventually bring in more people and more business for us."

Yancy fiddled with the chain of his gold watch. "I hear the government thinks the Pony might be vital in keeping communications open to the West if war breaks out."

"Reckon that's so," Oscar, the bearded one, bit off a chew of tobacco. "They say there's already Southern agents and spies trying to disrupt things. If there's war, I think the Rebs will want to try to come outa Texas and capture the gold and silver country so they can pay for guns and ammunition the French and British might be willing to sell them."

Quint thought about his sister with a frown. "There're always those willing to get a war going so they can profit from it. They don't care about either side."

Yancy nodded. "Ah reckon I'll say amen to that!"

Dallas stood up. "I promised to help mend some saddles and tack out at the barn, so I reckon I'll start."

Broken Tooth grinned. "Now there's the kind of boy I like. Most of them riders don't expect to do nothin' but carry the mail."

Quint glanced at her. "Dal is special, all right. Nice boy."

She glared at him. He knew she was annoyed that he wasn't taking her, but he thought she'd be safer here. Spirited? She certainly was! If capturing the stallion hadn't become such an obsession to him, they'd have ridden on, spent a few days of ease and luxury in San Francisco, and maybe taken a ship back to the East coast.

Quint waved good-bye to her, left her looking annoyed as he rode away from Williams' station. He rode for several hours, then, from a butte, turned and looked back, saw the gray smoke from the station chimney spiraling into the pale blue of the sky. Off in the distance, he made out a flurry of dust stirred up by a galloping horse heading toward the trading post, and knew the weekly Pony Express rider was coming by on the way to the relay point, Buckland's station.

Those wiry little mustangs might not be as fast as his thoroughbreds, which were being used on the Eastern end of the line, but they made up for that in stamina and sure-footedness.

Quint thought of the elusive stallion, then turned back toward the hostile arroyos and cliffs, hope beating high in his heart.

He rode for another couple of hours, spotting only a rattlesnake and the biggest scorpion he'd ever seen scurrying into the rocks. The sun beat down hotly and he reined in, sipped the tepid gyp water from his canteen, made a face. A man had to be plenty thirsty to drink gyp water with its strong mineral taste.

The holster hung heavy on his waist. He unbuckled it, hung it on his saddle horn, pulled his hat down over his eyes and rode on. Maybe the stallion didn't exist. Suppose he spent all this time and didn't even see it?

Then he spotted tracks of unshod ponies and horse drop-pings. An experienced tracker could tell how far ahead of him a herd was by the freshness of the droppings. Hope rose again as he realized a herd—or was it only an Indian war party—had passed this way less than an hour ago? Quint urged his mount on.

In a moment, he heard a scream of defiance, of challenge, and jerked up. He blinked, almost not believing what he saw. Watching him from atop a cliff was the biggest, most magnificent black and white pinto stud he had ever seen.

The pinto reared on powerful hind legs and whinnied again as if questioning Quint's right to invade its domain. He stared at the big horse, more than sixteen hands high and finely built, its long mane and tail blowing in the late afternoon wind as it reared and pawed the air in that peculiar climbing motion.

"Sky Climber," he whispered, and then realized he had been holding his breath as he stared at the great horse. A broken rawhide lariat dangled from the stallion's neck and the light gleamed on the unusual shield marking on its chest.

The wind came up again, bringing a coolness to Quint's perspiring brow and blowing the horse's mane and tail straight out like proud banners.

And Quint knew that, except for Dallas, he had never wanted anything as much as he wanted this horse. No wonder men had risked death and had spent fruitless months on vain attempts to capture the stud. He vowed right then that he would catch and break the horse, take it back to add its great bloodlines to those of his own fine horses.

He stared transfixed as the magnificent horse reared up and challenged him again, trying to climb the sky, and then wheeled and took off at a gallop.

That broke the spell. Quint spurred his own horse forward, knowing that unless he had incredible luck, he could never get close enough to lasso that stud. There was probably no horse that could outrun the big devil. His only chance might be to corner the stallion in a canyon, and the pinto knew the hills better than Quint did.

The herd. The Medicine Hat would have a little herd of mares nearby, colts and fillies grazing peacefully. That was why the big horse stood guard on the rise, to protect his harem. Quint reached for his lariat. The herd might slow the big stud down enough to get a rope on him.

The stallion stretched out into a lope. Quint spurred his horse even faster, galloping after him up the ridge. When he hit the flat plain, he saw the big horse running without effort ahead of him, nipping and urging on his mares, hanging back to stay between Quint and the little foals who ran on unsteady legs.

Quint almost cried out in exaltation. Because of that herd, he might manage to get close enough to get a loop over the stallion's head. Otherwise, he wouldn't have a snowflake's chance in hell of catching it.

The horses galloped across the small plain in a cloud of alkali dust, their hooves beating like war drums against the ground. The dust blew back, clinging to Quint's sweating skin and lips, but all he could think of was getting a rope on that horse. The Medicine Hat galloped so effortlessly that Quint began to appreciate why it was a legend in Nevada.

Closer. Even closer. He urged his weary gelding along, smelling the sweat of its lathered body, the dust that blew back at him from bay, black, and pinto mares. The little colts and fillies were tiring fast; the stallion seemed almost desperate now to keep itself between them and Quint. Several colts bore the medicine shield coloring of their sire.

Quint felt both excitement and shame that he might be taking the sire from the herd, leaving mares and colts unprotected. He told himself that sooner or later another stud would add the mares and babies to his own harem.

Closing ground fast on the great horse, Quint felt a deep admiration as he readied his loop. Sky Climber could avoid capture easily by galloping away and abandoning his family, but the big stud refused to do that.

The wind changed suddenly and whatever scent it brought to Quint's gelding caused it to start and lose stride, neigh and prick its ears in the direction from which the wind blew.

Damnit! Quint cursed and reined in, knowing the chase was over for that afternoon. His horse was too winded to take after the herd again now that Quint had lost that split second chance to get a loop over the stud's head. His shoulders slumped in defeat as he watched the little herd disappear down a ravine.

Quint took a deep breath, gasped at the sweet, decaying scent the hot wind carried. Something lay dead upwind, and the smell had startled his mount. Buzzards rose up and circled lazily, throwing black shadows across him as he squinted skyward.

What was it the filthy devils had been feeding on, or were about to feed on, when the galloping horses had startled them away? Whatever it was might not even be quite dead. They might be tearing at living flesh. *Suppose it was a man?*

Quint shuddered at the thought, urged his horse to lope over the ridge to investigate.

Lord, what was that? He didn't really need to ask. Even from here, he recognized the still form of a roan horse, a rider. They were both obviously dead and the buzzards had been feeding off the carcasses.

The thought made Quint a little sick. He'd at least bury the man. It wasn't decent to leave him for the buzzards.

He urged his gelding down the ridge, although the horse

shied from the reek of the rotting horse.

An Indian. Quint stared down at the half-naked, magnificent brown body. What had the warrior been doing out here alone and what had happened to him?

Then he noticed the broken rope tangled around the bodies, remembered the loop around Sky Climber's neck. The dead roan's head lay at an odd angle on the steep rise. Quint pictured the scene; the brave chasing the wild stallion, the roan tripping as the stallion broke the line, the fall.

The warrior's fingers moved ever so slightly. Good Lord, he was alive! Quint dismounted, ran over, felt for a pulse. When he touched the brave, dark eyes slowly opened, looked up at him for a moment as if not quite sure who Quint was or what had happened.

Then the Indian glared hatefully and managed to say in English, "I kill you, *tavibo,* if you don't kill me. . . ."

Quint knelt, frowned at him. "You've got more guts than sense." He studied the situation, realized the brave's leg was trapped under the dead horse. "For your sass, I ought to ride out and leave you lay."

The handsome face contorted in pain and fury. "I expect no better from a white."

"Then I'm going to disappoint you, Chief," Quint said, "I wouldn't leave a rattlesnake trapped for the buzzards to eat alive!" He went to his horse, got a canteen, and came back to kneel by the brave.

The Indian was all but dead. A less magnificent specimen would already have died under this hot sun. Quint gathered the big body into his arms, held the canteen to the Indian's lips.

The brave started to grab it, then turned his stoic face away. "You poison me."

Lord, why do I bother? Quint shook his head, "Look, I drink from it myself, see?" He took a sip then held it to the brave's lips.

The warrior grabbed it from his hands, gulped liquid down.

"Easy, not too much at first." Quint pulled the canteen away, wet his bandana, wiped dust from the brooding brave's face. Then he gave him another drink. "How long you been here?"

The brave blinked, found the strength to raise up on one elbow. "Yesterday I chased the great medicine horse. My horse slipped."

"Is your leg broken?"

The Indian considered, shook his head. "A big rock, the same one that ripped my canteen, is holding up most of its weight. Why do you stop to help me?"

Quint tipped his hat back. "Damned if I know! I'm beginning to think I must be *loco*."

He stood up, surveyed the situation for a moment, then strode over, took his loop, put it around the dead horse, and swung back up on his mount. "When I've dragged it far enough, you move quick." Quint backed his horse and dragged the roan just a few inches, but it was enough. The Indian managed to crawl free.

Quint swung down from the stirrup. Now what was he going to do? Two men, one horse. He couldn't leave the brave but he'd have to abandon his horse hunt if they rode double out of here. But when he turned around he saw that the Indian had crawled over and had picked up the knife and lance that had lain only a few feet away. He could throw either before Quint could move.

"And now, white dog, I take the horse and your scalp!"

Quint cursed himself for his carelessness. His guns were on his saddle. "I saved your life and you do this? Where is your honor?"

The brave hesitated. "You are right. I owe you my life."

Quint breathed a sigh of relief as the man slowly lowered the lance.

"You are very different from the whites I have known, except for the Mormons a long time ago," the warrior said in halting English as if he had not used the language in a very long time. "Who are you?"

"Quint Randolph."

The brave considered, then he seemed to notice the gold ring for the first time. "It is a sign." He gestured with the knife, "what does your name mean?"

Quint shrugged, still wary. The brave might change his mind and attack him with the long lance.

"Quint? It's a very old Latin name, meaning, 'five,' you know, the number. Randolph is Anglo-Saxon and it means—"

"Five? That is the magic number of my people, the *numa* that you whites call Paiute. The medicine vision is fulfilled!"

He staggered to his feet, and would have fallen but Quint caught him, lowered him to one knee. Very slowly the Indian held out his hand. "Quint Randolph, I am Timbi, a chieftan of the Paiute."

There was still conflict on his face as if it cost him a great deal to make this gesture of friendship to a white man. Quint wondered suddenly what had happened to create such hatred in him.

Quint took his hand. "Timbi?"

"It means 'the rock.' "

So this was the Paiute troublemaker who might create problems for the Pony Express and the whites pouring into the area What he should have done was put a bullet in the Indian's brain while he had him down and helpless. But even as he thought that, Quint knew he could never have done it. Like Timbi, he was a man of honor. "Well, Timbi, what am I supposed to do with you now?"

The Indian tried to scramble to his feet, but he was too weak. "If you think to capture me, take me to the whites so they can lock me in a filthy cage—"

"If I meant you harm, I would have let the buzzards finish you. It looked like they were about to eat you alive." Undecided, Quint glanced up at the sun. "I think you need food and rest. We could ride double back to the station—"

"No!" the dark face went grim, and Timbi pointed in the other direction. "Go Paiute camp."

Some other white man would probably ride out and leave the hostile chieftain. After all, Quint had gotten him out from under the dead horse; was it his responsibility to carry him back to the Indian camp? Suppose the Paiutes decided to take him prisoner or to kill him?

Timbi seemed to sense his hesitation. "I owe you my life, so

I am indebted to you more deeply than the brother I never had. You have my vow you will not be harmed in our camp. My honor demands I repay you or give you back the life you saved."

Quint grinned wryly, ran a hand through his hair. "I don't know how the hell you'd do that. But okay, I'll take you back to your camp. Maybe while I'm there, I can convince your people to let the Pony riders alone."

He put his shoulder under the Paiute's arm, helped Timbi up on the gelding. "As tired as my mount is, I reckon I'll have to walk."

Quint dug in his saddlebags, got out some beef jerky, handed a strip to Timbi, took one himself. It tasted salty, smoky, and delicious as he chewed on it and turned the horse in the direction the Indian had pointed. "Strange how I ended up finding you; it was almost as if the pinto led me to you." He started trudging along, leading the horse.

"I had a medicine vision," Timbi said behind him, biting off jerky. "It was almost as if I were the horse. We blended and became one; an eternal spirit of the desert running along the cliffs forever."

Quint shrugged as he walked. "Not a bad way to spend eternity."

"You were chasing the stallion? So was I. That is my broken loop on his neck."

Quint trudged on. It was late afternoon, but still hot. "I hear the Indians regard that horse as big medicine."

"Yes. Maybe no one is meant to capture the Spirit of the Sierra Nevada."

Quint looked back over his shoulder at the man in the saddle. "I hate to disappoint you, friend, since you think your soul is someday going to merge with his, but I have plans for that big stud. He would make a wonderful herd sire; bring new blood to my stock."

"You would lock him in a pen far from his mountains?" Timbi's face, when Quint looked back, was dark with disapproval.

"He'd have a good pasture, the best of food. He'd never have to look after himself anymore."

"And all he would have to give up is his freedom. That's what the white man has offered the Indian. Tell me, Quint Randolph, if you were Timbi, would you lead your people up to Pyramid Lake to join old Poito, the one the whites call Winnemucca, to live with his band like stupid sheep on a reservation?"

Quint didn't like the logic of the comparison. "The government is only thinking of the welfare of your people and of the safety of the Pony riders."

Timbi made a derisive sound. "When anyone offers to feed me, cloth me, look after me, I have to ask, what is it he wants? If my people, if any people accept, they should not be surprised to find out what they have traded away is their freedom, their right to come and go as they please."

"The whites mean you no harm, Timbi. There's room for all in this giant land."

"The desert may look big, but it is fragile as a butterfly's wings and can support only a few people. Besides, the Paiute are not the ones attacking the lonely outposts. The Pit River tribe does this, but I expect when the Paiute and their relatives council, we will vote to join them."

Quint felt troubled. Had he made a mistake in saving this savage chieftain? Would this act ultimately result in the deaths of whites? "Why do you hate us so?"

"The poison from the mines has already polluted a stream, killed my whole family, save one sister. For this, I have sworn to kill white men, to fight them to my last breath!"

Quint stopped and looked up into Timbi's hostile face. "I thought we were friends?"

Timbi looked back at him, stormy conflict in his dark eyes. "You and I are friends, Quint of the magic number who was sent to save my life by the horse spirit, but other white men and Timbi are not friends, can never be friends. If they come into my stronghold, I will kill them!"

He meant it, too. Quint had never seen such fury, such hatred in a man's face.

"You cannot win against the whites," Quint said softly. "They're as many as the sagebrush of the Great Basin. In the end, they will prevail."

"And did not the Mormons teach of whites who fought against terrible odds at places like Valley Forge and the Alamo, with no hope of winning or saving anything but their ideals and their honor?"

"You win, Timbi." Quint laughed as he walked. "The Mormons did a pretty good job of teaching you American history."

When he'd started out this morning, he'd never expected to end up headed to a Paiute village with a savage chieftain who knew enough to argue ideals with him. But Quint had a goal now. If he could make other Indian friends, get closer to Timbi, maybe the Paiutes would settle down and the rumors that they would hit the war trail would go unfulfilled.

He frowned at the rounded wickiups now visible on the far horizon. He might be remembered as the man who protected the Pony Express from Indian attacks or he might get himself killed. If so, what in God's name would happen to Dallas?

Chapter Sixteen

"Hurry up, kid, can't you hear him coming in?"

Dallas paused as she saddled the palomino horse, listened. Away in the distance, she heard the drumming of hooves as the Pony Express rider galloped toward Williams' station. Quickly, she finished, nodded to the bearded Oscar Williams as she led the horse outside.

Quint had ridden out a couple of hours before on his search for the Medicine Hat stallion, and Dallas was resigned to spending a couple of dull days disguised as a boy and working around the station.

She touched her pants pocket to make sure she still had the pearl earrings. The breeze blew against her face as the rider galloped toward them. He was only a tiny dot on the horizon, but the rhythmic pounding of the horse's hooves could be heard a long way in the desert.

The palomino she held by the bridle nickered and stamped, obviously realizing that it was about to start its run. Williams' station was a trading place and a minor relay post for a rider to get a fresh horse and gallop on.

The others came out of the adobe building to watch the transfer as the rider galloped closer. Dallas frowned now as she saw that the boy coming in was hunched low over his saddle horn, clinging to the horse's neck. "There's something wrong!"

She ran out to meet the weary dun gelding as it stumbled into camp, stood trembling and lathered. The rider lay on the horse's neck, his fingers clenched in the gelding's mane to

236

keep from falling off. "Somebody give me a hand! He's hurt!"

Yancy ran out and helped Dallas unclench the rider's hands, let the lad slide off the horse into his arms. "Boy, what happened?"

The broken shaft of an arrow protruded from the rider's shoulder. "Finally managed to outrun them . . . they ran off." He gasped. "Injuns . . ."

Oscar cursed as he knelt. "Dammit, it's been too quiet to last! Pit River or Paiutes?"

Dallas wiped the sweat from the boy's face and held a canteen to his lips. "Can't you see he's hurt too bad to answer questions? We've got to get him inside!"

The Williams brothers lifted the boy and carried him into the station, Dallas and Yancy trailing along behind.

Yancy drawled, "Damned shame! If the service is disrupted, the government isn't gonna be able to keep up communication with the West."

Why does he look so smug, so pleased? Dallas wondered. What has he been up to in the few days he's been out here? Her speculation was interrupted by Dave Williams. "Dal, boy, the mail has to go and there's no relay rider here."

She froze. "A war party on the loose and you want me to take that mail out?"

Yancy laughed cynically. "Kid, that's what they pay you for!"

"Yancy's right, boy," Oscar said. "Even if any of us was willin', we're too heavy and don't ride that well. It's up to you to get that mail on to the next station!" He reached for a bottle of whiskey, took a big swig before handing the bottle to the wounded rider. "Take a slug of this," he ordered. "You'll need it while we get the arrow out."

They were right. Deep in her heart, Dallas knew it. And she knew the mail had to go through. There might be important documents in that packet. But all she had to do was admit that she was a girl in disguise and no man, no matter how disreputable, would send her out into such danger.

But none of the men at the station were small enough to carry on. Besides, wasn't this her chance to slip away from

237

Quint?

"Okay, I'll go. When my friend, Quint comes back, tell him . . ." Tell him what? She'd wait for him in California? She was saying good-bye forever because she didn't think they could work things out? "Tell him I said good-bye."

Oscar frowned, scratched his beard. "Stops dawdling and get out of here, Dal! The mail's already been delayed ten minutes while we stand here jawin'. There's a schedule to meet."

"I-I don't know the route."

"There's bound to be a map in the saddlebags, you can study it as you ride."

Why was she being so hesitant?

"Sure, I can do it!" It suddenly occurred to her that she didn't really have all that far to go. A fresh rider was waiting at the next station some twenty miles down the trail. She'd hand the mail over to him and then make a decision as to whether to wait for Quint or catch the next stage to California.

She ran outside. A scraggly cottonwood tree grew in the station yard, and Dallas broke off a little switch to use because she wore no spurs. She retrieved the *mochila,* swung up on the palomino.

Yancy leaned on the doorjamb, sucking a gold toothpick with an amused smile. "Good-bye, kid, here's hopin' the Injuns don't get you and disrupt the Pony's service."

He was delighted with the turn of events. That showed in his eyes. Dallas gave him a curt nod, took the map out of the saddlebags, and swung up on the cream-colored horse. Using her little switch, she took off at a gallop for the next station.

I'm scared spitless, she thought as she galloped away. But she studied the map as she rode.

Horsefeathers, the Indians are back where that rider came from. Besides, vast as Nevada is, the chances of crossing a war party's trail are pretty small. But what if I do?

She shook her head stubbornly and hunched low over the cream-colored pony's neck. The mail she carried might be important to the government and since her family supported

238

Sam Houston and his efforts to keep Texas in the Union, she felt morally committed to get the mail through on time.

Twenty miles isn't a long way to ride, she told herself, concentrating on the desolate landscape ahead of her. Up there was another rider who would carry the mail on, then she could make a decision about what to do. The pony's drumming hooves seemed to say, Quint . . . Quint . . . Quint . . .

Should she go on to San Francisco and forget about him, knowing his snooty family would never accept her, or should she send a message back, suggesting they start fresh in a new place?

If only they'd never met . . . No, she wouldn't trade the hours of love and happiness she'd found in his arms for anything. But if only he hadn't turned out to be Lydia Huntington's brother . . . If only he hadn't ridden away to search for that wild mustang . . . *If only* . . .

Stop it, Dallas, she chided silently as he bent low over the pony's neck, galloping onward. Look into the future, don't waste time regretting the past.

The sun beat down on her small shoulders, and her mouth tasted dry; but she didn't slow to reach for the canteen on her saddle. She had about ten minutes to make up in order to get the mail back on schedule, and she had enough pride in her company to want to help them keep their contract. She'd get a long drink and a sandwich at the next station.

A jackrabbit jumped up almost under the palomino's feet, but the horse kept running, seeming as eager as she was to keep the mail on time. Up ahead at the next station, the relief rider was probably getting up from a nap, starting to saddle a fresh horse after having a bite of food.

The sagebrush-covered *playas,* the plain, was wild and beautiful, she thought as the horse galloped on, but so different from her own beloved Texas hill country. A wave of homesickness washed over her and she had to blink back the tears. When she reached California, she'd send another letter, hoping Papa's anger would have cooled. She couldn't imagine that Mama wouldn't have sent a message to St. Joe, but perhaps Papa was so angry, he hadn't even let her know he'd heard from Dallas.

Her shoulders ached from leaning over the horse's neck, but there was really no way to ease them until she finally dismounted at the next station. The minutes passed in a blur, and she was almost hypnotized by the rhythm of the pony's hooves. *Quint . . . Quint . . .* The pony lost stride for a moment, and the rhythm seemed to say: *If only . . . if only . . .*

Up ahead in the late afternoon, she saw smoke curling over the horizon. Thank God! She couldn't remember when smoke from a chimney had been such a welcoming sight. In a very short time, she'd be in the station yard where a new rider and a fresh horse would replace her and her own tired mount.

She leaned over and shouted in the palomino's ear as she tapped it lightly across the rump with the cottonwood switch. "Keep going, boy, we're almost there! They'll have grain for you and some hot food from that fireplace for me!"

It occurred to her as they galloped toward the column of smoke that it was an awfully warm day to have such a big fire going in the station, but maybe the manager was cooking up corn bread or smoking beef jerky. Either way, she was already looking forward to the meal.

She glanced up at the late afternoon sky. It wasn't long until twilight. Already the shadows were turning a pinkish lavender and orange. At least she wouldn't have to ride after dark. The other rider would go on through the night when she turned over the *mochila*. From the position of the smoke, it looked like the station was just over the next ridge.

She topped the little rise and saw the station up ahead. For a moment, she was so stunned that she couldn't even rein in her horse and it galloped ahead while she gaped in open-mouthed horror. The station was a mass of red and yellow flames, smoke curling up into the pale blue sky.

Oh, my God! Dallas reined in, looked around wildly. *Maybe it was an accident. Maybe someone had dropped a cigar on some hay. Maybe a spark from the fireplace . . .*

Logic told her if it were an accident, she'd see men running in every direction, toting water buckets and shouting instructions to each other as they tried to douse the blaze.

There was no living thing in sight; no sound save the crackling of the greedy flames. What had happened? What should she do? Instinct told her to gallop back the way she had come. Who knew what lay on the trail past the station? The hair on the back of Dallas's neck rose as she thought of the possibilities. *Indians.*

What was she to do? She clutched the little cottonwood switch so hard her fingers hurt. Riding slowly forward, she stayed ready to bolt and gallop away at the slightest sound or movement. *What had happened to everyone? Was there even a fresh horse?* The palomino she rode was lathered and blowing. Dallas took a deep breath, realizing that she might be facing another long ride on the tired pony on which she sat.

She reined in only a few hundred yards from the station and sat on her horse, undecided. Maybe the station tender and her relief rider had fled to safety at the next stop. Could there be anyone up there behind the wagons and the rocks? Suppose she was riding into an Indian ambush?

The bitter scent of smoke almost choked Dallas, and she blinked as it drifted into her eyes. She wheeled her horse to make a wide circle around the burning wreckage without risking riding into the station yard.

The wind shifted suddenly and she heard a moan as it blew at her, and she smelled not only smoke but gunpowder . . . and fresh blood.

The sound came again and she waited, straining to hear. *Is it a trap? Is it only the wind blowing around the almost burned building? Is it the moan of someone in agony?*

Instinct told her to get the hell out of this station as fast as her tired horse could carry her. She turned her horse to make a wide circle. The sound came again.

Horsefeathers. She just couldn't ride away if someone in that burned rubble was hurt. She wished she had her rosary and that she had been to confession more recently. But it was too late for all that. She nudged her horse forward, expecting painted braves to jump out from behind wagons and stacked firewood as she rode slowly into the station yard.

Nothing. Not a thing moved except the flames that leapt

241

toward the sky as the fire began to consume the roof. She still smelled blood and gunpowder, and she prayed as she rode in. *Holy Mary, Mother of God . . .*

A dead white horse lay on the other side of the woodpile, arrows sticking from it as if it were a perverted pincushion. She peered toward the burning station. Inside, she saw a slight boy sprawled out, gun in hand. Not far from him lay a fallen warrior in full war paint. She must get them out before the roof caved in. She must get help! She must . . . Even as she stared at the two lying inside the burning station, she realized they were both dead. The Pony rider, she thought in horror, the one who should have taken the mail on from here.

The Indian was small, slight, not much more than a boy himself. The bloody scene told its own story; they had killed each other in this attack on the station. Even as she stared, the roof burned furiously, then, with a crash, it collapsed. She stared numbly, watching the ruins burn, providing a funeral pyre for the two dead men. By the time the fire had burned another hour, no one would be able to recognize either of the two, they would be only two small charred mounds of blackened bones.

She heard the sound again as she absently tucked the switch in her saddle girth. Cautiously, Dallas dismounted and drew her Navy Colt, the only weapon she carried. Originally, like the others, she'd been issued a rifle, but like most riders, she'd discarded it after a few days because it was heavy and cumbersome to deal with on a galloping horse. The Pony riders figured it was easier to outrun a pursuer, considering the swift horses they rode. Now she cursed her carelessness and wished she were better armed.

Maybe she'd find some weapons or at least a fresh horse. But walking around the station yard, she realized the war party had left nothing behind but death.

She heard the sound again and gritted her teeth, fighting an urge to run back to her horse and gallop away. The only other noise was the crackling of the flames as fire consumed the station.

Gingerly, she moved around the silent yard, looking, her heart in her mouth. She kept her gun ready, expecting at any

242

time that a scarlet-painted warrior would jump out from behind something and grab her.

Following the whimper, she stepped around a wagon. And there she found him. It took a moment for the reality of the scene to register in her horrified brain. The station manager, no doubt, judging from his gray hair. A rifle lay flung away from him as if in disgust because it was useless without bullets, and his plump hands were pressed against his belly. When he breathed, crimson blood ran out between his fingers. *Gut shot*.

Dallas swallowed back the bile that rose in her throat as she knelt beside him. A gut-shot man couldn't be saved with the primitive medical care available in the West. But he could live a long time in great agony.

His eyes flickered open, and he looked up at Dallas, smiled with great effort. "Pit River war party . . . you'll have to carry the mail on. Water . . . please . . . water."

"You can't have water," Dallas said, brushing his gray hair back from his forehead, "You—"

"We both know it won't make no difference . . . please, water."

Dallas choked back tears. One never gave a gut-shot man water, but he was right; what difference did it make?

"I'll get you a dipperful, mister." She ran to the water barrel, brought the water, spilling a little in her haste. The heat of the roaring fire seemed almost to scorch her skin even from this distance. There wouldn't be much left of the two in the building to bury.

She stuck her pistol back in her belt, knelt to give the dying man a sip. The blood on his hands smeared the tin dipper as he grabbed it and drank greedily, then moaned in terrible agony that tore at Dallas's heart.

"I-I'll get you help." Should she go back to Williams' station and chance meeting up with the war party if it had ridden in that direction or should she ride on to the next station?

He shook his head, bit his lip until blood ran down his pale face. "No help for me, and you know it. Got to get the mail through. A lot of us have sacrificed for this idea . . . we believe in it . . . believe in this country."

Dying in slow agony, yet all he could think of was his commitment to the Pony. "I'll get it through, don't worry. I'll get the mail through."

"God, I hurt so bad! Son, do me one last favor and finish me off."

"Oh, God, no!" Dallas looked down at him, wide-eyed. Her religion made her recoil from doing such a terrible thing. "I-I can't help you do that!"

"Suppose they come back?" he whispered. "There's enough of me left alive to torture for hours."

That was true. She couldn't take him with her, and it would be awhile before she could get a rescue party from the next station to come back here. *Come back for what? To bury him or watch him finish dying. Holy Mary, mother of God . . . what should I do?*

Dallas wiped big drops of sweat from his face. "I'll tell you what I can do, I'll leave you my pistol in case they do come back. That way, you can defend yourself." She took it from her belt, put it in his bloody fingers.

He grabbed it the way a drowning man will grab at straws floating on the surface of the water. "You got another one? Don't want you to ride defenseless."

"Sure," she lied. "I got another one." She didn't, but what good would one pistol be against a war party? It would keep me from being captured alive, she thought with a shiver. In Texas, where the Comanche rode out to raid on autumn nights under a full moon, no man ever put himself in a position to be taken alive. And the legends were many of men who'd shot their women when the Comanches had them hopelessly surrounded, to keep them from falling into the hands of a war party. No one knew how to inflict torture like an Indian.

Many of the frontiersmen she'd known in Texas carried a fifty-caliber shell full of poison in case they were captured by Indians. If so, they could "bite the bullet" and commit suicide rather than be taken alive.

The man gestured weakly with a blood-stained hand, the other tightly clutching the pistol. "Get the hell outa here, boy, in case they come back. Get that mail through."

She stood up. "Can I do anything else for you, mister?"

He shook his head, grimacing in pain. "You've done enough. I'm much obliged."

He was dying, yet polite enough to thank her. She swallowed hard. "I'll send back help soon as I get there."

He nodded, both of them knowing how useless it was but the gesture had to be made. "Good luck to you, boy. Now, git!"

Dallas turned and walked swiftly away, too overcome to say more. She went back to her weary palomino, swung up in the saddle. "I'm sorry, hoss. I know I promised you a rest and some grain, but things have changed. We've got to get the mail on and bring back help for that poor man."

She turned the pony's head and took off at a lope. It was fifteen miles or so to the next station and almost dusk. The Milky Way seemed to almost touch the earth in the lavender stillness that comes just before the sun goes down completely. In less than an hour, it would be dark. Dark. The thought cheered her, when earlier it would have frightened her. Most Indians wouldn't fight at night, being afraid that if they were killed, their souls would wander the world forever, unable to find their way to heaven in the darkness. *Ekutsihimmiyo,* her Cheyenne mother called the starry trail, the Hanging Road to the Sky. The darkness would be a haven for Dallas. The chances that anyone would see her riding toward the next station would be minimized by riding through it.

For a split second, she worried about Quint, wondered if he had gotten back to the Williams station all right. Would the Pit River war party attack there? He was a good shot, and no doubt could take care of himself, but she loved him and couldn't help but worry.

She had ridden only a quarter of a mile or so, but she paused and looked behind her, seeing the distant smoke still drifting from the burned station. How long would that poor devil live in agony? At least, with her pistol, he could defend himself if the Indians returned.

The pistol shot rang out, echoed and reechoed across the desolate land, making Dallas start and the horse rear. Indi-

245

ans? But there were no more shots and Dallas knew then what the man had done. Unable to endure the agony and afraid of falling into the hands of a war party should the Indians return, he had taken his own life.

If only she had known what he intended, she wouldn't have left him the pistol. If only . . . No, she couldn't blame him even if it was a terrible sin.

That pistol still had five slugs in it and she needed it badly. Could she go back and take that gun from the old man's hand? She'd seen what a Colt could do at close range, and the thought sickened her.

No, she wouldn't go back. She'd have to try to outrun the war party if she was unlucky enough to cross its trail. That poor devil! All she could do now was go. She checked her map, tapped the pony lightly with the little cottonwood switch, urged him on. But tears blinded her, made it hard for her to see the trail.

Keep going, Dallas, she told herself to keep from breaking down completely. Up ahead, there's a station with safety and food and a bunk. Someone else can carry the mail on from there.

The sun began to sink behind the hills to the west, like a great, bloody ball. She rode on toward the station, praying for nightfall so she would have the safety of darkness.

It was then she noticed the fire on the next hilltop. *Oh, God, no, don't tell me the Indians got that station, too!*

Then she realized it was off to the right of where the station would be. She saw smoke rise in short puffs; then there was a long pause before it rose again. A chill went down her back, but she didn't break stride. *Smoke signals.* The Indians were sending messages. About what? Had they spotted her? Were they telling of their destruction of the station? Or signaling about an attack on the station ahead of her?

There was nothing to do but keep riding, hope they hadn't seen her. Besides, if the station ahead didn't yet know about the trouble, they needed to be alerted. She might save some lives.

Her heart hammering, Dallas watched the distant smoke as daylight began to fade. She reached out, patted her tired

246

horse, still absently clutching the cottonwood switch. "I know you're tired, boy, but we'll reach the station after a while and I'll see that you get a double measure of oats."

The palomino made a little noise as if he found that comforting. Of course, Dallas thought, his home stable is Williams' station, so if he ever gets loose, he'll probably return to that place.

"I didn't mean you were going home," she whispered to the gelding, trying to keep her mind off the smoke signals on the hills. "We're headed away from Williams' station."

And Quint Randolph, she thought. Oh, if he were only here. She might be a tomboy, but when it came right down to it, she was a woman first and she was scared. What she wanted most was to be able to throw herself into his powerful arms and have him hold her tight and whisper, Easy, angel, everything's going to be all right.

She loped her tired horse along the trail, hating to push him so hard, but afraid to slow down. Suppose she had been seen from a hilltop? It was almost dark now, the purple velvet of night slowly spreading across the sky as if some giant hand were pulling a blanket over the world. At least the smoke signals seemed to have stopped.

Craning to look, Dallas saw no hint of smoke. Maybe they had ridden on. In a few more minutes, it would be dark and she'd find refuge in the blackness until she made it to the next station. Her mouth tasted dry, but she didn't want to stop to get a drink from her canteen. She reached up to make sure the precious pearl earrings were still safely tucked in her pants pocket.

Think of dances, Dallas, she commanded herself, for every muscle in her slight body ached from fatigue. Think of attending a big dance in a new dress and wearing your pearl earrings.

That turned her thoughts to Quint. Would her family like him? Probably. But his wouldn't like her. She wouldn't think about impossible situations right now. She would concentrate on making it to the next station safely. She would think about a comfortable bunk to stretch out on and a big hunk of corn bread. Maybe they would even have butter.

She laughed a little as she rode, trying to cheer herself up. It wasn't far to the next station; she'd be there in an hour. Tomorrow a burial party would have to go back to that burned station, and the next time she ran across a *padre,* she would see that prayers were said for the dead.

And then the riders came up over the rise to her left. For a moment, in the purple twilight, she thought she had imagined the figures. Maybe . . .

They seemed to spot her and started forward at a run. A war party! For only a heartbeat, Dallas blinked, fighting back a scream. Then she lashed out at the palomino with the little switch.

"Run, boy. Run like the devil is after us!"

I must keep my head, she thought as she leaned low over the pony's neck and urged him on. She used her little switch, looked back over her shoulder at the braves. If only she'd kept her pistol! She could have at least taken a few of them with her before they got her!

She glanced back over her shoulder, not wanting to believe what her eyes told her. They were gaining on her, yelping, shouting as they rode. She heard the shots, hunched even lower in the saddle. But she felt a sting like that of a bee, looked down, and was stunned to see blood welling up on her arm, spilling onto her saddle, dripping crimson down the horse's light-colored hair.

If her poor horse hadn't already been worn out, he could easily have stayed ahead of the thin, grass-fed ponies of the Indians. But he faltered, stumbled. With her wounded arm almost useless, she was fighting to maintain her balance. When her horse stumbled again, she fell.

She scrambled to her feet, stood there in the middle of the meadow in the almost darkness. There was no running, no place to hide. Her palomino staggered to its feet, stood trembling, smeared with her bright blood.

The mail. It was her duty to protect it at all costs, get it to government officials in California. But there was no way to escape. The Indians were riding toward her at a gallop, their ugly leader's face still visible in the growing darkness. He caught sight of Dallas and yelled triumphantly. If nothing else, the mail must not fall into the wrong hands. Some of it might be secret and important. How could she save it?

She did the only thing possible. In a bare spot on the prairie, she knelt and scooped out a small hole, put the *mochila* in, quickly kicked dirt over it. She was terrified as they rode toward her, but she was honor bound to save the mail. Maybe by some miracle, the whites would find it when they followed her trail.

How could she mark the spot? She took the only thing she had, her little cottonwood switch, stuck it in the ground by the buried *mochila*. It was all she could do.

Maybe she could escape, hide in the sagebrush. She abandoned the exhausted and useless horse, took off at a run. It was dark now. With a lot of luck, she might stay hidden in the brush and the Indians wouldn't find her.

The war party, having reined to a halt, was yelping with disappointment like a bunch of coyotes when they realized she wasn't lying somewhere near her lathered horse. They started beating the bushes, poking at the sagebrush with sharp lances.

The moon came out, lighting up their painted, cruel faces and stars gradually flickered on like small lamps in the blackness above. *Nevada nights.* Once she had made love on a beautiful night like this and now she was going to die in the desert darkness.

The breeze brought her the scent of the braves. They smelled like sweat, smoke and rancid grease. She crouched, watching them spread out in a line, each with a lance, poking and prodding at every shadow. Her exhausted horse, stumbled away toward Williams' station.

One of the braves motioned toward the blood-smeared palomino and asked something in his language, obviously wondering whether to capture it or not.

The ugly leader shook his head, said something in a derisive tone. Obviously he thought the horse too exhausted to worry about. A war party would be riding fast and couldn't bother with an exhausted horse that might die on them if they pushed it too hard.

Well, if the horse made it home, at least Quint would

realize what had happened to her. Dallas's arm hurt and dried blood stiffened her shirt, but the wound did not seem as bad as it had looked. Was there any chance they'd overlook her and give up?

There is always morning, she thought, her pulse pounding so loudly, she was sure they must hear it. If they didn't find her tonight, they'd have all the light they needed to search at dawn.

Maybe, before then, she could slip away through the sagebrush and walk the rest of the way to the next station. Maybe . . .

Then the leader shouted in triumph, and his ugly face twisted in a triumphant smile as he suddenly seemed to look right at Dallas. He gave a shout and motioned his men forward.

There was no escape; he'd seen her. She turned to make a vain attempt to run. But hands reached out to grab her.

She wouldn't think of how it would feel when they killed and scalped her; she'd think of her love. I love you, Quint Randolph, she thought as hands closed on her, dragged her out of the sagebrush. I'll always love you!

Chapter Seventeen

Quint had mixed emotions as he led his horse with the chieftain on it into the Indian village. People came out of their wickiups, stood glaring at him silently as he passed. Even little children stopped their playing to stare wide-eyed. One little fellow with dark, solemn eyes trailed along beside him as Quint walked.

"Wovoka," said the child, touching his chest, "Wovoka." Then, seemingly overcome with shyness at his own boldness, the child fled.

Quint's heart went out to the Indians, who looked thin and poor.

He looked over his shoulder at Timbi. "I hope they know I mean well by bringing you in."

Timbi nodded. "It may take them awhile to get used to the idea of a white man saving a life instead of taking one. Stop here." He indicated a brush hut a little bigger and more luxurious than most of the others. "This is my *karnee*."

Indians gathered around, asking questions in their own language, obviously curious. Timbi launched into a long explanation, gesturing toward Quint. *"Nermerberah,"* he said.

They looked dubious at first, then slow smiles spread across the solemn faces and there were nods of welcome.

Quint raised one eyebrow. "What was all that?"

The chieftain gestured for help and Quint assisted him from the saddle. *"Nermerberah?* It means 'Indian's friend.' I tell them I owe you a life, that you are always welcome in this

251

village; that I intend to make you a blood brother."

Quint looked into the handsome, tragic face and felt deeply moved. "I appreciate the honor."

Timbi gave him a questioning look. "I do not understand some of your big words. Is this the same as 'much obliged'?"

Quint laughed in spite of himself as he helped the man inside the *karnee*. "You've picked up some Western talk. Yes." He nodded. "I'm much obliged."

Timbi collapsed on the floor with a tired sigh. "But you of the magic number—"

"Quint."

"Quint. You speak a different way from many of the others who come here, blowing our mountains apart with your medicine sticks to dig the gray rocks from the depths."

"Silver." Quint sat down cross-legged next to him by the fire. "It is of great value if war comes where white man fights white man."

The chieftain scowled, tragedy etched in every line of his brooding face. "More value than life? The poisoned runoff from the mines killed my family."

Quint leaned his elbows on his knees. "I am sorry the whites have done this thing. I, too, have been without a wife for a year now."

Timbi stared into the fire. "Then you know what it is to be alone. More than that, she carried my child. I think that perhaps we are much alike, Quint."

A pretty, dark Indian girl stuck her head in the *karnee*. "So, brother, you are back," she said in halting English, looking flustered. Quint saw sudden recognition on her face as if she recognized him, but to his knowledge, he had seen no Indian girls since he'd arrived at Williams' station.

Timbi smiled and then quickly frowned at her. "You disgrace me before my guest," he said. "Bring food for us." He glanced toward Quint. "The *tavibo* has no doubt been sent by the Great Spirit."

"I really ought to be getting back to the station," Quint put in. He was concerned about what Dallas would think when he didn't return. She'd be frantic, thinking something had happened to him. And what if some of those scruffy men

252

hanging around the trading post discovered she was a girl?

Timbi stared into the fire as the girl scampered away. "You would refuse my hospitality? Do you scorn to eat meat with Indians?"

His tone said he had run into prejudice before.

"No, of course not." Quint shook his head. "I am proud to share food with the Paiute, but there are those who will worry if I fail to return."

"With most of my people and our relatives, the Bannock and the Shoshoni, already gathering to decide whether to ride the war trail, I think it better you stay here until dawn when one of our people can give you safe escort back to your trading post."

The young girl brought the food in intricate baskets, set it before them, keeping her eyes demurely downcast, but sneaking peeks at Quint as she served him. She was fully dressed in antelope skin and red moccasins colored with natural dyes. She couldn't have been more than sixteen, but pretty, Quint thought as he helped himself to the gruel, dipping into it hesitantly. "Your wife?"

Timbi paused, a juicy piece of rabbit in his mouth. "No, my sister, Atsa. It means 'red' in our language and she loves the color."

Atsa blushed darkly and offered Quint a piece of roasted rabbit. He took it to eat with his piñon nut soup, and had a sudden, disturbing thought. "I'm not taking your food, am I, Atsa?"

She smiled with pleasure at his notice. "No, little Wovoka managed to kill it accidentally with a stone. It is our custom that a boy may not eat of the first meat that he kills, it must be given away after touching his wrists, elbows, and knees with the dead animal. We are eating little Wovoka's first kill."

Quint grinned at her in spite of himself. "Big name for such a small boy."

Timbi grunted. "It means the 'cutter.' He is an unusual little boy. Who knows what he thinks behind those dark, solemn eyes?"

He dismissed the girl with a wave of his hand, but Quint saw the fond smile that betrayed how much he cared for her.

"My sister is very pretty but a trifle silly. She has big dreams of wanting to live in the white man's town and have fine clothes and all the things a white girl has, maybe even a white husband. She thinks I do not realize all this, but she is the beat of my heart to me now that our whole family has been killed. I spoil her, I know."

Quint reached for a burning stick from the fire, lit his pipe. After a moment's thought, he offered a cigar to Timbi.

There was a long hesitation and then Timbi took it, let Quint light it. They smoked a long moment in silence.

Timbi inhaled and then took the cigar out of his mouth, stared at the glowing tip. "Once when I was a little boy, I went into this white settlement. The Paiutes were more friendly to the whites then, helped them as they went through with their wagons covered with white cloth. We did not know that some of them would stay."

"Most of us mean no harm," Quint said softly.

Timbi did not answer for a long moment, but stared at the cigar. "I saw an old Paiute man beaten and humiliated because he dared to pick up and smoke a cigar butt a white man had thrown in the street."

Quint said nothing, for he realized that perhaps this man was opening up his heart to him for this one time because he had saved his life. Tomorrow, things might be very different.

"That old man was my grandfather," Timbi said so softly that Quint had to lean forward to hear him.

"I apologize for my people," Quint said.

Timbi regarded him a long moment. "I believe you really mean that."

"There is no reason that we can't let bygones be bygones and start fresh."

Timbi laughed bitterly, took a deep puff of the fragrant cigar. "You and I are friends, Quint. You may come and go in this camp because I say you may. But the time comes soon, I think, when the Indians of the Great Basin will have to fight back before the white man destroys us."

"You cannot win, Timbi," Quint smoked and stared into the fire, thinking of this afternoon's conversation. "But I don't suppose that will stop you."

"Never!" The Indian's voice was hard, bitter. "We must all die sooner or later. The Indians have put up with too much already. Whenever I meet a white man from now on, I have vowed to kill him." Then he told Quint of all the injustice the whites had done to the Paiutes over his life span. "Winnemucca, like old Truckee, wants to keep the peace, but the tribes are gathering in now to council. I think the vote will be for war."

"After having heard you, I cannot blame you, Timbi, but it is wrong to dwell on the past. You should think of the future."

Timbi shrugged his broad shoulders, smoked, and stared into the fire. "I see our future. It is starvation and misery on a reservation, so the whites can dig for the gray rocks. Is the gray rock, this silver, what you come for?"

"No." Quint shook his head, enjoying the taste of the tobacco. "I come because of the pony riders. I sell them horses."

Timbi's dark eyes brightened with interest. "We have seen them. What is it that they carry that is so important to make them always gallop?"

Quint leaned back on one elbow and laughed. "Nothing that means harm to the Paiute. They carry only messages written on paper, back and forth."

"Is that why you chase the Medicine Hat?"

"Yes. I think he would sire swift-footed colts for me."

"I had a vision, a strange vision about that horse. It was as if I became him and ran wild and free forever, only. . . ."

Quint waited for Timbi to continue, realized he wouldn't. "You were chasing him yourself when your horse fell?"

Timbi ruefully rubbed his leg. "I should have known better. The Dreamers say the horse is big medicine and should be left alone."

"The Dreamers?"

"I think you would call it a new religion among the Paiutes. I know little of it myself. Young Wovoka's relatives follow it."

Drums began to beat far away in the silence.

Timbi looked at Quint. "Some of the tribes have gathered

255

over at Pyramid Lake to council and to discuss the whites."

"You think you could convince them not to go to war?" Quint felt hopeful.

But Timbi shook his head slowly. "I think we are all on a course we cannot change. It began long ago when many Paiutes saw an old man beaten over a cigar taken from the gutter, when some Washoe were murdered because the whites demanded justice for other white men who were killed."

Quint felt despair. "What happened?"

"The whites demanded our people turn over the killers. We knew nothing about this murder, but the whites would attack and kill many if the men weren't brought in. The tribal elders chose several young men who had no children to feed, sent them in even though all knew they had done nothing."

"I think I have heard of this thing." Quint grimaced. "Didn't it happen in the town of Carson City?"

The Indian scowled, nodded. "The young men were afraid they were going to be hanged. They tried to run away. The whites shot them down."

"Again I apologize for my people."

"What for?" Timbi said. "After all, they were only greasy Indians." His voice and face were bitter, sad. "Even we do not think much of Washoes."

Quint puffed his pipe. "Perhaps someday, Timbi, you will take another woman, have another child."

"If only I had been there that day," Timbi almost whispered, "I could have stopped my family from drinking the water. I knew about the poisons from the mining pits."

" 'If only' are the two saddest words in any language, Timbi, because no one can change the past. Once I thought my life was over, too, I had so much guilt over my woman's death. But then I found a new love, started to live again." He thought tenderly of Dallas, wondered what she was doing now that darkness was falling. Was she out under the stars, looking up at the beautiful Nevada night and thinking of him?

The Paiute shook his head. "I will never expect more from a woman than that she warm my blankets and give me sons."

Quint saw Dallas's dark eyes in his mind. "You have

256

missed much, Timbi, if you have never found a woman who becomes like the beat of your heart to you."

Timbi shrugged as if he did not believe it was possible. "Tell me of yourself, of the whites, and I will tell you about my people."

They talked for hours before Timbi finally stood up. "At dawn, you may go in peace, Quint Randolph, my *nermerberah*." He held out his hand awkwardly and Quint took it in both of his.

Quint said, "I never had a brother, Timbi, yet I feel as if I have found one in you. If things were different between our two peoples, perhaps we could become lifelong friends."

"But things are not different." Timbi said grimly and his hand dropped to his side. "I will hate the other whites no less, but I owe you a life, man of the magic number and medicine ring."

Quint looked down at the animal's head on the ring. "It's a family crest," he said by way of explanation, "it's not big medicine."

The Indian shrugged. "You alone, Quint Randolph, may come and go among the Paiutes because you have been honorable and brave in helping me. You might be in spirit, the brother I never had."

Timbi reached for a small knife. "Would you accept the honor of becoming my blood brother?"

Quint was deeply moved. "It is indeed an honor, Timbi, to mix my blood with yours."

The knife stung as Timbi made a small cut in both their wrists. They held them against each other while their blood mingled.

Timbi looked at him and his own hard face softened. "Quint, as long as we speak the truth—treat each other like brothers, live with honor—we will both prosper. Should either of us lie or do that which is without honor, the bad spirits will take swift vengeance."

They shook hands solemnly.

"Thank you, brother," Quint said. "I hope that gradually both our peoples will become brothers of the heart as you and I have done."

"I owe you a life, Quint Randolph, and I am in your debt for all time. It can only really be repaid by giving you a life."

Quint smiled and shook his head, his heart full of warmth for this simple savage. "I expect nothing, Timbi, but I hope for peace."

Timbi frowned. "Hundreds of our warriors are gathering to discuss this. I will have only a little part in the decision, and I hate the whites—except for you. If you ever have a need, something I can do for you, send word and I will do it."

"Thank you, brother."

"And now, sleep well, Quint," Timbi put his hand on Quint's shoulder. "Tomorrow we will give you a fresh horse, and send you back to the Pony station."

He called for a warrior, who led Quint to a comfortable *karnee*. Quint hadn't realized how tired he was until he stretched out on the pile of dried grass next to the little fire, dropped off to sleep. Tomorrow he would be back in Dallas's arms, and maybe he had done something to help the relationship between the two peoples.

In his dreams, he chased the great Medicine Hat stallion, but as he roped it, fought it, he saw Timbi's eyes looking back at him. Then it broke free, ran along the rim of the hills, no, floated along the cliffs as if it were not quite real, only a spirit horse that was kin to the wind and desert.

Quint awoke with a start, then heaved a sigh of relief that it had only been a dream after all. The Medicine Hat was just a horse, albeit a finer, faster specimen than most. The Paiute himself had been trying to capture it as Quint was still determined to. He was obsessed with the thought of adding the great horse to his herd, and now that he had truly seen the West, he was more determined than ever to reopen the old Wolf's Den ranch. He thought of Dallas, wondered if she would love Arizona when he took her there?

What had awakened him? It was very quiet and very late, he realized. Then he saw her. In the firelight, Atsa's naked body gleamed like brown satin as she sat on her knees watching him sleep.

"Atsa, what the hell are you doing here?" He rose up on his elbows in alarm. "Your brother would kill us both if he found you here!"

"I think not." She smiled as she came over, lay down next to him, pressed herself against him. "My brother has been asking me to choose a man and marry. I think he would be pleased if I chose the white man he has made his brother."

Before he could pull away, she pressed her ripe body against him, slipped her arms around his neck.

"Atsa, no, I already have a woman." Quint tried to break her grip on his neck, but his maleness reacted strongly to the pressure of full, firm breasts against his bare chest. He felt the swollen tips of her nipples brushing against thick hair, and her thighs were hot as she lay close to him.

"I have seen you with your woman, Quint Randolph, when I spied on the Pony Station. But many of our warriors have two wives. You are virile enough to keep two women full of your seed, their bellies swollen with your sons."

Before he could protest further, she reached to take his throbbing maleness in her hand and her tongue slipped between his lips and probed there.

He had not expected that his body would react so strongly to the ripe virginity she offered. But even as he found himself taking her in his arms, running his hands over her, Dallas's face came to his mind and he pulled back.

"I'm sorry, Atsa." He sat up on the grass matt, took a deep, shuddering breath. "You're very desirable, and if I weren't a man of honor, I'd say whatever it is you want to hear so I could have you tonight. But your brother is my friend so I won't lie to you. I have a woman named Dallas, and I love her as I never thought I could love a woman. She's my only woman. We are bound together by holy words until death do us part."

Atsa got up slowly, reluctantly. "You must love this Dallas very much, and you have as much honor as my brother. If someday, you want a second woman, would you desire me?"

He grinned and shrugged. "If that should happen, perhaps I would desire Timbi's sister. But I don't ever expect to lose my woman." He frowned suddenly at the thought. "If another man should try to take her, I'd kill him."

"I wish a man cared so much for me." Her pretty face was wistful as she reached for her antelope shift.

Quint had a sudden inspiration. "I have friends in Philadelphia who would be willing to send clothes. The Paiute seem to have so little."

"Dead peoples' clothes?"

"Well, the family I know had a daughter about your size, and lost her last year to a fever. They would be pleased that the clothes were put to good use."

"No dead peoples' clothes!" She jumped up, visibly angry. "White churches did this once, and we were deeply insulted. They called us stupid savages because we brought the clothes back, dumped them in the street. It is taboo to Paiutes to wear the clothes of the dead. Everything they owned must be destroyed and their names never mentioned again."

"Everything? But you have so little to begin with."

"Everything!" she answered haughtily. "Even a *karnee* must be burned if someone dies inside, so the dying are often carried out under the stars."

"I'm sorry, Atsa, that the whites offend because we don't know your customs. I'll tell you what; when I get to Virginia City, I'll buy you a fine dress, finer than any you have ever seen and send it to you."

She smiled, more child now than woman. "A red dress?"

He laughed, nodded. "I promise you the reddest dress that anyone ever saw! Now get out of here and let me sleep. Tomorrow I must get an early start."

"Then good-bye, white man." Before he could stop her, she leaned over, kissed him on the lips and scurried away.

Quint lay down. Many white men would think him a fool for not using the innocent girl for his own lust, telling her whatever she wanted to hear. Perhaps Timbi was right: they both had strict ideas of honor. He looked at the small, bloody cut on his arm. He had found more than a friend today.

Tomorrow he would ride back to Williams' station, tell Dallas he had given up the idea of capturing the stallion. They could leave immediately. If she wanted to live in Philadelphia in a fine mansion like his sister's, he would build her one, although the thought of staying in the crowded city, now that he had seen the West, sickened him. But it was up to Dallas. He would do whatever it took to make her happy.

The next morning, he said his good-byes and rode out. The other Paiutes looked at him with veiled hostility, and Quint knew that he was only safe because he was Timbi's friend. He tried one more time with the chieftain.

"Timbi, will you plead for peace at the council?"

The Paiute folded his arms across his broad chest and looked troubled. "I dislike to say no to my brother, but Quinton, I tell you this; I have no hesitation about killing any white man who crosses my trail. They all owe me the lives of my family."

"If you kill other whites, I don't see how you and I can maintain friendship," Quint said.

Timbi's face turned dark as thunder. "Then come no more to my camp, white brother! You alone are safe in these hills from the wrath of my people."

There was nothing else to say. Would Quint's decision to save Timbi's life cost other white men their lives? Perhaps, but if he had to do it over again, he still could not leave the savage chieftain to die in the desert. Quint mounted up and rode out. The last face he saw was Atsa's. She was staring after him wistfully.

He rode back to Williams' station. Yancy and a young boy with his arm in a sling came out to greet him.

Yancy sucked his gold toothpick. "Never expected to see you alive again. With the Injuns on a rampage, when you didn't come back, we thought they got you."

Quint shrugged and looked around for Dallas, wondering how much to tell them. It would take too long to explain. "Dark caught me. I managed just fine until morning." He dismounted, looked around. "Where's Dal?"

The boy with his arm in the sling said, "You mean the other Pony Express rider?"

Quint nodded. "Are you a rider?"

The boy held out his bandaged arm by way of explanation. "War party took after me yesterday, put an arrow in my shoulder. I was lucky to make it in here to the trading post."

Quint paused, thinking. This was the rider he had seen from a distance. At the time he had thought something was wrong. Suddenly, a horrible suspicion hit him. "You didn't carry the mail on?"

Yancy stuck his thumbs in his flowered vest. "With his arm in that shape? Looks like the Pony's about to get canceled or delayed because of Injun problems."

"Then who—?"

"Hey there, Randolph." The two Williams brothers came out of the building. "We'd all given you up for dead."

He looked around, the thought too horrifying to even be put into words.

Dave spat through the gap in his broken tooth. "That kid who came with you, Dal Dawson, took the mail out yesterday when Bob here was too hurt to ride."

Quint was stunned by shock and rage, for a long moment, he only stared back at Dave Williams. "You sent Dal? Good Lord!" He had to hold himself back to keep from rushing the man, battering him with his fists.

"Well, after all, he was a relief rider! The kid knew what he was gettin' into when he signed on with the Pony."

Quint wanted to scream and curse and strike out at someone, though he knew it was his own fault for leaving Dallas here alone while he went chasing a horse. "By God, I—"

"What's that?" Yancy drawled and they all turned to follow his gaze out across the *playas,* the barren plain.

A riderless horse stumbled wearily toward them. Quint swore under his breath as he recognized the palomino. No one moved. All were staring at the horse as if it were some kind of apparition. The young rider made a sound of dismay.

Quint groaned aloud as he ran out to meet the weary palomino walking into the station yard. The *mochila* was missing and dried blood smeared the saddle and the horse's light coat. "Look it over!" he ordered, frantically checking the horse himself. "It's hurt; see the blood? It's—"

"Randolph," Yancy drawled, "there's no wounds on that

horse."

"There's bound to be!" Quint was frantic now, stroking the horse, looking it over as the others gathered around. "See the blood?"

Oscar pulled at his beard thoughtfully. "That hoss ain't hurt. That only leaves one answer."

He was not going to accept the fact that she was dead, that he had gone off on a fool's errand to capture a horse and now Dallas was dead. "Damnit! Don't you realize . . . ?" *Realize what? They didn't even know Dal was a girl. Did it make any difference now?* He was too heartsick to do all the explaining.

The young rider said, "Maybe he ain't kilt. Reckon he could just be wounded and hiding in the grass someplace, waitin' for someone to send help?"

"Of course, that's it!" Quint grabbed onto the idea because he couldn't bear to live if she were gone. "Let's get out a search party."

Dave ran his tongue along the edge of his broken front tooth. "I ain't hankerin' to go prowlin' too far away. The kid here says it was Pit River Injuns, and them liquored up."

Quint had to fight himself to keep from pulling his gun and pistol-whipping the man. He needed all the help he could get. "There'll no doubt be a big reward from the Express owners. Besides, if Dal made it to the next relay station, it may still be under attack!"

With much grumbling, everyone admitted that might be true.

Quint distractedly ran a hand through his hair. "Then let's get mounted up, ride on over there!"

The young rider put the exhausted palomino in a stall with water and feed while the others saddled up, checked their weapons.

At least she was armed, Quint thought, and that gave him a little comfort as they rode at a gallop. He knew she carried the Navy Colt all the Pony riders had been given, and had scratched her initials on the butt.

He wouldn't even consider the possibility that something terrible might have happened to her. Melanie had died because of him and he'd felt guilty as hell, but he'd never loved her. Now Dallas might be dead, too, and he loved her more than life itself. If only he'd been here to stop her. If only he hadn't brought her out here. If only . . .

The two saddest words in any language. No, he would not think about the past right now, he would think about the future. Up at the next relay station, he'd find her, frightened but alive. She'd run into his arms and cry, Thank God you got here in time! We were almost out of ammunition but the war party fled when they saw the riders coming! And he would take her in his arms, kiss her tears away. . . .

Yancy rode to his left. "Reckon this closes down the Pony. The mail won't be able to go through. Now where would those Pit River savages get whiskey?"

"More importantly," Quint glared at him as they galloped on, "who would want to give it to them, knowing all the trouble it would cause?"

Yancy's cruel mouth smiled slightly. "Who indeed?"

If he could prove what he suspected, Quint would have gunned the gambler down on the spot. But suppose he was wrong and Yancy just happened to be passing through as he'd said?

"Hey!" Dave interrupted his thoughts. "I see just the barest wisp of smoke over the next rise!"

"Reckon it's smoke from the chimney and they'll invite us for breakfast?" Yancy drawled.

The thought cheered Quint. Sure, he was worried for nothing. They'd rode in and Dallas would meet him at the door with an ornery smile and a wink. She'd say in that Texas accent, Don't be too mad at me, I wanted to do it. We've got coffee made. Y'all come on in.

They rode over the little rise and looked down at the station. Smoldering ruins. No sign of life at all.

Quint lost his restraint. He felt as if some giant hand had reached into his chest, squeezed his heart to bursting. With a shout, he lashed his horse, galloped down the rise. Behind him, he heard the other horses picking up speed.

"Hello, the station!" he shouted as he galloped in, dismounted. They'd burned it down; but people must be hiding in the surrounding sagebrush. When they heard someone calling in English, they'd come out, knowing they were now safe. "Hello, the station!" Quint yelled more loudly as he stood there next to his horse.

The silence was deafening. Somewhere a bird called and in the ruins a burned timber collapsed, sending a flurry of gray ashes into the air. The others rode in, dismounted. No one said anything as they looked around.

"They're here all right!" Quint blustered to still his pounding heart. "They're just afraid to come out of the brush until they're sure we're white people and not Indians who speak English!"

He dropped his reins, turned, and walked around the deserted station yard. One lone chicken scratched in the dirt, cocking its head to look up at him as he approached. "Hello!" he shouted. "It's okay, you can come out now! We're from Williams' station."

The sound echoed back from the mountains: Williams' station . . . station . . . station. . . .

The hen clucked, went on scratching. The men spread out, began to look around.

If Dallas were dead, Quint didn't want to live anymore. He began to make deals with God. *If you'll make her be all right, I'll leave this place and never come back. If you'll work some miracle, I'll give big donations to the missions. If you'll just let me find her only slightly wounded, I'll—*

"Damn me!" Yancy drawled. "I think I see bodies inside the ruins . . . or what's left of 'em."

Oh, please, God, don't let it be her. If you'll let me find her alive, I promise I'll be a better person. . . .

Quint took a deep breath, drawing in the scents of smoke and gunpowder . . . and blood. He wouldn't go look at what the others were dragging out of the ashes because, of course, it couldn't be Dallas. Blindly, he walked around the wagon, and found the gray-haired man with the belly wound and half his head blown away.

"Oh, Lord!" he shouted as he stared down at the stiff body with a fly crawling across its disfigured face.

The others came running. Quint knelt next to the dead

man. Already, in the heat the body was beginning to smell.

The young rider took one look and left. Quint could hear him off in the brush, gagging and retching.

Dave Williams spat through his teeth. "The station manager, I knew him. That's just what I'd do if I had a belly wound — if I was lucky enough to have a gun to do it with."

Quint's fingers felt wooden as he took the pistol from the dead man's hand. He stared at it a long time, almost unable to breathe. *It was Dallas's Colt. It had her initials on the butt.*

Yancy rolled his toothpick from one side of his mouth to the other. "There's two bodies in the rubble, too burned to recognize. But I reckon it's Dal and his relief rider."

Quint turned on him savagely, almost hit him with the Colt. "No! There's survivors — got to be! Look some more!"

"If there is, where are they?" Yancy said. "We've made enough noise to be heard in Virginia City!"

Quint went for him then, relishing the feel of bone against his fist when it struck the handsome face, sending the Southerner stumbling backward. "This is your doing, you sonovabitch! You're behind this, somehow!"

The Williamses grabbed him, each seizing an arm. "You're talkin' *loco,* Randolph!"

One of the brothers clipped him across the temple and he lay in the dirt, stunned, head aching.

He saw the young boy come out of the brush, face ashen. "What's happening?"

From what seemed a long way away, he heard Dave Williams' voice. "Randolph went *loco.* Happens a lot when men first see something like this. Makes them scared and angry. They just strike out at the closest man."

Yancy clucked sympathetically, wiped the blood from his handsome face. "Reckon he and that kid were good friends."

Dave said, "I saw a shovel someplace. We got burying to do."

They were going to place his beloved Dallas in a crude hole out here in the wilderness without even a coffin to keep the dirt off her. Quint managed to sit up, although his head pounded. "Couldn't we take them into Virginia City?" Somehow, it seemed very important that she not be left out here in a grave with no marker and no one to ever bring flowers for her grave.

The Williams brothers looked at him. "Randolph, this ain't your back east, civilized way of living. Two of them bodies is burned so bad, they're just a mound of ashes. And this fella"—he gestured toward the suicide—"he'd smell a whole lot worse by the time we got him clear into town."

The logic of it was undeniable. Quint swayed to his feet, his head still pounding.

Yancy turned to the young rider, fingering his string tie absently. "Kid, you'd better ride on to Virginia City, have them alert everyone as to what's happened. I reckon as long as Injuns is on the warpath, the Pony won't be makin' any runs."

Maybe it was his imagination, but Quint would have sworn Yancy said it with satisfaction.

The boy rode out, and the rest of them got up a burial party.

"I want to help," Quint said stubbornly.

Yancy shook his head. "Damn me! You look sick enough to die, Randolph. Sit down on that rock before you collapse. We'll do it. Besides, I don't think an Eastern dude could stand the sight of what's in the ashes."

Quint slumped down heavily on the rock. No, he didn't want to see what lay in the ashes. He saw her in his mind the way she had been the night he'd met her, pretty and feisty, her black hair blowing around her face and almost obscuring the dainty earrings. *Mister, you're so drunk, you couldn't hit the ground with your hat in three tries!*

Dallas, oh, God, Dallas . . . He didn't even know how to reach her relatives so he could tell them what had happened. He closed his eyes and, head pounding, listened to the sounds of men digging.

Finally Oscar tossed his shovel to one side. "It's done. Let's get the hell outa here before it gets dark!"

Yancy laughed, sucked his gold toothpick. "You afraid of ghosts?"

Oscar wiped his sweating face. "I don't know. You stay out here long enough, you get to believin' the same things the

Injuns believe."

Quint stood up, weaving on his feet. "Shouldn't we say something over them?"

Dave spat on the ground. "Like what? You wanta say something, Randolph, you go right ahead."

But Quint didn't know what to say. He stood there, staring down at the graves while the lone chicken scratched around in the loose dirt, trying to think of something appropriate. But his soul was screaming at God for letting her die. His mouth couldn't form a prayer. "You're right, I suppose. Let's get out of here."

The others needed no urging. They mounted up, preparing to ride out. Quint looked back at the mounds of fresh dirt. He had not realized a man could hurt so much and not die of it. He had felt guilt when Melanie died, but he had not felt as if his insides were being torn out. He was not even sure which grave — which body — was Dallas's.

Good-bye, my dark angel. I'm leaving you out here alone. Will you be afraid without me here to protect you? Are you at peace?

In his memory, he heard her lilting laughter, saw the way she shook her hair back when she smiled. It was all he could do to keep from drawing his revolver, blowing his own head off. *No, she wouldn't approve of that.*

Resolutely, he turned and rode out at a slow pace. What was he going to do now? An anger began to build in him, fueled by his sorrow. He would stay in this area, close to her grave. He would hunt Indians down like coyotes, slaughter them without mercy. They owed him many, many lives to pay for hers.

The men took a slightly different route back to the trading post in case they had been trailed by a war party. Just before dark, they came to a place where many horses had trampled the grass down. There were signs of a struggle.

Her switch. Quint remembered that she liked to carry a little cottonwood switch instead of a big, cruel quirt. *Had she stuck it in the ground? And if so, for what purpose?* It looked out of place, poking up out of the flat, barren ground, but he didn't touch it. A slight smear of blood on the trampled grass made it plain that here was where she'd met the war party. No doubt she had turned and headed for the station, hoping the others could help her. But this was a little off the beaten path. Had she been lost?

What did it really matter?

Oscar spat on the ground. "I'll feel a helluva lot safer back at the trading post with some solid walls around me if there's going to be trouble."

Trouble? They'd think trouble when Quint Randolph started killing Indians. His vision blurred as he rode out behind them. Was it really that dark or was he blinded by tears? *Dallas. Oh my God, Dallas . . .*

Chapter Eighteen

Dallas had fought back as the war-painted braves dismounted and chased her down, dragging her out of the sagebrush. She was terrified and struggled to escape, knowing all the while it was useless.

At least she had buried the *mochila* and stuck her little switch in the ground to mark the spot. Perhaps later a search party backtracking her horse would find the mail. She'd done all she could do to save it from the savages.

The warriors grinned with pleasure at her futile efforts, ignoring her tired pony walking slowly away in the moonlight. Probably they thought it too exhausted to be worth bothering with. Eventually it would walk back to Williams' station and they would know the mail hadn't gotten through. But by then, it would be too late to help her.

The ugly leader twisted her arm cruelly. "So white boy, we catch!"

The others laughed, jabbered together in their language. She caught the scents of cheap whiskey, sweat, and rancid grease. Now why would anyone supply Indians with liquor, knowing they might go *loco* and run amok? *Someone who was trying to start an Indian war, shut down the Pony Express.*

She managed to twist out of his hand, took off running. They laughed and hooted, ran after her at an easy lope. They called out to each other in their language, obviously enjoying the diversion. Once she had seen a couple of cats playing with a mouse in just this way. It had run, terrified. The cats let it go

270

only a few feet, then pounced on it again.

Gasping for breath, knowing she couldn't escape without a horse, she ran anyway. Maybe one of them would shoot her. While she didn't want to die, the alternative, when they discovered she was a woman, was even more terrible. The ground was uneven beneath her boots and she stumbled, regained her balance, kept running as the Indians fanned out, slowly surrounding her. She wondered how it would feel to lie naked on that same rough ground with the relentless sun beating down on her and be slowly raped to death by the whole war party?

She wouldn't want Quint to find her that way, naked and without dignity, stinging ants crawling across her bare breasts, her body smeared with and reeking of their seed.

Her wounded arm stung and her head hurt, but their pain was nothing compared to the aching of lungs pulling air in desperate gasps. A horse could run itself to death; could a person? Certainly it beat the alternative.

The leader, obviously tiring of the game, barked a command behind her. Immediately, a couple of warriors ran over and grabbed her.

She would not give them the satisfaction of seeing her cry. She was Dallas Durango Randolph and her name meant 'spirited.' The blood of Spanish conquistadors and Cheyenne warriors ran in her veins; she would not show fear or beg mercy from this drunken group of Pit River braves.

When she finally faced the ugly leader, she spat full in his face. His eyes widened in surprise and his red paint smeared where her spittle ran in that split second before he struck her across the cheek.

She felt the pain in an explosion of little lights, tasted the blood from her cut lip, spat her own blood at him.

He grabbed her, reaching for his knife. Good. He was going to kill her quickly and without torture. But the other braves stopped him, and there was a hot verbal exchange. They seemed to be arguing that the captive should not be slain on the spot.

The leader swayed drunkenly on his feet. "They right, Pony boy. Not kill quick! Take you back to camp so all can

271

see how long it take you to die!"

So saying, they tied her hands behind her, threw her up behind the leader on the barebacked dun horse. Her own mount had wandered off into the darkness. Would it finally get back to camp?

The Indians took off at a leisurely pace, obviously not concerned about being pursued. To keep her balance with her hands tied behind her back, Dallas had to grip the horse with her legs, lean against the warrior. She felt his muscles against her bound breasts, the heat of his hips against the vee of her thighs. Soon, she thought, they will discover they have captured a woman, and those hard hips, that naked body will be between my thighs again in a brutal mating.

Dallas lost track of time and direction, but she was intensely aware of the sweat and stink of the man she leaned against. Once the Indians stopped to eat and water the horses, but they offered her nothing at all. After a few hours, her mind began to dwell on water—cold water.

She decided to escape, at least in her mind. She thought about her family's giant Triple D ranch in the Texas hill country. In the courtyard of the sprawling hacienda was a big fountain and a pool. The doves came there to drink, and many times as a child, she had splashed in the cold water of the fountain. In her mind, she once again played and splashed in that water, dove to the bottom of the pool like a little tadpole, came up laughing and splashing before her serene and beautiful mother, *Ojos de Pana,* and her proud, stern Spanish father.

Even gyp water began to seem appealing. There was a place on the range where that brackish water flowed. Even the cattle avoided it unless a drought dried up the deep artesian springs. Hard enough to float a horseshoe and tastes worse, she thought vaguely, attempting to wet her cracked lips with the tip of her tongue. If she had a bucket of gyp water now, she would drink every drop.

They stopped to sleep for a few hours and left her tied and thirsty while they rested. The sun was up now, and Dallas could no longer remember when it was she had been captured. Every bone in her body ached and she began to think she would welcome reaching the camp if for no other reason than to get her hurting body off this horse.

High noon, and the sun beat down on them. Then they topped a rise and suddenly another war party was only a few hundred yards away. But the Indians she rode with reacted with fear, and took off at a gallop.

The others shouted in triumph and raced after them. Was she better off to stay on the horse or fall off and hope the fall or the pursuers would kill her?

She didn't get to make that choice. The leader's horse was falling behind his comrades, struggling under the weight of two bodies. When he glanced back over his shoulder and saw that the enemy was gaining on him, he gave Dallas a sudden push.

Terrified, she tried to ball herself up in that split second before she hit the ground and rolled.

She wasn't dead. She realized that after the pain of the initial impact as she lay in a flurry of dust and movement as the pursuing horses galloped over her.

Prone in the straggly grass, Dallas stared after the running horses even as the pursuers caught up with the Pit River war party. The leader screamed as a thrown lance caught him in the back. The lance broke in half with a sharp sound as he hit the ground, but his dun pony kept running.

The pursuing warriors chased the others down. There was a brief fight, but within minutes, the original group lay dead in the blood-smeared sand while the second war party shouted in triumph.

She should try to get away while the Indians were occupied. Weakly, she swayed to her feet, took a few stumbling steps. But the tall leader of the second bunch saw her, urged his black pony after her with a triumphant yell.

Did it matter which tribe raped and tortured her? She was no better off than before except that she had had the satisfaction of witnessing the death of those who had raided the station.

The leader grabbed her, whirled her around. He was indeed tall for an Indian and wore only a breechcloth and knee-high rawhide moccasins. His black hair hung loose and straight to his broad shoulders, and he wore a red headband, Apache style.

She looked up into his handsome, hate-filled face, and felt too tired and hurt to fight anymore. "Go ahead and kill me, you bloody savage!"

The hatred in his tragic dark eyes did not lessen. "So Timbi catches a white boy! Why are you on Paiute lands, *tavibo?*"

"I-I carried the mail for the whites." Her mouth was so dry, she could barely speak.

He glared down at her. "The Pony Riders invade Timbi's land, plot to drive all of the Paiute to the reservation! Now that I have you, how shall I kill you?"

Desperation made Dallas bold. "I don't give a damn if you kill me! But give me water first!"

He threw back his head and laughed. "In two days I have met two brave whites! I would not have thought there were two so brave in your whole lot!"

He brought out his knife, stood looking at her.

She was past being afraid. *Horsefeathers!* He was going to cut her throat without giving her a drink! She glared back at him.

With one swift move, he whirled her around, cut the thongs that bound her. Then he yelled something to one of his men in a language she did not understand.

The circulation returned to her numb arms as she rubbed them, but her wrists were raw and stinging from the rawhide strips cutting into the flesh.

A warrior came running with a canteen made of watertight woven reeds and put it in her hands. For a moment, she blinked at it, not quite comprehending that she was actually being given water.

The leader nodded at her. "Drink, Pony boy, otherwise you may not survive to amuse our people back at the village!"

His tone was as hard and vengeful as his dark eyes, but Dallas cared for nothing at the moment but the water. Perhaps they were only tormenting her and would take it away before she could drink.

She threw back her head and gulped long swallows of the tepid liquid, strangling on it in her haste to drink. She had never realized how good water tasted. She closed her eyes and drank, feeling life flow back into her with each gulp.

The leader looked almost sympathetic. "It is the worst torture of all, to die of thirst. Only a couple of suns ago, I almost did, but a man came along. . . ." His voice trailed off, and the anger came back into his face. "Now, Pony Boy, Timbi takes you back to his camp where you will pay for everything the whites have done to my family, my people!"

Could she bargain for her life? "The Pony leaders will pay for my safe return."

He jerked the canteen from her hand, gave it to a brave. "Only blood can pay for what the whites owe me! If we kill enough of you, perhaps the whites will get off Paiute land and leave us in peace!"

She was desperate enough to try anything. "If you do not let me go, the Great White Chief in Washington will send soldiers to fight you!"

"That we already expect!"

She tried to argue more, but he dragged her to his black horse, threw her up on it, and climbed up behind her.

Well, at least she was still alive. Perhaps Quint and the men from the station would track her to wherever the Paiutes were taking her. That was all she could hope for.

They turned and rode off in the direction from whence they had come, leaving the dead enemy strewn on the bloody sand behind them.

Dallas was exhausted and hurt. She couldn't keep from leaning back against Timbi as they rode. He was all but naked except for breechcloth and tall moccasins and she felt the heat of him against her as his arms reached around her to rein the horse.

His chest felt hard and hot against her back through the boy's shirt she wore, and worse she felt the bulge of his big manhood against her hips through the loincloth. Her legs gripped the bareback black horse, but Timbi rode with one arm around her waist and the other on her thigh as if afraid she would make some sudden move and dislodge him from the horse.

She wasn't any better off than she had been except that the

Paiute leader had given her water to keep her from dying on him. When she reached the village and they discovered she was a girl, she most certainly would be raped and killed. Dallas was almost past caring what would happen. She wished they would just stop and rest awhile. Instead, they rode until late afternoon when they reached a camp of wickiup-type dwellings made of brush.

Dogs barked and people came running, jabbering in their native language. A pretty girl of about sixteen came out of a lodge, ran to greet Timbi. She wore red moccasins.

His woman. That girl must be his woman, Dallas thought as a crowd surrounded the incoming war party.

Timbi climbed down, reached up to jerk her unceremoniously from his horse and dump her in a heap at his feet. She was too weary to get up. If they were going to kill her, she hoped they would do it right here so she wouldn't have to move her aching body.

Judging from the laughter and the boastful tones, the warriors were telling of their fight with the other tribe. An older man walked up and said something to Timbi, then nudged Dallas with his foot.

Timbi's tone turned ugly. Obviously he was telling the older man not to interfere.

The chieftain grabbed her shoulder, hauled her to her feet. "The old one is afraid we bring trouble to our people by having you in camp. I tell him the whites have already brought us more trouble than we want, it is time to take vengeance!"

Timbi reached for the short quirt that hung from his saddle, began walking toward a lone, spindly tree, dragging her along. "I will punish you, Pony boy, for daring to trespass on our lands. Then I will kill you and send your body back to your people as a warning."

The pretty young girl said something in an angry tone; the handsome chieftain snapped back. To Dallas he said, "My sister, Atsa, wants me to spare you, but I owe the whites this for what they have done to my people, my family."

He pushed her up against the tree. The bark scratched her face as a warrior reached out, caught her arms, wrapped them around the tree in an uncomfortable embrace, and tied them.

She felt Timbi's hand reach out, catch the collar of the back of her shirt, tear it to the waist. He exclaimed in surprise at seeing the tight band she wore under the shirt, then she felt him take a knife to it, cut it away. The sun felt warm on her bare back and she clutched the tree, pressing her breasts against the bark. Would they do any less once they realized she was a girl?

All Indians admired bravery. Perhaps if she withstood the whipping without a murmur, he would be impressed, let her go free.

She heard the quirt snap back, sing through the air. She couldn't stop herself from gasping at the incredible pain she felt as the tip bit into her flesh, but she did not cry out. Timbi brought it back and hit her again. Wasps were stinging her all along her backbone. She gasped and buried her face against the tree, but she did not cry out.

"Pony Boy, why don't you scream?" Timbi shouted, obviously in a rage because his victim only clutched the tree and clung there.

She was afraid to unclench her jaw to answer, afraid she would start weeping and not be able to stop. A disapproving murmur came from the crowd.

Timbi's sister said in halting English, "If you are going to kill the boy, the men say kill him. He has shown his bravery; do not beat him like a dog!"

The whipping stopped. Dimly Dallas heard him say, "Maybe you are right, little sister. I intended to show what cowards the whites are. Instead, he is making our people believe the *tavibo* are brave and noble!"

He stepped around the small tree, cut her loose. She was not sure she could stand as he grabbed her shoulder, whirled her around. If they were going to kill her, she hoped it would be quick and merciful.

He reached out, grabbed the torn remnants of her shirt, ripped them away, leaving her standing naked to the waist. Immediately there were exclamations of surprise and much jabbering.

Timbi stared at her bare breasts in wonder. "So the Pony boy is a girl! Why would you do this thing?"

Dallas looked him straight in the eye, her chin high and defiant. "To show white women are as brave as our men, who would not do what you have just done!" Then her legs gave way under her and she collapsed.

Timbi reached out and caught her as she fell. She remembered the feel of his hard arm against the softness of her breasts for a split second, and then he swung her up in his arms. She closed her eyes as he carried her. Next would come the mass rape, but all she thought of now was how the welts on her back stung.

She felt him break stride and then stoop, and she was suddenly out of the sun. She opened her eyes as he placed her on some dry grass in the wickiup. He towered over her, looking embarrassed and chagrined. "Why did you not tell me you were a woman? I look the fool for beating a girl. That is not something a warrior should lower himself to. My sister, Atsa, will care for you, but do not try to escape."

She was too exhausted to leave even if he gave her a horse and turned her loose, but she didn't give him the satisfaction of knowing that. She rolled over onto her belly to stop him from looking at her breasts.

He went out and the pretty girl came in, hesitantly got down on her knees and began to rub a healing ointment into Dallas's back. Dallas sighed at the soothing feel of it. "Is the skin broken? Is there blood?"

"No, only welts that will go down fast," the Paiute girl said as she smeared the ointment on, then tended Dallas's wounded arm. "You make my brother look foolish. That is bad for a chieftain."

"Atsa," — Dallas craned her neck and looked earnestly at the girl — "what is to be done with me?"

"I don't know. We never had a white captive before. But the mood of the people is ugly. The miners have caused us much misery. They cut down the piñon trees that provide the nuts we eat, so now we often go hungry."

"But I'm not a miner." Dallas sat up. "Is there any chance he might let me go?"

"Why are you dressed like a boy?" Atsa appeared to be ignoring the question. "Do you not have pretty dresses and a carriage like all white women are supposed to have? Someday I will marry a white man, and he will take me away from this dirty village!"

What a foolish, vain girl you are. "What will happen to you if you aren't careful is this," Dallas snapped, "a white man will tell you a bunch of lies, take you to Virginia City, and put you to work servicing drunken, brutal men!"

Atsa looked annoyed. Probably she didn't believe Dallas. "You sound like my brother. He wants me to choose a warrior and spend the rest of my life looking for firewood and food. Life is too hard among the Paiute."

Could this girl be bribed? "Atsa, if you will get word back to the whites that I am still alive and tell them where I am, I will give you a red dress and these." She reached into her pants pocket and handed the girl her precious pearl earrings.

Atsa looked at them a long moment, then greedily closed her brown fist over the pearls and tucked them away in her own clothing. "I will think on this thing. But I would take a great risk of angering my brother. Besides, if soldiers came to this camp, some of my people might be killed or hurt."

Dallas had no answer for that. "I-I would try to keep that from happening."

"But you could not promise it."

Dallas bit her lip and looked away. "No. In truth, I couldn't promise it."

Atsa's face grew troubled. "I wasn't prepared to like you, but I find I do. I know. . . ."

Her voice trailed off and Dallas held her breath, waiting for the Indian girl to continue, but Atsa didn't finish. "I will speak to my brother, but not yet. I must choose the right time. He is often moody and angry since the great tragedy."

"What tragedy?"

Atsa didn't answer. She got up and left the hut.

Dallas shrugged. At least they hadn't killed her yet. And she was so weary, she didn't much care about anything right now. She lay down on the soft dried-grass mattress and slept.

* * *

When she awakened with a start, she realized that Timbi sat cross-legged, staring at her.

She rose up, crossed her arms over her bare breasts. "How long have you been here?"

His face was stoic. "A long time, watching you sleep. You are very pretty and dark. When your hair is long, there is probably not another girl anywhere as pretty as you are."

She flushed uncomfortably and kept her hands crossed over her breasts. "I am half-Cheyenne," she said.

"What is an Indian girl doing among the whites?"

She was uncomfortably aware that his gaze stayed on her hands. "My mother, Velvet Eyes, was rescued from the Comanche by my father, Don Diego de Durango, many years ago when she was only a very young girl and he married her."

She started to ask if Atsa had spoken to him yet about letting her go, decided to be cautious. He seemed terribly moody and unpredictable.

Abruptly, he reached out, caught her wrists, pulled her hands away from her breasts. "I own you. Do not hide yourself from me."

She jerked away from him, half turned away. "No man owns me! My name is Dallas which means 'spirited.' I give myself to my man, but no man owns me!"

He chuckled, and she saw a rare smile play about his grim mouth. "You are truly Indian, Dallas. What a shame to waste that fire on some weak, worthless white man."

"You'd think differently if he knew where I was!" she snapped, her eyes blazing. "He'd kill you for daring to take your quirt to me!"

"I . . . I . . ." He looked embarrassed, chagrined. "I thought I was whipping a man, an intruder into Paiute lands. The whites have brought us much trouble and, to me, more grief than I think sometimes I can live with."

"What do you intend to do with me?"

Timbi shrugged his broad shoulders. "I haven't decided. But until I do, you will be free to move about the village, help with the women's chores."

She looked down at her nakedness. "Like this?"

He actually smiled. "Most of our women wear nothing more than woven skirts. In the winter they also put on rabbit-fur cloaks against the cold. But you are right. I do not think I want the warriors looking at your breasts. It might give some of them ideas, and I would not want to kill any of them."

Slowly he reached behind him, brought out a very fine antelope-skin shift, held it out to her.

"Why, Timbi, it's beautiful!" Dallas took it and exclaimed over it. "This is some of the best beadwork I have ever seen." Like any woman, she could not help but admire something finely crafted and beautiful.

"My mother made it for. . . ." A dark shadow crossed his face, and he shook his head. "It does not matter. It will cover your nakedness."

He got up abruptly. "Do not try to escape, Pony Girl. The horse herd is closely guarded, and you would die of thirst out there in the wilderness if you should try to walk away from this village."

Timbi turned and was gone, leaving Dallas puzzling over this strange, moody man.

She was still stiff and sore, but she slipped the shift on, combed her black curls with her fingers. The antelope skin was of the finest. Timbi was obviously a skilled hunter. She had seen only a few people in the village wearing more than the scantiest of rags and coverings made of woven sagebrush bark. The Paiute looked as if they lived on the edge of starvation continually; the whites coming into the area must be upsetting the precarious balance of nature.

Atsa came into the hut just then, stopped, blinked in surprise. "Where did you get that shift? My brother will be very angry when he sees—"

"Your brother gave it to me. It is beautiful and very special, isn't it?" Dallas fingered the intricate beadwork. "He said your mother made it."

Tears came to Atsa'a dark eyes. "I find it hard to believe Timbi gave it to you. Our mother made it for a special gift. Timbi's wife was heavy with child. This was to be given to her after the birth."

Dallas stared down at the dress. *Such a strange, sullen*

man. "Atsa, tell me what happened."

The girl sighed. "We are the only two of our family left. My brother's wife and our parents were over visiting another band of our people. On the way back, they stopped to drink at a creek which flows through the mining area. Timbi was the one who found them. His wife died in his arms, screaming in agony from having drunk the polluted water."

"Oh, dear God!" Dallas felt a sudden rush of pity for the moody Indian. No wonder he was determined to extract justice from any white he met though that could only end in tragedy for him. "Atsa, have you spoken to him yet about letting me go?"

The girl looked away, and Dallas had a distinct feeling Atsa was hiding something. "Not yet. Must I give back the earrings?"

"No, keep them, but please talk to your brother for me."

"When the time is right," Atsa said. "And now let us go help the other women. There is much work to do around this camp."

As they went outside and joined a group of women cutting up fish, for the first time Dallas noticed the giant lake in the distance. They cleaned the fish, spread them to dry on racks in the sun.

As Dallas worked, her mind stayed busy. Well, at least she hadn't been raped or killed. Maybe if she would be patient, Timbi would decide to send her back to the whites. She had no idea where the camp was. She'd lost her map while being chased by that first war party and didn't know if she was twenty or a hundred miles from civilization. Were Quint and the men from Williams' trading post even now combing the area for her? Or had they already given her up for dead?

Quint. My husband. She thought of him with great love and longing. *What God hath joined together, let no man put asunder.*

And yet, she could not quite hate Timbi as she had when she had not known of his great loss. She pictured the pregnant girl dying in his arms, and him unable to save her. If that had happened to her, wouldn't Quint become an avenging fury, too?

She felt someone staring at her and looked up. Timbi sat cross-legged in a group of warriors. Obviously there was a discussion going on. But Timbi's eyes had strayed so that he stared at her with a troubled expression.

Later that day, she and Atsa carried water from the spring. Dallas's wounded arm still pained her so she had a difficult time. She had to set the water down and rest on the way back to camp.

Suddenly, Timbi was at her elbow. Without a word, he picked up the water, motioned her to follow as he started back along the path.

Dallas looked at him, her eyes wide. "You subject yourself to laughter from the men. Even in a Cheyenne camp, mother tells me men don't do women's chores."

He set the water down, looked at her gravely. "Any who would laugh at me might feel my blade in their throats and they know it." He extended a hand toward her, then seemed to think and drew back. "If anyone in this camp bothers you, Pony Girl, tell me and that person will answer to me."

Abruptly, he turned and strode away, leaving her staring after him. Something about the way he looked at her troubled Dallas. She had the distinct feeling that he had almost reached out to caress her face, then had changed his mind.

He never intends to let me go. She knew that suddenly, from the way he had looked at her. Tonight, she would try to steal a horse and escape. Even if she didn't know which direction to take, she would chance finding her way back to civilization and Quint.

And yet . . . she thought about the handsome, brooding chieftain. If she did not already love another, something tender and vulnerable beneath his hard exterior would have appealed to the woman in her. Unless his deep hurt was finally healed, there would be a great deal of bloodshed across Nevada.

Atsa waited until almost dark before approaching her

283

brother who sat alone, smoking and staring into the big council fire. Everyone else had already retired. Even the white girl had pleaded weariness and had stretched out in the *karnee* she and Atsa shared.

Atsa had promised to speak to her brother about the captive, but she had seen the way Timbi watched the white girl. He had not looked at a woman with such softness in his eyes since her sister-in-law had taken his heart many moons ago. There were Paiute girls who had tried to catch her brother's eye since his wife had died, but he did not even seem to see them.

Hesitantly, Atsa sat next to him, her hand reaching into the folds of her shift to feel the precious earrings. She could not wear them in good conscience until she had done what she had promised. Indeed, she was not sure when, if ever, she could use these baubles. She did not think her brother would approve of her wearing anything that reminded him of the hated white civilization.

She waited for him to speak, but he only nodded to her.

Finally, she summoned her courage and spoke in their language. "Timbi, what do you intend to do with the captive?"

He shrugged his broad shoulders. "Originally, I intended to give her as a plaything to my warriors for anyone to use who has need of a woman."

"And now?"

He looked at her, and his hard face softened. "Little sister, tonight you sleep at the *karnee* of your friend, Moponi, please."

She had known it deep in her heart from the way her brother had watched the white girl with desperate longing in his eyes. "Timbi, I . . . I must tell you something that only I know."

"Whatever it is, it won't change my mind," he snapped irritably, knocking his ceremonial pipe against a rock in the camp fire to dislodge the ashes.

"I think it will," Atsa said softly, "because you are a man of great honor. Only a few days ago, you made a blood brother of a white man with a magic name — a man who had saved

284

your life."

Timbi smiled, a rare occurrence. "Quint Randolph. Yes, he alone among all the white men have I liked and trusted. I owe him a great debt."

"You owe him more than that. Would you dishonor a brother by stealing his woman?"

"What is this lie you tell me?" His face was terrible to behold, and for a long moment, she thought he would strike her. His look made her wish she had kept her secret, but there was honor involved here and, ultimately, it was the warrior's decision to make.

"It is no lie." Atsa leaned closer. "When I spied on the trading post, I saw them together. At the time, I watched closely because I wondered why a man would kiss a boy. And then I saw him partially undress her, kiss her breasts—"

"Stop! I do not believe you!" But Timbi's eyes were full of a terrible reality, as if he might.

"Then ask her," Atsa said gently, because she saw the pain and, yes, tears gather in his dark eyes. "Ask her if her man is the one you call Quint before you dishonor her and yourself."

For a long time, he said nothing, staring into the fire. "Does she realize she is only a few miles from that place you spied on?"

Atsa shrugged. "I don't know; I don't think so. Otherwise, she would already have escaped and gone back to him."

She saw a terrible passion, a wanting in Timbi's face. "Does she know that I am blood brother to her man?"

"I haven't told her, so I would not think so. Do you think Quint will come here searching for her?"

Timbi shook his head. "She was first stolen by our enemy, the Pit River tribe. There is no way that Quint Randolph could know I have her."

"Unless you send him a message, brother," Atsa reminded him gently, "and tell him to come for her."

The fire crackled in the silence, and somewhere on a distant hill, a lonely lobo howled.

Timbi listened and frowned. "I have had a vision and I do not know what it means, but I think of it when I hear the wolf."

The trouble on his face, the inner turmoil she sensed grieved her, for she loved her brother. "Have you asked the shaman?"

"Yes, but he had no good answer except to say think carefully about all I know about wolves and then avoid them. I must not try to kill one or it will anger our god *Niminnaa* and my life will be forfeit."

"Then the answer is simple. Make sure you do no harm to that animal." She hesitated a long moment. "What do you intend to do about the girl?"

He looked at her, and his eyes were full of both passion and turmoil. "I want her, Atsa, more than I ever wanted my own wife! Since I first brought her back, I can think of nothing but holding her, mating her, keeping her with me for always."

He was her brother and she loved him but she winced at his words of dishonor. "What of Quint Randolph?"

"What of him?" Timbi said savagely, jumping to his feet. "He will think the Pit River tribe has killed her or carried her off. Finally, he will go away, back to his own people. He has other women to choose from, no doubt."

"As do you," she reminded him pointedly. "And what if he should come here?" She saw anguish on her brother's face.

"Then I will hide her until he leaves and lie to him, say we know nothing of her. None of our people, save the two of us, speak his language, and you are my sister, you would not tell him!"

Atsa was so stunned that for a moment she could not answer. "Oh, Timbi, think! You would lie to a blood brother, stain your chieftain's honor because you are so taken with this man's woman that you must couple with her? By white men's standards, it is wrong! By ours, even more so!"

"I care not!" He trembled with guilt and rage under her accusing words and stare. "I know only that I must have her! After she has been with me awhile, perhaps she will come to love me. And after my son sucks at her breast, perhaps she would not wish to go even if Quint Randolph came and tried to take her."

"Oh, Timbi! I never thought you could want a woman so badly that you would betray a friend, destroy your honor!"

286

"Besides" — he whirled on her defensively — "if she had my child, he wouldn't want her. No white man wants a woman who has been defiled by a lowly Indian. You know that. He would let me keep her."

"And what if he does want her?" Atsa challenged, standing up. "I have seen this man, and I think he, too, loves deeply and has much honor. I have also seen him with this woman in his arms. I remember the expression of his face as he looked into her eyes. What will you do if he finds out where she is and comes for her, wanting her anyway?"

He hesitated before answering savagely. "If Quint should come and try to take her, even though he is my blood brother and I owe him a life, I will kill him!"

She gasped in horror. Her brother was a man possessed. Nothing meant anything to him anymore except taking the spirited white girl into his bed.

Timbi looked long at her, and she saw grim resolve on his brooding face. "Tonight, Atsa, you stay with your friend, Moponi, because tonight I am going to take Dallas for my own!"

Chapter Nineteen

Dallas watched through a crack in the brush of the *karnee* as Atsa walked over and spoke to her brother, who was sitting by himself and staring into the council fire.

She had a feeling the girl would not make much headway with the brooding Paiute, and she feared she had wasted her precious Concho pearl earrings.

From her peephole, Dallas saw that the camp was asleep. Nothing moved anywhere under the starry sky. She might do better to take a chance on slipping away rather than wait and hope that Timbi would decide to let her go.

Very quietly she took a rawhide rope, a small canteen of water that she had hidden; and sneaking out of the hut, she stood in the shadows, watching. Whatever Timbi and Atsa were discussing must be serious from the looks on both their faces. She couldn't hear their words, but saw Timbi shake his head emphatically. Had the girl just asked him if he would let Dallas go? Why take the chance if she could slip away unnoticed? Maybe she could find her way by the stars.

The desert night had turned chill, and all the Paiutes seemed to be asleep in their *karnees*. Here and there, a camp fire dwindled to gray ash and red coals. A straggly dog walked by, sniffed at her. What would she do if it barked? But the dog wandered on past.

Off to the left of the camp, the pony herd grazed. Dallas knew there would be a guard. She got down on her hands and knees and crawled across the grass. A buckskin-colored mare raised its muzzle and sniffed the air, whinnied. Then the other horses moved restlessly. Holding her breath, Dallas froze against the ground like a frightened quail, waiting for the guard to come investigate. Nothing.

She took a deep breath, drawing in the scent of sagebrush and the pleasant smell of horses. Perhaps she could actually steal a horse and escape. Her Cheyenne ancestors were famous for taking horses.

Her mother had told her enemies were so afraid of losing horses to the Cheyenne raiders that sometimes a much-prized horse would be tied to its sleeping owner's wrist. Such horses were the ones the Cheyenne most delighted in stealing. More than one Pawnee or Ute had awakened to find his wrist tied to a log and moccasin tracks in the dew revealing that a cat-footed Cheyenne warrior had walked all the way around him without waking him, adding that insult to horse stealing.

Dallas searched the dark night for the guard, her heart beating so loudly she thought at any moment the pounding would alert someone in the sleeping camp. Suppose, while she looked around, the guard came right up behind her?

Taking a quick look over her shoulder to make sure this was not the case, she saw Timbi and his sister still in conversation. If they would keep talking long enough, she would have a headstart. Where was that guard?

The desert air made her shiver just a bit. Was the guard cold, too? And then she saw him, a fat Indian who had dismounted and now sat propped against a rock, his rabbit-fur cloak pulled around him.

What would Timbi do to her if he caught her trying to escape? Whip her again? Hand her over to his warriors? Maybe she should wait and see what Atsa found out. She thought of Quint. She wanted to get back to him, back to the safety of his arms. If he wanted to live in Philadelphia or Kentucky or wherever, she'd deal with his snooty sister somehow.

She took the rawhide rope and sneaked up to the inquisitive buckskin mare, slipped the noose over its neck. Then, holding its muzzle so it couldn't nicker, she led it away from the herd at a slow walk. She had to fight a terrible urge to jump on its bare back and gallop away, but the clatter of

289

hooves would alert the whole camp. No, she would have to stay calm until she led it far enough away.

As she walked from the camp, she expected at any moment to hear a shout as the guard awakened and discovered she was gone. If the horse herd should get too restless and start milling and whinnying, someone would come to see about the disturbance.

Finally, Dallas decided she was far enough from the camp. Remembering that Indians always mounted a horse from the right side, she grasped the buckskin's mane and swung up onto its bare back. Still, she was afraid to gallop across the rocks. Her mouth felt dry as the desert sand beneath her as she dug her heels into the mare's sides and quietly walked her away into the night.

Dallas broke into a slow lope once the camp fires were as dim as distant stars. Somewhere off on a crest, a big lobo howled and the sound reverberated through the velvet blackness of the night.

Dallas was a skilled horsewoman, and she had no trouble managing the horse with nothing more than a loop around its nose and no saddle.

She tried to get her bearings from the stars, but she still wasn't sure where she was or how many miles it might be to a lonely outpost or a Pony Express station. She'd had a good map of her route, but of course it had been lost.

Had anyone found her little switch and the *mochila?* She took pride in carrying the mail, as all the riders did, and she didn't like the idea that she was the first rider to lose a packet of letters that might be important to her country's future.

Finally, she took off at a ground-eating lope. Even if she ended up lost, it was a better gamble than staying with the Indians. She'd seen the way Timbi had been looking at her; that smoldering look needed no further explanation. If she didn't already have a man, she might have considered Timbi. But she had been raised as a white, and didn't think she could ever be happy in an Indian culture. Still, she couldn't help but sympathize with him because of his tragedy.

Why had he done little things like take burdens from her and carry them, knowing it would subject him to the ridicule of his men?

She heard the high scream of challenge before she actually saw the small band of wild horses; then the big stallion stood outlined against the full moon that was just now rising up behind him. Dallas reined in, staring in wonder at the great pinto stud, its bright black and white markings gleaming in the light. Her mare nickered nervously, danced a little.

"Easy, girl." She patted the buckskin's neck. "You can forget about him and what you've got in mind. We're moving on."

The Medicine Hat stallion. A thrill went over her as she recognized the markings on the big stud. The coloring meant big magic to the Cheyenne and some of the other tribes. And even if it weren't for that coloring, this was truly the finest stallion she had ever seen. No wonder Quint had yearned to own it! A horse like that was almost priceless as a ranch's herd sire. No amount of money could buy such a horse from the man who was ever lucky enough to capture it.

A broken lasso hung around its magnificent neck, and Dallas suddenly wondered if it was Quint's lasso. As she watched the stallion rear up, making that peculiar pawing motion at the heavens, she knew where he'd got his nickname.

Sky Climber. Yes, that was perfect for him. She could almost believe he really was a spirit horse about to gallop across the sky, the way he pawed with his front hooves at the blackness, rearing up on his powerful hind legs. When he shook his great head, his mane stood out in long, silken streamers.

But she needed to get out of there before he scented her mare. Now he whinnied and reared again, galloped straight toward her. She tried to turn the mare, ride away; but the mare would have none of it.

The buckskin made an answering noise in her throat and danced nervously around. *The mare.* The stallion wanted her mare.

Dallas cursed and tried to turn her mount away so they could ride off. The mare would not obey her. Nostrils flaring, ears pricked forward, she danced toward the stallion. Dallas kicked the mare in the ribs, trying to turn her, but the mare's entire attention was now on the stallion who galloped out to meet them.

In the moonlight, Dallas saw the silhouette of the stallion's big maleness standing hard and rigid from his body as he reared and danced toward the mare.

"Get away, damn you!" She slashed at him with the end of the rope, knowing full well she might be in danger from the great horse if she tried to stop him from mounting the eager mare. And at that moment, the buckskin reared, dumping Dallas in the dirt. The rope looped over the buckskin's muzzle slipped off as Dallas fell, and she scrambled to her feet, realizing that she was now afoot in hostile country, perhaps many miles from civilization and, worse yet, water. She only had the one small canteen.

The chill night seemed to warm suddenly, and she realized it was her own body reacting to the scene being played out before her. The big stallion moved toward the mare, his great maleness stiff and big as an iron bar beneath his belly.

The filly whinnied nervously, danced around him. He nipped at her flanks, her neck. She stood waiting. The stallion made soft noises in his throat before he reared up on the filly, biting at her neck, flaying her shoulders with his great hooves. And then he took her, humping over her in the mating ritual as old as time itself.

As Dallas watched from the ground, he plunged his iron-hard maleness deep into the filly, plunging again and again, his body slamming hard against hers in the stillness.

Dallas rose to her knees and watched the horses, frozen in place by the savagery and beauty of the ritual. There was a slight sound, and she turned. Timbi stepped out from behind the rocks, his eyes dark with emotion, his chest moving as he breathed deeply. In the moonlight, his muscular body shone with a fine sheen of perspiration. "I have come for you as Sky Climber comes for the mare."

"No!" Dallas scrambled to her feet, took off running. It was foolish, she knew. Somewhere behind those rocks, he had a horse tied. He'd ridden up on her because she'd been so absorbed in the mating of the horses. She couldn't outrun him on foot.

She fell and skinned her knee a little, but scrambled to her feet again, realized he was pursuing her on foot. She had a sudden image of the filly dancing around nervously, knowing the stallion would take her if he wished and she could not stop him.

Quint. She loved Quint. Dallas ran, fell, scrambled to her feet, ran again. Behind her, she heard Timbi moving lightly as a panther as he followed her through the night. Dallas staggered with weariness, slowed. She couldn't run anymore. Her lungs felt aflame. She would fight him, but she couldn't run anymore. Whirling, she faced him.

He stood staring at her, his loincloth stripped away, his manhood hard and big like the stallion's. "I will have you, Dallas. I will have you once if it costs me my life, and call it worth it!"

"No!" she gasped, backing away from him. But she was on the edge of a gully, and there was no room to retreat. His eyes turned dark and stormy as he stalked her, every bit as wild and as virile as the stallion.

In the distance, she was dimly aware of the stallion coming down off the filly, the two of them rejoining the herd. The night suddenly seemed sizzling, and she felt perspiration sheen her breasts under the antelope skin shift. She seemed bathed in it. His sinewy muscles gleamed hotly in the moonlight.

"No, please, no. . . ."

His breath came in aroused gasps. "Your blood runs as hot as mine from watching the horses." He reached out, caught the neck of the shift, ripped it down the front, and threw it to one side so that she stood there as vulnerable and helpless as the filly had been.

Quint. She thought of Quint. But all she saw was a great brown stallion of a man standing ready to block her should she try to run past him. "Timbi, no—"

But he reached out, jerked her to him, and his tongue slipped deep between lips that were half-open in pleading. His skin was as fiery and damp as her own as he locked her in his embrace. His hands held her against his chest as he kissed

293

her, and she could feel his manhood hard as any stallion's pulsating against her belly as he held her helpless in his grasp.

She hadn't realized how big and strong he was until he lifted her from the ground so that his lips found her breasts. Dallas gasped and tried to protest, but her body reacted to the hot, wet sucking on her nipple.

His breath was warm on her breast. "Tonight I put my son in your belly, and nine moons from now, he will share your rich milk with his sire!"

"No, Timbi!" Dallas tried to twist out of his iron grasp. "I have a man already. The magic words have been said over us, you do wrong!"

His face was deeply tragic as he held her, looked down into her eyes. "More than you know, Pony Girl, so much more than you know. But if I can have you only this one night, though it cost me my honor and my life, I will call it worth it!"

And so saying, he swept her up into his arms, carried her over to a little nest of rocks where soft grasses grew. She tried to fight him, but his mouth was all over her, teasing, sucking, caressing. She loved Quint Randolph, but she was half-savage and her body began to respond to Timbi's skillful hands and mouth in spite of herself.

"Dallas, I will make your body want me as I want you!"

"No!" She struggled again to get away from him. But with his great strength he held her, and now he spread her thighs and his mouth kissed and caressed deep inside her velvet place while his hands reached up to cup her breasts, catch the hard nubs of her nipples between his thumbs and forefingers.

She tried to think of Quint as she struggled, but her body moistened itself at the touch of this man's tongue. Tears ran in little crooked trails down her face. "Oh, Timbi, have mercy!"

But his face was aflame with passion, his eyes were dark and smoldering. "You will grow to love me, Dallas, once you carry my child, because I never intend to give you up. You'll never know how much my love of you has cost me!"

She struggled, but his greedy lips and hands were all over her; and then he was between her thighs, bending her knees so that her slim ankles slipped up over his wide shoulders so that she could no longer protect her velvet place from the hammer of his maleness. Even as she struggled, he grasped her hips, tilting her up for his coming thrust.

Like the virile male he was, he slammed hard into her, going deep and sure. She could not move with her legs over his broad shoulders, and he lifted her with his hands, pushed hard into her depths again, making noises in his throat like the stallion. He had her helpless, her weight against her own shoulders as he held her up off the ground.

She could feel him pulsating deep within her, big and hammer-hard, and they coupled like wild mustangs in the moonlight. She could not stop her passionate body from reacting to his raw virility, even though she did not love him. Her mind was faithful, but her senses reeled under the touch and taste and feel of him.

And then he began to climax deep within her, his hot, potent seed gushing into her womb.

He collapsed on her with a moan, and she lay there under him, shaking like the filly who could not have stopped the coupling with the great stallion if she'd wanted to. He had chosen to mate her, and he took her.

Dallas lay there with him sprawled across her, wept hot, salty tears and wished to die because she no longer belonged only to Quint. Another man had placed his body within hers, his tongue deep in her mouth. Worse yet, for a split second, she had given way to savage passion, arching up under him, her body unconsciously yearning for the potent seed the Indian stallion emptied into her waiting, eager womb. As he drove so deeply, she had felt the soft tip of him stroke and lunge against the very depths of her softness.

Now he lay spent on her trembling body.

She tried to push him off. "I hate you!" She gritted her teeth in rage. "If I were armed, I'd kill you!"

He raised up on one elbow, stroked her hair back from her face ever so gently. "I will do everything I can to change your mind," he whispered. "When you carry my child, you cannot help but love the father."

"Never!" Dallas fought to get out from under him. "My

man, Quint, would kill you if he were here, and you bring the wrath of God down on you for what you have done!"

Timbi sat up, and his eyes were full of sadness. "If only you knew it all, Pony Girl. If I should die tonight because of this, I would call it worth it!"

She got up from the ground, trying to hide her nakedness with her hands. His seed ran down her thighs. "I will never stop hating you! I will kill you if I get the chance!"

"I love you, Dallas." He stood up, reached out to her, but she slapped his hand away. "I meant to be gentle, but I wanted you too much and have been without a woman too long. Your man can't love you as much as I do and the whites owe me a woman and child, since they have killed mine." He tossed her torn shift to her, put on his breechcloth.

She slipped into it, knowing there was no place to run. She was his by right of possession, even as the stallion had taken the mare and run away with her.

He whistled for his gelding, and when it trotted up, mounted it. Then he reached out a hand to her. She hesitated.

"I think I would rather walk than ride with you."

"Would you, fiery Dallas? That can be arranged." He smiled ever so slightly. "There are times you let your temper outweigh your judgment."

He was right. What did it accomplish to walk all the way back to camp? She half turned, looking out at the barren landscape in the moonlight.

"If you think of escaping me on foot," Timbi said from behind her, "you should know better."

With a sigh, she conceded defeat, held her hand up to him; but she would not look him in the face.

He lifted her up before him on the black, held her very close against him, and kissed the back of her head. "I'm sorry I hurt you," he whispered. "I should have wooed you gently, but I have wanted you since the first moment. Like the stallion, I finally couldn't control myself."

She sat very rigid although she was cold and the heat of the big man felt good against her back. "I'll never stop hating you or trying to run away!"

"Then I am twice the fool for wanting you any way I can get

you when there are a dozen Paiute girls who would gladly be wife to a chieftain." His arms slipped around her possessively, holding her tightly against him as he nudged the horse and turned it back toward camp. "If I had any sense, I would give you to my men to amuse themselves."

The thought of being used by a dozen warriors to slake their lust frightened her. "Would you do that?"

She felt him shrug. "Perhaps. If you do not please me."

Dallas trembled at the thought, and he pulled her hard against him, one of his big hands warm on her small waist, the other on her thigh.

What was she going to do? To escape under his watchful eye would now be almost impossible. To defy a proud man and humiliate him in front of his people might lead him to give her to his warriors despite his avowals of love.

In silence, they rode back to camp.

"Where am I to sleep?"

"You know the answer to that; why do you ask? My sister has moved in with her friend, Moponi, until Atsa chooses a husband soon."

He turned the horse loose to graze with the others and swung Dallas up in his arms. "I have already scolded the guard. No one else will dare go to sleep and let you steal a horse."

She lay stiffly against his broad, bare chest as he carried her into the *karnee* and put her down on the grass mattress. "Don't fight me, Dallas. It won't do you any good. I have chosen you and I will not give you up, not even if it should anger the Gods."

Tears of anger gathered in her eyes. "You want me, knowing I love another and, if I get the chance, I will put a knife between your ribs?"

He reached out and touched her face, tenderness on his moody face. "I have already told you I want you any way I can get you. I only hope that when your belly is swollen with my son, you will come to love me as I care for you. And I'd think twice about that knife. Even if you should manage to get one, killing a chieftain would so anger my people, that they would torture you until you begged to die."

297

She scooted away from him as he sat down on the mat. "The Paiutes are a primitive people," she declared, "not as civilized as the Cheyenne."

He shrugged. "That's probably true. Do you know we stone to death women who are suspected of witchcraft or bad medicine?"

Her mouth fell open. "That hasn't been done since Biblical days."

"It's a Paiute custom." He shrugged. "And now, Dallas, until you decide to behave yourself, I'm afraid to turn my back on you or even sleep with you in case you manage to make good your threat." He reached for a rawhide thong.

"What are you going to do?"

"Take off that shift."

If she did not, he would strip it from her by sheer force. She took it off.

He reached out, grabbed both her small wrists, jerked them behind her. "You are like a small, wild pet that must be tamed. Until you are, I will do what I would do with any dangerous little animal." He tied her hands behind her back. Then he pushed her down on the dried-grass mattress and pulled the rabbit-fur cloak over both of them.

She lay helpless and bound, her chilled body pulled up against his big, warm one. He took her in his arms and kissed her, holding her very tightly against him. She was uncomfortable with her arms tied behind her back, although her head rested on his arm as he cradled her.

During the middle of the night, he awakened her, stroking her body with his hands, and because she was helpless and could not stop him, she lay there submissively while his lips kissed her all over, his hands stroking her skin into fire even though she hated him. Her body was too young and vital not to respond to his caresses, though tears gathered in her eyes and she hated herself for responding.

"Please, no . . ." she whispered, but he did not stop and she did not fight him, thinking that he might make good his threat to give her to his warriors.

"I would do anything for you, Pony Girl—except let you go or deny myself the pleasures of your beautiful body. I intend to take you several times a day and more at night until I am sure you carry my child." Then his mouth was on her breasts and he rolled over onto his back, pulling her up to straddle his lean hard body.

"I'll hurt you, I know, with your hands tied behind you back, so *you* must please me."

She glared down at him. "Suppose I won't?"

"If you push me too far, Dallas, I may forget how much I care for you. I command you to please me!"

She was helpless and afraid of his anger. She sat astride him, and his hands reached up and grabbed her shoulders, held her over his mouth so that he could enjoy her nipples.

"Now ride me," he demanded. She felt his hot maleness throb against her hips and did what she was told, raising up on her knees and letting him come up into her.

"Ride me," he said again and his big hands caught her small waist, ground her down on his maleness as if he were impaling her on a smoldering sword.

He could take her so much more deeply this way, she thought, feeling him pulsating almost up under her ribs. And then he seemed to explode within her, holding her very close and whispering, "Dallas, Spirited One, I love you. . . ."

And I hate you, she thought. Timbi must surely know that, but he gathered her into his arms and kissed her tears away ever so gently.

She lay wrapped in his embrace, her head on his shoulder, her arms still tied behind her, and listened to his easy breathing as he slept. Obviously this virile stud intended to keep her, to use her whenever he felt the urge, and he expected her to submit. His lovemaking was as savage as the man himself. Dallas thought of Quint's big arms and tender caresses, and she wept for him. What could she do?

An answer came to her. She would gradually pretend to like Timbi's kisses, pretend she wanted his lovemaking. In a week or two, when he was convinced she was happy to stay with him, she would steal a horse and run away again. That decided, she moved close to the Paiute's warmth and then slept, bound and helpless, in his embrace.

The day her monthly misery began, instead of being annoyed, Timbi grunted with satisfaction. "Now there will be no doubt when you are expecting a child that it is mine."

So she was spared his sexual appetites for three days. She moved into the *karnee* where menstruating women went until their time was up, because it was very bad medicine for a woman with her bleeding to be close to warriors. Three days. In that time, Atsa seemed to avoid her, and wouldn't meet her gaze. No doubt the girl was ashamed that she had taken Dallas's gift and had been unable to convince her brother to let the white girl go.

Dallas really couldn't fault the young girl for that. No doubt Atsa had tried to convince Timbi that night at the camp fire, the night Dallas had run away. Let the vain little thing keep the jewelry. Lavender pearls didn't mean much to Dallas in her predicament. She yearned to have Quint's wedding ring on her finger, to be returned to his arms.

Dallas began making her plans. She would do whatever it took to escape and get back to Quint, even if she had to pretend she liked being Timbi's woman so that he would let down his guard and she could escape.

The only thing that worried her was that Quint might have given her up for dead and gone away. That third night, when Timbi took her into his lodge again, she submitted without a fight. She must make him think she had changed. She must make him think her body wanted him. As he took her, she tried to hold the tears back, pretended she wanted him, yet thought of Quint.

Chapter Twenty

Quint was not sure he would survive the next day or so after they had buried what was left of the bodies at the stage station. And he didn't really want to. The Pony Express stopped running temporarily and then began again, much to Yancy's annoyance.

A cavalry patrol stopped by, said they'd found evidence of a battle up in the hills. Looked like the Paiutes had cornered and killed off a war party of their enemies, the Pit River tribe.

The Williams brothers laughed. They thought it was too bad the Indians didn't wipe each other out. They'd be glad when every damned Injun was dead or on a reservation.

Quint thought about the killings, wondered if his friend Timbi, had had anything to do with them. He should ride out and see Timbi, ask him. But he had no heart for it. The fact that his blood brother might have killed Dallas's killers gave him no comfort. Nothing would bring her back. Besides, he hadn't sorted out his own feelings yet, and he was a little afraid that the Paiutes might have been involved in the station raid.

There was nothing to hold him here, yet he could not bring himself to leave this wild Nevada area. He spent hours sitting on a rock some distance away from the station, staring into space, thinking of Dallas. When he slept, which was rarely, he seemed to see her lovely dark features in every dream. She called to him for help; so appealingly that he often sat up in bed, then felt sad and foolish because his beloved was dead.

If only he had been here that day to keep her from taking that run . . . if only he hadn't brought her out here in the first place . . . If only . . . *The two saddest words in any language because no one can change what's past*. He almost seemed to hear her deep, husky voice saying that to him.

He rode over to the massacre site and watered the wildflowers he had planted on the three graves. It made him feel useful and close to her while he planned what to do with the rest of his life.

He knew the Williams brothers, Yancy, and the occasional hunter or soldier who rode by considered him a bit insane. Quint had seen them whispering, tapping the sides of their heads knowingly. Once he'd overheard one of them say, "Greenhorn. First massacre he ever saw. Some of them dudes never quite get over that sight, I reckon."

Once he would have gone at the man with fists flying, now it did not matter. He felt nothing but emptiness . . . and a need for revenge.

There was a war coming between North and South. Everyone was sure of it, but no one knew what, if anything, could be done about it. Quint realized that since Kentucky was border country, his farm in the rich bluegrass might come under fire from both sides. In that case, he would need to move his horses to save them. With the elections due this fall, both sides held their breath awaiting the outcome. Southerners were grumbling that if Lincoln were elected, there would be war because of the way the man felt about slavery.

So Quint went back to Kentucky, hired some good wranglers to help him move his thoroughbreds to Arizona. A stack of letters from Lydia awaited him; scolding him for disappearing without letting her know where he'd gone and listing all the eligible women she had found to introduce him to. Always topping the list was the plump Miss Maude Peabody, ever so eligible and rich.

Quint dropped his sister a terse note, telling her he was handing the title of his farm over to his freed slaves, that he

302

was leaving the area forever and that she should stay the hell out of his life! Then he and the wranglers loaded the horses onto boxcars, took them as far as the tracks ran, and herded them the rest of the way to Wolf's Den ranch in Arizona. But Quint had to admit the stud he'd brought was not nearly so fine as the Medicine Hat that ran wild in the hills of Nevada.

His days were full but his nights were lonely and often sleepless. Sometimes, when the wolves howled as he slept, the howling mingled with his troubled dreams and he seemed to be one of the big lobos himself, running wild and free across the shadowy moonlit night, searching in vain for his mate who was gone forever.

He awoke, drenched with sweat, sat up on the side of the bed and reached for his pipe. He sat in the darkness, watching the glow of the burning tobacco and listened. How many years of lonely nights lay ahead of him? He must find something to occupy his mind before he went insane.

Quint decided then that he would put all his energy into raising the finest horses in all Arizona because if he did not take some interest in life, he would grieve himself to death and he was not that weak.

Revenge. The need for it haunted him. He began to think he would lose his mind if he didn't extract the vengeance the Indians of Nevada owed him. Then too, more and more, he thought about the Medicine Hat stallion, and felt driven to possess it. It had been some weeks since Dallas had been ambushed and killed. Could he bear to face going back to that area?

The Medicine Hat stallion had cost him his one and only love, and he was determined to own that horse; he had paid enough for it. Resolutely, he stood up, lit a lamp, and awakened the servants at the luxurious ranch, telling them to begin packing. He wanted revenge against Dallas's killers. They were someplace in the vicinity of Williams' trading post, as was the Medicine Hat stallion. So that was where Quint would go.

303

Dallas paused, leaning over the spring and looked at her reflection in the water. In the past weeks, her hair had begun to grow longer. She dipped her watertight reed basket into the spring, being very careful not to disturb the long, green strands of algae that floated lazily in the water. The Paiutes thought of water as a woman, and they were always careful not to anger her by disturbing her long green hair as they dipped out the life-giving liquid.

The small boy, Wovoka, came over, stood and watched her with dark, serious eyes.

She smiled at him. "Hello, Wovoka," she said in the boy's language. She now spoke a little Paiute. "Where's your mother?"

He pointed solemnly toward the camp. "Cooking," he said in his language. "I have been off sitting on a rock and thinking about the world the way the Dreamers tell of it."

She knew little of the Paiute Dreamers group and wanted to ask about them; but at that moment, Wovoka seemed overcome with shyness and ran back to the camp. She thought about the quiet little boy a moment. She was beginning to love these people, even though she was a prisoner in this place. And she was learning how hard it was to survive in this hostile environment. Any small thing the whites did to destroy food or habitat might mean that Indians starved during the winter.

It would soon be the last time she would take water from here, she thought, standing up and shouldering the jug with difficulty. This band was moving in a few days, just a few miles, over to the vast Pyramid Lake beside which the other tribes had been counciling for weeks as to what to do about the white invaders.

Timbi hurried to her side. "Here, let me carry that."

Except that he seemed to have an insatiable need to make love to her, he had been so kind and gentle that she found it harder to hate him with each day that passed. Still, she had been waiting for her chance to run away again. She had been too closely watched to try it, but in the confusion and disorder of the camp move, she hoped to be able to take a horse, escape.

"If the other warriors see you doing woman's work, they will laugh at you."

He scowled darkly as he lifted the heavy jug with ease. "As I told you before, Pony Girl, no man here would laugh at Timbi. Anything I do is all right."

That is true, she thought as she fell in beside him and they walked back to the camp. The chieftain was well liked and regarded with respect. Dallas herself was treated with deference because she was Timbi's woman.

She had felt slightly ill and sick this morning, and now she stumbled. Instantly, his hand reached out and caught her, lowered her to the ground. His eyes were grave, anxious as he put the water down, knelt beside her. "Are you all right?"

What was wrong with her? "I . . . I think I just tripped."

His hands were gentle on her shoulders. "Perhaps you are with child."

She felt her face flame. She had not even considered that possibility. "No! I haven't been here even a month yet!"

"You will know when your monthly time comes."

She flared at him. "I will not bear a child for you!"

He swung her up in his arms, carried her back to the camp. "You will, Dallas. I intend that you give me many sons. That will bind you to me in a way that nothing else can, so you will never leave me."

Dallas looked up at him in shocked silence as he carried her. The thought that he might manage to impregnate her had been pushed from her mind because it made escaping so much more difficult.

He reached the *karnee*, carried her inside, bent to kiss her forehead. "I pray it may be so. I know that once you carry my child in your belly, you can never leave me."

She felt angry because perhaps her own body had betrayed her. "I will leave!" She flung the words at him. "Quint will come for me, and he'll kill you for touching me!"

He winced at her words. "Your man has no doubt decided you are dead by now and has gone away. Anyway, would he want you if he knew a warrior had used you time and time again over the past weeks? Would he want to raise an Indian son? Would he look at your swollen belly and your breasts big with milk for my child and hate you because my son is not his?"

She looked away. "I think I know him better than that. He would want me anyway."

But Timbi pressed on mercilessly, reaching out to turn her face up to his. "Look at me, Dallas. What if he doesn't want you? What would you do? Where would you go? Would even your own family take you back when you bear a bastard Paiute baby?"

Tears gathered and ran down her face. "I . . . I don't know, I think my family would understand—"

"But you don't know for sure, do you?" He surrounded her with his cold logic. "You have told me your father is a proud man. What would his friends and neighbors say? Would they laugh and say you shamed him by not killing yourself instead of submitting?"

She burst into tears, knowing the hard reality of it. The whites were so prejudiced against Indians that a white woman who came back alive was the object of gossip, disgust, and pity. Whites thought a woman should kill herself rather than submit. "I hate you! I intended to leave, first chance I got! If I carry your child, I'm not sure I have any place to go!"

"You think I didn't know that? You always have a place in my *karnee,* in my arms," he whispered, and he held her close against him and kissed her as she wept. "I have wanted you badly enough to make sure I gave you a child to tie you to me forever."

She looked up at him and thought she had never seen such tragedy on a face.

"Pony Girl, I have given up more than you know to have you—honor, friendship. When I swim in the spring, I cannot even bear to look into the eyes of my own reflection."

She hadn't the least idea what he was talking about. She hated him still and yet she was not sure even Quint had loved her as much as this man did.

"Someday," she whispered, "the whites may find out you hold me and they will come for me."

"The whites owe me a woman and child, as I owe someone a life. . . ." His voice trailed off. Tipping her chin up, he looked down at her sternly. "Hear me, Dallas. I will kill anyone who tries to take you from me, because if you go you will take my heart with you and no man can live without a heart."

She looked up at him through her tears. "You have broken mine," she whispered, "knowing I belonged to another, yet forcing yourself on me anyway."

"Perhaps what I have done is wrong," he admitted, shame-faced, "but I have such a need for you, nothing means more than having you—nothing."

He stood up. "Rest awhile, and in the next few days, I will ask Atsa to do the final packing so that all will be ready when we move the camp. I would not want to endanger you and my son by heavy work."

Abruptly he turned and left.

Dallas knew then from the way he had looked at her that he had been bluffing about turning her over to his men if she did not submit without a fight. His stormy eyes had told her he would kill any man who touched her, yes, even one of his own people.

And his words had struck a response in her. At night, after Timbi had made love to her and gone to sleep, holding her close, he often thrashed about and cried out. What terrible things haunted him? Had the deaths of his woman, his parents been so terrible that he could never forget that tragedy. What else could it be? Even though she tried to fight it, she had softened a little toward this troubled, moody man.

Yet her own dreams weren't much better. Many nights, she saw Quint's face as he finally came for her. One night, he would say, It doesn't matter, I love you. On another, he would look at her accusingly and snarl, You let him touch you and you expect me to take you back? Why didn't you kill yourself rather than submit?

No. She shook her head. *Quint isn't like that . . . is he?*

307

She wasn't even sure anymore that she knew what he was like, deep inside. She had really spent so little time with him before she'd married him. And yet she had faith that her instincts had been correct and that he was as fine, honorable and loving as she had perceived him to be.

While she couldn't be certain, the possibility that she might be pregnant made her escape plans seem so futile that she pressed her face into the mat and wept.

But that night, in a rare show of courage, she defied Timbi when he tried to take her in his arms by the small fire in the *karnee*.

"All this time, you have terrified me into submitting by saying you would hand me over to your warriors! Well, I defy you! I will not submit anymore without a fight!" Dallas gestured toward the door. "Call your warriors!"

"Have you forgotten I am the chieftain, you are the captive? Do not anger me, Pony Girl!"

"You have threatened and threatened, now give me to your warriors!"

The firelight reflected off his anguished face, the gleam of her full, naked breasts.

"When did the master become the slave?" he whispered, so softly she barely heard him. "You know, don't you, Spirited One, how much power you hold over me? You know I would not hand you over to anyone, that I would kill the man who even looked at you with hunger in his eyes, much less touched you!"

He grabbed her by the shoulders, his chest heaving as he dragged her to him. "Does it make you feel better to know I am so bewitched by you? If my people knew how much I am under your spell, they would want to stone you to death for bad medicine!"

She turned her face away so that she felt his warm breath on her cheek, but she could not withdraw farther because he held her shoulders in a bruising grip. "Your people must be savages indeed!" She sneered.

Now it was his turn to scoff as he put his finger under her chin, forced her to look up at him. "Savages! You speak of savages? It was white people, not brown, who were marooned up in the Sierra Nevada a dozen years ago and ate each other, yet you call the Paiute savages?"

She winced, vulnerable. Even the Indians had heard of the ill-fated Donner party that had resorted to cannibalism when they ran out of food.

"I . . . I should not have said that about your people," she murmured. "You angered me."

"Oh, Dallas, Dallas, let us not quarrel! I love you enough for both of us, and if you'd let yourself, you could learn to want me, to like being my woman."

"I have a man already, and I will care for no other as long as Quint Randolph lives!"

"Then I wish him dead because his shadow stands between us!"

Timbi was visibly shaken by the words he had just blurted out. "Atsa is right," he whispered. "I have abandoned every shred of what's right and honorable for you. Damn you, Dallas!" He swore — white man's terrible oathes — and then dragged her to him, kissed her with wild abandonment. "If you must destroy me, at least make it worthwhile."

She didn't have any idea what he meant, but she found herself responding to his mouth, his seeking hands as he embraced her. Her heart belong to Quint, but she was of a passionate nature and she could not stop her traitorous body from arching against Timbi's hands as he stroked and kissed her.

Forgive me, Father, for I have sinned. . . . How could she even want a man to touch her as Timbi now did? She closed her eyes and saw Quint's face. It was not so terrible when Timbi took her because she pretended he was Quint and, as she convulsed under him, she cried out Quint's name.

Timbi sat up, his face terrible to see. For a split second, she thought he would strike her in his fury, and then he turned over in his blankets, his face to the wall. She thought she saw his shoulders shake, but she couldn't be sure. Devils drove him. He might even be going mad. She pitied him.

It occurred to her to wonder whether she would be able to love Timbi if Quint were dead or had abandoned her forever. Until now, she had kept watching the horizon, thinking that every horseman was her tall Kentuckian coming to carry her off into that eternal sunset. If he loved her, wanted her back, why hadn't he come? Now, as she lay in the darkness and wondered if she were pregnant with Timbi's child, she knew the brave had indeed tied her to him forever.

Atsa was certainly aware of her brother's total absorption with the white girl. She avoided Dallas as much as possible, partly because she was afraid Timbi's woman would want the precious earrings returned and partly because she was ashamed for the loss of her brother's honor and the part she herself had played in all this. She knew Dallas didn't realize they weren't that far from the trading post, that one could walk there in a couple of hours.

Atsa didn't dare wear the earrings, of course. Timbi would ask how she'd come by them. Then he would be angry with her because she had promised to help the white girl and had taken a bribe to do so, knowing that she was certainly going to fail. Atsa had to face the fact that she didn't have any more honor than her bother. Besides, she was a bit jealous. Where she had once been Timbi's pet, now he had shunted her over to her friend's *karnee,* and all were making broad hints that she should marry, get her own lodge and a man to hunt for her.

Yet Atsa would rather die than spend the rest of her life among the Paiute. She wanted a real house and a carriage and red dresses. She wanted to marry a white man.

If she were going to do anything about it, she must do it soon since the camp was being moved tomorrow, up to the giant lake that had once been an ancient sea that covered the whole basin. Once they were at Pyramid Lake, her brother would pressure her to choose a man from the many clans that were gathering. Atsa decided to slip away unnoticed and spy on the trading post one last time.

Good, Quint was back! She saw his tall frame leaning

against a hitching post. He was visiting with the others while he smoked his pipe. She could smell the good scent of the tobacco, even up in the rocks. The last time she had sneaked over, there had been no sign of him and she had been sad, thinking he had gone away forever.

Now just why had he returned? Her gladness turned to fear. Had he discovered somehow that her brother had captured his woman? Had he come to claim her and kill Timbi? She knew what her brother would have done were he in the same circumstances, and she was afraid for Timbi who behaved more and more like a lovesick fool than a Paiute chieftain.

But how would Quint have found out about Dallas? As Atsa considered this, she clutched the earrings she had never dared to wear.

Perhaps he hadn't. Perhaps he had returned for some other reason. Was there the slightest chance that if Atsa went down there and smiled with eyes of love, offering herself, he might want to marry her, take her to town to live like a white girl? Could she keep the shameful secret from him for the rest of her life, so that he need never know how his own blood brother who owed him a life had shamefully repaid him?

She would miss her brother, but if she could make Quint want her, take her away to live in that wonderful place called Virginia City, she decided she could keep the secret for as long as need be.

She brushed her black hair back, thought a long moment. She was no more honorable than her brother. *But some things were more important than honor—weren't they?*

She considered what she would do. What excuse could she use to go to the trading post? Certainly she had made some pretty baskets. Perhaps she could sell them to the white men, or trade them for red cloth to make a dress.

But even as she decided that she would go down there, her nerve failed at the idea of going alone. Who could she take with her? It couldn't be Dallas, of course, or her brother who would tell her to stay away from the traders. All the

Indians knew that bad Indians sometimes traded for whiskey at the post. There'd even been rumors that a handsome white man with a cruel, hard mouth and bright flowers on his vest had given the Pit River tribe whiskey to attack the settlers. The whites, being so stupid they couldn't tell one Indian from another, promptly blamed the attack on the Paiutes.

Atsa brightened. She knew who to take, the perfect person, one who spoke no English and couldn't slip and tell the whites about Dallas. She would invite her small friend, Moponi, to go with her to sell baskets. That would give Atsa a chance to smile at Quint Randolph and flirt with him. She scampered away, daydreaming of red dresses and furniture to sit on.

Chapter Twenty-one

Quint rode out to the burned station and put wild flowers on the three graves. He scattered the petals, stood lost in thought and sorrow. If only . . .

No, he must not think of what might have been or live in the past. Looking behind her was what had doomed Lot's wife in the Bible story. But every desert breeze seemed to whisper to him: *Dallas . . . Dallas . . . Dallas . . .*

Oh, my lost, dear angel. Her deep, throaty laughter seemed to echo in his mind, and when he closed his eyes, he saw her dark eyes, smoky and deep with passion as he made love to her.

He knew he would never marry again. Wolves mate for life, he thought, staring down at the big gold ring, and I have lost my mate. There would never be children for his empty ranch house in Arizona, although he longed for them. His sister Charlotte's youngsters would become his heirs.

On his return, as he dismounted at the hitching post in front of the Williams brothers' station, Quint heard the rhythmic drumming of hooves, turned to stare off at the horizon. A small figure on horseback galloped toward him.

Dave Williams came out of the barn, grinning. "Reckon the Pony rider's right on time. It got back running real fast, didn't it? Sure seemed to annoy the hell outa Yancy!"

Quint tied up his horse, watching the rider gallop toward the station yard. If he could have proven that Yancy had given those braves whiskey, caused Dallas's death through plotting to delay the Pony Express, Quint would have killed the gambler. But suppose it wasn't true? Even though he instinctively disliked the man from Mississippi, Quint was fair enough not to condemn a man without sufficient evidence of guilt.

The bay pony thundered into the yard in a cloud of dust, its young rider jerking it to a skidding halt. "Howdy! I've got a letter for someone here." He swung down, dug a letter out of the *mochila*.

Williams took the envelope in his hands and stared at it in wonder. "How about that! A real letter at a whole five dollars, clear from Philadelphia for Yancy!"

His brother came out of the station just then with a cold meat sandwich for the rider who was already swinging back into the saddle. "A real letter? Hey, Yancy," he called over his shoulder, "it's a real letter for you!"

Quint watched as the horse galloped away in a cloud of dust and was soon swallowed up over the horizon.

"Amazing," he said, staring after the boy, "to think a lone rider on a horse is what's linking the country together."

Yancy came out, took the letter. The gold toothpick extended from a corner of his mouth. "Mighty weak link; easy to break." He opened the letter, took some money from it, yawned as he read the message. Then he tore it into small pieces, tossed it to the winds.

"Hey!" Dave said, spitting through his broken tooth. "That cost five whole dollars for someone to send clear from Philadelphia and you tear it up?"

Yancy shrugged and leaned against the doorjamb, looking at Quint. "Just from a woman who's crazy about me, but I ain't interested—now that I got what I want." He grinned suggestively, holding up the money.

Oscar pulled at his beard, dropped to his knees to gather up the tiny pieces. "Well, you could have given her name to me. I'd be mighty pleased to get a real letter from a lady."

"I didn't say she was a *lady*." Yancy looked at Quint and fiddled with his string tie. "She's married, but she can be had."

Quint winced. "And you're no gentleman, Yancy. No man ought to smear a woman like that."

Yancy started to make a retort, then seemed to think

better of it.

Oscar was still trying to piece the tiny scraps together, but realizing they were too small, he threw them to the wind. "Dagnab it, Yancy! You could have given her name to me! I never had a letter in my whole life!"

His brother shrugged. "What does it matter, Oscar? You can't read nohow, and at five dollars, you couldn't afford to answer if she did write."

Everyone went into the trading post and leaned on the bar. Quint had stopped drinking, but the day had turned a little chill for the first few days of May.

"Give me a brandy," he said.

Dave sneered. "Listen to the fancy gent! You should remember we got nothin' but cheap redeye."

Yancy frowned and sucked on his toothpick. "Not a decent bourbon in the whole state," he drawled. "The rotgut y'all serve ain't fit for Injuns."

Quint sipped the cheap, raw liquor. "Somebody thought it was."

Yancy raised his eyebrows. "Was what?"

Quint couldn't prove it or he would have called the man out for a duel, shot him down like a dog. "I reckon I was thinking that if the Indians got liquored up again, stopped the Pony Express from keeping connections open with the gold and silver mines, it would sure make the South happy."

Yancy looked as if he was trying to decide whether to take offense. He glanced at the Colt strapped on Quint's hip, decided against it. "Closing down the Pony might help the Southern cause and that's a fact."

Quint sipped his drink, holding his anger in check. "Southerners may be noble, but they're fools if they decide to secede, they can't possibly win."

Yancy eyed him coldly, his cruel mouth a hard line. "We might," he drawled. "If the North should lose Nevada and California to invaders and England would decide to come in on the South's side because she needs our cotton for her mills."

Quint shook his head. "The Pony Express is determined to keep communications open, I hear; and England will never get involved. Her people are too opposed to slavery."

"Reckon we'll see, won't we?" Yancy brushed a speck off his flowered vest.

Oscar scratched his beard vigorously as if he might have fleas. "I have to tell you, Randolph, the word's come back that all the riders east of here's been sayin' your thoroughbreds is standing up to the pace as good or better'n our mustangs."

Quint nodded modestly. "Much obliged to you for telling me. I intend for my stock to get even better; I've come back to catch the Medicine Hat."

Dave spat through the hole in his teeth. "Don't tell me you believe that old Injun legend! You been out in the sun too long."

"He exists. I've seen him," Quint said softly.

Immediately he had every man's attention. "He's as big and magnificent as any horse I've ever seen. If I believed in reincarnation, it wouldn't be hard to convince me that he's the spirit of some great chief, running wild and free as the Nevada wind forever."

Dave grunted. "Don't sound like a bad idea of heaven, do it? Sometimes when I hear that Washoe zephyr blowing down from the mountains, it don't sound like no ordinary wind."

Yancy sneered. "And what makes you think you can catch him, Randolph?"

Quint glared at him, holding himself in check. Something about Yancy made Quint want to hit him. "It's worth a try. Sky Climber is priceless as a herd sire."

Oscar scratched himself again. "I'll go with you."

Quint shook his head. "One man makes less noise and I can travel faster alone."

The truth was, he wanted to be alone with the beauty of the desert, with his memories. *Nevada. Snow-capped.* The country brought back memories of the precious hours he'd spent with Dallas, and he didn't want to share them with anyone. No, there was one person who might understand his sorrow. For a long moment, he thought of riding up to the Paiute camp and visiting with Timbi. Strange, he'd known the chieftain only a short time, but the Indian seemed closer than a brother. Quint tried not to hold Dallas's death against all Indians; still, it was hard. . . .

Yancy sipped his drink. "I'd rather not be out there in that desert. You can never be sure if those Injuns will decide to go on the warpath again."

Quint gave him a long look. "They probably won't— unless someone gives them whiskey."

Yancy looked back at him and the tension between them hung in the air, heavy as the rank scents of greasy food and stale smoke. "You just never can tell when that might happen."

Dutch Phil came in just then, laughed, reached down to rub his hand over himself. "Damn, I wish one of them bucks would bring in a sweet little squaw and let me have at her for a few drinks of red-eye! I got a real hunger on me for a woman!"

Quint swore. "That's just the sort of thing that could put the Indians on the warpath, a white man bothering their women."

"Hell, man," Yancy drawled, "they're just squaws. They ought to feel it's a real compliment to lie down and spread out for a white man."

Quint gripped the edge of the bar to keep from hitting him in the mouth. He had a distinct feeling that Yancy knew something he'd like to tell Quint, but didn't have the nerve to do it.

Quint heard a noise behind him and whirled. Atsa and a shorter Indian girl stood in the doorway, regarding the men shyly.

Dutch Phil's dirty face brightened. "Well, looky here! Here we was wishing for something sweet and tasty to meet a hunger and it comes walking right in the door!"

Quint looked at the girls a long moment, felt his hatred melt. Maybe it wasn't in him to hate all Indians because of what had happened to Dallas. He walked over, gently put his hand on Atsa's shoulder. "Does your brother know you're here?"

She looked chagrined, turned to translate for her friend

317

who obviously didn't speak English. Then she stubbed the toe of one red moccasin against the rough floor. "No, he would not let us come if he knew." She looked around at the trade goods stacked everywhere, her eyes wide. "We bring baskets to trade."

"Baskets, hell!" Yancy drawled. "You got something sweeter than that!"

"Yancy," Quint ground out, "you say one more thing and I may shove that gold toothpick clear down your gullet."

He took each girl by the arm, led them outside. "Atsa, you'll get into big trouble here. Go back to camp. Give your brother my regards. Tell him someday I'll come visit him again."

She stared up at him, started to speak, looked away as if she were hiding something. "But, Quint, I wanted a red dress. Would you take me as a wife?"

He smiled sadly, started walking the girl across the station yard. "Atsa, I once had a woman, but she is dead and my heart is full of sorrow. I do not think I want another woman ever."

"You say your woman is dead?"

What was it in her face that disturbed him? Perhaps he only imagined it. He nodded, sighed. "I'm going to try one more time to capture Sky Climber and then I'm going away, never to return. But I will always think kindly of you and your brother, who was my friend."

She caught his arm. "Take me with you, Quint, I would be your woman. You could dress me like a white girl and we would live in a house with a carriage in the yard."

He frowned. "Stop thinking of that, Atsa. Be content to live as a Paiute, choose a warrior, have children by him. This yen to live like a white will bring you trouble."

Yancy came to the door behind him. "Hey, don't send them away. It looks like the weather might turn a little chilly."

Atsa looked at Quint blankly. "What does the white man mean?"

"Never mind." He turned away, and faced the other man. "Yancy, are you insane? This one is a chieftain's sister. You

318

defile a chief's sister and you'll find out how to die a slow death!"

Quint turned back to the girls. "You two go home," he ordered sternly. "Tell your brother what you were up to. And tell him I'm going away forever, but his blood brother sends warm regards."

Atsa didn't meet his eyes. "I . . . I will miss you, Quinton. I would still like to be your woman." Before he realized what she was up to, she stood on tiptoe, slipped her arms around his neck and kissed him.

In that split second, he realized she really was more of a woman than a child. Her mouth was soft and warm on his, her breasts pressed against his chest. He could feel the satin heat of her all the way down their bodies.

Very slowly, he reached up, unclasped her hands from around his neck and kissed her forehead. "I love you as a sister, Atsa, nothing more. Maybe when I go through Virginia City, I'll see if I can buy a red dress, send it back to you."

Atsa and her friend turned and started back up the trail. She stopped once, hesitated as if she were about to tell him something, stopped. "Good-bye, Quinton of the magic number."

He nodded. "Good-bye little Atsa of the red moccasins. I wish you and your people well."

He stood staring after the two young women until he was sure they were headed up the trail. Then he sighed and went back inside, brushing past Yancy to get through the doorway.

"Damn me!" Yancy said. "No wonder he ran them off; he don't want to share those sweet-as-sorghum Injun gals."

Quint hit him hard, throwing all his weight into the punch that sent Yancy stumbling backward over a pile of blankets and into copper pots that crashed to the floor in a jangle of metal.

But even as he tensed for a fight, wanting to take out his anger and frustrations on the man's handsome, grinning face, Yancy didn't get up. He just lay amid the copper pots, looking at Quint while blood ran down his face and onto his shirt.

"Get up!" Quint commanded. "Get up! I think you may have just pushed me far enough to kill you!"

But Yancy shook his head, made a gesture of appeasement. "I didn't mean to rile you, Randolph. I'm no street brawler, just a lover of pretty women. You took that awful personal. Them little gals would never tell if we sampled a little and give them a few trinkets."

"Is it worth your life?" Quint said. "I can tell you her brother dotes on her. He'd set this place on fire, kill everyone within a day's ride."

Yancy laughed, stood up, wiping the blood from his mouth. "Aren't you exaggerating a mite?"

"Let's just say I know her brother," Quint said with slow, cold emphasis.

He went outside to the wash basin. His hand felt stiff. It was swelling from hitting Yancy. Quint slipped the big gold ring off, laid it on the bench while he washed the blood off his knuckles.

Oscar came out of the station, and Quint whirled around.

"Randolph, you ain't going off alone, are you? Ain't you afraid of running into a war party?"

Quint nodded. "The Pony Express rider does it all the time. Besides, I'm armed. If anyone wants to tangle with me, I'd enjoy killing a couple of the Indians that got those poor devils at the relay station."

"Well, it's your life." Oscar shrugged, went back inside.

Quint headed to the barn, saddled up a bay gelding. Preoccupied, he gathered up some supplies and rode out. He was an hour away before he glanced down and realized he'd left his ring on the wash-up bench.

He swore under his breath, reined the horse around, then shook his head. It was too far back. He'd get the ring when he got back from his horse hunt.

He searched for track and sign of the wild herd for the rest of the afternoon, without much luck. Finally the pink shadows of the coming darkness spread across the lonely, barren area and he unsaddled his horse, built a fire.

Quint made a pot of coffee, roasted a fat rabbit he'd shot earlier in the day. Then he bedded down in his blankets, using his saddle for a backrest as he warmed his fingers on the tin cup holding his coffee. Relaxed, he lit his pipe, stared into the flickering flames, and took a deep breath, smelling the scent of burning sagebrush. He hadn't realized a man could love a country as passionately as he did a woman. Now that he had discovered the wide, free places of the West, he wasn't ever going back east.

His life would be complete if Dallas were snuggled down next to him as he puffed on his pipe, her dark head on his arm. *If only* . . . No, he must not think that way. He must not regret that which he could not change. He would think about tomorrow when he finally tracked down the great stallion.

He had an eerie feeling, as if he were being watched. He grabbed for his Colt, turned.

Up on a butte overlooking his camp, the Medicine Hat stallion stood poised on an outcrop, staring down at him. Anyone who doesn't believe in big medicine might change his mind at seeing you, Quint thought sheepishly, watching the horse. The light played on the stallion's spotted hide, and the relentless wind the locals called a Washoe zephyr blew Sky Climber's long mane and tail out so that they looked like wisps and swirls of clouds.

"Tomorrow, big fellow, I'm finally gonna rope you and make a friend of you. I've got a bunch of fine mares down in Arizona that would just love to make your acquaintance. There'll be plenty of good oats and the best stall. Life will be easy for you."

He frowned. *And all it's going to cost you is your freedom.* He was ashamed then, thinking he had no right to make that decision for the proud, wild horse. But never in all his years of breeding fine horses had Quint seen such a magnificent specimen. He would have sold his soul to own Sky Climber at that moment as the great horse reared up, pawing at the black night and whinnying a challenge. Watching the stud, Quint could easily believe a chief's spirit really could be reincarnated as a spirit horse.

The stallion reared up once more, issued a ringing challenge, and then took off running with his mares. Quint heard the drumming of their hooves long after the horses had vanished into the night. It almost sounded like Indian drums.

Somewhere in the hills, a giant lobo wolf howled. That has to be the loneliest sound in the whole world, Quint thought sadly. He wondered suddenly if the big lobo was running the hills forever alone.

Like me. He ruefully shook his head. *Well, the name Randolph—*

An answering howl drifted from another hill and Quint smiled in spite of himself as he sipped the hot coffee, took a deep puff of the fragrant smoke. *Well, old boy, you aren't alone after all, are you? You've got a mate.* The fact comforted him somehow.

He finished his coffee, knocked the ashes from his pipe, banked the coals of the fire, and curled up close to them. The foothills were unseasonably cool for early May.

Dawn found Quint already saddled up and tracking the big horse through the hills. The weather had turned cold enough for frost and the stallion had left hoof marks on the frozen, brittle grass.

Quint took a deep breath of cold air, feeling blood pump through his heart, inhaling the scents of hardy wild flowers and pungent sagebrush. In the distant hills, he saw stands of the piñons the Paiutes depended on for nuts. If the miners didn't stop cutting them . . .

A jackrabbit jumped under his gelding's hooves; causing it to snort and stamp. Quint watched the rabbit scamper away, long ears flopping.

He tried to stay downwind of the mustangs' trail. With the wind blowing toward Quint, the Medicine Hat wouldn't be able to smell the man approaching.

The herd was visible in the distance now, grazing quietly in the grass. Bay, sorrel, black. Mares nickered at bright pinto foals that showed their big sire's color pattern. The stallion himself stood watch on a rise, sniffing the air for the approach of enemies so he could warn the others.

For a long moment, Quint watched the horse, almost holding his breath at its beauty. More than anything, he wanted to possess the stallion, put his brand on it, brag about owning it. And yet, he felt ashamed of what he was about to do. The Medicine Hat was the personification of the West, and no one should ever own him or imprison him.

Well, you haven't done it yet, Quint, old boy, he chided himself, brushing his hair back and setting his hat firmly on his head so he wouldn't lose it when he took off running. *And I'm sure the Medicine Hat has other ideas.*

He spurred his horse and galloped after the stallion. The Medicine Hat reared once, neighing and shaking his head in challenge, and then he ran in a cloud of dust, driving his mares before him.

Quint followed, reaching for his lariat as he rode. He could never outrun the big horse, but maybe, because of the mares Sky Climber would not leave behind, he could get close enough to get a rope on him. Holding the stallion would be something else again.

Sky Climber was smart. He'd been chased many times, and at any other time of the year, he would have quickly outrun or outsmarted Quint. Quint knew that. But in early spring, the wobbly legs of the new foals slowed the herd down.

Quint was determined to own the great stallion. No horse that money could buy did he want as much as he wanted this one.

The chase stretched out mile after mile, all the horses blowing and lathered now. The colts and fillies were failing, falling behind. Only the stallion's sharp teeth kept them moving.

Quint felt a trace of regret and shame as he gained on the herd. Another stallion would move in and claim the Medicine Hat's harem after a few weeks, adding it to his own herd. *And why should he be ashamed when, on his ranch, the stud would have the most luxurious living it had ever known?*

Quint pictured himself riding into town on the beautiful horse while people turned to look. He was human enough to like the idea.

The black and white stallion lagged behind, a broken rope still dangling from his neck. Hardly daring to hope, Quint readied his lasso. There was a split second of heart-stopping suspense.

Now. *Now!* Quint thought and he threw the loop. For a heartbeat, it hung in the air before settling over the majestic head. *Good Lord! I've got him!*

Then the stud hit the end of the rope with his full weight, sending Quint's gelding stumbling.

He had not realized the pinto was so powerful. Timbi's accident flashed into his mind, and he knew now how that could happen to even the most skilled horseman with this stallion.

If I end up trapped under a dead horse, who will come along to save me? Quint silently asked himself.

But the bay gelding regained its footing, and Quint snubbed the rope around his saddle horn, being careful to keep his fingers free. Many an old roper in the West, he'd heard, had lost a finger or two that had been caught in the rope when a horse or steer hit the end and jerked it taut as a fiddle string.

He saw a dead mesquite tree sticking up out of the nearby rocks. Cautiously, he played the fighting horse, trying to work his way over to it. "Easy, big boy! Easy, Sky Climber, I'm not going to hurt you!"

But the horse reared and plunged, pawing with his hooves at the sky. Once he even charged directly at Quint, baring his teeth. Quint had a sudden, heart-stopping vision of going down in a tangle of loose rope as the big horse collided with the smaller gelding and attacked him with those gleaming teeth.

Skillfully, he managed to get the rope around the dead tree. For a few moments, he thought the Medicine Hat would jerk it up by its roots. But the stunted bush had sunk deep into the arid soil in its search for water, and though it trembled as the stallion lunged, it held.

It took most of the morning to secure the horse to the tree and stop its wild lunging and rearing. The herd stopped off in the distance, watched curiously for a while, snorting at Quint's scent and whinnying. Then the other horses went back to grazing.

"Easy, boy, I'm not going to hurt you!" Quint began to talk to the savage horse, caressing it with words. Finally it was too exhausted to do anything but stand and tremble.

"Thirsty, aren't you?" Quint poured some water from his canteen into his hat, approached cautiously, ready to run if the stallion attacked. But though Sky Climber bared his teeth, the lure of the water was too strong and presently he lowered his head and drank out of the hat. The horse pricked his ears forward, listening to Quint's voice as he drank.

Quint didn't try to touch the horse, but kept up a steady conversation with it, even as he went and picked tender bunches of fresh spring grass for the big stud. At first the horse would not touch the grass, but finally he ate.

Quint found a trickle of water coming through the rocks, icy cold runoff from the melting snow high in the Sierra Nevada, and watered the horse again. Then he built a fire no bigger than his hand and made himself some coffee as the day's shadows lengthened.

If there were any Pit River Indians or Paiutes who were not in Timbi's clan out there, Bannock or Shoshoni, he didn't want their sharp eyes to spot a wisp of smoke or their noses to smell the acrid scent of burning sagebrush.

Every muscle in his body ached from fighting the big horse that morning, but it had been worth it. He had captured the finest horse in all Nevada, and if he'd been offered a king's ransom for the Medicine Hat, he would have refused to sell him.

Night came on and Quint fried up a little bacon, got out some hardtack to go with his coffee. The big horse had stopped fighting the rope, and watched him curiously from where he was tied. Quint fed Sky Climber again and watered him. His own gelding grazed peacefully nearby, hobbled. Quint smoked and stared into his tiny fire, pulling his jacket up around his ears. Even in May, it was chilly here, and it wouldn't be unusual to get a little snow dusting the mountain tops as winter finally gave way to spring. Only one thing would now make his happiness complete. *Dallas.* If only she were here with him, snuggled close as they stared into the camp fire. *If only . . .*

He was doing it again and he had promised himself he would not. It was such a hard habit to break. "Tomorrow is going to be a long day," he said aloud. The big horse raised its head, looked at him, its neck rearing back as it smelled his scent, its nostrils flaring. "That's what I said, boy." Quint laughed. "Tomorrow, I'm going to try to get a halter on you, and we'll see whether I break you or you kill me."

He banked the fire and curled up in his blankets, then slept like a dead man.

The next few days were long and hard. At sunup each morning, Quint started working with the big horse, gentling him, feeding him. He was an expert with horses. By the end of the week, he had progressed to tying a blindfold over the stud's eyes and putting a saddle on him.

But the stallion almost killed his captor when Quint finally eased into the saddle and took the blindfold off. The great beast showed his rider why the Indians called him Sky Climber.

It was if Quint had saddled a Southwestern tornado. He was a skilled rider, but he'd never ridden such a horse. The stud bucked and sunfished, throwing his hind legs out and then bucking sideways, trying to rub Quint off into the dead tree stump. While Quint fought him, the horse reared up on his hind legs, pawing at the air as if he intended to go straight up.

Quint cursed, hanging on. For an instant, as the horse stood on his hind legs, he thought they might go over backward. The idea of half a ton of horse crashing down on him was enough to send the most experienced rider into heart failure, but Quint hung on. If this had been a bad horse in a paddock, he would have helped it go on over backward, then jumped clear. A horse wouldn't deliberately put itself through that experience twice. But in this situation, there was nothing to do but hang on and hope the stallion maintained his balance.

The stud crashed back down on all fours with a teeth-breaking, gut-wrenching jolt and took off running. Quint hung on, trying to rein him in, but to no avail. All he could hope for as the big horse ran was that there was no deep gully or prairie-dog holes out there that could break the horse's leg.

Finally Sky Climber stopped running and crow-hopped across the sparse brush, both he and his rider grunting with the impact each time he hit the ground.

Quint cursed and hung on. "You stubborn sonovabitch! You may kill me, but you won't pitch me in the dirt!"

Finally after what seemed like an eternity, the big horse wore out and stood blowing and lathered. With a sigh, Quint swung down, tied him in the shade of a gray-green sagebrush and got him a hatful of water.

Every bone in Quint's body seemed to cry out in protest as he moved, but he wouldn't give up. He eyed the big stallion. "After I rest and eat a bite, we'll try it again."

And so it went all week. Quint got so bruised, he could hardly find a comfortable position when he lay down at night. By day, he fed and watered the big horse and they had go-arounds with saddle and bridle.

After a few days, Quint decided he would be able to break the big horse after all—or at least get to a point where he could ride Sky Climber without the stud trying to pitch him into the cactus and stomp him to death.

He always talked to the horse and gradually reached out to stroke its head. At first Sky Climber bared his teeth and tried to bite him, but as days passed, the stallion began to act as if he might be enjoying the stroking.

On the day Quint rode without the Medicine Hat trying to buck him off, he smiled with satisfaction when he finally swung down at the end of the day. "You've still got some learning to do, Sky Climber, but you're green-broke enough for me to take you back to Williams' station. I want to pick up the ring I left there. After that, we'll make our way down to my ranch in Arizona. You'll like it there, it's not that much different from Nevada, except you'll have finer mares in your harem."

The little band of mares still grazed in the general area, but they no longer paid any attention to Quint and what went on in the meadow. If the big stud didn't return soon, another stallion would move in, add the herd to his own band.

That night Quint felt almost happy as he sat before his camp fire. The next day he would be leaving Nevada forever. Although he liked the wild country, it reminded him too much of the pain and sadness of losing the only woman he had ever really loved.

"Maybe in Arizona, I can finally put the past behind me, stop being haunted by her memory," he said softly to the stallion who stood tied to the stump. The horse nickered at the sound of Quint's voice.

Somewhere in the mountains, the wolves howled again and Quint sighed. He would never forget Dallas. She would be in his heart and soul forever. But maybe he could learn to live with his loss so that it didn't eat at him constantly. Perhaps someday the time would come when he could remember her velvet voice, her dark beauty, without blinking away the sudden moisture that came unbidden to his eyes.

Dark angel. I miss you so much. I miss you . . . He laid his head on his arm and stared into the tiny fire, listening to the pair of wolves howl as they ran through the hills.

Should he make one last trip to see Timbi? He thought about it as he smoked. Even though they were more than friends, the brooding Paiute might not like it that Quint had captured the Medicine Hat and was taking the stallion to another place. An Indian would think the great animal should roam the Sierra Nevada, wild and free forever, as it did in their legends.

Quint banked his fire and lay down in his blankets, shivering a little in the cold desert night. There was still a little snow on the mountain tops. It gleamed in the moonlight in an unearthly way.

He took a deep breath and sat up abruptly. The wind blowing from the hills brought the slight scent of smoke to his nose. And then he saw the signal fires on each hilltop; small at first, then growing to huge orange bonfires as men piled dry brush on the flames.

What was all that about? Had he been spotted? He shook his head. They wouldn't go to that much trouble if they were hostiles, they'd just ride down and kill him.

No, this was something more. There must be a dozen fires on hilltops now, their flames leaping toward the black sky.

Signal fires. Quint remembered something Timbi had told him. *When something really important happens the Paiutes call their people in; all the bands will come when they see the signal fires.*

Now just what had happened to cause the tribes of the Great Basin to call in all of their people? A little shiver went down Quint's back as he watched the fires and wondered. Maybe a thousand Indians or more would come riding in answer to that signal. Should he go investigate?

He realized it might cost him his life if he did. Certainly, except for Timbi, none of the Indians felt kindly toward Quint or any white man, and he wasn't sure he could blame them.

Whatever the fires meant, he realized with a heavy heart that they probably boded no good for the white settlers in the area or the Pony Express. He would get no sleep this night. What the hell was going on?

Chapter Twenty-two

"Damn me!" Yancy stood next to Oscar, staring after Quint Randolph as he rode away. "That uppity gent damn near broke my jaw!" He rubbed his swollen face.

The other man shrugged. "You pushed him too far, Reb. That kind may be quiet and have nice manners, but them's the very ones who can be dangerous as hell if pushed too hard!"

Yancy stuck the gold toothpick back in his mouth, wondering what Randolph would do or say if he knew a gambler from Biloxi had ended up in Quint's elegant sister's bed? He decided that was something he'd never tell.

The tall Kentuckian rode over the horizon. The sunlight glinted off an object on the bench by the wash basin. Yancy sauntered over, picked it up. "Look like he left his gold ring." He slipped it on, held it up to the light. "Just fits, too."

Oscar frowned. "If I was you, I'd let that be, Yancy. When he comes back, he won't like it if you've been wearing it."

Yancy grinned. "Now who's to tell him? You?"

"Not me." Oscar shook his head, pulled at his beard. "I don't like him no better than you do. I keep thinking how much fun we could have had with the two pretty Indian girls if he hadn't got so het up and cantankerous about it."

Yancy admired the ring again, the animal head profile. "He's a *loco* one, all right. I met him first in St. Joe—that

330

kid who got killed, too. There was something strange about them that I never quite figured out." He grinned. "Besides, maybe our uppity gentleman'll get hisself killed out there looking for that horse and I won't have to give it back at all."

Oscar shrugged, and they went back inside. Yancy felt bored and restless as he leaned on the bar, poured himself a drink. He'd left Clark in charge of the Naughty Lady, written out a will leaving the place to Margo and Rose if he didn't get back.

Yancy sipped the liquor, wondered if he'd have any trouble collecting the rest of his payment in San Francisco. Then he grinned. If so, Randolph's sister was good for it. All he had to do was write her a note telling her how much he missed her.

Anyways, he'd done what he could to disrupt the Pony Express by giving whiskey to the Pit River tribe, which hadn't created as much trouble as he'd hoped. He'd about run out of ideas to stir up the Indians. A man could only be so patriotic, even if he was being paid to disrupt things.

Yancy fingered his tie. He missed the excitement of a big town with all its women, gambling, and fun. He'd try to think of something more to stir up the Paiute, and then, pretty quick now, he was going on to San Francisco where a man could really find some excitement. He took a deck of cards from his pocket. "Anyone want to play?"

The Williams boys and Dutch Phil shook their heads, gestured him away as they drank. "Naw," Dave said, "you always win, Yancy. We know better than to play with you."

"You calling me a cheat?" he blustered, but he didn't really want to fight. His jaw still ached from Randolph's fist.

The others shook their heads and edged away down the bar, ignoring him. Yancy held his hand up and admired the gold ring. If he went off to San Francisco with it, would Randolph come after him?

He shook his head. Probably not. It was real gold and maybe a family heirloom by the worn look of it, but probably not worth trailing a man clear to California for.

Randolph was a rotten bastard for running those two girls off and spoiling an evening's entertainment. He deserved to lose his ring. Yancy wondered if there was any profit to be made off providing Injun girls to passing soldiers and miners? He'd had a nice income off the girls at the Naughty Lady.

He ran his tongue over his cut lip, cursing Quint Randolph and thinking about those two girls. That one in the red moccasins was pretty. Yancy wondered if Injun girls knew anything special to do to a man that he'd never experienced before?

Atsa hid behind the clump of sagebrush with her friend and watched Quint Randolph ride away from the trading post. Then she and Moponi went home, but they sneaked back several days later. Atsa looked for Quint's horse, didn't see it. *Good.*

She turned to Moponi and gestured. "He is still gone. Let's take our baskets and go back down to trade."

But little Mosquito hung back, fear and worry on her broad, brown face. "I think the white man is right. Didn't you say he told us this was a bad place and for us to stay home? Besides, my husband doesn't know where I am. He thinks I'm out gathering firewood."

Atsa sighed in disgust. Timbi didn't know where she was, either, or he would have stopped her from coming. Not that her brother paid all that much attention to her anymore. Between the troubles the tribe was having with the whites and the captive woman, Dallas, he didn't seem to worry about his sister much except to lecture her about choosing a husband and getting married.

She shook back her hair. *Her brother's woman.* What he'd done was dishonorable, yet he had the nerve to lecture a younger sister.

Grabbing up a bunch of baskets in one hand and taking Moponi's arm, Atsa nodded toward the station. "There's nothing to stop us now. If Quint won't marry me and take me to town, maybe one of those others will. That tall one with the hard mouth might."

She wanted to look very pretty, and she thought of Dallas's earrings. She hadn't dared wear them around Quint, he might recognize them. Then he'd know his woman was in the Paiute camp. But he had left. She put the earrings on.

"What are those?"

"Jewelry," Atsa said, exasperated. "I . . . I traded for them one time."

Moponi turned and looked uncertainly back up the trail. "I think we should go home."

"But, Moponi," she implored, "didn't you see the things inside? Just think how pleased your husband would be if you brought back something nice for him, a white man's shirt perhaps, in exchange for your baskets."

Her friend hesitated. "You really think it will be all right?"

"Do I look afraid?" Atsa said pompously. "Come along." She took her friend's hand, and the two of them went down the trail to the trading post.

Shyly, Atsa peered around the door. "May we come trade?"

The tall one looked up from his whiskey. "Damn me! This is our lucky night, boys. Look who's back!"

The other men in the place turned. Something about the way they looked at her and Moponi made Atsa uneasy. Maybe they should go back to the Paiute camp, she thought.

The bearded one motioned them in. "Come on in, girls. Don't be skairt." But the look on his face made her nervous. Although Atsa and Moponi had covered their breasts in the white way, the men were looking at them as if they wore no clothes at all.

Well, she wasn't afraid. Her brother was a chieftain. The white men would not dare harm her, knowing she would tell Timbi. Very importantly, she marched in, set her baskets on the bar. "I want a red dress and maybe some real shoes."

"You do, do ya?" The man spat tobacco juice through a hole left by a broken tooth. "What you got to trade?"

The tall one laughed. "Hell, Dave, you know what they got to trade, their soft little velvet —"

"Shut up, Yancy." The other man pulled at his beard. "You'll scare 'em and they'll fly out of here like frightened quail. Come on over, girls, we'll give you something good to drink and then we'll look at your baskets."

"Baskets, hell," the dirty-faced one at the bar said, "They got something I want to look at all right, and it ain't baskets."

The bearded one winked and said in a low voice. "After a couple of drinks, I'll wager they'll be ready to show us anything we want to look at."

The tall one with the tiny gold stick in the corner of his mouth grinned. "I intend to do more than look!"

All the men laughed. Atsa smiled back at them uncertainly. She spoke only a little English and Moponi none at all, so they didn't really understand why the men were laughing and winking at each other.

The tall one held out two cups. "Here, girls, try some of the white man's magic drink." His voice was slow, drawling.

Hesitantly, Atsa reached out, took the tin cups, turned and handed one to Moponi, who still stood shyly behind her. "Is it really big medicine?"

The one with the broken tooth snorted and laughed again. "Big medicine! Lordy, when I've had enough of it, sometimes I feel like I could fly!"

Atsa tasted hers and shuddered. "It does not taste good." Moponi's wry face agreed with her pronouncement.

"But that's what's magic about it." The tall one leaned closer. "The more you drink, the better it tastes!"

She looked at him uncertainly, dutifully took another sip. That ring he wore looked like Quint Randolph's. She wondered if he had traded for it?

The drink seemed to burn all the way down. She took another taste, smiled encouragingly at her friend who drank too. Maybe the white man was right. Atsa felt a little strange. She was not as shy or as worried as she had been. She drained the tin cup, looked around at the stacks of blankets, bundles of cloth, the ribbons and other wonderful things piled everywhere.

She reached out to touch a bright scarlet, flowered fabric.

The bearded one came over. "You like?"

He took the cloth, unfolded it, draped it over her shoulders, held up a small mirror. "See? It looks very pretty with your earrings."

Then he stopped, frowned. "Those are sort of unusual, honey. Where'd you get those?"

She put a hand to her ear guiltily. "I . . . I've had them a long time. One of the warriors once brought them from Virginia City."

The white man shrugged. "Unusual color. Don't 'member ever seeing anything like them before."

She must change the subject although she was sure if Dallas had been dressed as a boy when she'd been at the post, these men had never seen the earrings on the white girl. "How many baskets do I have to trade to get enough of this for a dress?"

The white men all broke into gales of laughter that sounded like a bunch of coyotes yipping although she couldn't see anything funny in what she'd said.

"Honey"—the man grinned, scratching his beard—"I'm gonna make you a gift of that there cloth. Now let's have another drink."

"For me?" It was too good to be true, but she didn't want to ask too many questions, he might change his mind. Why would he give her something so valuable? Maybe it was true that the whites were all very rich. Surely this bunch was. Just looking around at all the wonderful things they owned, Atsa knew these white men must have much money.

She translated for her friend who still stood near the door, looking uneasy.

Moponi shook her head. "I think we should go, Atsa. I think there is something very wrong with the way these men look at us. When anyone says he gives something away, I wonder what he expects in return?"

Atsa had never felt so recklessly happy as she drank from her tin cup. The white man was right. It did taste better with each sip. "Don't be so suspicious, Moponi, they are just

335

trying to keep a friendship with the Paiutes. Come choose some fabric for yourself before he changes his mind."

At her urging, little Mosquito came forward, stared at the good things piled up on the shelves, her eyes wide with wonder. The place smelled of tobacco and dust and new fabric.

Atsa had forgotten her manners. She turned to the grinning white men. What were the English words? Ah, yes. "Thank you," she said. "We are much honored. Now we will take our gifts and go." She put down her cup, carefully folded up the bright fabrics she had been given. The tall one with the string tie came over.

"Now what's your hurry? Why don't you and your friend stay and have another drink?"

Atsa realized she was having trouble keeping her thoughts straight. But something about the man's heavy breathing and the way he looked at her made her nervous. "I . . . I think we will go now. Moponi, have you chosen your gift?"

The broken-toothed one came over, stood close. "Ain't it polite among the Indians to give a gift in return?"

She nodded, gestured toward the baskets on the bar. "We have brought some of our best baskets for you."

The tall one's mouth became harder. "I don't want no damned baskets!"

His tone was even harder than his mouth. Little Moponi turned around from staring at the cluttered shelves. Although she did not speak English, even she had recognized that change in the man's voice. She looked from him to Atsa uncertainly.

Atsa started toward the door. "I think we'd better go."

The tall one stepped to block her path. "Now, sweet, don't be in such a hurry. You must know what I want." He put one hand on her shoulder in a familiar way that a warrior would never use with an unwed girl.

She remembered then that she had come here hoping to have a white man take her away to live in his city. If Quint Randolph didn't want her, maybe this one did. "Are you asking me to be your woman?"

336

He laughed as did the others although she didn't think there was anything funny about it. A marriage was serious business. "Yeah, sweet, you might say that. I want to sample the merchandise."

Out of the corner of her eye, she saw the bearded one advance on Moponi. "No," Atsa said sharply. "Moponi is already married to a warrior."

The bearded one paused, laughed. "I won't hold it against her."

The man over at the bar snorted. "I've got something big and hard I'd like to do more than hold against her."

The bearded one grabbed Moponi, who screamed and began to struggle.

Atsa tried to pull away from the tall one's hand to help her friend. "No, you don't understand. She must not be touched or it shames her husband. I am the one who wants a white husband."

"Then let's see what you have to offer!" The tall one drawled and grabbed her, pulling her against him. She was scared now with his mouth coming down on hers, Moponi screaming and struggling in the background. "No, let us go, please—"

"That's right, please us!" The man pulled her to him again, his hand fumbling with the antelope skin shift she wore. "Don't play innocent with me, you brown bitch, I know Injuns do it with anybody for a few cheap beads!"

She tried to tell him it was not true and that she was a virgin, but he wasn't listening, just pulling and tearing at her shift. The other men ran over, helping hold the two girls as they struggled.

"Hell, Yancy," one of them laughed, "Here, use my knife!"

She felt the blade ripping at her fine antelope-skin dress as she struggled.

"Damn me, if she ain't got the sweetest lookin' pair of little brown tits I ever saw in my life!"

The broken-toothed one held onto her other wrist and laughed. "Now, Yancy, how many brown ones you seen?"

"Seen lots of black ones," he drawled, and all the men

laughed. "Throw some of that trading stuff on the floor. I don't want to be down there on them bare boards."

"Hell, you'll have a good cushion under you!"

Atsa was terrified and screaming, as was her friend, but no one paid any attention.

The broken-toothed one frowned, paused. "You suppose we could get in trouble with the Paiutes for this?"

Yancy shrugged as he forced her toward the floor, "Suppose you don't ever let 'em go back? The Injuns might think they're just lost or carried off by the Pit River bunch. Could you keep 'em chained up and make a little money off passing soldiers?"

He had Atsa down on the floor now, the rough boards putting splinters into her back as she struggled. Somewhere in the background, she heard Moponi screaming. She felt dizzy with the white man's drink, and scared. "Let me go! I want to go back to my village!"

"You said you wanted to be a white man's woman, sweet, you're about to get your wish!" Yancy's hands and mouth were all over her while she fought him. She felt his lips and teeth on her throat, then on her nipple, sucking hard as his hands held her wrists against the floor above her head.

"Dave, hold her damn hands," he gasped, his breath hot on her breast. "I can't do it and hold her, too!"

The broken-toothed one grabbed her wrists, pinned them against the floor. That left the other one to run his hands and mouth all over her.

"Stop!" Atsa protested as she struggled. "I've never had a man before!"

He laughed as if he did not believe her. "Then it's time you did, bitch!" He was bruising her cruelly as she fought to get away, but both men were big and they didn't care if they hurt her.

Her nipples throbbed from Yancy's teeth and now his hands grabbed her thighs, forcing them apart. She had never been so frightened. If she could just get away, she would go back to the village, be an obedient sister, and marry any warrior Timbi chose for her. If only she hadn't been so greedy, if only . . .

She could feel him fumbling with the buttons on his pants as she gasped and fought. Moponi had stopped screaming and was sobbing somewhere far away.

Yancy's hard manhood was suddenly warm against her bare inner thigh and his fingers were stroking her. "She's dry as sand!"

The man holding her hands laughed. "She won't be after we get through with her!"

Atsa struggled to get away, but Yancy was between her thighs and she was powerless against the two men. She felt Yancy's seed hot and wet on her thigh.

The other one cursed. "Hurry up, so's I can have my turn. I'm hurtin', I want her so bad."

Both Yancy's hands cupped her breasts, his mouth came down on hers, his tongue pushing deep into her throat as he rose up on his knees. She felt his hard wetness throbbing against the lips of her velvet place. Then he came into her like a lance rammed deep and hard, breaking her virgin sheath in a rush of pain and tearing.

She could only lie there under him as he rode her hard, pressing her soft flesh against the rough boards. She hadn't thought it would be like this. She felt like a degraded animal as he grunted with the exertion of rising up and driving deep; his thrusts hard and hurting. Then he gasped and lay still.

Atsa's whole lower body felt as if it were on fire with pain, and she lay still and wept.

"Dang it, Yancy, get off and give me a turn," the other one grumbled.

The tall one in the flowered vest pulled out of her. "Damn me, look at the blood! Either she never had a man before or she's built small."

He stood up, looked down at his bloody manhood with smiling satisfaction. "An Injun virgin, didn't think there was such a thing."

She was weeping too much to speak. "Please . . . let us go . . ."

"Honey, we may never let you go." The broken-toothed one laughed as he exchanged places with Yancy. Now the tall one held her down while the other one got between her thighs. He was swollen big with his need. She could smell the rank scent of his seed already dripping as he shoved himself into her and rode her, the path easier now because of Yancy's smeared seed and her own blood. She hurt too badly to move as he rode her to a climax.

At least it was over. What warrior would want her for his woman now that she had been used like a captive, now that she was smeared with the seed of two men?

Dimly, she heard Moponi weeping in the background, but she couldn't help her; she couldn't even help herself.

She had only thought it was over. Now the four men exchanged places and the other two rode her, not caring that she was hurt and torn. She remembered the hairy-faced one's beard trailing across her bare breasts as his mouth sought her nipples. She stank of men's seed and her own bright virgin blood, and Moponi had black bruises on her face as the men dragged them to their feet.

Now the men laughed and offered them whiskey, but the girls wept and shook their heads, too shamed and hurt to speak or look at each other.

"Well, now," Yancy drawled, "let's chain 'em up in the barn so we'll know they're not going anywhere 'til we get ready to use 'em again."

"Which should be in about ten minutes after I finish this here drink." Dave laughed. "I'd forgotten how long I been without a woman."

His brother nodded. "Ain't that the truth! Yancy, I think you got a good idea there about making them whore for us. They're both pretty enough that the boys would pay right well."

They dragged Atsa and Moponi out to the barn, put ropes on their wrists, and secured them to a post. Then they went back inside to have another drink.

Atsa lay there, humiliated and hurting. No warrior would want her now that four white men had mated her. Her own blood and their seed was rank and stiff on her skin. She prayed to the spirits to die. "Moponi, are you hurt?"

There was a long pause. "Not as badly as you, I think.

I'm only bruised . . . and shamed."

Atsa burst into tears. "I was such a fool! And I got you into this. You wouldn't have come if I hadn't begged you—"

"Maybe we can get away while the white men drink."

Atsa shuddered as she sat up, and winced at the pain. "I . . . I'm not sure I could even walk, much less get all the way back to camp. And I know that after a while, they will come out and take us again."

They both listened for a moment as bawdy singing drifted from the station. The white men were obviously in high spirits and getting very drunk.

Atsa gritted her teeth. "Moponi, if I can manage to untie you, do you think you can go back for help?"

"If they come out and I am gone, they will be very angry, probably beat you; and all of them will use you."

"I am already shamed." Atsa thought about the possibilities, tried to stand, saw the fresh blood. It even dripped onto her moccasins. "You'll have to go, Moponi. I'm too hurt to walk. Here, turn and let me see if I can use my teeth on the thongs on your wrists. Maybe the white men will get so drunk, they will all go to sleep."

She saw her friend's worried face in the moonlight. "Atsa, I can't leave you behind. I'll try to carry you if we can get out of these ropes, and—"

"No, if you have to carry me, you'll never get back to camp before the whites catch us. Let me try to free you. You go for the warriors and my brother. Timbi will wreak vengeance on these men."

Moponi turned so that Atsa could use her teeth on the rawhide that bound her wrists behind her. "That one with the gold ring hit me in the mouth when I cried."

Yancy, Atsa thought, but her teeth were busy on the thongs. It seemed to take a long time, but finally she got the knot out and Moponi stood up.

"Now, I'll untie you," she said.

"No, don't worry about me. I can't run anyway. Get the warriors and tell my brother what happened. Go!"

"I'm afraid for you."

"Then get my brother before the white men come out here

341

and catch you again!"

Moponi hesitated, then slipped out the barn door and was gone into the darkness.

Atsa held her breath, listening, but all she heard was the pounding of her own heart. At any moment, she expected to hear a shout and cursing as one of the men looked outside and saw little Mosquito slipping away up the path. If they caught her . . . No, she mustn't think about that.

Her friend must bring help. Atsa lay there in pain, listening, for a long time. But there were no cries of discovery, no shouts or noises of a chase. Instead, only drunken singing and laughter drifted on the cold night air. She had never been so chilled as she was now, lying naked and bruised on the barn floor. She tried to burrow down in the hay for warmth but without much success. What a fool she had been, so vain, so trusting. Why hadn't she listened to Quint Randolph when he'd told her to stay home?

Atsa shivered as she listened to the noise coming from the trading post. After a while, it got very quiet. Were the white men all drunk and asleep or were they getting ready to come back outside and mount her again? She held her breath and listened.

Dallas lay on the grass mattress of her *karnee* and listened to the night noises. The men of the camp had been gone since late afternoon, up to Pyramid Lake to discuss the move and what they were going to do about the whites.

At first, she had thought the minute Timbi rode out, she would escape. But it soon became apparent that even the elderly warriors and the women had been told to keep an eye on her and prevent that.

Quint. She lay in the darkness thinking about him. That time seemed centuries behind her now, only a wonderful, distant memory. Even if she found him again, how could she expect him to want her back when she had been Timbi's woman? The Randolphs and their kin were proud people of the upper class. If she were with child, how could she and a baby fathered by a Paiute warrior fit into society?

Of the child, she had no thought yet. She still had not faced that possibility. She was not even sure anymore how she felt about its father.

Quint. Emotion seized her, making her chest so tight she couldn't breathe. There would never be another in her heart except Quint Randolph, not as long as he lived. If he were dead, she might someday come to terms with being Timbi's woman. It was hard not to be moved when he held her very close and looked into her eyes almost as if he worshipped her.

I love you enough for the both of us. I can wait, Pony Girl. Maybe someday you will decide you love me, too.

Never! She had cried that out at the time. But the more she saw of him—the more he adored her, hurried to help her, protect her—the more her heart whispered, Well, maybe someday . . .

But at the moment, that was not her biggest worry. Timbi's sister and Moponi had disappeared at about the same time he and the warriors had ridden out of the camp, and no one was quite sure who had seen them last or where they might have gone.

Dallas sat up and sighed. She couldn't hold the immature girl responsible for not convincing Timbi to free her. She now knew nothing could make the chieftain turn her loose; he wanted her too much.

But his little sister was so vain, so foolish. Where had she and Moponi gone? One minute they had been standing in the camp with a bunch of baskets. Then Dallas had begun to spread out fish for drying, and when she'd looked for Atsa because she'd needed help, the two had disappeared. No one seemed to have seen them leave, nor did anyone know what to do.

Now Dallas could only wait for Timbi and Moponi's husband to return. She had begged for a horse, promising that she wouldn't run away, that she would only ride out in the desert and search for the girls. But no, all shook their heads. Yes, they, too, were worried about Atsa and Moponi, but they were following orders. Timbi had commanded everyone not to let his beloved Pony Girl escape while he was gone. While the old ones and the women were concerned about the missing pair, they seemed to be even more afraid of incurring the moody chieftain's wrath should his woman get away.

So, for the past several hours, Dallas had tried to go about her chores and hope that the two would turn up at any moment with a reasonable explanation of where they had been. Without a horse, she wouldn't have much success in finding Atsa. And if she had the horse, would she run away? After she'd found the foolish pair, she might. At this point, she didn't know herself.

She lay in the *karnee,* listening to the wind blow.

Then she heard the rhythmic sound of horses coming from far off. She stood up, went outside. In the moonlight, she saw the warriors approaching, Timbi leading. She would have known him anywhere because of the size of him, the breadth of his shoulders silhouetted in the moonlight as he approached. With a puzzling mixture of pride, fear and uneasiness, she watched him leading his men in. He would be in a fury over his sister, but his rage would not be directed at Dallas. With her he was always gentle, sensitive. Sometimes when she looked up suddenly and caught him watching her, she saw some great tragedy in his dark face as if he harbored a sadness that could never be eased, as if he felt he were living on the edge of a cliff and it was only a matter of time before it crumbled under him.

Now the men rode into camp and people came out of their lodges with glad cries. Timbi's face shone with love as he saw her, reined in, and dismounted. For a moment, she thought he would hold out his arms to her, and in that instant, she was not sure whether, if he did, she would run into them or not.

But the moment passed. He handed the reins to a warrior, came to her. Dallas felt a great guilt at the emotion that had almost overcome her. *Quint.* She would love Quint as long as she knew he was alive out there, no matter if he forgot about her, found himself another woman. That was what always happened in Texas when a woman was carried off by the Indians. Usually, she was never seen again. In the rare

344

cases where one was finally returned, her white husband did not want her back, had usually given her up for dead and remarried.

Timbi took her arm and led her into the *karnee*. "It has been too long since I held you in my arms, Dallas. I don't want to be separated from you for even an hour."

She said nothing as he pulled her against him, kissed her forehead. It was hard to hate him in spite of everything when he worshipped her so. She let him hold her against him, feeling his heart beat against her breast.

His hand went to her belly. "Our son will be born in the late winter." He held her close, kissing her eyelids. "I have never known such happiness. Perhaps one has to experience great sadness to really appreciate the happiness you have brought me."

She must tell him about his sister. "Timbi, there's something you must know about Atsa."

She never got to finish what she had to say. At that moment, there came a long, horrible shout from outside, and Moponi's young husband's voice was raised in an anguished babble.

Timbi looked at her blankly, grabbed her hand, and dragged her outside. The young husband ran up to them, gesturing and babbling. She understood just enough of their language now to know he had found out.

Timbi whirled on her, his face stricken.

"I . . . I tried to tell you," Dallas said. "The girls took their baskets and said they were going off to pick berries, but they never came back. They—"

"How long have they been gone?" His face was dark as a gathering storm.

She told him. There was a long pause as the others gathered round, timidly telling what they knew.

Dallas nodded her head in agreement. "I didn't know what to do. No one would give me a horse to go look for her, and the old ones wouldn't do anything until you returned."

"The trading post," he said so softly that she wasn't sure she had heard him correctly.

345

"What trading post?"

But Timbi turned to Moponi's husband and the other warriors. "Light the bonfire signals to call our people in from all over the valley. We have been pushed far enough!"

Even Dallas knew that lighting the bonfires was only done when something of the greatest importance happened, such as the death of a chief.

"Light the bonfires!" Timbi commanded even louder, and she saw hatred and terrible anguish on his face.

Men hurried away to do his bidding.

At that moment, little Moponi stumbled into the camp and collapsed. Dallas ran to her, trying to hear her whispered words above the noise and shouting as people gathered around. One look told Dallas the worst.

As she held the young Indian girl in her arms, Timbi and Moponi's husband came through the crowd. The young warrior pushed Dallas aside, took his wife into his arms, his shoulders shaking with unheard sobs.

The Indian girl opened her eyes. "I—we—went to the trading post. I escaped. They still have Atsa."

The ensuing uproar almost drowned out her whispered words.

Timbi held up his hand for silence. "Tell all, Moponi."

Dallas winced as she saw the torn condition of the girl's worn shift, the bruises on her body and face, and the one eye that was swollen, nearly shut.

Moponi had a hard time getting the words through her torn lips. Blood ran from them. She reached up to touch the mark on her face, said something in Paiute about a tall man wearing a big gold ring.

Quint. Dallas gasped. The girl was describing Quint. "No," she said aloud, "no, he wouldn't—"

"Quiet!" Timbi commanded. Then he gently said to the injured girl, "Is Atsa still alive?"

At that point, the petite girl began to cry as if her heart would break. "We are shamed," she sobbed. "We go there foolishly, trusting, and we are shamed!"

No one needed to ask for an explanation. Dallas could smell the rank scent of men's seed on the girl.

346

She shook her head as she looked at Timbi across the girl's shaking body. "Quint wouldn't do that."

Timbi's face contorted with fury. "So he pays me back. I might have expected some vengeance for his honor, but I did not think it would be against my innocent sister!"

Dallas had no idea what he was talking about, but there was no time to talk now. Timbi turned and shouted orders to his men. "Paint your faces and get your weapons! Light the bonfires to ask the other bands for help! Before morning, we will make them pay for this!"

The young husband handed his weeping wife over to the women. Then he reached out and dipped his fingers in the blood that ran from her cut mouth. "Here is the scarlet paint I need!" He made the marks across his cheeks and forehead while the braves brandished their weapons and shouted in approval.

Timbi nodded as he looked at Dallas. She saw hate, anguish, and pain in his dark face. "From this moment on, he is my blood brother no more! We ride to destroy the trading post and all there! The *numa* have had as much as they can take from the whites. It is finally time to stop talking peace and give them war!"

"There must be some mistake!" Dallas said, grabbing Timbi's arm, but the shouting of the people as the drums began to beat drowned her out. Wherever they were going to attack, she must save Quint. Never would she believe him guilty of such a terrible thing.

Timbi shook her hand off. "You would do anything to save him, wouldn't you? Perhaps I deserve punishment for what I have done, but these girls did nothing!"

"Timbi, what are you talking about?"

He didn't answer. Instead, he turned to his warriors. "Tie this woman up and put her in my *karnee* until we return."

Dallas tried to protest, but the men dragged her away. As she lay bound in the hut, listening to the noise and confusion outside as warriors organized for an attack, she feared the worst for both Atsa and Quint. Deep in her heart, she knew Quint Randolph would never brutally rape a woman. Nothing would convince her otherwise. He was a man of

347

honor.

She heard the shouting, the drums beating as the men readied themselves. Then, too soon, she heard them mount up and Timbi shouted a reminder that they rode to spill blood and redeem Paiute honor. After a few minutes, she heard them gallop off. By tomorrow, all the clans would have come here in response to the signal fires. All Nevada would soon feel the Paiutes' wrath as warriors rode the war trail.

And what was going to happen to her? Dallas lay with her hands tied, obviously forgotten in the fury of the moment. Timbi had said he worshipped her—but that was before white men had raped, beaten, and maybe murdered his sister.

What would happen when he returned? If Atsa were dead, would he take his revenge on his white captive who might carry his child? At this moment, Dallas wasn't sure of anything except that she was dealing with a moody hate-filled man who might be capable of murder and torture. By morning, she might be begging for her own life when the Paiute chieftain rode back from his raid.

Chapter Twenty-three

Quint watched the signal fires burning on the faraway hills. Something important must be going on for the Paiute to be calling the people in. Had something happened that was causing an Indian war to break out? His first thought was for the Pony Express, so vulnerable in case of trouble out here in this desolate wasteland.

His second was that it wasn't so smart to be out here by himself in case a war party chanced upon him. Timbi might be his blood brother, but if warriors caught Quint alone, they might shoot first and ask for explanations later.

He studied the fires, trying to decide what to do. He'd been out here for days now without seeing another human being. Since he had to go back by Williams' station anyway to pick up his ring, he'd get the news and then ride on to Arizona. The big horse was what horsemen called green-broke now. Sky Climber still had much to learn, but that would come with time and gentle handling.

Quint shivered. It was cold for May, and seemed to be turning colder. It would be an uncomfortable all-night ride to the station but he'd feel safer traveling under cover of darkness if there were war parties roaming the barren land.

He began to pack his gear. The big stallion looked at him from where it grazed, tied to a stake.

"Hey, boy, you ready to go?" Quint reached for his saddle and bridle. Sky Climber was far superior to his own gelding, and it would be easier to ride him than to lead the half-wild horse. Besides, if he ran into any trouble, the speed and endurance of the Medicine Hat might mean the difference between life and death.

He kicked sand over his fire, then gathered up his things. In less than thirty minutes from the first moment he'd seen the signal fires, he was swinging into Sky Climber's saddle, headed to Williams' station.

It was just before dawn when Yancy came out to the barn. Atsa jerked up, too frightened even to speak.

"Damn me! So your friend got away!"

She winced, waiting for his fist to strike her, but he only laughed. "How long she been gone?"

Atsa thought quickly. Hours had passed since Moponi had fled into the darkness. She should even now be on her way back with Timbi and his warriors. "She just worked loose from her ropes a few minutes ago," Atsa said in halting English, trying to sound very stupid.

"She went to a lot of trouble for nothing. I was just coming out here to free y'all anyway." He went over, began to saddle a gray horse.

Atsa blinked in surprise. "You were going to turn us loose? I thought—"

"They're all asleep in there." Yancy nodded back over his shoulder. "Probably sleep for hours."

She hardly dared to hope. "You are going to turn me loose, why?"

"So you can go back and tell all the Injuns what happened and they'll get madder than hell and go on the warpath."

"And kill your friends?" She thought he might be crazed because she saw no logic to his words.

"Damned Yankees ain't no friends of mine! I'll be long gone before the Injun war puts an end to the Pony Express. That'll be bad for the Union, but I reckon it might be good for the South."

Atsa watched him saddle up, the gold ring catching the moonlight as he moved. She didn't have the least idea what the man was talking about. "You have hurt and shamed me, yet you seem to feel no remorse or guilt." Tears ran down her face.

He sneered as he came over, cut the rope that bound her. "Don't talk to me about shame and honor, you uppity red wench! Why everyone knows you Injuns are nothin' but red niggers!"

She didn't know what a "nigger" was, but his tone left no doubt as to what he thought of Indians. Yancy must not be allowed to escape the vengeance that was coming to him. She must delay him until Moponi arrived with the warriors.

She stood up slowly, painfully; naked except for her moccasins. "What about your friends asleep inside?" She nodded toward the station.

"I told you, they're not friends, just Yankees. Which means they deserve anything they get. I expect they'll sleep for hours! And by the time they wake up, it'll be too late. Those stupid Union bastards may die to help the Southern cause. Sort of ironic, ain't it?"

She didn't know what he meant. She only knew she had to delay this one until Moponi came with the braves. "Yancy"—Atsa tried to smile despite her swollen lips—"you have tried me, been my first man. Wouldn't you like to take me with you?"

He laughed in derision. "You were good, honey, and young. I always seem to end up with the old rich ones. But I feel the same about squaws and niggers." He went on saddling his horse.

Every inch of Atsa's body ached, but she saw that gray light streamed through the cracks in the barn. Dawn must be breaking. She went over, grabbed Yancy's arm. "Wouldn't you like to have me again, one more time? Then you might change your mind—"

"If you don't beat all." He brushed her away impatiently, went on with his chore. "I was so drunk and eager, I would have taken on a bitch dog. But this morning, I'm cold sober and I don't want no greasy, dirty Injun."

She must delay him. "I could wash in the river—"

"Don't you hear what I'm tellin' you, bitch? I got to clear out of here before your friend gets back." He untied the horse, started out of the barn with her limping after him.

She lost one of her moccasins, but didn't stop for it.

"Yancy, I'm shamed by your seed. No warrior will want me now. If you took me with you, I could wash your clothes, sleep with you."

"Just a brown whore after all, ain't you, after all that protestin' about not wantin' to do it? There's whores aplenty waitin' in San Francisco, then I'll catch a ship around the Horn, go back South. The money I'll be paid for this will keep me up for a while so I can stay away from old bitches with crepy skin and sagging tits."

"Yancy, please." Atsa trailed after him as he led his gray horse toward the river and away from the station. She lost the other moccasin near the riverbank.

"Shut up!" he snarled. "You'll wake the whole place before I can get outa here!"

She grabbed his arm, "Don't go—"

"Get your filthy hands off my sleeve!" He hit her then, knocking her backward, striking her again and again with his fists as if he were making her pay for the rage that had been building in him all his life.

She tried to cry out at the pain, but his fists were beating her to the ground. *She must not let him get away.* Weakly she reached out, grabbed his pants leg.

They were almost to the river now, and he turned, kicking her belly and soft breasts with the toe of his boot. "Let go, bitch! I'll teach you to bother me!"

Atsa hung on as long as she could while he kicked at her. He reached for the pistol in his belt, then seemed to think about the noise it would make. "I'll teach you to try to stop me from leavin'!"

She saw the flash of the knife, felt the sharp, sudden pain. Then she couldn't force her fingers to hang onto his leg anymore. He leaned over, wiped his bloody knife off on her hair as her eyes glazed, stuck it back in his belt. "Stupid bitch!"

As though from far away, she watched him swing up in the saddle, take off at a lope. He got to the river, splashed through it, came out on the other side.

She must stop him. With great effort, Atsa rolled over

onto her belly and began to crawl after Yancy. It was very hard to move through the gritty sand that tore at her bare skin. But she had to delay him. Only that thought kept her moving forward, an inch at a time. He seemed to be a long way ahead of her. She could at least trail him, see where he went. She realized she was on the bank of the river. It flowed swiftly, swirling with the runoff of melted snow from the mountains. Atsa wasn't sure she could cross the stream, but she knew she had to if she were going to follow him.

She put her hands in the wet gravel, dragged herself forward. The water was so cold, she gasped as it touched her bare skin. But it would cleanse her, wash away the stink of the men's seed. She took a deep breath, pulled her bruised, naked body into the icy, rushing river. It took her breath away, made her gasp, but the pain of the wound in her chest seemed lessened by the cold. All she had to do was get across the rushing water. She struggled toward the other side.

The cold water pulled at her, began to sweep her downstream. She wasn't going to make it, she realized dimly as the rushing force pulled her down. Her blood was red on the white foam of the surface. *Red. My favorite color.* The current caught her, took her under, washing her downriver. It was almost dawn, but it didn't matter anymore. All Atsa thought was that at last she was cleansed of her shame.

Timbi's rage made him shake as he had Dallas bound and put in his *karnee*. What kind of a man was he, after all, when he was more concerned with his white woman escaping while he was gone than with the fate of his own sister?

He was a man who had been willing to sacrifice everything for the love of a spirited girl who bewitched him with her beauty.

He watched the women lead Moponi away as she sobbed. Whether her husband would be able to overlook this insult to his honor and take the foolish girl to wife again was not for Timbi to say. Worse yet, suppose Moponi now carried a

353

white man's child?

Quickly, Timbi painted his face, motioned to his warriors. "Mount up! This dawn we finally move against the whites! We have taken as much as honorable men can stand!"

Honorable. He was no longer honorable, and he knew it. Nothing meant anything to him anymore except keeping the spirited Pony Girl as his own. Although he couldn't believe it, he half hoped Quint Randolph had been involved in this tragedy. It would ease his own conscience. Besides, if Quint were dead, perhaps Dallas would no longer think of him.

The warriors mounted up, garishly streaked with war paint, brandishing weapons so that the moonlight reflected off the metal. Then Timbi shrieked a challenge, a war cry to the darkness, and dug his heels into his black gelding's sides. It would be dawn in less than an hour and when daylight came, he expected to be attacking the trading post.

Even as his war party paused on the rise overlooking the station, the stars were winking out to be replaced by a gray dawn. Soon pale pink light would streak the eastern sky.

The trading post was quiet, a wisp of smoke drifting from the adobe chimney. Across the river, riding away from the post at a brisk pace, was a lone horseman. The rider was almost over the far horizon.

Timbi turned to Moponi's husband. "Take two of your best men and head that one off; bring him back!"

Revenge glittered in the young brave's eyes as he nodded, signaled to two men, and then took off at a gallop.

Timbi turned his attention back to the sleeping trading post. Moponi had said Atsa was being held prisoner in the barn. "Hear me, warriors of the Paiute, until we can rally the other clans and our relatives among the Bannock and Shoshoni, we will have to fight alone. When we finish here today, the whites will know that the Paiute are angry about all they have done to us and here we draw the line! From this day forward we say 'No more'! Even if we die for it, we will die like men!"

The Indians waved their weapons and shouted. "Aiyee! Aiyee!"

"They have stolen our land, destroyed our trees and animals, dishonored our women!" Timbi shouted. "Today we finally strike back! My sister may be in that barn, so do not burn it, but for the trading post itself, we are going to kill the men there and burn it to the ground!"

The war party set up shouts of victory and vengeance, charging down the hill as Timbi brought down his arm in an attacking motion.

The men inside Williams' station stumbled out the door at hearing the noise, looking disheveled and bewildered. A volley of shots greeted them, and they ran back inside, slammed the door.

Timbi signaled his men and they spread out, surrounding the building while he sent another man to check the barn.

The warriors sat on their nervous, stamping horses and waited for the man to return. Even before he reached him, Timbi knew by the expression on the brave's face that what he dreaded most had happened.

Silently, the man held up one bloody red moccasin. For a long moment, Timbi felt such pain in his chest, he thought he could not breathe. He took the small moccasin, blinked back the mist that gathered in his eyes. Then he turned and held the moccasin up so that all might see it.

"Hear me, warriors of the *numa!* Today it is my sister. Tomorrow it may be your sister or your wife! What answer do we give the white dogs for their Pony messenger to find when he rides through?"

The braves set up an angry shouting for revenge—for Atsa, for everything the whites had inflicted on them over the past years.

Timbi tucked the small moccasin into his shirt, next to his heart. "Avenge Atsa's death!" he shouted, and his warriors roared approval, then fired a volley of deadly gunfire into the station. The white men inside fired back, but Timbi kept his men at a distance so the rifles could not find their marks.

He hadn't known until now that rage and vengeance had

a taste; they tasted bitter as the weeds that grew in the sparse desert. He sat his stamping horse, listening to the gunfire that echoed throughout the hills as his men fired at the station and those in the station fired back.

Atsa had died for some of the clothes and trinkets in that trading post; now these things would be the instruments of the traders' deaths.

"Enough!" Timbi shouted, raising his hand. Instantly the Indians held their fire, although rifle shots still echoed from inside. He motioned for a fire to be built, watched it burn for a long moment. Then, very slowly, he leaned over, added the small, bloody moccasin to the flames.

His heart was so full as he watched the fire consume it, he could not speak. *Foolish, vain little sister. So pretty, so innocent.*

He turned to his men. "That place is full of cloth and blankets, whiskey, things that burn. Let every man who has suffered a wrong at the hands of whites come forward and light his arrow from this fire!"

The first gray light of dawn lit the scene as the warriors rode forward in a silent ceremony, waited respectfully for Timbi to dip his arrow in the flame. It sputtered, then caught fire. He fitted it to his bow, the scent of the flaming tip as acrid as the bitter pain in his heart.

"This is for Atsa," he intoned solemnly, and then, with a powerful arm, he drew back the bow and sent the arrow soaring through the gray sky.

He watched it wing its way through the air in silence, leaving a trail of smoke and red flame as it went. For an eternity it seemed to arch upward and then start back down. It hit the dry roof and stuck.

Around him, men set up a clamor as they, too, dipped their arrows in the fire, put them to their bows.

With grim satisfaction, Timbi watched half a hundred flaming arrows fly, hit the roof of the trading post. "We will burn them out. They will soon be like frightened rabbits fleeing a prairie fire!"

From inside, came shouts, noise and panic as the men tried vainly to fight the fires breaking out. But the roof was aflame in a dozen places, black smoke swirling and drifting. For long minutes the Indians watched the flames spread. Then part of the roof fell in and the cloth and trinkets inside caught fire. A man screamed and ran blindly out of the building, his clothes and beard in flames.

A brave raised his rifle, but Timbi held up his hand. "No, let him die slowly, as my sister must have died!"

The man ran a few yards toward the river, screaming and stumbling. Then he fell and lay still, only a mass of unrecognizable limbs as fire consumed him there in the sparse grass.

Timbi watched the burning building, his emotions in turmoil. Was Quint Randolph in there? He owed the man a life, and it was taboo to kill him. But it was not taboo to kill the others. He could still save Quint's life, give him back his woman. Yet nothing mattered to him but the fact that if Quint Randolph were dead, Timbi would never have to worry that the man would come to reclaim Dallas.

At that moment, two other men ran out, firing their rifles wildly, trying to make it to the barn and the horses. It was almost like shooting trapped rabbits. They went down and lay on the ground, jerking and moaning. Neither one was Quint. Timbi recognized that from a distance. He wasn't sure whether he was relieved or disappointed.

"Throw them back into the fire of their burning cloth and trinkets!" he ordered, and watched stoically as warriors ran to do his bidding.

The wounded men struggled and fought weakly as the rifles were kicked from their hands. They seemed to know what was coming, begged in English as they were dragged back toward the flames. Then the warriors picked the two men up, threw them through the burning door of the trading post. Their screams cut through the early dawn like a knife.

The three warriors Timbi had sent after the escaping white man rode back just then. Moponi's husband led a gray horse over which a white man's limp body hung. He was a big, wide-shouldered man with a gold ring glinting on his hand. *Quint?*

With a sense of dread, Timbi stared silently.

The young warrior made a gesture of apology. "You said to bring him in alive, but he fought and was escaping. We found this on the riverbank as we crossed back." He held up the other small, red moccasin.

Timbi raised his hand for silence. He strode over, grasped the head by the hair, raised it to look. The face had scratches from a woman's fingernails. But no, it was not Quint. *Why did he wear Quint's ring?*

Timbi took the ring from the dead man's hand, looked at it. How had he come by this, and what had happened to Quint? Had this man murdered him?

He took the pathetic, blood-smeared moccasin. "You found it near the water?"

The other nodded, not speaking.

"Search the river bank," Timbi said, certain it would do no good because of the rushing current. "Take him down!" he ordered, and the warriors lifted the dead man off the horse. He lay there, dead and bloody, his mouth and eyes open, on his face horror and surprise.

Very slowly, Timbi took Atsa's small moccasin, stared at it as if seeing it for the very first time. He had never realized what small feet she had when she'd run laughing through the camp, trailing after him as he went about his duties. Now he had no one and nothing but a white girl he had stolen from his friend.

Savagely, he took the moccasin, stuffed it into the dead man's mouth and choked back a sob. "Throw him into the fire!"

He ground his teeth in helpless rage and grief as he watched them carry the body, throw it into the flames. The black smoke curled upward into the gray light of dawn. It would be seen for a long, long way.

He and the others watched the place burn as the rest of the roof fell in, sending a shower of sparks and acrid ashes flying into the cold morning air.

He hadn't realized until this very moment that he clutched the ring so hard in his big fist that it cut into his flesh. But he relished the pain. It matched the one in his heart.

Slowly, he opened his palm, stared at the gold, wondered what had happened, and was ashamed that he felt relief at the possibility of Quint's death. If Quint Randolph was dead, there was no reason Timbi couldn't keep the girl who had made a captive of his heart.

He raised his head, saw that his men sat their ponies now, awaiting his orders as the spiral of smoke behind them drifted skyward. He put the ring in his shirt. "This is not the end, this is only a beginning! We must rally the other clans to drive the whites from our hills!"

They set up a howl of agreement, raising their weapons in gestures of defiance. Timbi took one last look at the burning trading post and turned his horse back toward the camp. With a sweeping motion, he led his warriors away from the battle site.

Against the white nation, they could not win, he knew. But a man must make some kind of gesture when he is backed to the wall. He must fight or die. Whatever time was left to them before the small force of poorly armed Paiute had to fight the whole white nation, it would be sweet. All a man could hope for was a woman who truly loved him, and a chance to die an honorable death. Timbi had thrown honor away. Nothing mattered to him anymore but whatever time he had left in Dallas's arms.

They rode back to the camp, setting up a victory chant as the people ran out to meet them so all would know the raid had been successful. The *numa* surrounded them as they dismounted, telling Timbi the other clans were sending messages calling all to gather and discuss the war plans. There would be much dancing and celebrating among the Paiute that night.

But Timbi felt only an emptiness, for his young, laughing sister was gone. He was a man alone . . . except for a white girl who loved another man.

He strode to his *karnee*, ignoring the jubilant people who swirled around him. Inside, Dallas lay tied, and he saw fear on her face as she looked at him.

359

He would never harm her; he loved her too much for that. Gently he untied her.

"What happened?"

Timbi shrugged, feeling as ancient and careworn as the eternal hills of his beloved country. "We have burned the trading post."

"And Atsa?"

For a long moment, he could not make himself say it. The noise and shouting from outside drifted faintly to them. "My sister is dead," he said softly, and swallowed hard. "We found no body. I think they threw her in the river."

"Oh, my God!" It was a soft prayer of anguish. Dallas began to sob softly, and then she seemed to think of his pain, came to put her arms around him. He had not realized until that moment that he was shaking.

His sister was dead and all he could think of was that he would do anything to keep the white girl with him. He took her in his arms, buried his face against her hair. She was his by right of capture; yet for her love, he would humble himself, cheat, lie—do anything to make her want him.

"There was another man," he gasped, stroking her hair. "A big, tall man with brown hair."

She pulled away, looking up at him with dread in her eyes.

He didn't look at her. "I told them to take him alive, but he was killed. There were scratches on his face where little Atsa had fought him." Very slowly, he reached into his leather shirt, handed her the gold ring. She stood there, staring and blinking in the early morning light, the ring in her palm. "No." Dallas shook her head as if denying it. "No, I don't believe it!"

Then the fact that the man was dead seemed to get through to her, and she threw back her head and screamed before she collapsed into Timbi's waiting arms.

Chapter Twenty-four

Quint rode through the night on the big stallion, hoping to reach the trading post by dawn. It was in that ghost-gray color between night and morning that he first saw the black smoke over the next horizon.

For a moment, he reined in, studied it drifting skyward like a black rope. *What the hell—?*

He blinked, looked again. Then the Washoe zephyr blew across the land, bringing him that unmistakable scent of smoke. It looked as if it might be coming from the Williams brothers' trading post. Had someone dropped a cigar in the bolts of cloth, or overturned a lantern in the barn's hay?

If so, the brothers needed help putting the fire out. Even then, carrying buckets of water from the river, they would have a big job containing the blaze. Quint took off at a ground-eating gallop, amazed at how fast the Medicine Hat stallion could run. But it was still almost an hour, and the sun was already up over the horizon before he drew close.

He reined in to rest the blowing horse, gave the fire more thought. Suppose it turned out to be another raid by the Pit River tribe and he galloped right into the midst of them? He'd better ride in cautiously.

Quint rode now at a slow canter, keeping his eyes on the column of smoke. If there was any trouble, he wanted to be able to make a dash for Buckland's, the Pony Express station down the river.

In another ten minutes, he topped the rise and looked down at what had been Williams' station.

Good Lord. He leaned forward in his saddle, squinting against the rising sun to look for signs of life. Nothing moved save the column of smoke drifting ever upward from the smoldering rubble.

If it had been an accident, wouldn't men still be running about, carrying buckets and shouting instructions? A bunch of buzzards circled overhead, slowly, as if scenting something dead but not finding it.

Suppose it was a trap? Suppose bandits or a war party hid in the barn, watching him? Quint reached for the Colt on his hip, and his rifle, checked them both to make sure they were loaded. Then he nudged the big horse forward.

The fire was only a few small flames licking at the edges of timbers as he rode in to a pile of smoking wreckage. He tied his horse to a stump, walked over to stare at all that was left of Williams' station. The unmistakable scent of burned flesh drifted to him along with the scent of smoke.

What in God's name had happened? He found himself reliving the horror of Dallas's death, told himself he must calm down and decide what to do. With shaking hands, Quint squatted down, absently reached for a burning splinter resting on a little pile of trade goods to light his pipe. Then, as he started to toss it away, he stared at the splinter. It looked almost like a man's finger bone. For the first time, he saw that the pile was the charred remnants of a man. The bare skull grinned back at him. There was something in its mouth. . . .

With an oath, Quint jerked the pipe from his own mouth, hurled it and the burning bone from him. For some moments, he had to struggle not to be sick. *Dallas. Oh, Dallas . . .*

It was then he saw the arrow embedded in a timber, the churned dust of unshod ponies in the station yard. *Indians. The Pit Rive tribe? The Paiute?* There was nothing he could do here except wait for the ashes to cool so he could bury whoever was in this funeral pyre. He looked around and realized all four of the men must have been caught unawares.

It occurred to him that if Indians were on the warpath here in western Nevada lands, he needed to get to Virginia City to spread the alarm so riders could be sent out to warn the isolated settlers. He'd lost track of what day it was, but thought it might be that time of the week when the Pony Express rode through. The riders and stations had to be warned.

Well, Yancy, you seemed to hope the Pony Express could be stopped, I hope you'll be happy when you hear about this. I wonder if you had anything to do with it?

The wind turned cold and Quint pulled his coat up around his neck, rode along the river. Maybe he should ride up to Timbi's camp, warn him about what had happened. The Paiute were surely innocent, but that wouldn't make any difference to a rowdy, drunken crowd of white miners. They'd have a tendency to shoot the first Indians they came across.

The river rushed wild and foamy below the station site as Quint rode along its bank. Something lay half in, half out of the water up ahead on a little spit of gravel, where the current had flung it.

He frowned, trying to decide what it was, and then it moved ever so slightly. *A body. A naked body.*

Quint swung down, splashed recklessly through the water, grabbed the slight form by the shoulders, dragged it free of the current. He was only aware that the brown skin was almost frozen, deathly cold to the touch. He turned the form over.

"Atsa! Good Lord, what happened here?"

When he saw the wound, he thought she was dead, but then her eyes flickered open ever so slightly. "Quinton?" Her voice was soft as a sigh.

"Yes, Atsa, it's me. What happened?" He held her very close, trying to bring warmth back into the bruised, torn body that was already growing stiff with approaching death.

"Yancy and the others . . ." — it took much effort for her to go on — "raped me and Moponi . . . she's gone to get

363

Timbi. Did they get here?"

Quint looked behind him at the devastated station. "Yes, they got here." They must not have found Atsa when they came on their quest for vengeance.

She smiled with great effort. "You promised me a red dress . . ."

Tears came to his eyes. "I . . . I didn't forget, little sister. I'll get you one yet."

"I'm so cold. . . . They shamed me. . . ."

He took off his coat, wrapped it around her. "I'll build a fire. You just hang on—"

"No." Her voice came fainter now. "I'm going where the wild horses run forever across ghost mountains . . . where no Indian woman is shamed . . . no child hungry. . . ."

He wept unashamedly as only a really strong man can. "Atsa, little sister, don't leave me. I can't bear to lose you, too!"

"She's alive, Quinton, alive. . . ."

"Who?" Atsa was losing touch with reason as she slowly died, that was all he could think. And then the early dawn light picked up the tiny lavender pink pearls she wore. *Rare pastel pearls found almost nowhere else in the world except the Concho River near Fort Concho, Texas.* Dallas's words seemed to ring in his ears. He found himself shaking her. "Atsa, where'd you get those earrings? Did you find them?"

She smiled up at him dreamily as if she were already beyond pain and cold. "Timbi. . . ." She was trying hard to tell him something, couldn't get the words out.

"Timbi what? How did he get them?" He almost shouted the questions at her. "Answer me!" In his confusion and agony, he shook her, trying to unlock the puzzle. "Atsa? Atsa, do you hear me?"

She smiled at him, but her eyes saw nothing. Whatever small flame of life that had been fighting to survive now flickered out.

He closed his eyes, rocking back and forth with her in his arms, holding her close as if the warmth of his body could bring her back. It was a long time before he faced the fact

364

that the fragile Indian girl was really dead.

What had she tried to tell him? How was Timbi involved? He looked down at her. There was no mistaking those tiny pearls. He'd have known them anywhere.

Very gently, he lay the dead girl down, stood up. The air was cold, but he was too numb to feel anything. Besides, he could not take his jacket and leave her lying here shamed and naked.

He walked back to his horse, trying to make some sense of her words. *Timbi.* He stood there staring into space. Had she been trying to tell him that her brother was in on that raid and had brought the earrings back to Atsa?

He looked behind him at the dead girl on the river bank. *Yes, those had to belong to Dallas.*

And as the truth came to him, another fact became unescapable. His blood brother, the honorable chieftain who owed him a life had ridden with the Pit River tribe. He had been there when they'd killed Dallas and taken the jewelry as a prize. Had they all raped her, too, before she'd died?

A rage began to build in Quint. He swung up on the big horse, turned it toward the Indian camp. He would ride in there, shoot Timbi down as the Indian came out of his *karnee.* And as the Paiute died, Quint would shout at him, blood brother, I now take back the life you owe me for the killing of my woman!

Then the warriors would overpower and kill Quint. Not that he cared or that it mattered. Nothing much mattered without Dallas; he had been fooling himself. *My blood brother, who swore undying friendship and loyalty, repays me by being in the war party that killed my woman.*

He had thought it hurt when he'd lost Melanie, but that was guilt, not love. And he had wanted to die when he'd lost Dallas. But perhaps the most painful thought of all was that he had saved the Paiute's life, which meant Timbi could be there to help kill Dallas.

If only he had been able to look into the future, he would have left Timbi to die a slow death under the dead horse. If only . . .

Stop that, Quint! You haven't time for the luxury of revenge right now. You need to ride in and warn the settlers that the Indians are on a rampage, so they can spread the alarm. Otherwise, helpless women and children will die. Later, you can go after Timbi.

He spurred the big stallion, headed at a gallop for Virginia City. After he spread the warning, he would go after Timbi, kill him. *My blood brother.* The revenge would be worth it even if it cost Quint his own life.

But when Quint finally arrived in the rough mining town some hours later, he discovered that the Pony Express rider had been to the trading post only minutes before he had arrived on the scene. The boy had raced on to spread the word.

The whole of Virginia City was in a panic, people running up and down, shouting, men standing on corners and holding discussions about what to do as word spread that there'd been another Indian uprising with dozens massacred by the savages out at Williams' station.

Quint tied up in front of the saloon. That the town existed at all was a minor miracle. For some years, Quint had heard, prospectors had cursed the gray sticky clay that clung to everything while they dug for gold. It was only accidentally discovered that the gray nuisance tested out high-grade silver. If newspaper accounts were to be believed, this past winter had been one of the worst in history, with the town snowed in and isolated. White people had run out of supplies, and many had gone as hungry as the Indians.

Quint pushed through the rough crowd and into the saloon, leaned on the bar. "Brandy."

The rough crowd grew silent at the approach of this stranger. The barkeep had heavy hair growing on the backs of his hands, and looked as if he hadn't had a complete bath in years. "Brandy? You must be jokin', mister. We don't keep anything that fancy."

Quint was still in a fury at Timbi, and tired now. He

clenched his fist, thought seriously about hitting the man's sneering mouth, decided the barkeep had meant no harm. He tipped his hat back. "Give me whatever you got then."

He took a big drink out of the smudged glass the man slid down the bar, shuddered. He'd heard in some of these Western saloons, they made their own liquor, threw in pepper and rattlesnake heads to give it "body." He wouldn't think about that now.

The miners gathered around him. "Where you from, mister?"

Wearily Quint reached for his pipe, remembered. "Originally, Kentucky. Just now, Williams' station."

There was immediate silence as the men crowded close. He could smell their unwashed bodies as he breathed.

"Williams' station? Then tell us the news, stranger. All we got is wild rumors—"

"It's burned to the ground." Quint sighed. "Everyone there dead. I think they were crazy enough to capture some Indian women, use them. The Paiute didn't take kindly to it."

There was a buzz of noisy talk.

"From what I remember of the Williams boys," an old man sucked his teeth thoughtfully, "I'd say it couldn't happen to a more deservin' bunch!"

"Hush, Willie." Another man, obviously someone of importance from the quality of his clothes, held up his hands for silence. "Stranger, tell us, you think there's a likelihood the Injuns will attack here? Some's wantin' to get outa town, others is turning one of the stone buildings into a fortress for the women and kids."

Quint shrugged, thinking of Timbi. "Who knows what they'll do? I'd like to lead a force out there and attack their camp, kill their leader."

"We're all pretty nigh indignant, too, stranger." The well-dressed one stuck his thumbs in his vest importantly. "As one of Virginia City's leading citizens, I say it's a shame two peace-lovin' businessmen like the Williams boys couldn't be protected against red savages—"

"Oh, stop that foolishness!" old Willie said. "Businessmen, my grandmother's sweet patootie! Them thieves'd cheat a blind beggar—and sell whiskey and powder to the Injuns if they knew the redskins was about to attack a Sunday school!"

"Well, they was gonna buy it someplace," the other man said self-righteously. "Might as well keep the money in the area, rather than have it go into the tax coffers of some other town. Now, men, you heard the stranger. He confirms what the Pony Rider told us about the massacre—"

"I didn't say it was a massacre," Quint said, leaning on the bar. He'd come in here to warn these people and get help in going after Timbi's warriors. But he didn't like this motley crew.

The well-dressed citizen looked at him. "If there was white men killed, that's what it was, all right. Let's remember we expect Nevada to be a legal Territory next year after the new president takes office, and maybe soon we'll be a state. Now that's progress!" He held onto his lapels. "We got to show Congress we ain't wild and uncivilized anymore. We got to do something about them Injuns. Ain't that right?"

A chorus of agreement went up from the crowd.

The bartender said, "We already sent a call for help to California. And riders have gone out to Carson City and Genoa."

Quint stared into his glass. All he could think of was getting his blood brother in his gun sights. Quint had always been a civilized man but he could see now how anyone could be driven to killing, torture. He would take his vengeance out on Timbi for what had happened to Dallas.

He drank deep, ignoring the men around him as they took turns making speeches.

"So tell us again what you saw, stranger."

Quint jerked back to reality. In his mind's eye flashed a picture of a naked, bruised Indian girl lying frozen and dead on the edge of the river. "Is there a dry-goods store in town?"

The pompous man smiled. "Sure, we got a dry-goods

368

store, and next year, we'll have another and a school. That's progress and growth for our fair city. But if we're gonna get to be an official Territory, we need to do something about those Injuns."

"Did you say help is coming?" Quint asked, staring into space. He needed help in tracking Timbi to his lair.

"If you call the Carson and Silver City bunch 'help,' " old Willie said acidly. "Think they're all interested in a lark. It won't be no army, it'll be a drunken mob."

Someone in the crowd laughed. "Well, they's just Paiutes. A mob'll put those cowardly Injuns on the run without waitin' a week for help from California."

"Hear! Hear!" The men cheered.

Quint finished the bad whiskey, realized how exhausted he was. "I'll find myself a room. When the Californians get here and you're ready to ride out, I know where the Paiute camp is."

The pompous one clutched his lapels and looked at Quint with interest. "Who are you, mister? You don't look like no miner."

"Randolph," Quint said. "I supply horses for the Eastern end of the Pony Express."

"And that's another thing," a drunk said, weaving over to the bar, "with all this Injun war, the Pony'll stop runnin'."

Quint closed his eyes, in his mind seeing Dallas with her short, tomboy hair and laughing eyes as she rode away carrying the mail. If only . . .

"Hey." A burly fellow pushed through the saloon doors. "Who came in on the Medicine Hat stallion?"

A whisper swept through the crowd.

"The Medicine Hat. The Medicine Hat?"

"What's he talkin' about?"

"You know, the mustang that's such a legend."

"I always thought that was just an old Indian tale."

The pompous man's eyes grew round. "I got to see this."

All the men pushed outside behind Quint and stood staring at the fine stud tied to the hitching rail.

Quint reached out, stroked the stud's nose thoughtfully.

The pompous one whistled loud and low. "Stranger, I got half-interest in a gold mine I'll trade you for that hoss."

Immediately, half a dozen voices yelled offers. But Quint shook his head. "Gentlemen, this horse means more to me than almost anything in the world. If I were starving, I wouldn't sell him."

One of the miners spat a stream of tobacco juice. "I got money and no hoss. It ain't fair; them Paiutes got hosses."

A drunk laughed. "After we get through killin' Paiutes, we'll all have us plenty of hosses."

"An Indian for breakfast and a pony to ride!" Another shouted.

The rough crowd cheered in approval.

"I tell you what I'd like to ride," the businessman said with a broad wink, "one of them little brown fillies."

Again, Quint had a sudden vision of Atsa, all naked and shamed, covered with bruises. He brought back his fist and hit the man, sent him crashing across the wooden sidewalk and into the glass window with a tinkle of glass. The man got up, rubbed his jaw. "Didja see that? What got into him?"

Quint swung into the saddle. "As I said, when the so-called army is ready to go, I'll be there, but don't underestimate the Paiutes."

A couple of miners laughed. "Aw, it'll be a lot of fun, and maybe we'll get some horses and some women."

Quint turned his big horse away from the hitching post and started down the street. He hated the brutish mob, but he hated Timbi more. When the ragtag army got itself together, he'd be with them.

Down the way, he found a small general store, tied up his horse. There must still be lots of rumors flying; people stood talking in little groups on the street.

Quint went into the cramped store. It smelled of pickles and unwashed bodies, spices and leather horse gear. "You got a man's pipe and a red dress?"

The man behind the counter shrugged his stooped shoulders. "Well, yes, but it's been special ordered for Mrs. Haskins."

Quint frowned. "Who?"

"You know, the bigshot. His wife."

"In that case, I'll take it."

The storekeeper looked bewildered, scratched his nose. "You didn't hear me, stranger, I said it was ordered for Mrs. Haskins. I'm waitin' for her to come get it."

Quint frowned. "She anything like her husband?"

"More so."

"In that case, I'll take the damned dress." He reached into his vest for silver dollars, threw a handful to the counter.

"But you ain't even seen it!" The man's eyes were wide at the amount of money Quint had thrown out.

"Is it pretty? Is it something a rich white girl might wear to a ball?"

The man looked at him a long moment as if he'd lost his mind. "That's just what she was gonna do with it. It came all the way from San Francisco for a party."

Quint was suddenly very tired, and his head hurt. "Mister, let me have the dress or I may kill you for it! I've been pushed as far as I'll allow this day."

The storekeeper's face blanched, and he reached under the counter, brought out a box.

Quint opened it, smiled sadly. "It'll do." He picked up the box, the pipe; started toward the door.

"But what'll I tell Mrs. Haskins?"

Quint thought about it a minute. "Tell her a greasy, savage Paiute girl needed it to be buried in."

Outside, noise and drunken singing drifted onto the street as the miners' bravery increased with each drink.

The storekeeper looked from the door back to Quint. "You going with that mob when they finally get organized and go out after the Paiutes?"

Quint nodded.

"But you care enough about a dead Injun girl to buy a fancy dress to bury her in? That's kinda unusual."

"I'm only after one man." The anger came back into Quint's soul. In his mind, he imagined Dallas trying vainly to outrun the war party. Had she screamed and begged for

371

mercy? Had Timbi raped her before he killed her?

"This fella an old enemy?"

Quint shook his head, saw Timbi's handsome, brooding face in his mind. "No, a friend."

Then he picked up the package and strode out before the shopkeeper could say anything more.

Chapter Twenty-five

Dallas held the ring in her clenched fist and screamed as she collapsed. "No! Quint wouldn't do something like that!"

Dimly, she felt Timbi's arms catch her, swing her up and hold her close. "I'm sorry, Pony Girl, so sorry."

She fought to get out of his arms, beating against his massive chest, striking his face. "You! You did this! You killed him!"

He stood her on her feet, caught her flexing arms with his hands. "No, Dallas, I didn't. My orders were disobeyed! I told them to capture him so we could find out the truth, but I never gave an order to kill him!"

She didn't care how it had happened, she only cared that Quint was dead. She struck at him while he held her, realizing even then that he could have killed her with one hard blow. But he held her against him while she fought him until she was too exhausted to fight more.

Then she collapsed in his arms, put her face against his chest and wept and wept. "Oh, he's dead! I don't want to live! You can't know how this hurts!"

"Don't I?"

She looked up at him, saw the tragedy in his dark eyes, and remembered that he had just lost his sister. "Oh, Timbi, I . . . I'm sorry! I forgot about Atsa. What happened?"

He swallowed hard. "The white men raped and killed her. We found blood marks that showed she'd been dragged, thrown in the river."

Dallas saw the girl in her mind's eye; laughing, foolish, vain. Yet Atsa had been so full of life, and her brother had adored her. "How terrible! It was selfish of me to think of nothing but my own loss!"

He held her very close, and she felt his big body shake with unshed tears. Through no fault of theirs, they had both lost someone they loved. They clung together for comfort because there was no one else to comfort either of them.

"Pony Girl," he whispered against her hair, his voice thick with grief, "I was wrong to hold you captive—so wrong. If only—"

"No, don't say that." She reached up, put one finger against his lips. "It does no good to regret the past. If it helped, I would torture myself by thinking Atsa might not have died had I done a better job of looking after her."

He kept her against the shelter of his chest, stroking her hair. "Don't feel guilty, Dallas. Sooner or later, Atsa was headed for trouble."

"Maybe not." She began to weep again, the ring clasped tightly in her hand. "I . . . I just couldn't believe he would do that. The man who owned this ring was my man, Quint Randolph."

Timbi didn't look her in the eye. "You never really know what people will do . . . for love. I'm sorry about everything; the wrong I did you by holding you prisoner. If I said you could leave now, would you?"

She did not move away from his embrace. He, too, was hurting, and the warmth of his arms gave her comfort. Did she want to leave? "I . . . I don't know," she answered truthfully. "My man is gone, and I don't know whether I would be welcome at my father's home."

"I am sorry I have shamed you." He brushed her short curls out of her eyes with a tender gesture. "I thought only of taking you, not knowing that before it was over, I would be the slave, willing to do whatever it took to keep you. Whenever you think of me in the future, Dallas, remember this; I loved you enough to forget everything else, sacrifice all because of you." She had such an ache inside because of her loss of Quint, she did not think the pain would ever end. And yet, she was touched by this man's simple declaration. "Are you saying I can leave if I want to?"

He seemed to be fighting some great battle with himself as he reached out, took her face between his two big hands. "Oh, Dallas. If you go, I . . . I think I cannot live."

She looked up into his dark face, realized he adored her. Once she would have plunged a knife in his heart if she'd had the chance, but now she was unsure of her feelings for him.

"If you don't want my child, I'm sorry you must bear it." He kissed her forehead. "But I want you, Dallas. You will never know how much I've wanted you, how much I've sacrificed to keep you. I never knew a man could care as much for a woman as I have come to care for you."

She had just lost the man she loved, yet she stood here in the embrace of another who begged for a chance to take his place in her affections. Tears started again. "I could never love you as I loved him."

He held her against him while she sobbed. "I don't even ask that. I just hope you won't hate me, Dallas, I love you so!"

She should hate him and push away from him, but the warmth and the strength of his arms around her was so comforting. She let him hold her tightly while she cried for Quint Randolph.

He picked her up, carried her to the grass mattress, lay down with her, held her, stroked her gently. "Someday, when you finally stop hurting, maybe you will know that I love you more than the white man ever could."

She put her face against his big chest and wept for Quint, for Atsa, and even for Timbi who worshipped her with an ardor she could not return. But most of all, she wept for herself because Quint had died and left her without the comfort of his love, and she didn't know what to do or where to turn—except to the comfort of Timbi's arms as he held her and whispered that he'd do anything to make her happy.

She wept until she had no tears left and her eyes were almost swollen shut, while Timbi held her. Finally she slept.

When she awakened, sunlight streamed through the door of the *karnee*. She lay blinking, trying to remember why her eyes felt so swollen. Something terrible had happened.

Then she remembered with a sigh. Quint Randolph was dead. Maybe she had dreamed it. But no, as she sat up, unclenched her fist, she saw the ring with his old family crest on it. She'd held it so tightly there were red marks on her palm. Tears started afresh as she looked down at the ring.

She wanted to keep the gold band forever close to her heart. She rummaged through baskets, found a thin strip of rawhide, tied the ring around her neck. Besides being tired, she didn't feel very well. She thought about that for a moment. Even at this early stage, she was certain she was with child. She felt nothing as she considered the fact — not hate, not love, nothing at all for the child. *If only it could have been Quint's* . . .

Tears started fresh as she gripped the ring. She heard the soft sound of moccasins outside in time to make one swipe across her wet eyes with the back of her hand.

Timbi came in with a small bowl of rich broth, set it down. "Are you all right?"

She saw him frown as he looked at the ring hanging against the antelope-skin shift.

"I . . . I'm all right." She said it with more assurance than she felt, and reached out to take the broth. The rich, meaty scent of it made her stomach uneasy, but she knew she should eat.

She thought about his sister, looked at his slumped shoulders. He seemed to be carrying the world's weight on his shoulders. "Timbi, are you all right?"

He nodded, but didn't look at her. "And you?"

"I . . . I suppose eventually people learn to live with tragedy." She didn't see how she could go on without her husband, but she was strong, too strong to just lie down

376

and give up. She drank the broth. It tasted steamy and good. She knew somehow that there had been a mistake; Quint couldn't have been guilty of such a crime. And yet Timbi had had Quint's ring.

"All the clans are gathering," he said, "to decide what to do. Old Winnemucca, the war chief, Numaga, and Saaba, who the whites call Smoke Creek Sam; everyone."

She finished the broth and felt stronger. "Does this mean war with the whites?"

"That depends on them, Dallas. We've been pushed as far as we can go. But it's been a long time coming. We must stand and fight now, or let the white men push us right into Pyramid Lake."

She got up, went to stand at the *karnee* door. The grave little boy, Wovoka, walked past and nodded to her, smiling slightly. Somewhere women laughed as they went about their chores. The whole camp seemed peaceful enough except that she knew the warriors must be readying weapons, planning for a big council. Strange, she wasn't even sure where her sympathies lay. Certainly she'd seen enough of the drunken Williams brothers to know they probably deserved to die.

She turned back to him. "The whites have many soldiers, more than you can even imagine if they decide to bring them in from the surrounding areas. The Paiute cannot win this fight."

"We know that." He stared into the little fire. "That's what makes it so sad. In the long run, we know we cannot win, and yet we seem to have no choice. Honorable men can be pushed only so far, no farther."

Dallas sighed, reached up to clasp the ring. "So the Paiute will fight, the Pony Express will be stopped, and many people will die."

"Yes." He didn't sound like a war leader, he sounded very tired and worn with care. Timbi was her master, her jailer, and yet her heart went out to him and his people. Without thinking, she reached out and put her hand on his shoulder.

Timbi felt her small hand on his shoulder, and knew such guilt that he could not look into her eyes. What had happened to Quint Randolph, he did not know, and yet he had deliberately led Dallas to believe the man was dead. Would she eternally remind him of his blood brother by wearing that ring? He had a terrible urge to tear it from her neck, throw it as far as he could.

The drums began to beat outside.

"They are calling the men to council," he said, and stood up. He paused, looking down at her for a long moment, his heart torn by the anguish in her eyes that he had caused with his lie.

And yet if through this lie he could eventually wipe Quinton from her heart and mind, he would count it worthwhile. If she thought Quint dead, perhaps she would finally turn to Timbi and give him her love, if he waited patiently. He was glad she hadn't persisted in her questions about allowing her to leave. He had given up his honor, risked bad medicine in retaliation from the Gods. He would never let her go. She would leave only when he was dead and could not stop her.

He walked with dignity to the circle where the leaders took their places around the fire, sat down cross-legged and stared into the flames, waiting for the old ones to open the ceremony.

But all he could think of was Dallas. The white girl had bewitched him, and he didn't care. What would he have done if she had said she wanted to leave him? He frowned. Never had he loved a woman so, no, not even his pretty Paiute wife. He hadn't known it could be like this between man and woman.

Timbi looked around the big circle. There was old Chief Winnemucca and War Chief Numaga from the local tribes, and Chief Wahe, Winnemucca's brother, from Walker Lake. From the most desolate of the Paiute country, that to the north, Black Rock Desert, had come Chief Sequinata and his men. Yes, they had all come in. In the circle sat Chief Hazabok from Antelope Valley and Chief Yurdy from the Big Bend of the Carson River to the southeast.

From the northeast, Humboldt Meadows, Chief Moguan-noga and his people were here.

Even the Shoshoni Chief, Qudazoboeat, who was married to a Paiute girl, had come from far to the east. And Chiefs Hozia and Nojomud of Honey Lake Valley were here with their men. All the way from the Powder River country had come Chief Sawadabebo, who was half Bannock and half Paiute. And of course, Chief Saaba, the one the whites called Smoke Creek Sam, had been here and talking war since February when he'd had a run-in with the whites.

Everyone waited for the ceremonies to begin. In the silence, at distant Pyramid Lake, the water birds on Anahoe Island called out and the white pelicans flew across the sky. It was spring, mating season, and the birds that lived off the bountiful fish of the giant lake had gathered in by the thousands.

Timbi shifted his weight uneasily. It was not good medicine for one who had lost his honor to take part in the gathering of the chiefs. To do so might bring bad fortune to his people. But how could he stand up and declare that he had thrown away everything that had meant so much to him because of his love for a white girl whom he had stolen from a blood brother?

Not only would he be disgraced, the chiefs might decide Dallas was guilty of magic and order her stoned to death. Above all, even if it brought misfortune to his people, Timbi would not endanger the life of the woman he loved.

The ritual began as wrinkled old Chief Winnemucca called on the Buhagant, the spiritual leader to offer a prayer to the Great Spirit.

And now Winnemucca, with dignity, took his pipe, filled it, and lit it with a burning stick from the fire. He drew in deeply and let the smoke drift from his mouth, then turned and handed the pipe to the man on his right. That man also smoked and slowly passed the pipe to the man on his right. And so it went about the big circle. Timbi looked at the pipe a long moment before he put it to his mouth, let the smoke drift, and passed the pipe on.

The Paiutes' sacred number was five, and the pipe went around the circle five times. Quint, Timbit thought, Quint of the magic number name. I knew you would have a great effect on my life, but I did not know it was because I would love your woman.

After the pipe had made the circle five times, the group sang five medicine songs, and the wind carried their voices across the lake and the hills.

Now the talk began as each man stood and told his grievances and whether he was for war or peace. The discussion went on for hours.

Timbi stood. "This has come to a final decision because of me." He paused. "Perhaps I should have waited before I attacked the station, but I have lost all my family because of the whites." He thought of Atsa, running through the camp in her red moccasins, and his voice almost broke. "All! You have heard what happened at the trading post from Atsa's friend, Moponi. This one last thing I could not stand by and do nothing about."

A murmur went around the circle. A man's honor was the most important thing he had. To shame the sister reflected on Timbi's honor. He had done what any warrior would have done.

"I have taken my vengeance! But it is not enough! I want to drive the whites out of Paiute lands, drive the Pony riders away!"

"Does that include the white girl you have taken to wife?" a brave asked pointedly.

The others glared at the man with evident disapproval. It was not polite to interrupt another at council. Each must wait his turn to speak.

Timbi, too, glared at the man. "You may think her white, but she is half-Cheyenne and so is Indian in her heart."

A murmur of approval at his choice of words came from the men.

Timbi finished telling about finding the bloody moccasins, about how his braves had killed the men and burned the trading post down. He spoke for war.

The young husband of Atsa's friend stood and told of his shame that could not be erased since the white men had mounted his wife like coyotes with a bitch dog. He voted for war.

A brave stood. The whites had polluted the streams with their mining so that people and animals died from drinking it. He voted for war.

The whites had carried off Indian girls and made them whores in their towns. When they did, finally, let them go, often the girls carried disease back to the men of the Paiute. The chief who said that demanded war.

The whites cut the pine trees for fuel and mine timbers, the piñon that the Indians depended on for the nuts that were such a large part of their diet. So saying, that warrior voted to fight.

A chief spoke. The whites shot the rabbits and the deer indiscriminately so that they disappeared and the Indians starved. He was for war.

Timbi stared off into the distance, past an old chief's shoulder, no longer listening to the long list of grievances. The somber little boy, Wovoka, stood outside the circle, listening instead of running and playing with the other children. Timbi felt a dark cloud cross the sun and had a sudden foreboding. *Someday this small, solemn boy would bring a great change, perhaps a tragedy to Indian people. But how?* Then the sun came out from behind the clouds and Timbi's feeling passed. Perhaps it had only been his own moodiness that had given him that thought.

One by one the warriors stood, talked and made their wishes known. The Paiutes would want a unanimous vote from their leaders to undertake a war, Timbi knew. But when it came time for War Chief Numaga to speak, he surprised all by urging caution and voted for peace.

Timbi looked at him with disgust. When he glanced around the circle, he saw the disdain of the others. Numaga had spent much time among the whites. Perhaps he was becoming a white man in brown skin. That thought seemed to be on every face. But because they did not now have a unanimous decision, and because Numaga was a top war leader, the plan for war had to be postponed. The meeting broke up. Timbi went up to Numaga, gestured angrily. "You have a white heart! The others will not vote for war unless you vote with them."

Numaga looked at him calmly. "I foresee terrible things for our people if we take this revenge. Remember, I have spent time among the whites, and know how strong they are. I will do whatever is possible to keep the clans from going to war."

As Timbi watched, the young war leader mounted his sorrel horse. "I will go to each clan, see if I can convince them it will bring us tragedy if they vote for war."

He rode out.

Over the next several days, Timbi heard that the young leader had called on each chief, asking that he vote against war. That Numaga had little success was evident from his drawn features when he returned and walked to his *karnee*. He sat in front of it for a long moment and then spread out on his face in the sand. Passing women stopped and stared.

Timbi walked over. "Numaga, what is this that you do?"

"I can think of no other way to protest what I see as suicide for my people. I will lie here as a silent protest until they all change their minds . . . or I die."

Timbi sneered at him. "You do not deserve to be called a Paiute. In an hour, you will get tired and get up out of the dirt."

At the end of the first day, Numaga still lay without moving on his face in the dirt. Dallas came out of the *karnee,* stood with the other women, looking and gossiping. "What is it Numaga does? What is it he wants?"

Timbi was in a fury. "He is weak and loves the whites! He will not lie there long."

But the next morning, Numaga still lay in the dirt. His woman tried to give him food, water—she brought him a blanket—but he refused her offerings.

Timbi glared at him. "He will get bored with people staring at him and will get up."

But the man did not move all that day, either.

By now, everyone in camp was worried that Numaga would die lying on his face in the dirt.

"Get up!" Timbi and the others yelled at him. "What do you prove if you lie there and die?"

"I prove I have honor," Numaga said through cracked lips, and Timbi flushed guiltily, thinking that perhaps the man knew that he had no honor.

The third day, even Dallas was frantic. "Can't someone do something for him? He will lie there until he dies!"

Timbi went over the the prone Numaga, furious with him because the war chief had more honor, more ideals than he himself. "The chiefs have called another meeting," he said. "Now get up before I kill you!"

"Kill me," Numaga said faintly. "If I save my people with my protest, it is worth my life."

But then a brave came galloping into the camp. "I have been close to the city, heard them talk! Because of what has happened at the trading post, the whites are organizing an army to ride out and attack us!"

Timbi turned, looked down at Numaga, smiled in bitter triumph. "Do you hear? There is no chance for peace."

Numaga sat up slowly. "It is done then. We can do nothing but prepare to fight!"

The men gathered ceremonially around the fire, but there was no discussion now. They had been pushed as far as they could go. The happening at the trading post was the final climax to a long history of troubles. They must fight, even though in the long run, they could not defeat the many whites who would come against them. They could only buy a little time to breathe the air, see the new spring flowers, and think how precious life was when one is about to lose it. And they would die like men, honorably.

Timbi spent the next several days like the others, readying his weapons, praying for luck in his battles.

Not that he expected any. He had gone against the accepted behavior of his people and he expected nothing but death.

That last night, he sat before the little fire in the center of the *karnee* with Dallas, each silently involved in personal thoughts.

He said, "If I am killed, you can go over to the whites and they will help you get back to your family."

She winced as if she did not want to think of his death, and fingered the ring she still wore on a thong. "I have lost Quint Randolph. Will I now lose you, too?"

He looked at her, loving her more than his honor, his life. "Does it matter?"

She reached out, put a hand on his arm. "I have changed much over the past few days, Timbi. At first I hated you, hated your people."

"And now?"

Her hand on his arm trembled ever so slightly. "I have seen how the Paiute suffer. I feel for them and it grows harder each day for me to hate a man who adores me as you do. Besides, it is difficult for a woman to hate a man if she carries his child."

He looked at her a long moment, loving her as he had never loved anyone. He had sacrificed everything for this woman, and may the Gods forgive him, he would do it again if she would only love him in return. "Tomorrow we will probably face a hundred whites who are better armed than we are, if our scouts are to be believed."

He heard her swallow hard. "Must you go?"

"Dallas, I must. Whatever I have done to hurt you or cause you sorrow, I want you to know now that it was only because I worshipped you, I would have lied, cheated, even killed to keep from losing you."

Her expression told him how touched she was by his words. "What you say has such a ring of finality about it. You don't expect to live through this war, do you?"

He shrugged and did not meet her eyes. "Let us say I owe the spirits a debt for things that I have done, and I think they will demand payment with my life."

Her hand felt very warm on his arm, but he would not take her by force. He wanted her, oh, how he wanted her in his arms one last time. He had not touched her since he had told the lie about Quint Randolph's death.

"It is late," he said softly, "and we fight tomorrow." He looked at her, wanting to take her in his arms, hold onto her as if the reality of the child she might carry could keep him from going to his death in battle. But he only lay down on the mat and pulled the fur robe over him. He heard her lie down, too, but he didn't think she slept. Both of them lay there, staring up at the thatched roof of the *karnee*.

Dallas was very aware of the big man lying next to her, knew he was awake. He was so sure he would die on the morrow, she wondered how that would feel to a man. Maybe she no longer hated him, but she did not really love him. Her heart would always belong to Quint Randolph, even though she thought her body carried Timbi's child.

Perhaps not. It had not been long enough to know that for certain. And yet her heart was sure. Tears gathered in her eyes. *In love with a dead man and carrying another man's child. Funny how life turns out. If only Timbi were dead and I carried Quint's child.* She felt guilty over the thought. She could not hate the chieftain when he loved her so.

Timbi sighed heavily, and she felt a terrible need to comfort this man who would surely die against superior forces on the morrow.

"Timbi, are you asleep?"

"You know I'm not."

She was cold, or at least she was shivering.

He reached out hesitantly as if afraid she would stiffen and resist. She let him pull her against his wide chest, cradle her in his arms until she stopped trembling. Somewhere in the distance, a big lobo howled, and she snuggled even deeper into the protection of his strong arms.

Timbi cocked his head, listening. "I wonder if he howls to let me know he's coming for me."

"Who?"

"The lobo. I've had a vision, Dallas, that I am the great Medicine Hat stallion and I am attacked by a giant lobo."

She thought about it a long moment, lying in his arms, listening to his heart beat against her ear. She knew all tribes set great store by such things. "And do you kill it?"

"I . . . I don't know. I never see the end of the dream. I have the big lobo down and I am rearing up, about to kill it. Then its mate attacks me from behind. I'm not expecting that, so I am helpless as I turn to fight her off. . . ."

She waited for him to finish. "Is that all?"

"I always wake up before it ends, but the *shaman* says it doesn't sound like a good omen."

Dallas thought about Quint. Her mate was dead even though they'd been joined for life.

Timbi held her very close as if taking comfort in the warmth of her body. She closed her eyes and thought of Quint, pretended that she was in his arms. She feared the morrow, and was uncertain as to whether the man who held her would be alive when night came again. She pictured Timbi lying dead in the desert.

Tonight, she wanted comfort herself, the comfort of a man's arms. *Quint.* She wanted Quint. But he was dead. Dallas closed her eyes, feeling deeply saddened and bereft, yet also feeling pity for this man who held her, who loved her as much or more than Quint had. She closed her eyes and opened her lips to Timbi.

"Dallas, are you sure? I . . . I won't force you, but I want you more than anything in the world tonight."

Was it wrong to close her eyes and let him make love to her? Did he need to know she saw chestnut hair and hazel eyes in her mind? Maybe it was disloyal to the dead, but she would not look back tonight. She would take what this man offered in case there was no tomorrow for either of them.

His hands were warm on her bare shoulders, and his lips found nipples that were already beginning to swell with the milk they would someday carry for his child. She pulled him tightly against her, feeling his manhood hard and throbbing with need against her belly. Her own body suddenly was dewy wet as Timbi stroked her there with his fingers, making her arch with aching need against his hand. She put her hand on him and felt his seed hot on her fingers as he pushed against them, needing relief.

They were both so sad, bereft and tragic, she thought. So

alone except for each other. Tonight they would comfort each other.

He took her ever so gently, and she wept in his arms, "Oh, Quint . . . oh, Quint!"

He held her very close and kissed her face. "It is punishment of the cruelest sort," he whispered. "I make love to you, and in your passion, his name is on your lips. It is all I deserve, I suppose."

"I . . . I'm sorry. I never meant to do that."

"It doesn't matter, Dallas. I want you any way I can get you. That has been my downfall from the first."

And he took her in his arms, cradled her against his chest, and dropped off to sleep holding her as if he couldn't bear to ever let her go.

Chapter Twenty-six

Quint had grave misgivings as he rode out of Virginia City ahead of the hastily gathered army.

He took the red dress with him. There was a dead girl lying on the bank of the Carson River that he had given a promise.

As far as the drunken and unmilitary crowd that was gathering to go out and fight the Paiute, Quint wasn't sure he wanted any part of them. Only a few had had any military training, and they all seemed to be overly armed and full of liquor. In short, it was a drunken mob of over a hundred men, all shouting, "An Injun for breakfast and a pony to ride!"

Quint had tried to tell them he had seem some of the warriors and this was not going to be any turkey shoot. The Paiute would be prepared to defend themselves.

Nobody believed him; that was apparent as they drank themselves limber-legged and galloped their horses up and down the main street, yelping like coyotes and shooting at signs and windows. They were going out there to Pyramid Lake, shoot those cowardly braves, rape the pretty Injun gals, and steal all the fine horse herds.

Archie McDonald and the young lawyer, Henry Meredith, led the Virginia City volunteers. The Silver City Guards arrived to join them, led by one-legged R. G. Watkins who had to be strapped to his horse.

From Carson City, under the leadership of Major William Ormsby came the Carson City Rangers. Captain

Thomas F. Condon, Jr., led the Genoa Rangers in to join the rest of the rowdy, drunken volunteers.

Quint looked back at the boisterous men standing around on the streets as he pulled the coat collar of his new jacket up around his ears. Then he rode out to take care of his sad chore.

Even though it was May, the weather had turned cold and it looked as if snow might fall up there in the hills. If his urge for vengeance against Timbi hadn't been so strong, Quint would have listened to his instincts and ridden out of Nevada without a backward look. But in his soul burned a hatred for his good friend, his blood brother who had been in on the killing of Dallas. No matter what happened when the white men went out to attack the Indian camp, as long as he managed to kill Timbi, nothing else mattered to him.

He rode out alone into the growing cold, his thoughts on a small body lying defenseless on the frozen ground.

It was late afternoon when he reached the Big Bend of the Carson River and rode up onto the plateau overlooking the burned-out ruins of Williams' station. He looked up and down the steep-walled canyon where the river ran. Nothing moved.

It might snow tonight, he thought as he rode down into the canyon. In a few hours that drunken rabble would arrive, if the leaders could ever get them organized enough to mount up and leave town.

Quint tied the big Medicine Hat stallion to a straggly bush, took a short-handled spade, the package with the red dress, and a blanket from his saddlebags. There hadn't been a coffin in town, and he couldn't have carried one anyway.

The small, brown body lay crumpled where he had left it. Atsa looked younger now, but at peace. How could he get the dress on a body already stiff in death? He thought about it a minute, then took his knife, cut the dress down the back, and slipped it over her. "I promised you a red dress, Atsa. Lord, I didn't think I'd be keeping my promise like this."

He brushed her hair out of her eyes, noticed she wore no moccasins. It didn't seem right to bury her in a fancy red party dress and barefooted. But he hadn't thought of shoes and there was no help for it now. *What did it matter anyhow?*

The earrings. She still wore them. What should he do about them? They had obviously meant much to her, and he couldn't bring himself to take them from her dead body. But he looked at them, thought of Dallas and gritted his teeth until it hurt, swearing that he would get Timbi for his part in Dallas's death. Funny how things turned out, he thought as he began to dig. A pair of rare lavender pearls from the Concho River of Texas were going to end up buried forever in the barren soil of Nevada, in an unmarked grave by the Carson River.

Very carefully, he wrapped the body in the blanket he had brought. Atsa almost looked asleep now. But her skin was so cold. All she had wanted was a red dress, a carriage, and to live like a white girl.

"Good-bye, little Atsa, maybe someday we'll meet again."

He finished digging the hole and put the body in it, filled the dirt back in. From the riverbank, he got big rocks to cover the grave, keep wild animals from digging it up. Should he say something? He wasn't sure what was appropriate.

"Great Spirit, let her go now to your spirit land where at last people treat each other with kindness and dignity, and there is no pain, no hurt—and no one will mistreat her because of the color of her skin. . . ." Quint broke off awkwardly, not quite sure what else to say. He swallowed hard. "Good-bye, little sister."

With a sob and a curse, he went over, sat down on a rock, and buried his face in his hands. After a while, he stared up at the hills where the Paiutes camped. I'm coming for you, Timbi, he swore silently. *With the others or without them, I'm coming for you. My blood brother who owes me a life—my very good friend. You owe me a life and I'm coming to claim it.*

Quint glanced up at the sky. It was almost dark and getting colder. Somewhere behind him was the motley army if the leaders had managed to get them on their horses and out of town. The men were all treating the foray like some giant picnic. This cold should cause some of them to wonder how much fun it would be.

He swung up on the stallion, realizing suddenly that he was in a very vulnerable position should a war party catch him out alone. Before, he'd been so concerned with seeing Atsa decently buried that he hadn't thought about the risks of riding out here by himself.

Then he heard the shouting and singing. The Virginia City volunteers rode in, to camp near the burned-out station, and were soon joined by the Carson City Rangers. Now all they had to do was await the arrival of the Silver City Guards and the Genoa Rangers.

Quint was disgusted with that crowd, and obviously some of the leaders were, too. Fires were built that could have been seen all the way to San Francisco and more whiskey bottles came out.

Quint stood in the background and listened to portly old Judge Cradlebaugh. "Men, I've come along reluctantly, and my good sense tells me we ought to investigate a little more."

"Investigate, hell, Judge!" someone yelled. "You see that burned-out building? That's all we need to know!"

The judge signaled for silence. "Now most of you knew the Williams as well as I did. They'd steal the pennies off dead men's eyes—and you know it. No telling what they did to bring this on themselves!"

The crowd set up an ugly rumble. "Judge, these was white men, and that's all that counts with us. We'll teach those damned Injuns a lesson!" a bearded man said.

The others shouted their agreement. "Yeah, that's all we want to know. There's no use talking to the Paiute. What they will listen to is killin'!"

Any other time, Quint would have been one of those

pleading for cool heads and discussion, but now he was like the others. Timbi had been involved in Dallas's death, and Quint wouldn't be satisfied until that brave's blood smeared his knife.

Only a few people listened to the judge ask for calm and reasoning. The others wanted to kill Indians. In his heart, Quint knew the judge was right, but all he could think of was what Dallas must have suffered when she died. He would take his pound of flesh from Timbi very slowly and painfully.

A scout had found many tracks north of the camp, and some wanted to follow them, to go charging up into the hills in the darkness. But they were talked out of doing it by those with cooler heads. After all, it was dark and the wind was cold. What they did was pile more wood on the fire to make a gigantic blaze — never mind that it could be seen for a dozen miles — eat, drink whiskey, and tell tales about how they would kill Injuns come dawn.

It was a miserable night. By morning, most of the men were sober and wishing they'd stayed home. They sat holding their throbbing heads and wishing they had refrained from yesterday's wild celebration. *It was the damned Injuns' fault they were here and that was a fact!*

Judge Cradlebaugh and his few followers pleaded again for reason and investigation. After being shouted down, these men declared they wanted no part of what was going to be a slaughter, and they mounted up and rode back to town.

Quint's instincts told him to ride out with them. This was going to be a disaster. With one or two exceptions, these were poorly trained men. The Paiutes would have to be deaf, dumb, and blind not to realize the army of volunteers was on its way to attack the Indian stronghold. The whites thought the braves would scatter in panic. Quint, who had seen the warriors up close, wasn't so sure.

The leaders finally got everyone mounted up. Then the men rode to that place where the Truckee River turned north toward Pyramid Lake.

Mostly now the men were sober and silent, obviously thinking more about aching heads and chilled bodies than stealing horses and pretty squaws.

Quint reined in Sky Climber, looked from the well-defined trails of unshod pony tracks back to Major Ormsby. "There's something wrong here, and I don't like it."

"What do you mean?"

"The trail's too plain, like an invitation, laid out carefully as if they were afraid we'd miss the tracks, go off in the wrong direction."

A man behind him laughed. "You scared of a few greasy Indians, Randolph? If so, you still got time to catch up with the judge and his bunch riding back to town."

Quint turned in his saddle. "I've been in that camp. Hundreds of Paiutes have been coming in over the past few weeks as well as other tribes. We may be facing a couple of thousand braves when we get where we're going."

The man shrugged, spat tobacco juice. "So what? There's over a hundred of us, and we're not skairt of a bunch of cowardly Injuns. They'll run when they see us coming!"

Quint leaned on his saddle horn and frowned. "You may be surprised. The Paiute don't have anything left to lose by standing and fighting."

"If you're skairt, turn and go back," a beefy fellow yelled.

Quint's instincts told him to do just that. He had good reason to believe the Paiute knew they were coming, would set a trap for them in the narrow valley of this river.

But he thought of someone else getting to kill Timbi and knew he wanted that pleasure himself. "I'll stick," he said.

He heard a whinny, looked up. On a ridge, the wild horse herd grazed. Some of them had stopped, were watching with curiosity. The Medicine Hat's ears went up, and he whinnied low in his throat, looking at the herd longingly.

"Easy, boy." Quint patted the stallion's neck. "You'll like

it on my ranch with plenty of hay."

But no more running wild and free, he thought with a pang of guilt. The stallion belonged on this range, but Quint wanted him too much to turn him loose.

The wild herd took off running, and the stallion stared after them, pulling at the bit.

A bearded man swore under his breath. "Eventually, we need to shoot all them mustangs. They're eatin' up grass we could be feedin' to cattle."

Quint clenched his fist. "If you say that again, I'll knock you out of that saddle!"

Major Ormsby gestured to both of them. "You two stop it! You want a fight, you may get one when we finally corner those Indians."

They followed the tracks. The weather worsened and the wind blew colder. Men began to complain as the sky turned the color of lead and began to spit snow. Slowly at first, and then the flakes fell faster, became bigger.

By midafternoon, the weather had turned so bad and the column was moving so slowly, it was decided that the motley group would camp on the great curve of the Truckee River to wait for the storm to pass. Men were griping and complaining openly now, talking about going back to town. But it was as far to it as it was to the Paiute camp, and at least here there was a roaring fire and some hot coffee.

Major Ormsby said maybe the fires should be kept small so as not to be seen.

Quint laughed, hunching his shoulders against the driving wind. "Don't kid yourself, Major. Their scouts have known we're coming since we left town. We haven't exactly been moving quiet and swift."

The others glowered at him, glum and miserable. What had started out as a lark, a picnic to kill Injuns, had been turned into a miserable thing by the unpredictable weather of the mountains, blown in by the Washoe zephyr.

Quint stomped his feet, trying to keep the circulation

going and warmed his hands around a tin cup containing hot coffee. The horses, their tails turned to the wind, stood waiting for the storm to blow itself out.

The men hunched down around the fire, and cursed. They'd make the Paiute pay tomorrow for all the inconvenience the filthy savages had caused them.

Major Ormsby sent out scouts, and they didn't return. Gloom descended on the camp. This was turning into serious business. Quint got a hard knot in his belly. Something was very wrong.

But finally the scouts rode in. "Seen lots of tracks like before, but no Injuns."

That didn't make sense to Quint. "You sure?"

They nodded, swung down from their horses. Quint stared into the fire. The Paiutes must know their whereabouts. The drunken volunteers had made lots of noise, and they'd built big fires that could be seen for miles. More puzzling to Quint was the wide trail the Indians had left. Even with the snow deepening, the tracks were still visible.

"Major," Quint said, "I still think we're riding into a trap."

"Oh, the Paiutes aren't that smart or that brave," Ormsby said.

"Maybe, but they are desperate. And they've been pushed as far as they can go," Quint reminded him.

They bedded down as best they could, no one able to stay warm and got up to a frozen dawn. But at least it had stopped snowing. The men stood around drinking coffee and stamping their feet, cursing the weather.

As Major Ormsby poured the last sip of his coffee on the fire, there was a hiss. He looked at Quint. "Pyramid Lake is about ten miles to the north. What do you think, Randolph?"

The men grew quiet. They had come to respect the Kentuckian's opinion. Quint reached for his saddle, looked around. They had camped on a narrow slope that angled steeply down to the river. "I think here'd be a good place to leave a handful of crack rifle shots to cover our retreat in case anything should go wrong."

Someone in the group snorted derisively about taking such precautions when the whites were going to scatter the Injuns from here to breakfast, but Quint glared at the man and he shut up.

Major Ormsby motioned to another fellow. "You, Lake! Get a half-dozen men who know how to handle a rifle and put them up above in those rocks, just in case we should need a covering fire."

"From this far away?" the man looked outraged.

"Do like I tell you! The rest of you get mounted up."

Finally the ragged column of amateur Indian killers was on the march again. The gradual slope down to the river extended for about five miles, Quint figured. That still gave them another five miles to go to the Indian camp.

Quint reined in near the river, studied the small clumps of scraggly cottonwoods and willows that might hide men, looked back up at the slope. The hair on the back of his neck seemed to rise up.

Major Ormsby stopped next to him. "What's the matter?"

"I was just thinking that with us on the low ground next to the river, if a war party gets above, on that ridge, it'll be like shooting fish in a barrel for them. With the river running full and deep behind us, we don't have any place to escape to."

Ormsby frowned. "It would take real military tactics for the Indians to think of that, Randolph. These are just simple savages."

Quint shook his head. "I know one of their chieftains. If you think they're just going to sit there at Pyramid Lake doing nothing while we walk in and start shooting, you've underestimated them. Anytime you underestimate the enemy, you're in trouble."

The major and the men around him gave Quint skeptical looks. Obviously he thought the Injuns were as smart as white men and, of course, that couldn't be true.

Although there was a broad meadow on each side of the river, clifflike bluffs bordered the stream to the west and to the southwest by the long trail down which they'd just descended.

Quint's uneasiness grew. He put his hand on the cantle of the saddle, craned his neck to look around. To the south, the river curved into a narrow canyon and to the north, it rushed on toward Pyramid Lake where the Indian camp lay.

He couldn't shake the instinct that warned him almost as a wild animal is warned of danger. "I hate to keep mentioning it, Major, but this is a helluva good place to get trapped."

The major looked behind him at the trail they'd just descended. "If we're gonna change our minds and go back, this is probably our last chance to do it."

He was waiting for advice, Quint knew. But all Quint could think of was that in a few more minutes, he was going to get a chance to kill Timbi. Revenge was more important to him than anything else at that moment. "Let's go on. Maybe we're just being a couple of nervous old maids."

The men buzzed and gestured, their excitement growing as they realized they were only a few miles from capturing pretty Paiute women and fine horses, becoming heroes, by God!

Quint glanced over at the grove of willows and cottonwoods growing near the river, their new spring leaves shimmering in the late afternoon sun that was finally making an appearance. If he were Timbi, he'd have a big war party hidden in that grove, ready to ride out and hit the straggling line of volunteers broadside. And he'd have more up above on the ridge, firing down on the white men. He wondered where Timbi was at this moment, what he was doing, what he was thinking. Was he anywhere nearby?

From the camouflage of the cottonwood trees, Timbi

watched the straggly line of whites ride even nearer. He saw only a bunch of men with their coat collars turned up against the wind, their faces hidden. Still, there was something vaguely familiar about that big one riding near the front of the force.

There was something familiar about the pinto the man rode, too, but of course it couldn't be the Medicine Hat stallion. It was only a very fine quality horse that was spotted with a similar pattern. Before this day ended, Timbi decided he would own that horse when he had killed its rider.

Timbi stood holding his hand over his own black gelding's muzzle so it would not whinny at the strangers and alert them to the trap. The other warriors did the same. The whites were still out of rifle range. Besides, the closer they came, the easier it was going to be to close the trap behind them, with the war party that waited out of sight on the other side of the ridge.

Timbi's heart beat fast with the thrill of the coming battle. He had a thousand warriors, braves from all the clans, with him, and there were no more than a hundred white men. The Indians would kill them as easily as they did the rabbits when they had an annual drive and surrounded the helpless animals, running them in blind panic into the nets and then clubbing them to death.

Aiee! What a cold day to do battle! But maybe if they massacred the whites, it would send a message to the Great White Father in Washington that the Paiute deserved to be treated like men. Then maybe the whites would sit down in the circle and smoke the pipe five times, listen to all the grievances—and they were many.

Now he gave a silent signal with his hand, and a small war party of his men rose up out of a gully ahead of the whites, pretended to see the white men for the first time, fled. The whites set up a cry like dogs on a scent, and whipped their horses, taking after the small group, galloping deeper and deeper into the trap even though the two men who led them shouted and tried to stop them.

Like a bunch of mindless hounds, the whites galloped

after the decoy war party, shouting with the excitement of the chase, thirsting for blood. There were only a handful of fleeing Indians, and the whites were many. Deeper into the ambush, the whites rode. The war party was under orders not to turn and fight but to lead the white pursuers on down the gully.

Timbi smiled. It was time to close the trap. Behind the high ridge to the south, a big party of warriors stayed hidden, waiting for the decoys to lead the white men to them.

This was for Atsa and his parents, his wife and unborn child. It was for every Paiute murdered, mistreated, and raped since the whites had come here looking for the silver metal.

Timbi's heart was full of emotion as he swung up on his pony, looked back at his men. For only a moment, he wondered if he did the right thing, if any part of his plan could have been done differently; if he would die this day.

If only . . . No, he must not think of things that could not be changed. He would think of the honor to be gained in fighting, the warmth of Dallas's arms, and how he would make love to her tonight when the tribes did victory dances around the big fires.

Now he signaled his men and took off at a gallop behind the whites, riding to the top of the ridge to seal off the escape back up the trail. They had taken the high ground, and the whites were trapped.

There was no looking back from this moment on. Timbi brandished his rifle, shouting to the sky for the good wishes of the spirits, urging his men on to victory. They had the rabbits in the trap. Now they would slaughter them!

At the war cry, Quint reined in, startled, took in the scene in a heartbeat. Ahead of them where the reckless volunteers had galloped forward, a wall of Indians seemed to rise up out of the ground from behind the ridge. The warriors sat their war-painted ponies, waiting. The late afternoon sun glinted off their spear points and rifle barrels.

He turned in his saddle, cursed out loud. "Lord, we should have known it was a trap!"

Behind them, galloping riders came out of the cottonwoods, charged up and across, cutting off the only avenue of escape.

But Quint's heart sang in exaltation as he recognized the tall, proud leader of that line on the shining ebony horse. If he died today, it didn't matter. His life hadn't meant anything to him since he'd lost Dallas, and if it was the price he must pay for killing Timbi, he'd count it worthwhile.

Quint looked at Major Ormsby, whose face had gone white. "The only chance we have is to fight our way back up the slope!"

Ormsby shook his head. "That's no chance, that's suicide! There must be a thousand Indians on those ridges looking down at us!"

The white volunteers were screaming in panic, milling their horses; unsure what to do. *An Injun for breakfast and a pony to ride!* But they hadn't counted on this! Some of them were shouting to others to ride for the shelter of the cottonwoods, too panicked to realize they'd still be surrounded.

Quint shook his head, motioning them forward. His own fear was that he would be killed before he could collect the life Timbi owed him.

"Don't panic!" he shouted over the yelping of the Indians, cries of the terrified, milling volunteers. "Our only chance is to charge and break through their lines, get out of this trap!"

Ormsby looked at him. "Anytime you're ready, Randolph!"

Quint had the best horse in the battle, and he knew it. If anyone could break through the line, then outrun the braves, it would be him. He pulled his pistol, started firing as he and the major led the charge up the steep slope. He was halfway up before he realized that most of the panic-stricken men had not moved. Less than half were behind him and the major as they struggled up the slope. And of that small number, some had horses that were so exhausted they might not make it all the way to the top.

It seemed to Quint the slope was a million miles, almost straight up. A million miles of echoing shots that rang in his ears, men's shouts and screams, and the smells of hot blood and gunsmoke. The great horse between his thighs fought its way up the rocks in a shower of gravel while around them horses screamed and died, rolling all the way to the bottom, crushing hapless riders who couldn't get free of stirrups in time to jump clear.

The smoke stung Quint's eyes and nostrils as he fought for air, and his throat ached from shouting orders that panic-stricken men didn't seem to hear. By this time, his mouth was so dry, he could no longer scream orders. And still he had not reached the top of the slope as Paiutes coolly used the trapped whites for target practice.

Quint tried to organize the retreat, but the men were too ill trained, too terrified. No man thought of any life but his own. They ran over each other, trampled those who were afoot as they tried to get up the slope that led away from this field of death.

"Help each other!" Quint shouted, "Double up on the horses and protect our flanks! We'll get out yet!" He tried to protect the stragglers, shooting a Paiute who was picking them off with a rifle.

But the men still fled mindlessly like rabbits. The cross fire was deadly, taking men from their saddles, killing horses. Here and there a wounded animal stumbled, fell all the way back down, taking the men and animals behind it crashing down the snowy slopes.

Quint fired, took a warrior down, fired again. If he was going to die, he would sell his life dearly. He didn't mind dying, but not until he'd had his revenge on Timbi.

In spite of the cold, his body was wet with sweat. He didn't look down, afraid it might not be sweat at all but his own blood. The wind blew and the sweat almost seemed to freeze on his skin, but at least he was still alive.

He was almost to the top of the slope. Any second now he expected to feel a lance tear into his chest, a rifle bullet burst his heart. If taken alive, he knew he'd be tortured.

Finally, he made it to the top of the slope, and turned to lay a covering fire to help luckless devils behind him. But some of those who reached the top were so terrified, they didn't stop to help anyone. They just fled up the trail, leaving their friends to die in the frozen mud near Pyramid Lake.

The gun smoke swirled so thickly, Quint couldn't be sure of what had happened to anyone else. He looked around, searching for Timbi on the big black gelding. Killing him was foremost in his mind.

A lathered, riderless roan galloped past him, smeared with blood. Quint wondered if it was human blood or the horse's own? A man lay in the mud near his stallion's hooves. Quint saw him, moved his horse closer. The man reached up a hand to Quint, but then a lance flew through the air and impaled him against the frozen mud.

Up ahead was a gully. If Quint could just get his men to that protection, maybe he could reorganize them, put up enough of a defense to get a few out alive.

Major Ormsby was wounded, but still trying gallantly to give orders. Even as Quint watched, Ormsby caught another bullet in the face. He galloped to Quint, blood running red down his pale features. "I don't think any of us will get out alive, but do what you can!"

There seemed to be literally thousands of Paiute, Bannock, and Shoshoni rising up out of the brush to fire at fleeing whites.

All around Quint, men lay dead or dying. Yelping braves galloped after the survivors, reaching out to pull them from their saddles, throw them to the ground, and impale them with their lances.

If only they could fight their way to where that small group waited a couple of miles back to cover them with rifle fire! If only night would fall . . . But there was still another hour of daylight, another hour to kill white men.

Now all who were left alive had made it to the top of the ridge. Quint tried to rally them for an orderly retreat, but the men were too frightened to even listen when he shouted

orders. They trampled wounded friend and foe while trying to escape.

Some even tried to swim their tired horses across the
rushing river to escape the Indians. But the stream, swollen
from melting winter snows, ran full force and swept them
away to drown or threw them back up on shore where
warriors waited to kill them.

Quint tried to wave the men away from the river, shouting at them that it was suicide to try to escape that way. But
panicked men rushed headlong in any direction—over gul-
lies, their horses crashing on the rocks below; into the
rushing water that swept them end over end in a tangle of
flailing hooves, boots, and bridle reins.

He did manage to rally one small group, keep them
together as they fought their way to a small grove of
cottonwoods that offered a little protection. Here maybe
they could make a stand. Behind him, a terrified boy on a
bay horse plunged into the water to avoid being trapped
against the shore. For only a split second, the horse's head
bobbed up and down as the beast fought the current, then
it and its rider were swept away.

Major Ormsby was still alive, though reeling in the
saddle. Quint sized up the situation. He couldn't believe
there were so few men left. If he didn't organize them into
an orderly retreat, get them back up the trail where the
covering rifle fire could protect them, they were all going to
die pinned down here.

The Indians were attacking those on the outside edge of
the cottonwoods with battle axes and lances. He heard a
man scream in agony as he was impaled against a tree.

So this is where I will die, Quint thought with detach-
ment; thousands of miles from home in a small valley of
the Truckee River in a battle that will not make the history
books. But he was past feeling fear now, he loaded his rifle
and pulled the trigger, searching the horizon for Timbi. If
he could just get him . . .

He was weary and cold. He thought if he could only
have a cup of hot coffee and lie down and rest for a
minute, he wouldn't care if he had to die for it. It seemed

he had been here forever with smoke swirling around him and horses screaming as they went down and lay kicking.

His own great stallion was still on its feet and able to run. Many of the others' mounts were not.

A garishly painted warrior galloped right up to Quint screaming in defiance, a knife glinting in his hand. Quint shot him in the face with his pistol at point-blank range.

He had to get what was left of the force out, or they would all die in this little grove of trees.

Major Ormsby bled from half a dozen wounds, yet he stayed in the saddle.

Quint signaled the men, pointed toward the line of savages. They were going to have to run the gauntlet, get through that deadly fire and then try to outrun the warriors.

Quint spurred the gallant stallion and it gave him everything it had, charging straight at the painted, screaming braves. Here and there a horse shied from the Indians and when it did, that man was shot down and his horse galloped away in panic with no rider in the saddle.

It was a rout. Even though Quint hung back and tried to protect the stragglers, most of the few who made it through the deadly line galloped on, thinking only of saving their own necks, oblivious to the fates of their comrades and friends. *Such a small group.* Perhaps not as many as twenty-five out of the original one hundred. And some of them, such as Ormsby, were gravely wounded.

If they could just make it back to where the riflemen held the pass, they would be safe. But some of the horses were exhausted. They stumbled and fell. And when they went down, Indians were waiting with lances and knives.

The little group fled blindly back toward the pass in spite of everything Quint could do to rally them. Here and there, warriors galloped close, overtook them, pulled men from their horses, killed them.

A couple of more miles, Quint thought, looking behind him as he brought up the rear. If we can just make it a couple of more miles to the riflemen in the rocks. A couple of miles. It might as well be a million, he reflected grimly as another man clutched his chest, blood spurting from it, and tumbled from his saddle.

It was nearly dark and Quint prayed for the sun to sink, for the covering safety of darkness. Major Ormsby had fought gallantly, but now, bleeding from many wounds, he fell and the yelping Paiutes stopped to strip his body.

The Medicine Hat stallion performed gallantly and Quint suddenly realized that he alone had a good enough mount to outdistance the Indians, to ride to safety. Yet he had too much honor to desert the others. He would die trying to save them even though many were the dregs of humanity, not worth saving. But Quint was an honorable man.

It was dusk-dark now. Up ahead were the rocks. Quint cried out with relief. "We've made it, men. We've made it!" He galloped on, listening for the sudden deadly rifle fire that would save them, drive the Paiute back. Perhaps he had miscalculated and they weren't yet close enough to be in range, for there was no sudden echo of gunfire from the rocks.

Any second now. Still nothing. He wanted to shout at the men in the rocks: Look alive there, don't you see us coming? Don't you hear the Paiute guns? Help us! Help us!

He was among the rocks now, looking around frantically for the help they had counted on as they'd fought their way back to this spot.

Nothing. There was no one here. No men. No horses. No lifesaving cover fire.

Even as the others straggled into the rocks, thinking they had made it to safety, he wouldn't believe it. Then he faced reality; Lake and the others had panicked and deserted them. There was no one here to help. The handful of survivors was on its own.

Quint had never felt such rage and terror. They had fought their way this far only to discover they were still not safe. Miles of bloody ground had been covered and now they had no rescue.

He led his horse into the cover of rocks and dismounted,

cursing and praying. The only hope for all of them was the descending darkness. If they hid like frightened rabbits maybe the Paiutes would stop looking for this last few and go back to their camp.

Night came on. Quint hid in the rocks, listening to the Paiutes talk to each other as they searched out the survivors, killed them. His own gun was empty. He could do nothing but hide like the others, wait for the braves to leave.

It was a long, cold night. Somewhere out there in the sagebrush, he knew a few more survivors of the Pyramid Lake Massacre hid and trembled, praying that at dawn they would be able to ride back to Virginia City.

The stunned population turned out to gape at the handful of tired and wounded men who finally rode back in. Out of over a hundred, less than twenty-five had returned and some of those were wounded.

Quint hadn't gotten Timbi. It was his biggest regret as he slid from his horse in exhaustion.

Already those around him were talking about troops coming from California to attack the Paiutes. In the meantime, the townspeople went into a panic, thinking the victorious Indians might overrun Virginia City.

Quint frowned wryly as he limped into the saloon and gulped a whiskey to warm his chilled body. The Pony Express had been shut down indefinitely. His mouth formed a grim line as he stared into the bottom of his empty glass, thinking about the gambler from Biloxi. If Yancy's intent had been to break off communications between the North and West, it seemed he had accomplished his purpose.

Chapter Twenty-seven

Dallas listened as echoing gunfire cut through the cold afternoon. Only a few miles away, Indians fought whites, and her very soul was in turmoil because she was not sure where her heart lay, which side she hoped would win.

But there would be no real winners, she knew. In the long run, the Indians would lose even if they won today. Sooner or later, the government would send a great army to vanquish the warring tribes, force them onto reservations. And yet, even though the warriors knew what the final outcome must be, they had ridden into battle because a man does what he must do to protect his honor and his family.

All afternoon, Dallas, the other women, the old people, and even the small children, listened to the gunfire and wondered about the outcome. If the warriors were victorious, there would be much feasting and dancing tonight, if the whites won, the white men would enter the Indian camp and there would be rape and pillaging.

If the whites came, Dallas would be free to go. *To go where?* She thought about that. If she were free, it would be because Timbi and his men had lost the fight and he was dead. When she thought of his possible death, tears came to her eyes. She had lost one man she loved more than life itself. While she did not love Timbi in the same way, it was impossible not to feel something for him when he adored her. Besides, she knew in her heart she carried his child. She could not carry the child without feeling

407

something for the sire.

Yet, if she were freed by a victorious white army, where would she go? A woman who had lived with an Indian was scorned, ostracized by whites, treated as the lowest of the low. The feeling was that a woman should kill herself rather than submit. But those who believed that had never been captives of Indians. Dallas was no weak, whimpering soul, not the type to do such a thing; and if she had been, it was against her religion to kill herself.

Would her parents want her back, pregnant by an Indian, but the widow of a white man? She couldn't be sure. He papa was a proud and well-respected man in the Texas hill country. And she had never gotten an answer to the letter she had sent home.

So as the gunfire echoed, she tried to go about her chores as women do when waiting for word they fear to hear. Somewhere out there in the snow, both Paiute and whites were dying. Dallas wept for both sides and feared for Timbi who loved her above all else.

If only Quint had lived, it might be his son I carry. If only . . . Stop that, Dallas she told herself. It's a waste to look behind you, you can't change the past. Do you want to be like Lot's wife?

It was almost dark, the sky the color of lead and diluted blood when the Paiute men rode back into camp, exhausted and victorious.

Dallas went outside as she heard the noise and shouting. Women ran to meet each incoming group. Here and there, a woman screamed in pain and loss as she searched, realized that her man lay back dead and bloody on a snowy battlefield.

Timbi. Where is Timbi? Dallas looked at each paint-smeared face as the men rode in and dismounted, boasting of the day's events, telling how many whites they had killed.

From the smattering of Paiute Dallas had learned she knew the whites had been outnumbered, outsmarted. Most of the attacking force lay dead back there along the river, where the Indians had lured them into a trap and then slaughtered them like so many terrified rabbits.

She pictured the scene in her mind, winced at the images of death and pain. And yet she sympathized with the brown women in this camp who ran about, searching for a beloved husband or son, and upon not finding their menfolk, tore their clothes, inflicted gashes of mourning on their bodies and then collapsed in the frozen mud, screaming and crying.

Women are much the same whatever the race, Dallas thought. Back in Virginia City and the other white settlements, there will also be weeping and moaning tonight.

Timbi. Where is he? Then she saw him riding in with the other chieftains, tall and strong and proud. Without even realizing she did so, she ran to meet him, crying out his name in sheer relief.

He slid down from his horse, swung her up in his arms, and she put her face against his broad shoulder and wept.

"It's all right, Pony Girl." He brushed her short, black curls back, pushed through the jubilant crowds that congratulated him on the clever strategy of the victory, carried her into their *karnee.*

Timbi looked down at her as he let her slide to the floor. Yes, those were really tears in her eyes. He wondered if they were for him or for the slain whites. For now, it was enough that she was in his arms and he could hold her, savoring this moment. If tomorrow never came for him, this night would be enough.

"Dallas, I was afraid when I first heard the guns, saw the white soldiers. Somehow, I also heard my name called by the Great Spirit, and I turned and looked up at the heavens and whispered, 'Oh, give me just a few more weeks to love her; then if you want to take me, I will go willingly enough'."

"Oh, don't say that!" Dallas laid her face against his chest, and he held her very close and stroked her hair.

Somewhere in Timbi's mind, the giant lobo howled a warning, but the warrior did not understand nor did he care.

Today he had almost been certain that in the swirling smoke and snow, he had seen Quinton Randolph mounted on the great Medicine Hat stallion. But he had not seen that form again during the frenzied battle, and he wasn't at all sure that his guilty mind hadn't created it. Even so, he had searched the battlefield, half hoping, half dreading that he would find Quint's body. Perhaps the man had gone away, never to return.

Dallas turned her face up to his. She would never love him as she had loved Quint, but she knew many a woman started life with another man when the one she loved was gone. At first it is as though you cannot bear to live, Dallas thought, and then you find that the wound partially heals itself so that you can pick up the pieces of a life and go on.

"I was afraid for you," she whispered, "afraid that you were dead out there on the field. I have lost one man already." She felt him stiffen in her arms and regretted instantly what she had blurted out.

"Do not mention him again," Timbi said. "Do you know what it does to me to imagine you in the arms of another man?"

"But that was before you came into my life. That has nothing to do with us."

He didn't answer for a long moment. "Anything that has to do with you concerns me."

She was content to stand there in his arms with her face against his wide chest, listening to the joyful sounds coming from outside. *Tonight there will be singing, dancing and feasting. And tomorrow* . . .

Dallas imagined the men of both races lying dead in the frost and mud. "The white men will come again when they have reorganized."

"I know that, but my people are a simple people. They

410

think that once the enemy is defeated, it is ended." He kissed her forehead. "They think the whites will now gather up their mining equipment and go away. They think that with the Pony messenger stopped for a while, we have won."

"There is something more powerful than the pony rider," she said. "Soon the magic wires will be in place from one side of the land to the other. Then messages will move like lightning through the wire and, gradually, more people will come to this land."

"Then we have tonight and whatever days are left until the whites reorganize their army to send against us. For those few precious hours, we will live as if we do not expect to be here when autumn turns the grass brown and the new snow flies."

She turned her lips up for his kiss. "Which makes that little time all the more precious, knowing that it's all we have."

His lips sought hers. "In the next few days as we ready ourselves for the coming fight, we will send the women and children to Black Rock desert, away from here. Even if the men are defeated, our families will live."

She turned away with bitterness. "But the whites will come there for them, gather them up. Do you call being sent to a reservation 'living'?"

He caught her arm, pulled her back into his arms. "You are white, Dallas. They won't send you there."

"You and I could run away from this place. We could take refuge with the Bannock or the Shoshoni."

"And desert my people?" He shook his head. "Old Winnemucca and Numaga cannot deal with all this alone. I cannot leave. My place is with my people. I must share their fate, whatever that is. But I will send you with the other women to the east until the fighting is over."

Dallas shook her head. "I won't go. You are all that binds me to the Paiute, Timbi, you and the child I may carry. If you stay, I stay."

"Then we are in this together, Spirited One. I have given up nearly all because of you, and perhaps it is meant that

411

we should be together at the last."

She frowned, sadness on her face. "You sound as if sure you will die."

"I have had a vision. . . ." His voice trailed off. "I hear the wolf howling for me, in my mind."

"That's superstitious nonsense!" Dallas flounced away from him, annoyed with his primitive beliefs.

"Perhaps. But I am, after all, as the whites would say, only a simple, superstitious savage."

She colored, aware he chided her for her thoughtless remark. "Timbi, what is it we do to each other? We seem to be living on borrowed time. Knowing that, every moment should be sweet. Soon the white men will come with more men, and the next time, the outcome will be different."

"Then let us live for the moment, savor each precious second we have as it disappears like sand washed away by the water. I have no regrets, Dallas. If you should ever wonder, know that whatever I did, I did for love, and I wouldn't go back and change anything. If that is dishonor, then let it be so."

Dallas wasn't sure what he meant, but it didn't matter. She was satisfied to be in his arms as he pulled her to him, ran his big hands down her back.

She didn't want to lose him as she had lost Quint. "It isn't fair that you will probably not live to see your son draw his first breath. Think again of leaving here, just the two of us. We could start over someplace else."

He kissed her, oh, so very gently. "You think I'm not tempted, Pony Girl? I don't want to die, and those of us who lead most surely will when the whites come again. When I have had to choose before between you and my honor, I chose you, but this time, I cannot. My people need me. And perhaps it is right that I now sacrifice my life. Perhaps I can redeem my honor."

She was angry that she could not sway him. "I care nothing for your honor, I want you to live."

He brushed her hair from her eyes. "Spoken like a woman. Only men care about honor. We cannot live without it. I know, I have tried in the last few weeks, and even though I deny it, I find that it is after all important to me."

The tears came then. She wept for the Paiutes who were doomed even though tonight they danced the victory dances, and for the dead white men who lay sprawled and frozen out there alone in the late spring snow. She wept for Quint and Atsa and Timbi, for herself, and perhaps most of all for her unborn child who would be born into such tragedy.

"Don't cry, Pony Girl, or else I might cry, too, and it is not seemly that a warrior should shed tears like a woman."

"I . . . I can't help it. It isn't fair. If only—"

"Life isn't fair," he whispered, "but that doesn't matter to me anymore. I have a few days left to love you, and if that's all I get, then it's been worth it!" He kissed the corners of her mouth and then her eyelids.

She wanted him as she had never thought she could want him, because she knew they had so little time left before the white soldiers came. "Make love to me," she whispered, holding him close and trying not to imagine that she held Quint Randolph in her arms. Did Timbi suspect that she thought of another? Perhaps, if he did, he didn't care.

"I fear to hurt the child," he whispered, but she felt his manhood swelling strongly against her belly.

"It will be all right," she whispered. "I need you tonight. I think you need me, too."

She pulled off the butter-soft rawhide shift, stood naked before him.

"Your breasts already swell." He picked her up in his arms, took her nipple in his mouth until she moaned and pulled his head against her, urging him to suck still harder.

"Take me," she said, and he lay her down on the mattress by the fire.

He shook his head. "I fear for the child." But he slipped his fingers deep within her and her body shuddered with longing at his touch.

He went down on his knees in homage to her femininity, and then his mouth was on her, touching the hard ridge

413

with the tip of his tongue, sucking and teasing, his tongue alternately thrusting and caressing. She clasped his face against her body, driven wild with longing.

She reached out and grasped his manhood in her hand, feeling the wetness of it, the surging of its power. Then she stroked him with her fingers while he thrust against them and his own hand teased her velvet place until she clutched at his hand with her body, convulsing in her own need.

Then he moaned and stiffened, his seed pulsating out onto her hand. He reached down, dipped his finger in it, smeared it across her swollen pink nipples. "I mark you mine as a stallion marks a mare. With the scent of me on you, no other stallion will try to take you."

"Then *really* take me," she whispered, and felt him grow hard again.

This time, she spread her thighs and tilted her body up to receive him so that everything he offered plunged deep into her depths.

In the next battle, he might die, but tonight he was alive and coupling with her in a frenzied celebration of life.

Dallas was not even completely aware that, when she climaxed under him, she cried out Quint's name.

Chapter Twenty-eight

Quint straggled back to Virginia City along with the other exhausted survivors. First he found a doctor and got his arm bandaged.

Next he sought out C. T. Lake, the man who had deserted his post in the rocks. Lake had rushed back to Virginia City and was in the saloon, talking about the fight as if he had been a part of it. Men were buying drinks for the "hero."

Quint walked up to him in front of a crowd of wide-eyed men, sloshed a beer in Lake's face, and then struck him awkwardly with his left hand. "You yellow-bellied coward! Get out of town before I kill you! You deserted, and better men than you lie out there dead while you fight your battle in the saloon!"

Meekly, Lake and his cohorts turned tail and left.

Quint went back out on the street. The whole town was in a panic as the stragglers drifted in, wounded and weary. No one seemed quite able to grasp the enormity of the massacre. Over a hundred men had ridden out to teach the Indians a lesson. At least seventy-five of those were lying dead and mutilated in the snowy mud back along the trail to Pyramid Lake.

People gathered in little groups on the street, trying to decide what to do. Rumors flew. The Indians were massing to attack the towns and torture every living soul. The Indians had already hit every town in the Great Basin but this one, and they'd be here in the morning to rape the

415

women and carry off the children.

Men suddenly remembered important business in California and took off on fast horses, putting distance between them and the warring savages.

Terrified townspeople "forted up," putting the women and children in the strongest buildings in town where they could be protected when thousands of screaming braves attacked the town.

Help. That was what they needed, help. But a majority of the able-bodied men had been killed or were wounded or still missing out there in the wilderness. Word was immediately sent over the mountains to California. Indignant people out there called meetings, got volunteers organized, and raised donations to buy guns and ammunition for the beleaguered settlers in the Nevada desert.

One brave man, Warren Wasson, rode a hundred miles through Paiute country to warn the settlers of the Honey Lake area and to ask assistance from the cavalry stationed there.

The Pony Express was shut down. Word drifted in of stations under attack, riders and stocktenders dead in burning ruins.

Quint, knowing it would take time for reinforcements and ammunition to arrive, retreated to his rented room to rest and let his wounded arm begin to heal. He had missed his chance to kill Timbi. If that leader had fallen, perhaps the Paiute would have left the field and many lives on both sides would have been spared.

In the meantime, the governor of the state of California sent word that help was on the way if they could just hold the bloodthirsty savages at bay until men could cover the distance to them.

Old Colonel Jack Hayes, the famous former Texas ranger, arrived to take charge of the volunteers. The grateful population quickly took up a collection and presented him with a fine horse, complete with saddle and bridle, then waited for him to make a speech.

But Hayes, like many frontiersmen was taciturn and shy.

The closest he came to making a speech was to say, "He's a mighty fine horse and I'm much obliged." Then he sat down.

It took more than three weeks to assemble the men from California and reequip the ones already at Virginia City. During that time, the Paiutes were raiding in isolated areas, the Pony Express no longer ran, and the men who had been killed in the Pyramid Lake Massacre lay rotting because no one would venture out to the scene of the battle to bury them.

Quint's arm began to heal slowly, although the doctor warned him to go easy for another few weeks because any stress might tear the wound open again.

As he watched the hundreds of men gathering and drilling on the streets, he knew that there was going to be yet more slaughter. They were expecting five or six hundred volunteers and two hundred cavalry to gather under Jack Hayes's leadership.

That means more wholesale bloodshed, Quint thought with a sinking heart. Many would die on both sides, and if the troops stormed the Paiute village, Indian women and children and old people would be killed.

If Timbi were dead, the Paiute might flee to the desert rather than stay and fight. Many lives could be saved if that happened. Quint considered riding out alone, challenging Timbi to a life and death fight. He examined his arm critically, knowing it was healing slowly. He wasn't sure he could fight a man as powerful as his blood brother with that drawback. If he were killed, it wouldn't matter, but if he managed to kill Timbi, he might save many lives on both sides when the Indians fled instead of fighting to the death.

Although it was now the month of June, the weather turned cool and rainy as the attack force made its final preparations. Quint mounted Sky Climber and rode alongside Colonel Hayes, Captain Storey, and Lieutenant Lyon, leading the eager, but poorly trained volunteers.

The first night they camped at Buckland's Station where the ill-fated militia had camped. That alone made the more superstitious nervous as they huddled around the camp fires, imagining a savage brave signaling at every bird's chirp.

The next morning, they moved out slowly, making poor time in the slick mud as they rode toward Pyramid Lake where the Indians were surely waiting. The only other place for them to go was the desolate Black Rock Desert and all knew the Paiute would probably defend the more strategic lake area rather than fight on the desert with little water and no good cover.

Quint mulled his idea over, decided it was a worthwhile gamble. He shifted in his saddle. "Colonel Hayes, the Paiute are mostly an honorable people. If I were to get their chieftain to agree to a fight to the death, I might save a lot of lives on both sides."

The grizzled old frontiersman shook his head. "That arm wound puts you at a big disadvantage—"

"It's healing."

"Yep, but it's not healed yet. Suppose it reopens while you fight him? And besides, you can't know for sure that the Injuns would just let you walk out of there if you killed him. You'd most likely be signing your own death warrant."

Quint scowled, took off his hat, ran his hand through his hair in agitation. "I'll admit there's something else involved. I've sworn to kill Timbi for personal reasons. If I do that, and he gets me, I won't care much. In the meantime, his people would scatter and there wouldn't be any battle this afternoon."

Hayes looked at him a long moment. "You must hate him very much."

Quint stared into the distance. "He's my blood brother. Once I saved his life; then he helped kill my wife. Frankly, I don't want someone else to have the pleasure of killing him and doing me out of it."

"That won't bring her back, son," the old Texan drawled softly.

"No, but I'll feel a helluva lot better!"

Hayes looked at him. "Will you? I wonder."

Quint ground his teeth. "Let me be the judge of that."

If he were lucky enough to kill Timbi, the men wouldn't have to fight. If he were killed, they wouldn't be any worse off than they were already, going up against a thousand crack warriors.

Now as the whites moved forward, they began to find the bodies of those who had been killed more than three weeks before and who had lain unburied all this time. The buzzards rose up from the slain, great wings flapping.

The sweet scent of decay and the sight of the bloated corpses were enough to set the most hardened men to retching and gagging.

They left a burial detail behind and moved on in the late afternoon.

Quint frowned, thinking. "I'm riding ahead, Colonel. Maybe I can stop this. Don't come in until you hear me fire a signal that I've killed their chieftain."

"And suppose he kills you?"

Quint shrugged. "Then you won't be any the worse off, will you? I have nothing against the women and children, I'd like to save them if I can."

A scout galloped back to them. "They're out there all right, sir; holed up at Pinnacle Mount! Lots of rocks, good place to make a stand."

Quint frowned. "See? It's better if I can get him to agree to a fight between just the two of us."

Hayes protested. "But your arm—"

"I've got to do it," Quint said. "You wait here for me. If I don't come back alive, you can bring your troops in and try to run them out of those rocks."

Hayes leaned on his saddle horn. "I don't like it, but we can always do it my way if yours doesn't work."

Quint nodded and rode out at a canter, leaving almost eight hundred men behind him. He had never felt so alone as he did then, riding to Pinnacle Mount. The Paiute were prowling up there like a bunch of cougars, desperate enough to make a last stand and die fighting the white army.

Dallas had lived every moment of the last three weeks as if it were the last, knowing the soldiers would soon be sent against them. Every breath she drew, every memory was precious to her. Almost all the women and children had been sent to the desolate Black Rock Desert in the last day or two. Even somber little Wovoka had gone, although his warrior father, Tavivo, was up there in the rocks with the others.

Timbi tried to insist that Dallas go with the other women, but she refused. The only real link she had with the Paiute was her man, and she flatly refused to leave him.

"Pony Girl, if you stay, you might get caught in the firing."

She shrugged. "What would I do among the Paiute if something happens to you? I will stay with the father of my child for whatever time we have left together."

He was visibly moved by her words, although he frowned when he looked at Quint's big ring hanging from the thong around her neck.

He came over, put his arm about her shoulders and they stood watching the last of the women and children ride out. "I wish you would go, Dallas. My men and I are prepared to stay here, die in this place to hold the whites back until our families get safely out into the desert. I would feel better knowing you and my child will live."

She looked up at him, loving him because he loved her so completely, so passionately. It wasn't like it had been with Quint, but a woman can only love that much once in a lifetime and Dallas considered herself luckier than most because she had had the adoration of two brave men.

"No, Timbi. I'll stay with you for whatever time is left."

She had no doubt that, when the Indians were besieged this time, everyone here would be slaughtered. But she did not want him to die alone if he must sacrifice himself for this hopeless cause.

He turned to his men. "See that! My woman is as brave as any warrior! Though she carries my child, she is determined to stay and share my fate."

There was an approving murmur at the bravery of the pony girl.

It was late afternoon and now the slate-colored sky had finally started to clear although the ground was still wet and slick from cold rain.

A brave shouted from the rocks. "A white man rides toward us!"

She felt Timbi stiffen. "A white? Is he a scout?"

"He does not try to hide. He rides boldly as if he wants us to see him. Shall I shoot him?" The man raised his rifle.

Dallas knew Timbi was about to assent from the look on his stern face. "Oh, Timbi, don't murder him! Perhaps he wants to parley."

He smiled. "I will humor you, my spirited one." Then he turned and yelled up at the man in the rocks. "Let him ride in. We will see what it is this bold one wants."

They waited, watching the man up in the rocks, little Wovoka's father, squinting to perceive the rider they could not yet see.

"Timbi," the man yelled, "there is something more. The white man rides the medicine horse!"

Amid a flurry of excited talk, more men climbed up into the rocks to stare at the man moving closer.

Timbi frowned. "The Medicine Hat stallion? But of course that's impossible. You are wrong!"

But the man turned and yelled again, "Timbi, it is our *nermerberah*—your blood brother!"

Even as Dallas stared curiously, Timbi seemed to falter. "N-no, that can't be so! He must only resemble him!"

"I thought you didn't have a brother? A white man?"

Timbi shook his head, not looking at her, staring into

space. "I owe him my life, so it's taboo to kill him."

Dallas stared at Timbi, horrified. "Kill him? Why would you want to kill him?"

"Because I'm sure he comes to kill me!"

"Timbi," shouted a warrior, "what shall we do? He will be in the camp within a few heartbeats."

"Does he come alone?"

"He comes alone."

"Then let him come," Timbi said with grim finality. "It is time we ended this so I won't have to spend the rest of my life listening for every footstep, awaiting that time when we will fight to the death."

She ran over, grabbed his arm. "Timbi, what is this all about? Surely this can be settled without bloodshed—"

"No, it can not." As he looked at her, deep sorrow etched lines in his face. "He comes for you, Dallas, and because of you, one of us will kill the other."

"Me?" She touched her chest in surprise. "But I've never even met your blood brother!"

He came over and put both his hands on her small shoulders. "Listen to me, Spirited One, and know this; what I have done, I did for love of you, and I would do it again, no matter how dishonorable it may seem."

She looked up into his dark, tragic face. "You're talking in riddles. I don't understand—"

"Dallas, listen." He took her small face between his two big hands. "I tell you, he comes for you. But when he finds out you carry my child, he won't want you. No white man wants a woman who has been a brave's squaw."

She looked past his shoulder, saw the barest outline of a big man on a pinto stallion just at the edge of the camp. Then she looked up at Timbi, not understanding. "Why would he want to take me? I don't know him."

His face seemed grim as death. "Hear me! I did it for love of you, and would do it all over again. I hope you will understand and not hate me."

"Hate you, Timbi? I don't hate you!"

"But you will soon. When you see him, you must tell

him to turn around and ride out, that you carry my child and that you love me and want to stay with me."

What on earth was he talking about? It didn't make any sense to Dallas. "Why must I tell him this?"

"Pony Girl, I lied when I let you think I might let you leave." His expression was tragic. "If he tries to take you out of here, my men up in the rocks will shoot him down. He will never leave this camp alive!"

Dallas pulled away from him, turning to look in puzzlement at the big man riding into the camp. "But no white man knows I'm here, and—"

"Somehow he found out. Remember, if you value his life, you must pretend that you care nothing for him so he will ride away without you."

She was utterly bewildered as she turned and stared at the big man riding closer. She felt Timbi's hand tighten on her arm.

"Remember," he whispered.

She stared at the profile of the big man on the giant stallion, blinked, stared again.

It couldn't be. . . .

The man dismounted at a distance, tied up the strangely marked horse.

No, it was a mistake, something she had prayed for so hard, she now imagined it. He was tall and broad-shouldered; that was why he reminded her so much of . . . But Quint was dead. Her hand went to the ring she wore on a thong.

Then he strode toward them in that easy, long-legged gait that was so familiar to her. It couldn't be! Tears blinded her so that she could see nothing but his vague outline.

She felt Timbi's hand tighten on her arm, saw the warriors up in the rocks ready their weapons.

"Remember," Timbi whispered, "convince him to leave this camp if you value his life!"

Quint? Quint! It was a good thing Timbi had hold of her because her first impulse was to race toward the big man, screaming his name.

She whirled on Timbi. "What is this about? You told me he was dead! You told me—"

"Silence!" he commanded, and they both turned to face the white man as he strode up.

Dallas's heart was in such turmoil, she was not sure she could stop herself from racing into Quint's arms. She looked at the Paiute's grim face. She had never hated a man as much as she did at that moment, knowing that she was going to have to deny her real love to save his life.

Then Quint stopped, stared at her, his mouth opening in surprise. "Dallas?" For a split second, she thought he would run to her. "Angel, I thought you were dead, and—"

"No, I just ran away," she answered coldly, folding her arms across her chest to keep from throwing herself into his arms. "I . . . I decided our marriage was a mistake."

Mistake? Never! she thought. 'Til death do us part. But I will make this sacrifice, dear one, to save your life.

He stared at her, wide-eyed, and the hand that he ran through his hair trembled. "Good Lord! Dallas, you can't mean that!" He turned and smiled at the warrior. "Brother, I can't thank you enough for finding her. Here I thought you'd been involved in her death! Why if I hadn't found out in time—"

"Save your thanks," Timbi said coolly. "She has something else to tell you."

Quint looked from one to the other. "What is all this?"

Dallas didn't look him in the face. She knew if she did, he'd know she lied. "Actually, Quint . . . well, I can't think of an easy way to tell you."

"Tell me what?" His voice had a decided edge to it as he looked down at her. He began to curse. "I ride in here, find my woman alive, and my blood brother hasn't bothered to send me word—"

"Tell him, Pony Girl," Timbi said.

The lie. She was going to lie to him to save his life. He would ride out of here hating her forever, cursing each time he thought of her. But nothing was more important then saving Quint's life. Dallas took a deep breath, forced herself to stare into Quint's eyes. "Quint, I . . . I'm Timbi's woman now."

He reacted as if she'd hit him hard across the face with a gun butt, staggered backward two steps. "What the hell — ? What did you say?"

Timbi nudged her. "Tell him again, Dallas."

"God damn it, I heard her! I just don't believe what I hear!"

For a split second, she thought he would throw himself at Timbi. She glanced up at the warriors in the rocks with their rifles, stepped between the two men, wanting to throw herself into Quint's arms, to kiss away the anguish in his eyes. "It . . . it just happened Quint. Timbi saved me from the Pit River tribe after they captured me."

Timbi reached out, put an arm around her shoulders. "You heard her, Quinton. She's my woman now, and has stayed of her own free will when she could have come back to you if she'd wanted to. Isn't that right, Dallas?"

My love's life might depend on what I say, whether I manage to convince him. She could feel the tension in Timbi's arm. "That's right." She even managed to look Quint in the eye without blinking.

Dearly beloved, we are gathered here today before God and these witnesses. . . .

"Dallas, my God! How could you? You're my wife!"

She knew if she hadn't been standing between the two men, Quint would already have thrown himself at the Paiute. Pain battled fury on his face. "We're married!"

Do you, Dallas Durango, take this man . . . ? Oh, yes, yes, yes!

"Not as far as I'm concerned, Quint," she answered coldly, and Timbi pulled her close against him. She could feel the big knife he wore pressing against her side. She must get Quint out of here before Timbi and his men killed him. "Quint, I . . . I think you should know that I'm happy here and I intend to stay."

425

What God hath joined together, let no man put asunder.
"Besides, I . . . I'm expecting Timbi's child."

The sound he made was halfway between a curse and a sob. His face turned ashen. "My blood brother. My woman. Why, I ought to—!"

"No! Quint!" Again Dallas moved between them. "I . . . I've made my choice. I made a mistake, marrying you! I'm half-Indian myself, you know, and Timbi and I have much in common."

We've both betrayed you, she thought in anguish, but I never meant to.

"I loved you, Dallas, more than anything in this world!" He gestured toward Timbi. "And I saved his life! If only I'd known then—"

"Remember what we said about never looking behind you," she snapped. "Now why don't you get on your horse and ride out of here?"

He stood staring at her, fists clenched. "I love you, angel, and I'd do anything in the world to make you happy. If you want him, I won't try to force you to leave with me."

His shoulders slumped as he turned back toward the big stallion.

Dallas felt Timbi's arm relax on her shoulders, yet she was so blinded by tears she could barely see Quint's big form as he walked toward his horse. The love of her life was leaving her behind—forever. But she had saved his life, and that was all that mattered.

A warrior grabbed the stallion's bridle, and the horse laid back its ears, snapping, hooves flaying. The man stumbled backward, and the rifle he held slammed against the ground and discharged, the shot going wild and echoing through the hills.

Quint grabbed the reins. "Sky Climber lets no one but me get too close to him!"

Then one of the braves on the rocks yelled, "The white army comes at a gallop!"

Timbi let go of Dallas, pushed her away, jerked out his

knife. "My white brother whom I trusted!" he snarled. "You said you came in peace, but you actually bring the white army to kill us!"

"Quint, look out!" Dallas screamed.

He turned. "Timbi, no. I told them to wait while I parleyed so no one would die!" Quint unbuckled his gun belt, let it drop to the ground. "I disarm myself to prove my good faith! I'll ride out and try to stop them—"

"No, I will not be fooled by your lies!" Timbi advanced on him, knife flashing in the light as the late afternoon storm clouds parted and the sun broke through.

Dallas clasped her hands over her mouth to hold back her sobs. "Timbi, let him go! I promised I'd stay if you let him live! Let's escape before the soldiers come!"

In that split second, Quint seemed to read her face, to understand the sacrifice she had been willing to make. "Why, you rotten—!"

He charged Timbi, and they meshed, fought; Timbi slashing with his knife.

"Stop it, both of you!" Dallas cried, but all she could do was watch helplessly as they fought a life and death battle. The warriors in the rocks were now pre-occupied with the white men galloping toward them. The firing between the two groups began, rifles echoing through the hills.

But Dallas cared only about the fight between the two men who loved her. She watched them, torn by her emotions as they struggled, went down, rolled in the dirt as they fought—her husband against the father of her unborn child. And she didn't want either of them to die.

Timbi regained his feet, slashed at Quint. Quint dodged.

"White dog, you'll never take her away from me! I'll kill you first!"

Quint grabbed Timbi's wrist, stopping the sharp blade in midswing, and they seemed poised for a heart-stopping minute as they struggled. Both men were big and powerful. They were evenly matched, and they fought for more than their lives, they fought for possession of the woman they both loved.

She didn't know what to do. There was no way to stop them. All she could do was watch as they fought. In the distance now, she saw the cavalry and the volunteers galloping forward, shooting at the braves up in the rocks. The Indians were shooting back. It would all be over before anyone could get here to stop the battle.

And now Quint lunged, throwing Timbi off balance, the knife clattering away into the rocks. Timbi went down, slamming his head against the ground, temporarily stunned.

She saw the rage on Quint's face as he grabbed up a stone, stood for a long moment over the fallen man. She held her breath, helplessly watching as Quint brought the rock back to crush Timbi's skull.

"My blood brother," he said softly. Then, very slowly, he let his hands drop and tossed the rock to one side. "Even now, I can't kill you!"

With a sigh, he turned away, clutching at his arm. His blood-soaked shirtsleeve was evidence that an old wound had reopened during the fight.

"I won't let you leave here alive!" Timbi stumbled to his feet. "Only if you are dead can I make her mine forever!" He grabbed up the knife, charged blindly at Quint's undefended back.

"Look out!" Dallas screamed, and Quint half turned, throwing up his arm to defend himself but the knife caught him in the shoulder. He was fighting now for his very life.

Dallas didn't know what she could do. The noise increased as the army overran the Indians' positions in the rocks, charged forward, the Paiutes scattering. But the white force wouldn't get to her in time.

She ran over, picked up Quint's holstered pistol from the ground. She would scare Timbi, demand that he drop the knife, let Quint go.

Timbi's face was distorted with insane jealousy and fury. "And now, white dog, I kill you, claim the woman and the stallion!"

She cocked the pistol, aiming it at the two men. "Timbi, no!"

He looked at her even as he brought the knife down in a final swing toward Quint's heart. She saw the surprise on his dark features as if he had not thought of the gun or of Dallas turning on him.

In that split second as the knife flashed down toward Quint, Dallas chose between the two men.

What God hath joined together, let no man put asunder.

She didn't even realize for a moment that she had aimed and pulled the trigger.

From a long way off, she seemed to hear the shot echoing in her ears, to smell the acrid scent of powder.

Timbi's eyes widened in surprise as the impact of the .44 bullet caught him full in the chest. He dropped the knife, clutching at the ragged hole, scarlet blood pumping between his fingers.

He stood there just a moment, staring into Dallas's face as she dropped the gun in horror. Quint staggered to his feet, holding his bleeding arm.

Then Timbi fell. Dallas stared at the gun in her hands, suddenly realizing what she had done. With a scream of anguish, she dropped the pistol, ran to Timbi's side, knelt there. Quint came to his other side. The white army swirled around them in a blur of noise and gun smoke, but to Dallas nothing mattered but the three of them. Between them, she and Quint gathered Timbi into their arms.

Tears ran down Dallas's face and she clutched his hand. "Oh, Timbi, why did you make me do it? I never meant to! If only you had let him go unharmed, I would have stayed with you to protect him!"

His eyes flickered open and he looked up at her, blood coming in a thin trickle from his lips. His gaze seemed to fasten on the big ring she still wore around her neck. "I broke the taboo, wanting to kill my blood brother, steal his woman. I loved you too much to care about honor . . . I know it was wrong. . . ."

Quint took his other hand. "Timbi, I'm sorry it came to

429

this. I couldn't kill you—"

"You're an honorable man, Quinton of the magic name," the chieftain whispered. "My *nermerberah*. The vision . . . I had a vision. Tell me what your name means . . . ?"

Quint looked over at Dallas in puzzlement, and she saw the tragedy in his eyes. "Randolph? Why would you ask that now?"

". . . Must know . . ."

And then the knowledge hit her. Unknowingly, she had fulfilled the dream.

Quint shrugged and looked at her. They both knew Timbi was dying in their arms. "Randolph? It's an old Anglo-Saxon name," he said, obviously mystified. "The wolf is on my family coat of arms."

Then Dallas knew. "Oh, God!" She reached up, clutched the ring with the wolf's head engraved on it.

Timbi smiled faintly. "The meaning . . ."

"Why, it means 'protected and advised by wolves.' "

Timbi nodded, satisfied. "I stole the wolf's mate . . . Should have heeded the warning. . . . Thought I could keep her as my own . . . forgot wolves mate for life. . . ."

He looked up at Quint and tried to say something, but his dying words came so softly in the noise of the fighting around them that they both had to lean closer to hear. "Now, my blood brother, I give you back the life I owe you, and one more. My child's. I have no right to ask. . . ."

Quint swallowed hard, nodded. "I know what you want, my brother. You know the answer."

The stallion whinnied in the background, and all three turned their heads. The wild herd was poised on the hill overlooking the battle.

Timbi frowned. "My spirit animal should not wear any man's saddle . . . should run the hills wild and free. . . ."

Very slowly, Quint rose, stood looking down at Dallas and the dying chieftain.

Tears ran from her eyes as she realized what it was that

430

Timbi wanted. He could not expect it. No one could expect that. Quint had wanted the great horse too badly, had gone through too much to get him. Freeing the stallion was too great a sacrifice to make.

But even as she thought that, Quint turned, strode over to the Medicine Hat stallion, and stripped off its saddle and the bridle. The powerful horse looked at him a long moment as if not quite believing it was free.

Quint waved him away. "Go on, boy, I'm sending you back to the wild, to run wild and free forever!"

The great stallion paused, looking around. Then the wild horses called to him again and he reared up, neighing an answer. Sky Climber's great hooves churned the air, and then he took off for the hills.

Dallas watched him for a moment; then she leaned over Timbi. "He's done it!" she cried. "He's turned him loose!"

Timbi tried to sit up and could not, but she helped turn the brave so he could see the great horse gallop away.

The dying chief looked at Dallas. "I'm going now, too, my Pony Girl. Always remember that what I did, I did for love . . . just as you did . . . for love of Quint. . . ."

The great horse gained the top of the rise and paused, looking out over the valley, the wild horses around him. At that moment, the sun broke through the clouds, creating a halo behind the big horse as he reared up. And a rainbow shone from hill to hill across the Great Basin of Nevada.

"Oh, look, Timbi!" Dallas whispered as the horse reared again and then took off with the wild herd, galloping into the snow-capped mountains. "Isn't it wonderful? He's free! Free!"

He didn't answer, and she looked down. Timbi was gone, too; gone with his spirit animal across the hills, wild and free forever. Untamed and savage as he was, he could never have lived on a white man's reservation.

She held him close, rocked back and forth, and wept for all the pain and sorrow of her own life, but especially for the Paiutes and the primitive chieftain who had loved her more than honor, more than life itself.

Quint came over, bent down, and she saw that his eyes were not dry. The noise had stopped, except for an occasional shot, as the warriors retreated to the hostile desert where they would eventually be rounded up before being herded to a reservation. "I'm sorry, Dallas."

She sobbed uncontrollably. "If only all this hadn't happened! If only I had shot above his head! If only—"

"Remember you once told me those are the two saddest words in any language?" He reached out a hand to her. She took it, and he gently helped her to her feet. "We who loved him will give him a chief's burial up on the crest of the hill."

Dallas got some of the finest blankets to wrap the body. It was quiet now, the whites had chased after the warriors who had fled. The two of them buried Timbi up in the rocks, where the stallion frequently stood guard.

"He will like it here," she whispered. "The whole of the Great Basin lies before him."

Finally they were finished. The sun was setting on the western hills as Dallas turned away with a sigh. Quint would not want her now that she had been Timbi's woman, now that she carried the other man's child.

She was not quite sure what to do. "If you'll help me get back to Virginia City so I can get a stage to California, I'd be much obliged."

"If that's what you want to do," he said softly.

She didn't look at him, loving him too much and knowing he wouldn't want her; no white man would under these circumstances. "I . . . I don't know what I'm going to do. Maybe see if I can get a letter through to my family. Maybe go back to Texas. I don't know."

"I see." He walked over, caught a loose white cavalry horse, brought it back. "Have you ever thought about going to Arizona?"

"Arizona? I don't think I have any reason to go there." She turned away, wondering how she would pay the stage fare from Virginia City.

He hesitated, fumbling with the reins. "A lot has happened, Dallas, and we'd be lying to each other if we tried to pretend it hasn't. But I know a lonely fella who has a ranch in Arizona called the Wolf's Den."

Perhaps he hadn't understood. "Quint, I . . . I'm carrying another man's child. I couldn't expect you—"

"Didn't you hear Timbi tell me he was handing over the care of that life to me?"

She looked up at him, not daring to hope. "You're not obligated because of his request. I wouldn't want you to feel it's your duty to take me—"

"Duty? Good Lord, Dallas, you're my wife! What's happened can't change that! Don't you remember the preacher said, 'til death do us part'?"

"Oh, Quint! Quint!"

They were in each other's arms now, and he held her so close she could scarcely breathe as he kissed away her tears. "I love you, angel, nothing can change that! We'll make a fresh start, and no one, not even the child, need ever know of the past! I'll raise Timbi's child as my own. He was, after all, my brother!"

Quint lifted Dallas, swung her up on the white horse, and mounted behind her. They looked back only once when they heard the ringing neigh of the great Medicine Hat stallion. The big horse poised on the crest of a hill, watching them as the glow of the setting sun spread out behind him. Then he reared up, shaking his long mane as if he approved of them being together.

Tears blinded Dallas. "Oh, good-bye . . . good-bye. I . . . I'm sorry! I never meant to hurt you, Timbi. If only—"

But Quint gently stopped her words by brushing her lips with his. "Remember, angel, no matter how much you regret it, the past can't be changed. Timbi's happy now. This is the way he would choose, rather than going to a reservation."

The big horse reared again, almost as if it heard his

words and agreed with them. Then, with a final whinny, the stallion turned and galloped away into the blinding gold and red of the sunset.

For the sake of the child she carried and for the man who loved her, as well as the man who had loved her, Dallas knew she would go on. With a sigh, she leaned back into the protection of Quint's big arms.

He kissed the top of her head and held her tightly in his embrace. "We'll make it, Dallas, far from here in our own Eden. Don't cry. Please don't cry. I love you, and he loved you; think only of that."

Her small chin came up bravely. "I . . . I'll try not to have regrets."

Then Quint nudged the horse into a walk, still holding Dallas close to his heart. In the pale pink and lavender dusk of the coming Nevada night, they turned their backs on the past and rode into the future.

To My Readers

The Pony Express lasted only eighteen months before the new telegraph line put it out of business and it passed into Western legend forever. The most important news it would ever carry was the election of Abraham Lincoln in November, 1860. The Southern states would secede, plunging the nation into war in April of 1861, just as Dallas was planning to take her baby and husband to visit her parents in Texas. Since the area that would finally be known as Arizona was Union land and Texas was now an enemy, she couldn't get home until the war ended. Someday I'll tell you what happened when her child grew up and discovered the past's secret. And of course, Lydia Huntington will eventually get what's coming to her.

When the Pony Express closed down in October of 1861, the *Sacramento Bee,* a newspaper, published this emotional salute:

> *Our little friend, the Pony, is to run no more. . . . Farewell forever, thou staunch, wilderness-overcoming, swift-footed messenger . . . thou wert the pioneer in the rapid transmission of intelligence between the people of this continent and you have dragged in your train the lightning itself, which in good time, will be followed by a connection by rail. Rest upon your honors; be satisfied with them. Your destiny has been fulfilled—a new and higher power has superseded you.*

The *Bee* was right. The telegraph lines had already been strung along the Pony Express route, and when the transcontinental railroad finally united the country in 1869, its track followed the Pony's trail.

During the Pony Express's brief moment of glory, its riders covered a distance equal to twenty-four times the circumference of the world, carrying 34,753 pieces of mail. Only one *mochila* was lost during that time period. It might interest you to know that not one original *mochila* still exists. For the Pony Express museum in St. Joe, a replica *mochila* had to be made.

But despite its accomplishments the Pony venture bankrupted its three owners. Regardless of the high cost of $5.00 a half-ounce, the Pony Express lost money the whole time. The owners had banked on landing the government mail contract. But when the government finally saw the wisdom of using the central route for mail, the firm of Russell, Majors, and Waddell didn't get the contract because of a financial scandal involving Russell.

During the Paiute War, sixteen employees of the Pony Express were killed. What happened to the others? Most faded into oblivion after they returned to daily life. Several became Mormon bishops. Others were killed in the Civil War. One, Samuel Gilson, became a U.S. Marshal. Another, William Carr, was the first man legally hanged for murder in the new Territory of Nevada. "Happy Tom" Ranahan ended up as an army scout at the famous Beecher's Island Indian battle in 1868; someday I'll tell you about that in another book.

One rider's great-grandson, William F. Fisher, an astronaut, took a Pony Express map along on his space flight, Discovery, in 1985.

Big Jim Hickok of the Rock Creek station, killed the McCanless gang at that same location in 1861. A writer named Ned Buntline turned him into a Western legend under a new name: Wild Bill Hickok. "Wild Bill" would cut quite a swath through the West before being gunned down in a Deadwood saloon in 1876 while holding the now infamous "dead man's hand," aces and eights.

The young boy rider, Will Cody, would also become a legend several years in the future under the name, Buffalo Bill Cody. Cody held the Pony Express record for the longest single ride, 322 miles, undertaken in the summer of 1860 at the height of the Paiute trouble, when no replacement rider could be found along his route.

The last surviving rider, William Campbell, died in 1932 at Stockton, California, having lived to be ninety years old.

One more young man was important in enlarging the Pony Express legend. When President Lincoln appointed Orion Clemens secretary of Nevada Territory, Clemens brought his younger brother, Sam, with him. Sam had been a riverboat pilot, and in 1862 would start writing for the Virginia City newspaper, the *Territorial Enterprise*. He took a pen name from his riverboat days, and went on to write a book called: *Roughing It*, in which he described the thrill of actually seeing a galloping Pony Express rider.

Sam wrote: ". . . Away across the endless dead level of the prairie a black speck appears against the sky, and it is plain that it moves. Well, I should think so! In a second or two it becomes a horse and rider, rising and falling, rising and falling, rising and falling—sweeping toward us nearer and nearer—growing more and more distinct, more and more sharply defined, nearer and still nearer, and the flutter of the hooves comes faintly to the ear—another instant a whoop and a hurrah from our upper deck, a wave of the rider's hand, but no reply, and man and horse burst past our excited faces, and go winging away like a belated fragment of a storm!"

If you don't recognize him under his real name, maybe you will recognize his pen name, Mark Twain. Twain was the author of such classics as: *Tom Sawyer* and *Huckleberry Finn*.

Did a woman ever ride for the Pony Express in a man's disguise? Calamity Jane always claimed that she did, but

I don't think anyone took her seriously. Yet, you might be intrigued to know that historians are not sure of the identity of that first rider out of St. Joe.

That's right. They can tell you the name of the bay mare, Sylph, who carried the first rider, but they are still arguing over who rode her.

When I uncovered that fact, I thought the rider might as well be Dallas. Dallas was first mentioned in a previous book of this series, *Cheyenne Princess,* #2176, my best-selling Zebra Heartfire, about the Great Outbreak of 1864 Indian battles in Texas.

I didn't tell everything I knew about the Pony Express; space wouldn't permit it. I also left out many of the characters and legends, but did include the "Lone Tree" tale of the switch that stuck in the dirt, took root, and became a huge tree over the passing years. The giant cottonwood finally had to be cut down because it had become a danger to the ranch house built in its shade.

That part of Utah Territory that was already called Nevada became an official Territory in 1861, and a state in 1864 because the Union needed its silver to finance the Civil War. Nevada has the distinction of having the smallest capital city of any state, Carson City, named for the famous scout, Kit Carson. Three of its sixteen counties, Onmsby, Storey and Lyon are named for men killed or involved in the Paiute War.

It is true that the Paiute's magic number is five. What I told you of their stoning people to death is also true. Probably the last time it happened was in 1882 when old Chief Winnemucca lay dying and his people stoned his wife to death, thinking her witchcraft caused his demise. It didn't seem to matter that the old man was ninety years old at the time.

What happened to the Paiutes? Unfortunately, they met about the same fate as other tribes; bad Indian agents cheated and mistreated them. The Paiutes and their relatives, the Bannock and the Shoshoni, did battle the whites again, but without much success.

I included the little Paiute boy, Wovoka, for a reason. His warrior father would be killed soon, and the child would be raised by a devout Christian family, the Wilsons. Gradually, he would combine the old Paiute "Dreamer" legends with Christian beliefs, and would create a new religion, the Ghost Dance. The Ghost Dance religion would draw many tribes to it, particularly the Dakotas (Sioux). The final great Indian massacre at Wounded Knee in 1890 would come about because of Wovoka's Ghost Dance, and the reaction of panicky whites. But I'll tell you more about all that someday in another book.

If you wonder what happened to the young half-breed Comanche boy, Eagle's Flight, who was in the war party that destroyed the mail stage, I'll tell you. He grew up and ran away to join white civilization. Under his new name, Maverick Durango, he had his own Zebra Hologram book, *Comanche Cowboy,* #2449.

What I told you about the songs; "Dixie" and "The Yellow Rose of Texas," is true, as is the interesting information about the editor of *Godey's,* Sarah Hale. She convinced President Lincoln to declare Thanksgiving a national holiday. But she is still best known for writing, "Mary Had a Little Lamb."

Yes, there really are unusual lavender and pink pearls in the Concho River in San Angelo, Texas. Matter of fact, I'm lucky enough to own one, set in a small gold and silver spur pendant. I've mentioned these pearls before in my last book, *Bandit's Embrace,* Hologram #2596.

That was the tale about the famous Colonel Ranald McKenzie's cavalry raid on warring Indians south of the Rio Grande, the swaggering *pistolero,* Bandit, from Bandera, Texas; and an elegant, but sheltered, Spanish *señorita* who was on the run when she met the part-Apache gunfighter.

If you missed any of my past novels, you can order them, just as you order any of the others listed in the ads

439

in this book, by writing to Zebra Books. Be sure to include the book ISBN number. Heartfires are $3.75, the Holograms are $3.95. Yes, there are going to be more books in this series, probably two a year. Watch for them.

If you're ever in Missouri, you might want to stop in St. Joe at the Pony Express museum. I'd also recommend you go about fifty miles to the southwest and see Lawrence, Kansas. Yes, that's the site of the massacre committed by Quantrill's guerrillas during the Civil War.

But the most interesting thing in Lawrence to a Western buff is an item on display in the Museum of Natural History Building at the University of Kansas. What is it? A stuffed horse.

Who'd want to see a stuffed horse? Oh, but this is the famous Comanche, supposedly the only U.S. Cavalry survivor of Custer's last stand. He wasn't really the only survivor, of course, but he lived to a ripe old age as the cherished mascot of the Seventh Cavalry.

Someday as I continue this Panorama of the Old West Series, maybe I'll tell you about The Little Big Horn, Custer, and how Comanche ended up stuffed and standing in a glass display case in Kansas. That old bay gelding looks so very lifelike in his Seventh Cavalry saddle and bridle, you may be as overcome with emotion as I was when I saw him.

By the way, Comanche was ridden into battle by Captain Myles Keogh. Don't believe novelists who write that Custer rode Comanche. Those writers haven't done their homework.

Speaking of horses, I will tell you the Medicine Hat coloring really does denote big medicine to several tribes, and I had a photo of an actual wild Medicine Hat stallion, from a book about mustangs. Yes, there are still wild mustangs in America, the majority of them roaming the state of Nevada. If you write the Tourist Bureau at the State Capitol in Carson City, Zip 89710, and tell them you are interested in the horses, they will send you information on the most likely places to see the wild herds.

Before they became tourist attractions, the wild horses were considered a nuisance by ranchers who begrudged them grass that might feed profit-making cattle. As I write this in 1988, almost 300 mustangs have been found shot to death this year in Nevada. We may never know if it was done by ranchers, drunken hunters, or just some deranged person using them for target practice.

I won't tell you all the horror stories about how wild horses have been mistreated over the years. If you saw the movie, *The Misfits,* you know what I'm talking about.

But I will give you one grim statistic: In the year 1925, probably the largest single shipment in history of the luckless horses — six thousand mustangs — filled an entire freight train that carried them from the Elko, Nevada area to slaughterhouses in Petaluma, California. They were processed into chicken feed.

And the slaughter continued for years until one brave woman living near Reno, Nevada — she was nicknamed Wild Horse Annie — set out to save the mustangs that were being killed for pet food. If you've read Marguerite Henry's classic children's book, *Mustang, Wild Spirit of the West,* you know she succeeded — maybe too well.

At the moment, the mustangs are multiplying faster than the environment can support them. The government has rounded up thousands of them, and is trying to get them adopted. Unfortunately, not many people are offering homes so the government is spending almost ten million dollars a year on feeding the horses. If homes are not found, some of them may eventually be killed.

If you're interested in adopting a wild mustang or burro, you should contact your nearest Federal Bureau of Land Management office and ask about the program. You will have to meet some requirements, and you must pay $125.00 for a horse or $75.00 for a burro, plus other expenses. If you can't find your nearest office, write me c/o Zebra books.

Zebra books is kind enough to forward all your letters

out here to my remote home in the old Cross Timbers region of central Oklahoma. If you will include a stamped, self-addressed envelope, I will be happy to reply eventually. But I'll tell you the answers to the most frequently asked questions now.

Is Georgina Gentry Indian? No, she's a petite, blue-eyed blonde, married to a mixed-blood Choctaw whose ancestors hid out in the South to keep from being sent on the bloody Trail of Tears. My brother-in-law is one of the most prominent Chickasaw Indians in this state. He's here because his ancestor survived the Trail of Tears.

I'm what's known up in the Osage country as a "Heart-stay." My roots go too deep in the Sooner state's red dirt to ever leave, but I spend a lot of time in Texas and other Western states.

What about all this cowboy lore in your books? My grandmother was a pioneer Texan who married a cowboy and came to Oklahoma. The family has been here ever since. I spend a lot of time at powwows and rodeos because of my children. My daughter was the local 4H Horse Club Queen and my son was a member of the Future Farmers of America. Many of the horses that show up in my books, under their own names, are ones that we or members of our family have actually owned.

To the Cheyenne, a story is a possession, like a pony or a blanket. None but the owner may tell it. And the magic tales can only be told at night because of the taboos. So the Ancient Ones gather the people around the camp fire by beating the drums, and tell their tales in the darkness. As each one finishes his story, he says: "That is my tale. Can someone tie another to it?"

Then another will stand and begin weaving his magic tale of the old days when the warriors ruled the plains. Sometimes the tales go on all night, but they must stop at dawn because it is taboo to tell the medicine tales in daylight.

Oh, yes, Ancient Ones, I have heard the drums beat late at the powwows, heard them echo through the shadowy hills of the warrior's land. Yes, I can repeat the tales and legends I have heard around your camp fires.

So what story will I tell next? Would you like to hear about a famous Indian battle involving the outlaw Cheyenne Dog Soldiers and the U.S. Cavalry? This was the last great Indian battle fought in Colorado. Nine years have passed since young Bill Cody rode for the Pony Express. He is now known as Buffallo Will and rides as a scout for the army. But this is really an Indian romance about a half-breed Cheyenne girl and a Pawnee scout who helped track the renegade warriors to their camp.

Now they came from two tribes that hated each other. Why? A long time ago, the Pawnee had captured the Cheyenne's Sacred Medicine Arrows and wouldn't return them. But I've already told you all that in my very first best-selling Heartfire book, *Cheyenne Captive,* #1980, the book that won two prestigious awards because of its authenticity.

The Pawnee had one fascinating custom: they were the only American tribe to practice human sacrifice. Every year in an elaborate ceremony, they killed a captured enemy maiden to insure a good harvest.

If you read Captive, you may remember the Pawnee villain, Kiri-kuruks, Bear's Eyes, who was finally slain by the hero in 1858. Bear's Eyes left sons who grew up to ride as scouts for the U.S. Cavalry. No one made better scouts that the Pawnee "wolves for the blue soldiers."

Now what do you think will happen when one of those sons falls in love with the half-breed Cheyenne girl who is scheduled to be the human sacrifice? And how can she love a hated enemy who leads the soldiers against her people?

If you like passion, fast-paced conflict, and authentic Indian tales, return with me to Colorado in the year 1869. We're going back in time to relive every heart-pounding moment of that love story, and be on the scene for the last great Dog Soldier battle, Summit Springs. When the darkness falls and the drums echo through the stillness, I'll begin my next tale. . . .

And for those who have written to tell me you like my stories, I'll say to you as the cowboys do . . .

I'm much obliged,

Georgina Gentry

Author's Note: As we go to press, arrests have been made in the 1988 slaughter of the Nevada wild mustangs.

Although my research involved some twenty-eight books, I'd like to recommend these in particular for further reading:

America's Last Wild Horses, by Hope Ryden
E. P. Dutton & Co.

Pony Express, by Fred Reinfeld
University of Nebraska Press

Saddles and Spurs, The Pony Express Saga, by Raymond W. Settle and Mary Lund Settle
University of Nebraska Press

Sand in a Whirlwind, the Paiute Indian War of 1860, by Ferol Egan
University of Nevada Press

Sarah Winnemucca of the Northern Paiutes, by Gae Whitney Canfield
University of Oklahoma Press

Survival Arts of the Primitive Paiutes, by Margaret M. Wheat
University of Nevada Press

ROMANCE REIGNS
WITH ZEBRA BOOKS!